In a M
They Made T
But Success Couldn't Quench
Their Hunger for Love . . .

ELLA KOVAC: Driven by a painful passion for the one man who could never be hers, she found solace in the embrace of a secret lover. She would do anything to keep her son Greg from uncovering her scandalous past—anything . . .

STEPHANIE BONHAM: Determined to close the deal of the century, she seduced the powerful, arrogant man who could help her. But even she could not predict the twist of fate that would threaten all she had gained—and all she had to lose . . .

MARGOT HAIGH: The half-Korean, half-English finance mogul had given up on romance . . . until she found it with a lover whose passion was deeply fulfilling—and totally forbidden . . .

AARON CONNORS: The golden hero of Ella's girlhood, he alone knew the sordid truth behind her respectable facade—and only he could turn her most precious fantasies into glorious reality . . .

GREG KOVAC: Burning to discover the mystery of his fatherless past, he plunged instead into the future—with a woman old enough to be his mother . . .

TIM IRVINE: The model of British gentility, his ambitious wife's neglect drove him into the bed of her most trusted business partner—and friend . . .

ALEX MEYER: Heir to a glittering hotel empire, the international playboy had met his match in a woman whose high-fashion looks hid dark—and explosive—desires . . .

Books by Deborah Fowler

Deal
Ripples

Published by POCKET BOOKS

DEAL

DEBORAH FOWLER

POCKET BOOKS
New York London Toronto Sydney Tokyo Singapore

This book is a work of fiction. Names, characters, places and incidents are either the product of the author's imagination or are used fictitiously. Any resemblance to actual events or locales or persons, living or dead, is entirely coincidental.

An *Original* Publication of POCKET BOOKS

POCKET BOOKS, a division of Simon & Schuster Inc.
1230 Avenue of the Americas, New York, NY 10020

ISBN: 0-671-70238-6

First Pocket Books printing October 1990

10 9 8 7 6 5 4 3 2 1

Cover photo by Franco Accornero

Printed in the U.S.A.

Prologue

Silver Springs, Kentucky—*July 1956*

To Ella, it seemed that the world had turned upside down. Someone must have tripped her as she had lunged forward to strike that fat, freckled face with its twisted smile, taunting and cruel. A hot, sharp pain shot up the side of her cheek where it made contact with the dirty, dusty ground. Above her she could see the clear, blue Kentucky sky and a mass of brown arms and legs. She gave a roar of frustrated anger and struck out—kicking, biting, scratching at whatever was within her reach. All reason had left her; she wanted to do damage, to hurt as she had been hurt. The dust cloyed at the back of her throat and made her eyes stream with tears, but she felt no pain, although she knew she should. She was in a seething, scarlet world of her own.

"Stop that!" The words rang out high above the chaos around her. "Stop that, and stop it now!" The weight of bodies was suddenly lifted off her; the sunlight burned directly into her eyes, causing her to shut them tight. Strong hands gripped her arms. She struggled to be free of them the moment she was set on her feet, but she could not break away, nor could she open her eyes, which were caked with dust.

"Leave me be, leave me be," she screamed, twisting this way and that like a caged animal.

"You kids beat it, and next time pick on someone your own size." The calm, authoritative voice was not directed at her, but it quieted Ella, too. She made an attempt to rub the dust from her eyes and squinted up into a bronzed, smiling face below a thatch of white-gold hair. She knew who he was, of course, and, momentarily intimidated, she ceased to struggle. "You're Ella Kovac, aren't you?" She nodded dumbly. "My name's Aaron Connors. My pa's the doctor," he added unnecessarily. "I guess we better take you along to Pa right now. You're a real mess." He chuckled, apparently amused by the sight of her.

His laughter irritated Ella, snapping her out of her temporary inertia. "I'm OK, I'm going home." She tried to wrench herself from his grasp, but he retained a firm grip on her arm.

Aaron studied the dirty little urchin before him. She was not badly hurt, only bruised and scratched. He understood, or thought he understood, her reluctance to see his father—there would be no money to pay for any treatment. "OK," he said, cheerfully, "but I'll walk you home."

"There's no need for that."

"Yes, there is. I'll walk you home, or I'll take you to my pa—it's your choice."

Without a word Ella shrugged her thin shoulders and, turning, began walking down the dusty street that led northward out of town. Aaron walked beside her, unselfconsciously still holding onto her arm. "How old are you?" he asked after some minutes of silence.

"Eight," Ella replied.

"I'm fifteen." He could not resist the note of pride. "Why were you fighting?" Ella did not reply. Aaron deliberately slowed his pace, forcing Ella to do the same. "Tell me why," he insisted.

"No matter," Ella replied stubbornly.

"It matters to me."

The sincerity of his voice made Ella glance up. Their eyes met and held for a moment, and what Ella saw in his face brought a sudden rush of comfort, so unexpected and so unfamiliar that it shocked her into responding. "They called my ma names."

"What names?" Aaron demanded.

"I can't say, I won't use those words." She hesitated. "They say she goes with men, goes to their beds, does things."

"What do you think?" Aaron asked gently.

Ella shrugged her shoulders. "I guess she does some of the things they say, but that don't give them no right"—Ella hesitated—"I wish she was like other mothers."

"Have you told her that?" Aaron asked with interest.

"Hell, no, she'd just belt me."

"Do you have a pa?" Aaron asked.

"No," Ella replied, "and I don't want one neither. Ma's enough trouble."

Aaron laughed. He liked her, this funny little kid in her torn dirty dress. She had something, a kind of—he searched for the word—dignity. Yes, that was it. Despite everything, she was not letting her circumstances drag her down.

They had reached the end of the street, which had become nothing more than a track—dirty and dusty in summer, muddy in winter. At the end of the track stood the Kovacs' wooden shack, with a few pitiful items of clothing hanging limply from a line outside.

"Say, Ella." Aaron at last released his grip on her arm. "Things must be kind of tough for you. Look, I'll pass the word around that no one is to hurt you, or they'll have to answer to me. What do you say?"

Ella raised her head and met his gaze defiantly. Her huge brown eyes regarded him in silence for a moment, the expression in them unreadable. "I can take care of myself."

Aaron laughed. "Oh, sure, like you were doing just now."

A look of anger washed across Ella's face. "I've got to go." She pushed past him and ran off on down the track toward her home without another word. Yet before she reached the shack her pace slowed, and she glanced fleetingly over her shoulder. Aaron, watching her, raised an arm in farewell. Ella hesitated and then did the same.

Chapter 1

Paris—*August 1977*

Ella fumbled with the unfamiliar francs and handed the cab driver what seemed an appropriate amount. His surly face broke into a warm smile, which left Ella in no doubt that she had grossly overpaid him. Still, what the hell—it was summer, and she was in Paris. It was the first holiday she and Greg had ever spent together, and besides, it wasn't as if she couldn't afford it. She turned and surveyed the building in front of her. Joshkers Bank—their trademark of gold lettering on marble was instantly reassuring, a home away from home. It would be good to be on familiar ground. For as long as she could remember Ella had longed for a trip to Europe, to Paris in particular, but she found her inability to cope with the language oddly nerve-wracking. Communication had never been a problem for Ella; in fact, her ability to establish a good dialogue with just about anyone was probably one of her greatest assets. But as she struggled to understand what was being said to her she cursed the fact that her formal education had finished at twelve, and certainly French had been no part of it.

"Good morning, madame." The doorman clearly did not mistake her for a French woman, not for a moment.

With a sigh of relief Ella stepped into Joshkers' elaborate, marbled banking hall, identical in style to the branches in New York, Washington, and London. She started toward the information desk when a dark young man in a neat gray suit stepped forward to greet her. "Miss Kovac?"

"Yes," said Ella.

"If you'd like to come this way, Miss Kovac, Miss Haigh is expecting you. Did you have a good flight?" The American accent, although slight, was music to her ears.

"Yes, it was fine," said Ella, "although I've been in France for over a week now. My son and I have been in Provence."

"Oh, I didn't realize. Did you have a good time?"

"Great, thanks," said Ella.

They took the elevator in silence to the fifth floor. It was unusual for Margot to have someone greet her like this. Ella grinned—clearly Margot wanted something, for she never did anything without a reason. Theirs was an odd relationship. Margot Haigh had given Ella her first break by lending her sufficient money to take her initial, tentative steps into the world of real estate. To this day Ella wondered at the decision. Eight years ago she had been so naïve. Margot, older, already an experienced banker, must have known that. Still, Margot had backed her hunch, and, thought Ella with satisfaction, it was a decision that had proved to be more than justified.

The elevator doors slid open. "This way, Miss Kovac."

For a moment the room, luxurious to the point of ostentation, held Ella's full attention. An enormous chandelier dominated the room, lavish drapes hung at the windows, and the conference table, following Joshkers' tradition, was a marble oval of vast dimensions. Her absorption with the room and its splendors, however, was quickly diverted by the two women who rose to their feet as she entered. Margot—tall, elegant, with her distinctive, sleek auburn hair—came forward to greet her and planted a cool kiss on her cheek. "Ella, welcome to Paris. How lovely to see you. I'd like you to meet Lady Stephanie Bonham. Stephanie, this is Ella Kovac."

The two women shook hands warmly enough, but immediately Ella felt on edge—wary, almost uneasy. It was not just her title—one look at Stephanie Bonham was enough to see she was a force to be reckoned with. Tall, slim, dressed casually in a cool summer dress, she had a natural confidence, an air of authority—that distinct, very individual prerogative of the English upper classes. Ella noted her pale blond hair, her perfect English complexion, and her small, heart-shaped face. Stephanie Bonham looked as though she had just stepped out of the pages of *Harpers & Queen.* Only her eyes were different—only her eyes showed she was not some empty-headed debutante living off her parents' wealth and status. Unexpectedly, in contrast to her coloring, her eyes were hazel, almost green—piercing, calculating, and even now, Ella was aware, scrutinizing her thoroughly. "I'm sorry I'm late," Ella found herself saying. "It was difficult to find my son something to do while I was away. His French isn't good enough to get much out of TV."

"Stephanie has children, too," Margot said, almost ingratiatingly.

"Oh, do you?" said Ella. "How many?"

"Two girls," said Stephanie, "but I keep them well away from my business."

The implied criticism rankled. "Me, too," said Ella defensively, "but I'm not on business at the moment. I'm here in France for a holiday."

"At least you thought you were," said Margot, smiling, "which brings me to the purpose of this meeting. I suppose you're both wondering why I wanted to see you so urgently."

"Intrigued, certainly," said Stephanie. She leaned back in her chair. Ella envied her cool poise.

"I should perhaps begin by explaining my role in both your lives," began Margot, "and in the process introduce you, in a commercial sense, to each other. Through the offices of Joshkers Bank, I have helped you both with your businesses for approximately the same amount of time. I have known Stephanie slightly longer—nine years to be precise—and you, Ella, for eight. Whereas I was in on the ground floor with Ella, Stephanie was already in business when we were introduced. You are both in real estate, and in many ways your activities are not dissimilar, except in two major respects. Firstly, you operate on different sides of the Atlantic—Ella in the States, Stephanie in Britain—and secondly, while Ella concentrates her interests on apartments and office blocks, Stephanie is into hotels and leisure centers."

Ella and Stephanie regarded each other with sudden interest. Until this moment, neither had ever met another woman in real estate, at least not on the kind of scale they had established for themselves. Whereas a moment before there had been slight antagonism, now there was a mutual quickening of interest—almost a bond. Their areas of interest might be different, but each instinctively knew what the other must have come through to be sitting there, in the boardroom of Joshkers Bank, at the invitation of Margot Haigh, director of corporate finance.

"OK," Margot was saying, "are you with me so far?" Both women nodded. "The reason for inviting you here today is a unique and exciting project that has landed upon my desk. I have spent a couple of days searching my mind for someone suitable to handle it, and the conclusion I came to is that it's a venture that needs two talents, not one, for it incorporates leisure interests and the requirement for offices and apartments."

Ella frowned slightly. "You're suggesting that Lady Bonham and I join forces in some way?"

"Hear me out," said Margot. "About five years ago a project began to be put together, here in Paris, to create an enormous complex on the south bank of the Seine, just east of the Eiffel Tower. It was the brainchild of the *enfant terrible* of the French architectural world, a brilliant young man called Gaston Balois. You may have heard of him, perhaps, Stephanie."

"Yes, I have," said Stephanie. "In fact, I met him once—very charming, very chic." She raised an eyebrow and laughed, suddenly looking young and girlish. Ella found herself smiling back.

"The idea of the complex, known as the Centre des Arts, is to provide a playground for people of taste, coupled with living and working accommodations for people with both taste and money." Margot leaned forward in her chair and began doodling earnestly on the pad in front of her. If both women had not known her so well, they might have been surprised by the gesture, but endless discussions over many deals had taught them that this little eccentricity meant Margot was starting to talk serious business. "Currently the complex has been granted all the necessary permissions and licenses. The whole scheme is ready to go. The trouble is, it's not going to happen."

"Why?" Stephanie asked.

"The principal moneybags behind the whole scheme is an Englishman named Ronald Slater. He has a first-class reputation for successful investment in all sorts of schemes, not necessarily connected with real estate, and is much respected in the City generally. Neither of you will have heard of him because he tends to keep a low profile, but as far as the banks are concerned, Ronald Slater's good for whatever he needs. The trouble is, in the case of the Centre des Arts, he's made the first mistake of his career."

Margot, now totally caught up in the project she was describing, continued. "The problem is that Ronald Slater is gay, and so is Gaston Balois. Ronald is in his fifties and has quite literally fallen in love with the young Frenchman, with the result that for once his impeccable judgment has been impaired. It has taken far too long to put the scheme together. Gaston has been given enough rope to hang himself, and although the fundamental design is excellent, the whole project is unworkable."

"But why?" asked Ella.

"It's simply not commercial enough," Margot replied. "Gaston, in his enthusiasm, has provided vast areas of public amenity that produce absolutely no revenue. It's all wonderful stuff, but the cost of the project is just too great to be that philanthropic."

"So," said Stephanie, "Gaston will just have to change his ideas."

"That's just it," said Margot, "he won't. He's thrown a complete artistic fit, and Ronald—poor, besotted fool—is backing him to the hilt. The situation is further aggravated by the fact that the multinational corporation that was going to invest in the majority of the office space has pulled out. So far as Ronald's bank is concerned, it's the final straw, and they're withdrawing their support."

"Wow," said Ella. "Poor old Ronald."

"Yes, indeed," Margot agreed.

Stephanie stood up and wandered over to the window. "So let me get this straight, Margot. You're suggesting that Ella and I take over this project?"

"Yes, I am," said Margot. "Your unique experience in two different fields makes you the obvious candidates. It's an enormously prestigious job, it would absolutely make your reputations worldwide, and it's well within both your capabilities. So far as financing the operation is concerned, it goes without saying that Joshkers would be prepared to back you, or I wouldn't be putting the proposal to you at all."

"How much?" Ella asked.

Margot sidestepped the question. "It depends on whether we take over the existing mortgages, whether we keep Gaston on the job or fire him, and, of course, how radically you wish to change the design. I have all the existing figures, the plans, and a positive fleet of lawyers and architects available to discuss the project with you. What's vital is that if the idea appeals to you both, you have to move fast. No one outside these four walls knows as yet that Ronald's support is being withdrawn, and that includes Ronald."

"Jesus!" said Ella.

"What I am offering you is first bite. What you also have on your side is the fact that it's August and there's no self-respecting Frenchman left in Paris. I suspect that the authorities would like the project to go to a French company, so by the time everyone returns from their holidays, I would like to have the deal stitched up. To use the vernacular, it will be a fait accompli, and the authorities will just have to lump it." She smiled triumphantly, pushing back her great curtain of auburn hair.

Stephanie looked across the room to Ella. "Well, I suppose we'd be foolish not to look at it."

"Guess so," said Ella, "though I'm not sure it's really for me."

"How can you say that?" said Margot. "It's tailor-made for you. Just imagine what it will do for your prestige in New York. Ella Kovac, developer of the Centre des Arts, Paris—it'll knock them cold."

"I guess you're right," said Ella, "and certainly I would be crazy not to take a look at it, but I do have reservations."

"Like what?" said Stephanie.

"Logistically," said Ella, looking at Stephanie. "You're based in London, right?" Stephanie nodded. "So great, an hour's hop and you're here in Paris. For me it's a completely different ball game. Then, of course, there's the question of Laurence, I don't know how he'll feel about it."

"Laurence? Who's Laurence?" Stephanie asked. "Another of your children?" Her voice was heavy with irony.

"No," Ella said, vehemently. "Laurence Merman is vice president of my corporation and has a small stake in the business."

"How awful," said Stephanie. "I couldn't bear to defer to anyone on a business decision. My husband Tim's a co-director of my company, but in name only. I certainly don't have to ask his permission to do anything."

"Laurence doesn't interfere," said Ella defensively.

"Laurence is no problem," Margot cut in. "I've already spoken to him about the project—not in detail, of course—and he says it's fine with him. In fact, he said he'd be very happy to keep an eye on the New York office so that you can spend more time over here."

For a highly intelligent woman, Margot had all the sensitivity of a bull elephant, Ella thought angrily. Margot had introduced her to Laurence all those years ago, and without them both, she certainly would not be in business today. She was well aware of the debt she owed them, but why did Margot always have to rub her nose in the fact by highlighting her easy access to Laurence, and her apparent right to discuss Ella's affairs with him? "All right," she said sullenly, "so where do we go from here?"

"You're both staying at the Meyer Hotel, I understand, so I've taken the liberty of booking a boardroom for you, and I would suggest you spend the next few days looking at the plans and discussing them together. You're going to have to rework the whole internal design structure if it's to pay, but between you, I would imagine that represents no problem. When you have satisfied yourselves as to the viability of the project—as I'm sure you will—then I suggest the three of us meet and talk again."

"I'm on holiday," Ella said, "and there's no one to look after Greg. I suppose I can give you until the weekend, but no more."

"That won't be long enough," said Margot. "It's not simply a question of coming to grips with the details of the project; you need to get to know each other. If this scheme is to work, it is imperative that you like and respect one another and feel confident that you can work well together."

"I tell you what, Ella," said Stephanie, "let's spend the next two days here, viewing the site and getting a feel as to the contribution the Centre des Arts could make to Paris. Once we've done that, we don't need to do our thinking in Paris, particularly in August. What I suggest is that you and your son come to England and stay with us in Gloucestershire. I'm sure Greg will get on with my children—they're only a couple of years younger than he—and my husband's marvelous with children. He'll look after them while we discuss business."

"I hadn't planned on going to England," said Ella defensively.

"That is an appalling omission," said Margot. "Of course, you must accept Stephanie's offer. She has the most wonderful house in the country. You'll love it, and so will Greg. There's a farm and horses—after New York, the boy will think he's in paradise."

She was right, of course, Ella knew. Greg had never really enjoyed city life. "OK, Stephanie, Greg and I would love to accept your invitation."

"Well," said Margot, leaping to her feet and striding across the room, "I think this calls for a celebration, don't you?" A little mahogany cupboard concealed a fridge, from which Margot produced a bottle of champagne. She popped the cork and filled three glasses to the brim. She raised her glass. "It seems to me the only toast appropriate is the Centre des Arts."

"And perhaps a new partnership?" Stephanie looked inquiringly at Ella.

"Why not?" said Ella. "I'll drink to that."

Chapter 2

Ella surveyed herself in front of the long mirror in her hotel bedroom. The long, hard years of her youth had passed slowly, and Ella felt every inch of twenty-nine, though she knew she did not look it. Her hair was cut very short into tight, dark curls. Her face, cherubic like a choirboy's, was dominated by huge brown eyes that stared back at her balefully. She was not beautiful. Pretty, yes—vibrant, intelligent. Despite the circumstances of her life and the passage of years, there was an innocent quality to her looks that had enabled her to conclude many a sharp business deal, leaving behind a trail of bemused victims who had rated her little more than a child. No, her face was all right; it was her height that disappointed her. At barely five feet it was difficult to be taken seriously, particularly in a man's world. Still, the light tan she had acquired suited her, and the cream silk suit that she had bought in the Champs Elysees the day before more than did her justice. The telephone by her bed interrupted her thoughts. She walked over and picked up the receiver, watching her reflection as she did so. At least she was slim—the years of malnutrition had seen to that.

"Ella?"

Ella recognized Laurence Merman's gruff voice and felt the usual rush of warm affection at the sound. "Hi, Laurence. How are you?"

"OK, sweetheart. How's Gay Paree?"

"Fine, fine, though I'm missing you, of course." She kept her voice neutral, not knowing whether he was at home or in the office. "What's new?"

"I heard a buzz in the café today. Two guys, having lunch, from ADC Engineering. Ring any bells with you?"

Ella dragged her tired mind away from Centre des Arts to consider her New York properties. "ADC Engineering . . . aren't they the guys who are taking over the ninth and tenth floors of that new building on Park?"

"Precisely. There's my girl, always got a finger on the pulse."

"So what's the problem?" said Ella.

"The lease is drawn up wrong. There's been a mistake somewhere. The rent's been fixed at less than fifty percent of what you originally quoted them, and they were out to lunch to celebrate. They've signed, apparently, so I guess there's nothing you can do except kick Henry's ass all over town. I assume it was Henry's fault."

"Shit," said Ella, "I don't believe this! That lease is for fifteen years!"

"I know, I know. You're going to lose your shirt unless you can wriggle your way out of it."

"I doubt that," said Ella. "If Henry entered the wrong figures and they've signed, it's legal and binding. How could that idiot have made such a mistake? Thanks, Laurence, I'll call him right away."

"No need," said Laurence. "I called because I thought you should know what's going on, but leave me to fix the mess for you. I'll call the lawyers, get Henry over here with a copy of the lease, and see if I can't persuade ADC to play fair. It's worth a try."

"Bless you, Laurence. It just goes to show that it doesn't pay to take a vacation."

"Rubbish. You deserved this vacation, sweetheart, you and Greg. You have fun now. The business will keep."

"I love you, Laurence," said Ella.

"I love you, too, little girl. Hey, how's this deal Margot's cooked up? Any good?"

"I don't know yet," said Ella, "but I think so. I gather she's already spoken to you about it."

"Yeah, and I thought she was a bit pushy. Take the advice of an old sinner and keep a cool head on this one. Margot's real eager to do the deal for some reason—too eager. Either there's a catch or there's something in it for her. Oh, shit, there's the other phone. Bye, sweetheart. See you in a couple of weeks."

Ella put down the phone thoughtfully, and, as she did so, the door to her suite burst open. "Hi, Mom. Hey, you look great."

Ella laughed as she put her hands up on his broad shoulders and kissed her son. It was hardly surprising that most people mistook them for brother and sister. Greg had inherited his mother's dark brown curly hair, but in all other respects he was quite different—tall for his age and powerfully built, with an open, freckled face and a strong jaw. He would be a handsome man, and he already looked older than his years. "Greg, I'm sorry if I've neglected you the last couple of days."

"It's been OK, Mom. In fact, today was great." While Ella and Stephanie had been poring over designs and figures, Greg had taken a series of excursions around Paris. Today's had been a river trip.

"I'm glad. So you saw all the sights?"

"Yeah, a few, and I got to meet a really neat family. They're American, and they have a son, Stephen, a couple of months older than me. They're staying at the Astoria, and they've asked me over for dinner tonight. It's OK, isn't it?"

"I don't like you wandering all over Paris on your own," said Ella.

"Look, I'll take a cab from here to the hotel and one back again, I promise."

"OK, OK. I'm too protective, right?"

"Yep," said Greg, without rancor, "but I guess you could be worse. Hey, what's the time?"

"A little after seven."

"Jesus, I'm supposed to be there in twenty minutes—I'd better go and change."

"Do you have cab money?"

"Yes, ma'am," said Greg, with a mock salute at the door. "Just relax, OK? You have fun at the old drawing board, and think of me being wined and dined at the Astoria."

"I want you back here by ten-thirty," said Ella.

"Oh, Mom!"

"OK, eleven, but come and see me before you go to bed so I know you're back safe."

"Mothers!" Greg raised his eyes to heaven, dashed across the room, and slammed the door behind him.

Ella was left grinning foolishly. How she loved him, and how lucky she was! He was such a friend—kind, loving, clever at school, good at games, popular with his peers. Yet with the start he'd had—they'd both had—he could have been such a mess. Still, he would never know the circumstances of his birth, and what he didn't know couldn't hurt him. It was not easy, though. The older he became, the more he questioned her about his father. How could she tell him that she was unable to reveal the identity of his father because she did not know which one he was . . .

The bar of the Meyer Hotel, Paris, was a lavish affair. It was built around a little piazza in which fountains played and flower beds were awash with colorful blooms twelve months of the year. In winter a glass roof protected the piazza from the harshness of the weather, but tonight it was drawn back, and the soft evening air was a relief after the heat of the day. Stephanie was waiting for Ella at a table in a quiet corner of the piazza, two glasses of kir royale waiting.

"Hi," said Ella. "Boy, I need this. It's been a long day, hasn't it?"

"Yes," said Stephanie, "and I'll have to admit this is my second. I came down here sneakily early, to get one ahead of you, but my natural honesty has shone through, and I feel forced to admit it." The women raised their glasses in a silent toast.

"Talking about natural honesty," said Ella, "I was speaking just now to Laurence, the stockholder I mentioned to you—he rang from New York because I've a few problems back there, and he made a rather interesting observation about Margot."

"What did he say?" Stephanie asked.

"That she seems a little overeager to do this deal. He thinks there must be something in it for her, and now he's got me wondering."

"Go on," said Stephanie. "What's on your mind?"

"Well, if you think about what Margot actually said to us, she gave us the impression that the bank pulling the rug out from under Ronald Slater was some bank other than Joshkers. Well, suppose Joshkers is in dead trouble over this guy Slater. What do they do? They search through their client list, they come up with a couple of suckers they figure they dump the project on—at the full price. This gets Slater and his boyfriend off the hook, but—far more important—saves the bank from losing any money as well."

"So you're saying that far from Margot doing us a favor, she may be playing us for a couple of foolish women who might just solve the bank's problems for her." Stephanie's voice was full of indignation.

"Just a thought," said Ella.

"Margot *was* unnaturally obsequious," said Stephanie thoughtfully. "I don't know what she's like with you normally, but she's fairly cool with me. And what about the boardroom and the champagne? Have you ever had that treatment before, Ella?"

"Never," said Ella.

"I tell you what. Before we go to dinner I'll give Tim a ring and see if he can do some undercover work for us."

So far, all that Ella knew about Tim Irvine, Stephanie's husband, was that he had an obsession with farming and insisted on burying himself in Gloucestershire, which clearly irritated Stephanie. "How can Tim help?" Ella felt compelled to ask.

"Tim had a friend at Cirencester Agricultural College named Jeremy Colquhoun. When Jeremy left Cirencester he decided to go into banking instead of farming, mainly because he had a job waiting at the family firm. I'm quite convinced the real reason he went into banking was because nobody else would give him a job. Anyway, he's deputy managing director of Joshkers UK now."

"I thought you said family business," said Ella. "Joshkers is an American firm."

"Yes, but Joshkers bought out Charles Colquhoun and Company, a small English bank, about ten years ago, forming the basis of their UK operation. Jeremy, I assume, just went with the package."

"So, this Jeremy of yours is, in effect, Margot's boss," said Ella.

"Yes, more or less. If I get Tim to go to London and take

Jeremy out for lunch, we might learn a thing or two. What do you say?"

"Sounds excellent," said Ella, "if Tim won't mind."

"Tim won't mind," said Stephanie.

The tables at Langham's Brasserie were filling up. Tim Irvine sat gloomily at a table in the window, waiting for his guest. It was a stifling day, making the unaccustomed restriction of his suit all the more unbearable. He found himself asking yet again why he allowed Stephanie to impose her will upon him with such apparent ease. He had promised to take their daughters to a gymkhana today, but the call from their mother had put his plans in disarray, and here he was lunching with a man with whom he had nothing in common and whom, when he came to think about it, he actively disliked. Why did he always assent to his wife's wishes? Was it because he recognized how much he owed her, or was it a concession to the memory of how much he had once loved her? Loving her was becoming a thing of the past; he recognized that now. You could not indefinitely love someone who was a stranger to you.

"Tim, old man, how nice to see you. You seem to be deep in thought."

At the sound of Jeremy Colquhoun's voice Tim forced his thoughts away from Stephanie and stood up with a trace of a smile. "Hello, Jeremy. Thanks for coming on such short notice."

They dealt with the pleasantries and ordered both food and wine, and at last Tim was able to turn the conversation to Joshkers. "The reason I asked you to join me today, Jeremy, is to ask your valuable advice." Jeremy's appalling susceptibility to flattery was already written all over his stupid face, Tim thought with satisfaction. "Stephanie is having trouble with Margot Haigh, and we just wondered if you could help."

There was an instant quickening of interest at the mention of Margot's name. "What sort of trouble?"

"Stephanie has a feeling that Margot isn't being straight with her. Since our company has been a very satisfactory, long-standing customer of the bank, Stephanie feels more than a little affronted at the thought that she can't trust a senior member of Joshkers."

"I think you'd better explain some more, Tim."

Got him, thought Tim gleefully. "It appears that Margot is trying to persuade Stephanie to go into partnership with an American real estate dealer to develop a site in Paris known as the Centre des Arts. Although Margot has introduced the project to Stephanie as a golden opportunity, Stephanie has since discovered that the original project was funded by Joshkers Bank, and that they have withdrawn their support from the existing developer. This would suggest that the bank is trying to slide a sticky problem onto Stephanie's shoulders." He spoke with absolute authority and conviction, praying that Stephanie's hunch was right.

He was well rewarded. As anticipated, Jeremy, in his anxiety to discredit Margot, completely overlooked all banker's discretion and took the bait. "Stephanie's absolutely right, old boy. Margot's really in trouble with the Centre des Arts. She's been messing around with that project for years, dealing with a little poofter called Ronald Slater. The upshot of it all is that the whole thing's gone sour, and she's got to get out and get out fast. It's not that easy, of course, and between you and me, I think her job's on the line. The bank could lose a couple of million on this one if she can't sort herself out."

Hurriedly, in case Jeremy regretted his disclosure, Tim changed the subject and limped through the rest of lunch, trying to show the right degree of interest in Jeremy's long catalog of amorous conquests.

It was after four before they left Langham's. Tim was exhausted but oddly triumphant. It was by choice he excluded himself from his wife's business world, but now and again he quite enjoyed a brief foray. It was not the real world, of course—more a game, really, but surprisingly easy to play.

Stephanie, Ella, and Greg sat in a cab on their way to Joshkers Bank. It was late Friday afternoon, and the Paris traffic was building up for the weekend exodus. "That bitch!" said Stephanie. "To expect us to take on f30,000,000 worth of commitment just to get her off the hook—it's not only unprofessional, it's positively unethical."

"The question is," said Ella, "do we want to do the deal at her price or not?"

"If she's in as much trouble as Jeremy says she is, I think we should offer her f15,000,000, and she should consider herself lucky. It will halve the bank's losses—what more can she expect?" Stephanie's normally full lips were set in a firm, straight line.

"If she's going to take that sort of drop, wouldn't she do better to put the whole project on the open market?" suggested Ella.

"I doubt it," said Stephanie. "As she said herself, the French are going to make a stink about the project going to anyone other than a French company, and you know how the French like to drag the last franc out of any deal. They'll smell her desperation and really take her to the cleaners, you can be sure of that. Let's face it, if she's going to be screwed, she might as well be screwed by us."

Ella laughed. "I can't argue with that."

Greg sat mutely in the cab. He had heard enough of the Centre des Arts in the past few days to last him a lifetime, but he already knew better than to interrupt. Stephanie Bonham had made it clear that he was to speak when spoken to, or else keep quiet.

"So how are you two getting along?" Margot greeted them as they walked into her office, Greg having been left to wait in the reception area.

"We're getting along just fine," said Ella. "What we're not crazy about is being taken for a couple of idiots."

Margot frowned. "You've lost me."

"We've done some checking," said Stephanie. "We find that the bank backing Ronald Slater is none other than Joshkers, and that the original deal was set up by none other than Margot Haigh. Given that information, I don't think it unreasonable of us to be just a little suspicious that we may have been set up."

"Don't be ridiculous," said Margot. "It's a wonderful opportunity for you both. I can assure you that was my sole motive for getting you two together."

"I'm sorry," said Ella, "but we just can't buy that. You made a mess of this deal, and now you need to bail out. Being honest and telling us the true position would clearly have affected the price. You haven't exactly behaved ethically, have you? If you wanted to shed a difficult deal at the full price, you should have approached somebody who was not a bank customer."

"The site is worth at least the asking price," said Margot, apparently unruffled. "There's nothing unethical about suggesting you pay a fair price."

"If that's the case, why didn't you explain the full position to us in the first place?" said Stephanie.

"Because I was protecting a colleague," said Margot defensively.

"Within the bank?" said Ella.

Margot nodded.

"Jeremy Colquhoun?" said Stephanie.

"Yes!" said Margot, clearly surprised. "What on earth prompted you to mention him?"

"You may be interested to know," said Stephanie, "that Jeremy Colquhoun informs us that *you* were in charge of the project, and that the whole mess is *your* error of judgment, not his."

"That's outrageous," said Margot.

"Well, one of you has to be lying," said Ella.

"Fine," said Margot. "I'll put a call through to our chairman right now. You ask him any question you like about the background of this deal, and I'll leave the room so you don't feel embarrassed discussing it frankly."

Sir Nicholas Goddard, UK chairman of Joshkers Bank, courteously suffered a ten-minute telephone interrogation by Stephanie, with whispered asides from Ella. "Well," said Stephanie, replacing the receiver, "it seems Margot told the truth. It's Jeremy's mistake, and all she's trying to do is sort out the problem for the bank. To that extent, I suppose, she has no personal ax to grind, though obviously she's going to be quite a hero if she succeeds in extracting the bank from the mess."

"I accept all that," said Ella slowly, "but I don't see how it changes anything as far as our attitude toward the price is concerned. The bank needs out, and they need out fast. Whether it was Margot's fault or Jeremy's is simply not relevant. I don't see why the hell we should pick up their pieces for them without a substantial incentive—do you?"

"You know something, Ella?" said Stephanie. "You're a woman after my own heart."

"You have to be joking," said Margot. "That's half the asking price!"

"It's a risky project fraught with complications," said Ella. "Clearly, the trap we must not fall into is to delay the development further. We have to develop the site within the confines of the existing building permits. The scheme we have worked out does away with the theater, the library, the art gallery, and the recreation area. We have increased the size of the hotel, the number of apartments, and the office space, but working within the existing framework is far from ideal, and there's a great deal of space to sell. We could fall flat on our faces over this one."

"Stephanie?" Margot looked inquiringly at her.

"I agree with everything Ella says."

"I'd agree to a f5,000,000 reduction," said Margot, "for a quick deal."

"No," said Stephanie and Ella in unison.

There was a tense silence in the room. "All right," said Margot, "f20,000,000 for completion by the end of the month. That really has to be my final offer."

Stephanie stood up. "We'll think about it over the weekend. Will you be in London next week?" Margot nodded. "We'll telephone you."

Ella and Stephanie swept out of the room, well aware that they were leaving a thundercloud behind them.

"How did it go?" Greg asked as they walked through reception.

"Your mother and I have just saved ourselves f10,000,000," said Stephanie.

"That's great. Well done, Mom." Greg slipped an arm around his mother's shoulders and kissed her.

Stephanie watched them, feeling a brief stab of envy. Ella seemed to have achieved the impossible—a successful career and a close relationship with her son. Stephanie's own daughters were little more than strangers to her. Still, she reminded herself, it was a question of choices, and she had made hers long ago.

Chapter 3

The first major choice Lady Stephanie Bonham had to make in her life had occurred when she was eleven years old. Her father, the Marquis of Burford, remarried just a few months after the death of Stephanie's mother. His bride was a young model named Pamela Hunt, less than half his age and only four years older than his elder child. The controversial move split the family down the middle. Stephanie's brother George, who was fifteen, had adored his mother, had watched her take three painful years to die of cancer, and could not begin to come to terms with the idea of a nineteen-year-old stepmother. To George, his father's remarriage represented the utter betrayal of his mother. Stephanie was less sure. She had loved her mother, of course, but she could not help being attracted to Pamela; and Pamela, for her part, sensing a potential ally, went out of her way to be charming to the child. Pamela was fun, Pamela was pretty; she helped Stephanie with her hair and took her shopping for clothes that Stephanie's mother would have considered quite unsuitable. In any event, it was fun to have a "big sister," and after the melancholy of her mother's slow decline, it was a relief to have the house cheerful again.

George did his best to recruit his sister's disapproval. "Surely you can see it's revolting, Steph," he said. "Have you seen the newspapers? He's nothing but a dirty old man."

"She is Father's wife," Stephanie said. "In any case, George, I like her. She's fun." It was Stephanie's first experience of openly defying her elder brother on a major issue—a heady, if terrifying, feeling.

"You're hopeless," said George angrily. "All you can think about is enjoying yourself and having fun. As soon as I'm old enough, I'm going to leave Wickham and never come back. Not while *she's* here, at any rate."

"You can't leave Wickham," said Stephanie, genuinely appalled at the suggestion.

"I can and I will," said George. "Thank heavens I'm back at school next week."

Wickham was the one true passion of Stephanie's life. It had been the family seat of the Burfords for nearly four centuries. The land, in rich Gloucestershire countryside, had been gifted by a grateful king to the first marquis. The original building had been a relatively modest affair—a central dwelling house surrounded by a moat and fortified by a high wall and gatehouse. After the Civil War the fortifications had been removed, and in the early 1700s the house had been greatly improved and extended. Subsequent generations had made their contribution, and by the time George and Stephanie were growing up in the house it had become an imposing twenty-bedroom mansion, still retaining many of its eighteenth-century features. Despite its size, the house managed to be a cozy family home, and Stephanie adored it.

The rest of the estate was comprised of just over a thousand acres of mixed-quality land and, unusually, a complete village. The village of Wickham included a church, a vicarage, a rather drab public house, and sixteen cottages. There were also two working farms on the estate. Every day Stephanie went riding on a fat little pony across the much-loved acres and back through the village. She knew everyone; everyone knew and liked her. Wickham was her life; she could not imagine anyone wanting to leave it.

When, shortly after his marriage, her father had suggested boarding school, Stephanie had been horrified and was grateful for Pamela's intervention, which resulted in her receiving a very unspectacular education at a local convent school. The years drifted by happily enough for Stephanie. The early teenage years were no problem to her—she suffered neither from adolescent awkwardness nor a lack of eager young men wishing to squire her to local dances. In her safe, secure, self-centered little world, however, she was unaware of the deepening cracks in her family life. She never stopped to ask herself why Pamela actively sought her company so often in preference to her father's. She liked Pamela, admired her, tried to emulate her stylish dressing and easy charm. Stephanie simply saw her father's increasing absences from home as opportunities to spend jolly, girlish evenings with Pamela. George, too, was a comparative stranger at home. He had moved on from school to university, and apart from turning up at Wickham for the obligatory festivities—Christmas, Easter, and the occasional birthday—he spent his vacations with friends.

When Stephanie was sixteen she left school with two poor O levels, much to her father's disgust. She had no idea of what she wanted to do and an apparent lack of ambition, but her father insisted that after the summer vacation she would enroll at a local secretarial college and at least acquire some shorthand and typing skills. Stephanie agreed because she could think of no alternative and settled down to enjoy a carefree summer at Wickham. However, it was not to be. One afternoon in the first week of July, Stephanie returned from a ride to find her stepmother waiting for her in the hall. One look at Pamela's tearstained face and Stephanie knew something was terribly wrong. "What is it?" she asked apprehensively.

Pamela took her hand. "Darling, you're going to have to be very brave. Something awful has happened."

"What?" said Stephanie.

"It . . . it's George. We didn't know it, but apparently he's been on drugs for some time."

"Drugs!" said Stephanie. "I'd never have suspected stuffy old George of taking drugs. I suppose he'll have to go into hospital to be dried out."

"I'm afraid it's too late for that," said Pamela. "He went to a party with some friends in London last night. He must have drunk quite a lot and then injected himself with too much heroin. I'm terribly sorry, darling, but I'm afraid he's dead."

The words had no meaning for Stephanie. She stared at Pamela, trying to imagine her childhood companion robbed of life. It was impossible. "W-where's Father?" she managed.

"In his study."

"I'd better—" Stephanie began.

"I wouldn't go near him, darling, I really wouldn't. He's in the most terrible state, and I don't think you'll do each other any good at the moment. Let's go into the drawing room and have a stiff drink, and I'll tell you all I know about it."

For two days Robert, Marquis of Burford, locked himself

away from the rest of his family. When he emerged he was in control of himself but completely unable to give any form of comfort to his remaining family. The three of them moved in a dream world, which took them through the inquest, the funeral, and the unwelcome but persistent interest of the press.

Without consulting Stephanie her father enrolled her in a Swiss finishing school. Stephanie did not wish to go, but this time Pamela did not intervene on her behalf, and so two months after her brother's death she found herself entering the world outside Wickham for the first time.

Robert never recovered from his son's death, nor did his marriage. With Stephanie in Switzerland and a husband who had suddenly become an old man overnight, Pamela began an affair with a local farmer. Robert was aware of what was happening, but rather than make any attempt to win back his wife, he simply took solace in the bottle. When Stephanie returned from Switzerland it was to a very different household. Pamela had become remote, involved in a secret life of her own. Her father seemed barely to remember who she was, and any intelligent conversation with him after midday was quite impossible.

Switzerland had been good for Stephanie. She had grown up, and a new and stimulating environment had jerked her out of her inertia. Rather than live with two unhappy people, apparently hell-bent on self-destruction, she found no difficulty in making the decision to move into a flat in London with a group of friends, from where she embarked on a frivolous but enjoyable life-style. A generous allowance from her father needed only the occasional top-up from the odd temporary job, and the rest of the time she concentrated on her social life.

Looking back on her life, Stephanie was often to wonder why she did not marry during this period. There were plenty of proposals and potentially serious relationships, but she always shied away. Whether the pattern of her father's life had put her off marriage or whether she already sensed that she was not a person suited to family life, it was hard to tell, but somehow she managed to live in London for three years without committing herself to anyone. It was not until 1965, when she was twenty-one, that the second major choice in Stephanie's life presented itself.

It was a cold day in early January. Robert fortified himself with the best part of a bottle of brandy before taking to the hunting field. He had been out for less than an hour when, taking a jump badly, he lost his seat, fell awkwardly, and broke his neck—mercifully relieving him of a life that had become a burden to him.

The will was hopeless, for it had not been altered since George's death. The estate had declined, and while it undoubtedly represented an enormous asset, there was virtually no money with which to maintain it. The easy friendship Pamela and Stephanie had once enjoyed was gone. Pamela, now in her early thirties, felt that the Burfords had taken the best part of her youth and so was determined to get something tangible out of the marriage. Stephanie was equally determined that Wickham should not be sold. The battle raged, and undoubtedly Wickham would have been lost had not Stephanie met quite by chance at a party a young Cirencester graduate named Tim Irvine, who offered to help her sort out the mess.

"Tell me about your husband," said Ella. Their flight had been delayed, and as soon as they had boarded, Greg had fallen asleep. Ella and Stephanie sat companionably sipping champagne on the British Airways flight to Heathrow.

Stephanie, jolted from her thoughts of the past, looked at Ella, surprised. "Tim? He's a nice, kind man. You'll like him."

Ella smiled. "Nice, kind . . . the way you say it almost sounds insulting."

Stephanie laughed. "Well, I love him dearly, of course, but to be honest, he is just a tiny bit of a bore on occasions. Is it dreadful of me to say so?"

"No . . . but in what way?" Ella began, then said, "Oh, excuse me, it's none of my business."

"I don't mind talking about him," said Stephanie. "After all, you're going to spend the weekend with us, so you might as well know something about us. Tim helped me sort out Wickham, the family estate, after my father died. We worked very closely together and turned what was an absolute financial disaster into a commercial success. You know what it's like when you're working on a project with somebody, how close you become"—she touched Ella's arm—"anyway, it was like that. It took us three years to get things really established, and during that time we sort of drifted into marriage. As far as Tim was concerned, once Wickham was saved that was the end of it, but for me, I'm afraid I was bitten by the real estate bug"—she grinned engagingly at Ella—"and you know all about that. In our business we wouldn't have got where we have without steely personal ambition. That's where Tim and I differ. Tim is totally content with his life. He has his fields and his stock, the seasons come and go, and now he has the children. He doesn't want to go onward or upward—he's perfectly happy as he is."

Stephanie's obvious agitation surprised Ella. "Surely, in view of the children, his attitude to life has to be a positive advantage—it leaves you free to pursue your career."

"Yes, indeed," said Stephanie, "but everyone makes me feel so guilty—his parents, the children's schoolteachers, our friends—they spend all their time saying how wonderful Tim is, playing the role of both mother and father, and—by inference, of course—how useless I am."

"You could change things," said Ella.

"Yes, but that's the problem," said Stephanie. "I don't want to. I love my life, and I adore wheeling and dealing. I'm really not suited to being purely a wife and mother, yet everybody makes me feel so damned guilty."

"How do your children feel about it all?"

"I don't really know. They look to Tim for everything, and of course I go along with all his decisions on their well-being. I wouldn't dream of interfering—it wouldn't be fair."

"How old are the children?" Ella asked.

"Eleven and ten. Millie, the elder one, has much the same temperament as me, God help her. The little one, Belinda, is very much Tim's child—in both looks and attitude."

"I suppose I have rather an idealistic view of marriage, since I've never been married," said Ella, "but it must be kind of tough on you both, seeing so little of each other."

"We've been married for twelve years now," said Stephanie. "It's hardly love's young dream anymore. Don't get me wrong; I think we're faithful to each other—at least I am to Tim—I've never had time to be anything else. And Tim, somehow, isn't the type to have affairs. For one thing, he'd give himself away in a moment. He's far too honest and open a person." It should have been a compliment, but to Ella it sounded strangely like a criticism. "Anyway," said Stephanie, "enough of me. What about you? Do you live with Greg's father, or is it a thing of the past?"

"A thing of the past," said Ella, and clearly that was the end of the conversation.

At Heathrow the two women parted. Stephanie was staying overnight in London in order to attend a meeting the following morning. It was proposed, therefore, that Ella and Greg should travel on to Gloucestershire alone in the chauffeur-driven Bentley thoughtfully provided by Stephanie to meet the plane.

"Why don't we stay over in London and travel to Gloucestershire with you tomorrow?" Ella suggested, uncharacteristically shy at the thought of meeting Tim Irvine.

"Not a good idea," said Stephanie. "For one thing, London is hell this time of year, and in any event, I'm not sure how long I'll be with Lord Rainham. I've only met him a couple of times, but from what I can recall, he's a tedious old bore—the meeting may go on all day."

It was early evening, the end of a beautiful, sun-drenched day, as Ella and Greg barreled down the M4. The surrounding countryside charmed them, but it was nothing compared with their delight in the little Gloucestershire villages through which they passed once they turned off the motorway.

Greg was ecstatic. "Hey, Mom, why don't we live in England? I love it here."

"Darling, we've only been in the country an hour."

"So? You know I hate New York."

"Many people consider it to be the most exciting city in the world," Ella said valiantly.

"I still don't like it—just look at all this country, Mom. Isn't it great?"

Despite the splendors of their journey, neither of them was prepared for the beauty of Stephanie's home. They traveled through the village of Wickham first and then turned off the lane, through stone pillars, onto a driveway flanked by massive chestnut trees. After about half a mile the driveway opened out, and there stood the house. Bathed in evening light, the pale yellow stone glowed almost apricot. Long and low, the house was built in the shape of an E with the center prong missing. The roof was turreted, the windows all had tiny leaded panes, and the great oak front door was thrown open in welcome.

"I just don't know how she can ever leave this place," Ella said quietly, and that was before she had even met Tim Irvine.

Chapter 4

Gloucestershire—*August 1977*

He was already in the driveway to greet them by the time the chauffeur had opened the door for Ella. The imposing house and the fatigue of the journey had Ella suddenly feeling self-conscious and longing for the anonymity of a hotel room where she and Greg could just collapse. All these feelings of awkwardness vanished, however, at the sight of Tim Irvine. He was not at all as Ella had imagined. He was not particularly tall, probably no taller than Stephanie herself. He had bright blue eyes, light brown hair, and an open, humorous face creased with laughter lines. He wore a checked shirt and faded cords, and he stepped forward with outstretched hands, taking hers in both of his, exuding warmth and welcome. "Miss Kovac, how very nice to meet you. You look wonderful. I thought you'd be frazzled from a journey in all this heat. And this must be Greg—how do you do, Greg? It's lovely to have you both here at Wickham."

"Hi," said Greg awkwardly.

Ella, momentarily stunned, made an effort to pull herself together. "It's very kind of you to invite us," she said. "This is wonderful." She gestured around her.

"It is rather splendid, isn't it? Come inside, I'll take you straight up to your rooms so that you can wash and relax. Supper's in half an hour. No need to dress, as you can see. Oh, and there have been two phone calls for you—one from a Laurence Merman in New York and the other from the indomitable Margot. She said she was happy to speak to either you or Stephanie, it didn't matter who. She was a little curt with me, so I think she must have found out about my lunch with Jeremy."

Ella's room was simply furnished, with spectacular views across the Gloucestershire countryside. She stood by the window for a long time, drinking in the scene—she had never expected England to be so beautiful.

At last she remembered her telephone calls. Laurence was brief and to the point. "I'm sorry, Ella, but I thought I'd better let you know you're stuck with that lease. Henry should lose his job over this."

"Are you sure there's no way around it?" Ella asked.

"None," said Laurence. "It appears that no letter was exchanged between you and ADC confirming the rental fees. Had there been, it's possible it could have been used as evidence. Henry said it was all very last minute and agreed verbally."

"Yes, that's right," said Ella. "I did the deal just before leaving for Europe. Oh, hell, it was a good deal, too. I think ADC have behaved like rats."

"Not really," said Laurie. "They've got prime office space for practically nothing. It's not their fault that you have inadequate staff in your office."

"I still think—" said Ella.

"Forget it, sweetheart. It's business, and this is one you lost. I think we need to have a talk when you get back to the States. The one thing I know about is staff—in the catering business they make or break you. If you're going ahead with this Paris deal, you're going to need some people who can keep you out of the shit, not drop you right in it."

"Yes, yes, all right, Laurence," said Ella, suddenly feeling very weary. "I must go now. I have to call the bank."

The London number Tim had written down for her was not Joshkers, so Ella presumed correctly she had been given Margot's home number. Margot was such an enigma—no one Ella had ever spoken to, who'd had dealings with Margot Haigh, felt they really knew her personally. Her private life was a closed book, and the barrier Margot presented to the world kept any inquisitiveness at bay. Disclosing her home number in this way seemed a chink in the armor and quite out of character. Ella dialed the number and waited.

"Margot Haigh." The familiar brusque voice echoed down the line.

"Margot, it's Ella. I had a message to call you."

"Thanks for calling, Ella. Where are you?"

"I'm at Wickham, and Stephanie's still in London."

"That's fine, but you're going to meet her over the weekend, I trust?"

"Yes, of course. She'll be down tomorrow."

"Good." Margot hesitated for a moment. "I've had a word with my chairman about Centre des Arts, and he's not unsympathetic to your view."

"What view?" said Ella, knowing perfectly well, but wanting Margot to spell it out.

"That I should have been more frank with you initially and explained the bank's involvement."

"Yeah, you should have," said Ella. It was a heady feeling having Margot on the run for once.

"Anyway, we've sat down and done some sums, and the result is that while we can't agree to your proposed price of f15,000,000, we would be prepared to split the difference with you at f17,500,000. I thought I'd ring you and mention this because it is bound to affect your thinking. Since this weekend is decision time, it's clearly important that you have all the facts."

"Thank you," said Ella, "I appreciate it." She tried to sound nonchalant, but it was difficult to keep the smile out of her voice—it was one hell of an about-face. She couldn't wait to tell Stephanie.

"I would like to make one thing clear, however," said Margot a trifle tartly. "There is absolutely no room for any further negotiation. There is no point in your coming back to me to try and screw the price a little lower. This is our *final* offer, and it depends on you completing by the end of August. I should also add that if you have not made a decision by Wednesday, then the project will be offered on the open market."

"I understand, Margot," said Ella meekly. "I'll pass the information on to Stephanie."

"Fine, OK, have a good weekend. What do you think of Wickham, by the way?"

"It's wonderful," said Ella.

"And Tim?"

"Very charming."

"Yes, he is," said Margot, "but he's no match for Stephanie."

Tim met Ella and Greg at the bottom of the great mahogany staircase that dominated the central hall of Wickham. "Come out onto the terrace," he said, "we're serving supper there because it's too nice an evening to be inside. I'll pour you a much-needed drink, and then I'll call the brats."

Millie and Belinda Irvine came running across the lawn in swimsuits as Tim was dispensing drinks. They were attractive children, very fair, slim and athletic, with healthy outdoor tans. Millie was clearly going to be a great beauty, even better-looking than her mother, while Belinda had the same open, cheerful face as her father. After remaining quiet just long enough to be introduced, their chatter was incessant. Greg, who had been a little shy, opened up immediately as they plagued him with questions about America.

Tim immediately came to his rescue. "Greg, when you can't stand these two any longer and prefer a little adult conversation, just tell them to shut up and come and join us. Would you like a beer?"

"A beer?" said Millie, scandalized. "He's not grown-up enough to drink beer."

"He certainly is," Tim corrected her.

Greg flushed with pleasure. "Yes, please, sir."

"Good lad." Drinks dispensed, the children wandered off to see the stables, giving Ella and Tim a few minutes of peace. "You made your phone calls," said Tim. "No problems, I hope."

Ella made a face. "I have a few problems back in New York. I've never left my business before, and it seems the moment I do, everything falls apart."

"Oh, I'm sorry. Is it serious?"

"Expensive," said Ella. "The other call was interesting, though."

"To Margot?"

"Yes. Amazingly, she's dropped the price again. I don't know whether Stephanie told you, but as a result of the information you gave us she immediately came down by f10,000,000."

Tim shook his head. "No, I haven't spoken to Stephanie since. I just had a message via our housekeeper that she wouldn't be home tonight, and that you and Greg would be arriving in time for supper."

Ella tried not to show surprise. Tim's role had been crucial—it seemed extraordinary that Stephanie had not told him so. She felt compelled to explain. "The original price was set at f30,000,000. As an immediate result of your lunch with Jeremy Margot dropped to f20,000,000. We rejected the price, and that call was to say she has agreed with her chairman on a final price of f17,500,000."

Tim grinned. "That's great. So do you think in the circumstances I can justify charging my lunch to the business?"

Ella laughed. "I most certainly think you should." She hesitated and then asked the question, although she already knew the answer. "Are you much involved in the business?"

Tim shook his head. "No, normally not at all. I was initially with Stephanie's original project here at Wickham. We planned the whole thing together, but all her schemes since have been of her own making. She's a clever girl."

"Yes, she is," said Ella.

"People knock her, you know, for spending so little time at home, but we're all different, and what's right for some is not for others. I miss her, of course, and so do the children, but she has a right to respond to this ambition that seems to drive her on." He smiled—a little wistfully, Ella thought.

"Though I can't help hoping that every deal she does will be the last."

"You can't be too pleased about Paris, then," said Ella.

"Certainly it's going to be a long and difficult job. It will be far from easy to administer from your point of view, I would have thought."

Ella nodded. Tim had immediately spotted the predicament Margot and Stephanie chose to ignore. "To be honest, I've been thinking a lot about that angle—how I'm going to cope from the other side of the Atlantic. Obviously, now that the price has dropped so low, it would seem to be crazy not to go ahead, but I clearly can't afford to neglect my New York business . . . and then, of course, there's Greg."

"He's a nice boy."

"Yes, he is," said Ella, "but you know what kids are like—they need stability more than anything else. Although my business is demanding, up till now it's all been based in New York. We have a nice roomy apartment there, in the same building as the office, and Greg goes to school nearby. I'm always there for him at the end of the day, and I'm reluctant to alter that. It's a funny age, fourteen—such a time of change."

Supper, a simple meal of shepherd's pie and salad, was served on the terrace by a strange little woman with peroxide-bleached hair. "This is Mrs. Maggs," Tim explained. "She cooks, cleans, and looks after us in a most wonderful way and keeps the children in order."

"Oh, no, she doesn't," said Millie, "we keep Maggs in order."

"You mind your tongue, Miss Millie, or I'll beat your bum." Clearly, Mrs. Maggs was one of the family.

Greg was full of enthusiasm. "Mom, they have horses and a swimming pool. Belinda says I can go riding tomorrow. Is that all right, sir?" He looked at Tim expectantly.

"Yes, of course. In fact, we can make a good long day of it. Why don't I give you a call at six o'clock? You can come and watch the milking."

"I'd really like that," said Greg.

"You can't," said Millie, appalled. "It's much too early."

"I love the country and farming," said Greg. "I don't want to miss a single minute."

"Then we'll get up, too," said Belinda.

"Oh, no, you don't," said Tim. "You're going to be spending all day with Greg, and with you two around I won't get a word in edgewise. I'd like to spend some time with him, too, you know—I don't see why he should be your friend and not mine."

Again, Tim had hit just the right note with Greg, Ella thought. The only men her son knew well were Laurence, who was gentle and kind to him but still treated him as a baby, and Aaron, his godfather, who, because of his work, was rather a remote figure. To be placed on an equal footing with this man, whom he clearly already admired, had to be very good for him.

The next day was wonderful—they rode and swam, walked and talked, and the easy friendship that developed among the five of them was uncanny in the swiftness of its growth. There were no squabbles among the children, but there was a great deal of laughter, and both Greg and Ella relaxed and blossomed in the warmth of this happy family—indeed, it felt as though they had known Wickham and the Irvines for ever.

Stephanie was bone-weary as she turned her MG into the driveway of Wickham. She had spent a long, restless night haggling over the details of the Paris deal, followed by a long, tiresome day with Lord Rainham. He was an irritating little man who knew nothing about the commercial viability of stately houses but behaved as if hc knew everything. If it was not for the magnificence of his property, Stephanie would have abandoned the project. No, that was not true, she thought as she brought the car to a halt by the front door. She was restless. She'd had no new project for some months, and while the Paris deal looked as if it was coming together, she could not rely upon it. She eased herself out of the car and straightened her aching back. Her head thumped, and she felt sticky and dirty from the twin effects of London and the heat. She was about to enter the house when she heard the sound of laughter coming from the direction of the swimming pool. Changing direction, she walked around the side of the house.

Tim and Ella were sitting by the pool, a bottle of champagne between them, while the children splashed about in the water. The scene was so perfect, it looked like something out of *Homes & Gardens*—the happy, laughing children, the relaxed couple enjoying their drinks. Stephanie felt a stab of irritation. Her resentment swelled as she dragged herself across the lawn toward them—the swimming pool had been paid for by the proceeds of a project Stephanie had undertaken for Lord Montague several years before; the champagne they were drinking had been a gift from a grateful client; and how was it that she and Ella were about to embark upon the biggest project of their respective careers, yet Ella could sit there like any housewife, relaxed and apparently without a care in the world?

Stephanie strode into their midst. "Very cozy, I must say."

"Darling." Tim leapt to his feet and kissed Stephanie's cheek, which she offered to him coolly. "You look absolutely exhausted. Let me pour you a glass of champagne."

Stephanie ignored his offer and turned her venom on Ella. "I expected to find you hard at work."

Ella shook her head. "I've spent most of this week hard at work, and I am supposed to be on vacation—I guess I've earned a day off."

"You're lucky you feel you can afford one," Stephanie said.

"I don't know about *afford,*" said Ella mildly, "but *earned,* certainly. Besides, I have some great news for you that is going to make our sums one hell of a lot easier. Margot's dropped to f17,500,000."

"Certainly, that's good news," said Stephanie, "but it's hardly a reason to abandon our calculations."

Ella was irritated. "I'm not suggesting it is, but let's face it, the whole project suddenly looks a great deal more attractive than it did."

Stephanie turned away. "I'm going to change. What time's dinner?"

"Eight o'clock," said Tim.

"Eight o'clock! But it's only half past six, and I'm absolutely starving."

"I'll see if Mrs. Maggs can move it forward, only I didn't dare make it any earlier because I didn't know what time you'd be back," said Tim.

"Oh, don't worry," said Stephanie, striding away, "I wouldn't want to disrupt the domestic arrangements." She stepped off the terrace, almost tripping with a combination of anger and fatigue. She knew she had behaved badly, but the compulsion to destroy the evident easy happiness around the pool had been too strong an instinct to fight.

It was only as Stephanie opened the front door that she realized her children had not even acknowledged her arrival home.

Chapter 5

"Bye, Stephanie, see you tomorrow," Ella called as she, Tim, and the children stood at the front door of Wickham. With an elegant wave of the hand Stephanie slipped into gear and sent her little MG hurtling down the driveway.

Ella and Stephanie had planned to spend most of Sunday working on figures to see how Margot's new offer affected their budget. However, on Sunday morning Stephanie had received a telephone call from Lord Rainham asking her to come up to Derbyshire immediately, as he had thought through her proposals and wished to sign the deal immediately. Stephanie, eager to secure the deal, felt it important to respond positively to his request, which was why on Sunday evening she was leaving her family again and heading for Derbyshire. "I'll be back by Monday evening," she assured Ella. "We can spend all Tuesday on the project and telephone Margot on Wednesday morning in order to meet her deadline."

The little group dispersed as soon as Stephanie had left—the children to play tennis, Tim to inspect the stock before sunset, and Ella to do some work. At Tim's insistence Ella settled herself in his study—an elegant room facing due south, with wonderful views over the estate. His desk was made of polished oak, solid and dependable. There was a photograph of the children on their ponies, another of his sheepdog, yet another of himself and Stephanie, clearly taken some years before—they were leaning over a gate, arms around each other, laughing, and for a reason Ella could not define, the photograph disturbed her. She had just started going through one of the interminable lists of building costs when the telephone rang. She hesitated and then picked it up. "Wickham"—she glanced at the instrument—"253."

"Ella?" The voice sounded vaguely incredulous but was nonetheless instantly recognizable. As always, Ella felt her heart flip.

"Aaron! How are you? How lovely to hear from you."

"I'm OK, Ella. I didn't expect to get through to you this easy. I understand you're staying at some grand stately home, and so I guess I thought the butler would answer."

Ella laughed. "It's not that kind of stately home—very old, very impressive, but inhabited by nice, simple people. It's great to hear from you. How are Alice and the kids?"

"Fine, just fine."

There was a silence on the line, and Ella instantly felt a sense of apprehension. "Aaron, is everything OK?"

"That's why I'm calling, Ella. It's your mother. She's had a stroke."

Ella waited to feel something, but the news seemed to have no impact on her at all. "Is she dead?"

"No," said Aaron carefully, "but she's in a coma, and Pa reckons it's unlikely she'll come out of it—in fact, she's slipping away, which is why he asked me to call you."

Ella had a sick feeling in the pit of her stomach. "He wants me to go to her?" she asked incredulously.

"That's right," said Aaron. "Although it's unlikely she will regain consciousness before she goes, it's a possibility, and just because she can't communicate herself, it doesn't mean she doesn't know what's going on. You know Pa, he loves playing the amateur psychiatrist. He reckons you should be with her when she goes, as much for your sake as for hers."

"I can't come, Aaron—I'm in the middle of finalizing a big deal, and I have a deadline set for Wednesday."

"OK," said Aaron, "so you're in the middle of a deal. There are plenty of deals in the world, Ella, but you only have one mother, and Pa doesn't think she'll be around after Wednesday. You may regret it if you don't come immediately."

"I can't come, Aaron, I really can't."

"Sure you can—shall I tell Pa you're on your way?"

"I'll never get a flight at such short notice."

"You'll get a flight," said Aaron, "but I must know you're definitely coming. It would be wrong for Pa to tell your ma you're on your way if you're not going to show."

"I thought you said she was in a coma," said Ella.

"She is, but as I said, who knows what she can hear? I understand how you feel about her, but she's dying, Ella. You're the only good thing that's come out of her rotten life. Don't deprive her of that—not now, not at the end."

"I can't go back, I can't face it," Ella said, hot tears in her eyes. "Surely, Aaron Connors, you of all people should understand why I can't ever go back home."

"Ella, you can do anything—you're the bravest person I've ever met."

"What about Greg?" Ella said faintly.

"Bring Greg, too."

"But I couldn't—he'll ask questions. What'll I tell him?"

"Ella, Greg is fourteen years old. So far you've managed to avoid telling him about his family and your past, but you can't put it off for much longer. This trip back to Silver Springs could be just what both of you need. You've been running away from your past ever since you left. You should turn around and face it."

"I can't, Aaron." Ella was crying in earnest now.

"You can, brave girl. You must. You owe it to yourself, to Greg, and to your mother."

"I owe Ma nothing," Ella almost shouted at him.

"She gave you life, Ella."

Another silence followed.

"Look," said Aaron, "one thing at a time. Call the airline

and book a flight as early tomorrow morning as you can make it. Then call me with the details, and I'll arrange for a car to pick you up from Cincinnati. Delay your deal, whatever it is, for a few days, and when you have it all arranged and have had a chance to clear your mind, call me back, and we'll talk about how to handle Greg."

Slowly Ella replaced the receiver. Wickham and the balmy English summer's evening had receded. She was back in the steamy, dusty heat of Kentucky, and all the superficial achievements of her life seemed suddenly to count for nothing. Only the echo of Aaron's voice sustained her—her rock, her secret love. In a trance she telephoned the American Airways office and booked two seats on a flight to Cincinnati, leaving Heathrow at 8:30 the following morning. She arranged for a car to collect her from Wickham at 5:30 and then, taking a deep breath, she dialed Margot's home number.

"Margot Haigh."

"Margot, it's Ella. I'm sorry to trouble you on your home number again."

"That's no problem, Ella." Margot sounded unusually friendly.

"Something's come up," said Ella. "I've just had a call from a childhood friend of mine to say that my mother's dying. She's had a stroke."

"Oh, I'm sorry," said Margot, a little guardedly.

Ella hurried on. "I'm going to have to fly back to Kentucky to be with her. The doctor says she probably only has twenty-four hours, thirty-six at the most."

"Is she in a coma?" Margot asked.

"Yes."

"Then she's unlikely to know you're even there, I suppose."

"Possibly not," said Ella, angry at having to defend a decision that was not of her own making, "but I have to go anyway."

"I understand, of course," said Margot, "and there's no

problem provided you and Stephanie can give me the go-ahead on the Centre des Arts project before you leave."

"We can't do that," said Ella. "We need at least another day on the figures, and Stephanie's not here right now—she's in Derbyshire on business."

"I'm not extending my deadline. Either you'll have to delay going to Kentucky, or Stephanie will have to cut short her business in Derbyshire. The decision's yours, of course," said Margot, her voice steely. "I'm just telling you the facts. The drop in price I've offered you is withdrawn at 5:30 London time on Wednesday."

Ella just managed to cope with supper, but when the children had gone off to bed Tim poured two hefty brandies and handed one to her. They were still sitting at the kitchen table over the remains of supper. "Take a hefty swig," said Tim, "and then tell me what's wrong."

Ella did as she was told. Strangely, his intuition did not surprise her. "How can you tell anything is wrong?" she wondered aloud.

Tim smiled gently. "Oh, come, come, the effervescent girl we know and love is nowhere to be seen. It's been forced jollity tonight, and a real strain, by the look of it."

"I hope the girls didn't notice." Ella's dark eyes looked huge and haunted in the evening shadows.

"Greg might have, but the girls didn't. You're evading the issue, Ella."

"I've had a call from Aaron Connors. He's a childhood friend of mine. We grew up together in Kentucky. He's now a gynecologist in New York."

"Go on," said Tim encouragingly.

"He called to say my mother's had a stroke and is in a coma."

"I'm terribly sorry," said Tim. "Are you close?"

Ella shook her head vehemently. "I should be with her, though, Tim, so I've booked a flight to Cincinnati for Greg and me. The car's going to pick us up at 5:30 tomorrow morning."

"I could have arranged for the chauffeur to take you to the airport," said Tim.

"No, no, I wouldn't dream of troubling you. It's all fixed, but it does leave us with a problem."

Tim lowered his brandy glass. "Of course, the Centres des Arts—the deadline's Wednesday, isn't it? Still, under the circumstances, I'm sure Margot will extend it."

"She won't," said Ella. "I've already spoken to her on the phone, and she won't budge."

"That woman's impossible. Look, let's go and say good night to the kids, then I'll make some coffee, and we'll talk this through."

It was good to have someone else taking charge for once. They kissed the children good night, and when they came downstairs Tim felt in the pocket of his trousers and threw a lighter to Ella. "The fire's laid in my study. You light it while I make the coffee. I'll be with you in a moment."

At night Tim's room came into its own. The lighting from two charming standard lamps gave the room a soft glow. The flames from the fire sent shadows flickering around the wood-paneled walls. Ella collapsed onto a battered old sofa that was pulled up in front of the fire. By the time Tim joined her she was starting to relax a little. "So let me get this straight," Tim said, sitting down beside her. "You've spoken to Margot, and she won't extend the deadline, but you haven't yet spoken to Stephanie?" Ella shook her head. "Are you prepared to take the risk of going ahead without spending any more time on the deal?"

"No," said Ella quickly.

"Is that because you're unsure as to the viability of the project or because you're still uncertain about your personal commitment?"

Ella smiled at the shrewdness of the question. "A little of the former and a great deal of the latter," she admitted. "Margot and Stephanie between them seem to have swung me along with their enthusiasm, and certainly it is a marvelous opportunity. In my view, though, we need more time. There's a lot of money involved, and a great many implications—both commercial and personal—to consider. For example, we have yet to finalize the terms of the funding."

"It seems to me Margot's being more than a little unreasonable."

"Possibly, yes, but I've never known her to change her mind, and honestly I don't think I can make a decision before I've seen my mother."

"No, of course you can't," said Tim. "Look, leave it to me. I'll talk to Stephanie in the morning, and between us we'll see if we can persuade Margot to wait a few days. I know this is a ghastly question to ask, but assuming your doctor's prognosis is right and your mother does die Wednesday, how long will it be before you can be back in England?"

"I won't want to stay," said Ella hurriedly, "but I suppose there's the funeral to consider. I could be back by next weekend, I guess."

"We'll see if we can get a week's extension, then. Here, let me top up your brandy."

"I shouldn't. I have a very early start in the morning."

"Rubbish, it will do you good. Tell me, are there any other arrangements you should be making?"

Ella considered for a moment. "I have to call Aaron back and tell him what time I'll be at Cincinnati, and then he'll arrange for a car to meet me."

"Give me Aaron's number, and I'll do that for you."

"You're very kind, Tim," Ella said. "You know, it's strange—three days ago I didn't even know you." She grinned, the tension in her suddenly easing. "I knew *of* you, of course, but I suppose I imagined some pompous, frightfully British guy who could talk about nothing but horses and shooting small animals. I couldn't have been more wrong—you're so kind, a true friend."

Tim laughed. "It's not difficult to be kind to you, Ella, and I hope we'll be friends for a long time. I admire you very much—the way you handle your business and still manage to be a full-time mother to Greg—it can't be easy."

"We muddle through," said Ella, "but thank you for the vote of confidence."

"Speaking of friendship"—Tim hesitated, swirling his brandy in the glass to catch the light from the fire, and carefully not looking at Ella as he spoke—"if we are to be friends, why don't you tell me what's really worrying you about going back to Kentucky?"

The suddenness of the question astonished Ella. "W-what makes you think that there is anything worrying me?"

"I'm only guessing, and tell me to mind my own business if you want, but you haven't told Greg you're going, have you?" Ella shook her head. "For a normally efficient woman it doesn't make much sense. The boy has to be packed up and ready to leave at 5:30 tomorrow morning, and yet he doesn't even know he's leaving. That can only mean you have grave doubts about taking him." Ella still said nothing. "Well, let me approach the problem from a different angle," said Tim. "If, for whatever reason, you don't want to take him to Kentucky, leave him here with us. The girls would love to have him—you know that—and so would I. I'll make sure he has a good time. Certainly, deathbeds and fourteen-year-old boys aren't really very compatible."

Ella felt her spirits soar at the unexpectedly easy solution to her problem. "Oh, Tim, that's so kind of you."

"Are you saying yes, then?"

Acceptance was on Ella's lips when Aaron's words came back to her. "I—I don't know. I'll have to think about it."

Tim got up and threw another log on the fire. The sparks fanned out, and the shadows created by the flames leapt onto the ceiling. "Ella, something's worrying you a great deal. There's probably a hell of a lot of other people it would be better to talk to than me, but I'm here now. Tell me what's troubling you, and I promise I will never pass it on to a living soul."

The warmth of the fire, the brandy, the tranquillity of the room, and the still quietness of the countryside outside the windows combined to lull Ella into a sense of peace and security. This subtle blend of atmosphere, combined with her instinctive trust in this man, this comparative stranger, made it suddenly seem possible to let someone glimpse the turmoil that seethed beneath her apparently easygoing, good-natured exterior. When she spoke at last her voice was low, barely above a whisper. "You're right," she said, "I am worrying about taking Greg back to Kentucky."

"I am guessing here," said Tim, "but does your worry concern Greg's father?" Ella nodded. "You're worried you'll meet him again, is that it? Are you still married, or is he likely to cause trouble?"

"No, and I'm not worried I'll run into him again—well, not exactly," said Ella. "You see, I—I don't know who he is."

Tim frowned. "I don't understand."

Ella stared at the fire, unable to meet Tim's eyes. "To say I don't know who he is is wrong. I don't know which one he was—you see, I was gang-raped."

When she left school at fourteen Ella Kovac was certain of one thing: She had to find a means of escape—from her life, from her mother, from Silver Springs, from Kentucky—but escape equaled money. Ostracized from society, the Kovacs had no friends, but since the day she had fallen under Aaron Connor's protection no one had actually abused or fought with Ella—neither, though, had they befriended her. The mothers saw to that. Mollie Kovac was a threat to every woman in Silver Springs. If one had a fight with her man, he would likely go to a bar, get drunk, and from there, almost inevitably, end up at Mollie Kovac's.

The backdrop to Ella's nights as a child was a noisy one. The sounds of fornication she blocked out, but the drunken arrivals and departures woke her up regularly, every hour or so right through the night. It was not until she moved out that she experienced the luxury of a full night's sleep for the first time.

Money was the key to escape; how to get it was the question. Working in town did not appeal to her. She could imagine the mean, critical eyes of the inhabitants following her every move. It was Dr. Andrew Connors, Aaron's father, who provided the answer. Like most country doctors of the time he relied heavily on the mixing of his own prescriptions to provide medicines for the community. In return for a nine-hour day during which Ella answered the telephone and prepared Dr. Connors's home cures she received $10 a week. It seemed a fortune to the fourteen-year-old, who'd never had a dime of her own, and with great foresight she lied to her mother about the amount of her earnings. Each week she handed over the bulk of her money to her mother, but she kept $4 for herself, which she kept in a little cash box in Doc's study.

In addition to the money, the job had the advantage of keeping Ella in touch with Aaron. The bond between them had grown steadily since the day Aaron had become her champion and on Ella's part had developed into adolescent love. She knew there was no future for them—she was not good enough for him—but no one could take away her dreams.

Doc Connors liked his waiting room to be a welcoming place. There were always fresh flowers on the windowsill, the curtains were washed each week, the paintwork was kept spick-and-span, and on the table by the door there was a selection of magazines and a copy of the *Wall Street Journal.* Though nearly a week out of date by the time it reached Silver Springs, the paper was changed on a daily basis, as though it contained the most up-to-the-minute news. In idle moments Ella took to reading the paper, thirsting for knowledge of the outside world she longed to reach. With an inherent love of figures the local school had been quite unable to encourage, she discovered investment among the pages of the *Wall Street Journal.* Fascinated day after day, she plotted the rise and fall of stocks and bonds, watched and fretted over the Dow Jones, and began to understand the workings of the international money markets.

One evening Andrew Connors caught her poring over the

Journal. "Well, I'll be darned," he said, "Aaron told me you'd taken a liking to the stock market, but I didn't believe him."

"It fascinates me," Ella admitted. "I hope you don't mind me reading the paper now that everyone's gone."

"Of course not, child—so, are you going to tell me where to place my money?"

"The United Railroad Company," said Ella promptly.

Dr. Connors laughed. "Show me."

Ella ran her finger down the column. "There."

"But the stock is dropping, honey."

"Yes, I know, I know," said Ella patiently, "it's been dropping for three months—in fact, it's half the price it was three months ago."

"So why do you want me to throw my money away? It sounds like your red-hot tip is going bust."

"I read an article in the *Journal* a month back that said there's going to be a big shake-up in the railroads and a lot of these small companies are going to be bought up. Just think what would happen to the stock."

"And just think what would happen to the price if it didn't happen."

"I think it's worth a gamble," said Ella stubbornly.

"Do you now," said Dr. Connors. "Tell me, how much are your savings worth these days?"

"I have nearly $110."

"OK, here's what I'll do. When I'm in Cincinnati next week for that medical conference I'll invest $100 of your money and $200 of mine. If your hunch pays off, then we'll split the profits fifty-fifty. If we lose, well, we lose."

"That's not fair to you," Ella protested.

"I'm happy with the deal," said Doc Connors, laughing. "You've given me the tip, so I'm paying for privileged information."

Five weeks later, after days of nail-biting and watching the price plummet even further, the United Railroad Company was bought out. After a further three months Ella and Doc

Connors's $300 investment was worth about $4,000. They cashed in and split the proceeds, and Ella reinvested. At fifteen she owned one pair of shoes and three dresses and slept in a bug-infested shack with her prostitute mother, but she was launched on the American stock market.

One evening that summer, shortly after Ella's fifteenth birthday, she had been working late and decided to take the long way home, by the river. It had been stifling hot all day, threatening a storm that never materialized. The air was still humid, but with night coming there was a gentle breeze, and the cool air off the river was infinitely comforting. She was reluctant to go home. Now that the family had two incomes, Mollie Kovac's love affair with the rye bottle had become even more profound, and the sessions at the shack accordingly less discreet. Ella sat down on a tree stump at the edge of the river, enjoying the peace and solitude.

"Why, if it's not little Miss Kovac, out looking for a man just like her momma." Ella swung around. There were three—no, four—boys walking along the bank toward her. They had all been her classmates at school. They were an irritant, but they did not worry her; she knew how to handle them.

"You hush up, Jim Keeting," she spat back. "I just want a little peace and quiet. Some of us have been working hard instead of lounging around bars all day."

"Will you listen to that," Jim said. "Miss High-and-Mighty, yet I do hear that she and Mamma Mollie are a double act now—two for the price of one and a half. Maybe we should sample the goods sometime." The other three sniggered a little self-consciously.

The boys had reached Ella now, and she automatically stood up so as not to be at a disadvantage. At Jim's words Ella felt the control on her temper ebb away, and she drew back her hand and slapped him viciously across the face. He caught her wrist in his hands. He was surprisingly strong despite his small stature. Without warning, his lips crushed onto hers, forcing the breath from her body.

Ella had been in so many fights during her short life that one more seemed of no particular significance . . . until she felt Jim Keeting's mouth on hers. Then she recognized the difference.

Panic rose as if to smother her. She fought for control of this new, terrifying fear, but the trembling weakness of her body betrayed her.

"See that, boys? She likes it!" Jim still had hold of her shoulders. She tried to tear herself away, but she no longer had the strength.

"Leave me be, just leave me be," she said. There was a pleading note in her tone that appalled her. Terror was recognizable in the high tremors of her voice, and she shuddered with a sudden unexplained chill.

Like every predator, Jim scented her fear. For a moment common sense prevailed, but the warmth of the night, the feel of Ella's warm flesh, and the surfeit of beer in his belly proved too much for him. He kissed her again, and as he did so his inexperienced fingers fumbled with the buttons of her dress. She fought him, but she was no match for his strength, and her very resistance seemed to goad him.

Angry, agitated, driven by lust, he tore away her dress, the well-washed cotton giving easily to expose her bare breasts. The other boys stood rooted to the spot.

"Stop him," Ella yelled at them. They did nothing.

He threw her to the ground with a cry of triumph and tried to hold her down as he fumbled unsuccessfully with her pants and then his. Ella recognized her chance. With a supreme effort she tried to tear herself from his grasp.

"Hold her down. I said hold her down, dammit!" Jim could barely speak for shortness of breath, but they heard him all right.

Silently, and therefore all the more menacingly, the three moved forward. One pinned her arms above her head; the other two held her thrashing legs while Jim tore away her pants. Naked, spread-eagled before him, Ella watched in paralyzing horror as Jim stood up and leisurely began to remove his trousers. His white teeth gleamed in the darkness, and she realized he was smiling.

Each took a turn with her. The last one turned her on her front, spread her legs wide, and sodomized her. Only he could not be the father of her son, but by then she could not distinguish one from the other, for a sea of pain had engulfed her.

The quiet of his room for once brought Tim no comfort. There was a long silence after Ella had finished speaking, broken only by the occasional shifting of the logs as they burned in the grate. It seemed incredible to Tim that this warm, intelligent, humorous woman, with whom he felt he had so much in common, could have been through such an experience—yet he did not doubt her for a moment. The horror of that night still showed on her face as she spoke, and now, sitting in a corner of the sofa, she seemed to have shrunk. The bold, dazzling exterior she showed to the world was nowhere to be seen. The scars were still very near the surface, he realized. "What did you do?" he asked at last.

"It—it took me a long time to gain any sort of control of myself and find what was left of my dress," Ella said. "I couldn't go home somehow, so I went back to the Connors place. I was lucky, if you can call anything about that night lucky. Aaron was home from college and had been to a party in Lexington. We arrived at his house together, and he led me inside and called his father. Doc Connors patched me up and put me to bed in a spare room. He gave me a shot, and I slept. When I woke up crying he gave me another shot, and I slept some more." Ella grinned faintly. "It went on like that for some time."

"At least you knew who the boys were, so they didn't go unpunished," said Tim confidently.

Ella laughed aloud, a small, brittle laugh that made Tim wince. "The law in Kentucky isn't quite as automatic as it is in some places," she said, "particularly if your mother's the local whore. The fathers of the boys got together and paid off my mother so she wouldn't press charges, and being only fifteen, there was nothing I could do about it."

"I don't believe I'm hearing this—your own mother sold your . . . your innocence?"

"If you like, yes," said Ella. "I didn't realize it at first. Doc called in the law immediately after he put me to bed. He assumed that the four boys would be picked up because I'd been able to tell him who they were. I don't know how things went from there exactly, but every time I asked Doc what was happening he became more and more tight-lipped, and finally he burst out with the news that charges weren't being pressed. It wasn't until sometime later I found out that my mother had been paid off, and by then, of course, I realized I was pregnant."

Tim sighed. "So of course you're worried that you may meet these men again when you go back to Silver Springs."

"I don't mind if I do," said Ella. "That's not what worries me. It'll be they who won't be able to meet my eye, not the other way around. I haven't forgotten them—Jim Keeting, Gregory Daingerfield, Sam Morgan, and Warren Clay." She spoke the names slowly, deliberately, and Tim recognized her hatred for them was burned into her very soul. He shuddered slightly at the depth of feeling he saw there.

"You're worried that Greg will start asking too many questions, is that it?" Ella nodded. "What have you told him so far?"

"I told him that his pa took off when he was just a baby, and that I didn't know where he was. I hinted, though, that we had been married." Tim frowned. "Oh, I know what you're thinking. You think I'm doing the wrong thing, bringing him up on a fairy tale."

"No, I'm not thinking that," said Tim.

"It's what Aaron thinks. He thinks I have to start telling Greg something."

"Aaron's right there," said Tim, "but the way I see it, Ella, you can't ever tell him the truth either."

Ella leaned forward, elbows on her knees, her face suddenly alert and alive again. "Oh, Tim, do you really believe that?"

"Of course I do. It would destroy the boy."

"I can't tell you how much it means to me to hear you say that," said Ella. "You see, it's something I've never discussed with anybody in the world except Aaron, and he—well, he believes in dealing with the realities of life."

"I do think you should tell Greg the truth about as much of your background as you can," said Tim thoughtfully, "but you're going to have to lie about the circumstances of his birth. You have to lie to him to protect him. There's no risk of anyone telling him the truth, is there, provided the Connorses know what you've said to him?"

Ella shook her head. "No," she said. "It was an odd thing—the town's attitude toward me changed completely afterwards. When I found I was pregnant Doc offered me an abortion, but I wouldn't take it. It didn't seem right somehow. Greg can remember very little of the five years we spent in Silver Springs before moving to New York, but his childhood was very different from my own. We lived with the Connorses. I worked for them, and Greg mixed with other kids without any problems. All the old sly remarks were a thing of the past—everyone was too ashamed, I guess."

"Then," said Tim, suddenly decisive, "this is what I would do. Take him with you to Kentucky, because you could do with his support, and he's old enough now to give it. Tell him about your mother, who and what she was, and about your childhood and how tough it was. I take it that'll be news to him?" Ella nodded. "Tell him that you and his father weren't married, that you spent one imprudent night together, and that you parted the following day without your knowing where his father was going, and of course without either of you being aware that you were pregnant. Maybe that doesn't put you in the best of all possible lights, but it saves Greg from any feeling of rejection."

Ella stood up and walked to Tim where he stood in front

of the fire. She put a hand on his shoulder and kissed his cheek. "I won't ever forget our talk, Tim, and I'm going to follow your advice precisely. I will take Greg with me tomorrow, and I'll tell him every detail of my background except that one night. I know I've been a little overprotective of him in the past, but—well, now that he's older, perhaps my telling him about my life will help him to understand why his mother is so odd."

"Odd, yes," said Tim, his eyes filled with frank admiration, "oddly magnificent."

Greg was unusually quiet on the flight. As an only child he was not particularly gregarious, but despite her own worries and preoccupations, Ella became increasingly aware that his silence was not natural. After a meal he slept for a while. When he woke she took a deep breath and asked him what was wrong. He shrugged his shoulders. "Nothing's wrong, really, Mom."

"Something is," said Ella. "Are you sad at leaving Wickham?"

"Yes, very," said Greg. "I liked it there."

"Is that the problem, then?" There was silence. "Come on Greg, tell me what's bugging you."

"Why aren't we like a normal family?" Greg burst out.

"You mean mother, father, and children?" said Ella with a sinking heart.

"I guess so, and grandparents, too. Millie and Belinda see their grandparents all the time. I don't have a father, so I don't know his parents, and you've never talked about your mother—not until now, when she's dying." His voice was full of contempt.

"We didn't get along," said Ella, aware of the inadequacy of her answer.

Greg appeared not to have heard. "I've been trying to remember her from when we lived in Kentucky. I can remember Doc Connors and, of course, Aaron, and most of all I remember Mrs. Connors—she was so kind. I don't remember my grandma, though—did we used to visit her?"

Ella shook her head. "No. She came to see you once after you were born. We got into a kind of argument, and I was very upset. Doc thought it was better if we didn't see each other anymore, so we didn't." Greg remained silent. "Look," said Ella, "there are a lot of things I ought to tell you about my past, about our lives in Kentucky, but it seems right now on the plane just isn't a good time. Trust me, Greg—once we're in Silver Springs and we have a little time on our own, I'll tell you all about it."

"OK," said Greg affably enough, and, with the resilience of youth, he was soon flipping through a magazine, apparently unconcerned.

Their brief conversation, however, had left Ella in a turmoil. Her past was at odds with the image she tried to project to Greg and to the world. To have to face what she had once been was agony to Ella, and as always, she found herself blaming her mother. It was typical that her mother should have fallen into a terminal coma rather than dying outright, forcing Ella to return to Silver Springs—the one place on earth she wished never to see again.

Chapter 6

Silver Springs, Kentucky—*August 1977*

Since Ella and Greg had left Wickham with only overnight bags, they were off the plane quickly. "Aaron said he would arrange for a car to meet us," Ella said to Greg. "Can you see anyone holding up a card with our name on it?"

"No," said Greg, and then he laughed aloud. "But I can see Uncle Aaron." He let out a whoop and ran to Aaron.

"Hi, Greg." Aaron shook Greg's hand, and Greg turned to Aaron's wife, Alice, who embraced him warmly.

Ella stood for a second watching the scene, a great feeling of relief flooding through her. With Aaron and Alice around, she could cope. Aaron was suddenly beside her. "Hey, you don't look too pleased to see us."

"Oh, Aaron," said Ella, and uncharacteristically she burst into tears.

The journey from Cincinnati airport to Silver Springs was uneventful, but for Greg it was a complete eye-opener. His passion for country living had him craning out of the window, pointing out the virtues of Kentucky in high summer. It was a sweltering day, and by the time they finally reached Silver Springs they were all wringing wet and exhausted. Aaron drove the car slowly up thc main street, giving Ella time to take in her surroundings. "Nothing's changed," she said, "absolutely nothing."

"You're practically right," said Aaron. "There's another bar now, a ladies' hairdresser, my mother tells me, and there's some new housing development out beyond—beyond your mother's old home. We'll stop off at Pa's first, and when you've had a chance to change and rest, I'll take you up to the hospital."

The welcome from Andrew and Irene Connors was equally warm, although Ella had only seen them twice since she had left Silver Springs. Irene looked at Greg in amazement. "Is this truly my baby boy?" Greg shifted uneasily and grinned self-consciously.

"Some baby, eh?" said Ella, ruffling his hair.

"My, you've turned into a handsome young man. Come here and give your Aunt Irene a kiss."

It was early evening before Ella and Aaron made the pilgrimage to the hospital. In some dark corner of her mind Ella had almost hoped her mother would be dead by the time she arrived in Silver Springs. She was not proud of the thought, but the idea of confronting her mother, even in a coma, appalled her.

"Can I come, too?" Greg asked as she was leaving.

Ella shook her head. "Not until I see how she is, Greg, but I promise you, tomorrow."

"OK," he said grudgingly.

They drove in silence for some minutes. "Tell me what you're thinking," Aaron said as they turned up the dusty driveway to the hospital.

"I was counting my blessings," said Ella. "I just don't know what I would have done at the various stages of my life without the love and support of the Connorses. You're all so good to me—just imagine you and Alice coming out here to be with us, and leaving your practice and your kids behind." She was close to tears at that moment, painfully aware of the depths of her feelings for Aaron.

"It's nothing," said Aaron. "Actually, it was Alice's idea. She didn't think you should go through this alone, and she's right, of course—as she always is."

"You're lucky to have her," Ella forced herself to say. It was true, of course. Alice was just right for him in a way she, Ella, never could have been.

Aaron grinned. "Don't I know it." They drew up outside the hospital entrance. "Shall I drop you off?" he asked.

Ella shook her head. "I'd like you to come with me, if you would, Aaron."

Aaron Connors was something of a celebrity at Silver Springs County Hospital. His father was enormously admired and respected, of course, but his son was the big-time consultant from New York. The nurses lowered their eyes and spoke in hushed whispers as he passed. In different circumstances Ella would have been amused.

Because of Aaron's status they were shown into the head nurse's office. "How is she?" Aaron asked. Ella seemed incapable of speech.

"Much the same, Dr. Connors, I'm afraid." The nurse was a thin, scrawny, middle-aged woman whose best feature was a pair of warm brown eyes. "She's showing no signs of coming out of the coma."

"D-do you think there's any chance of her regaining consciousness?" Ella asked.

"To be frank, I doubt it, but you never know. We've seen some strange sights here over the years when people were close to death." The nurse looked suddenly uncomfortable. "I'm sorry, Miss Kovac, I take it you've been told that there is little chance of your mother surviving this."

"Yes, yes I understand," said Ella.

"Would you like to see her now?"

Ella took a deep breath. "Yes, please."

"Shall I come with you?" Aaron asked quietly.

Ella shook her head. Up to that moment she had needed him. Now, suddenly, she didn't want anyone to witness her seeing her mother. She was unsure as to how she would react.

"Call me if you need me," said Aaron. "I'll be in the waiting room."

Aaron had arranged for her mother to be moved to a private room. A nurse opened the door for her, ushered her in, and closed it quietly behind her. Beams of sunlight played on the walls, and there were several bunches of flowers on the window ledge. The paintwork, white and yellow, made the room bright and airy. For a long time Ella stood staring out of the window, unable to look at the figure in the bed. At last, her heart beating as loudly as a drum, she turned and gazed at her mother.

She was a stranger—a tiny, wizened old woman. Her hair had gone completely white, a pretty color, brushed back from her face and fanning out onto the pillow. Her face was lined, but her good bone structure still showed through, and it was possible to see that this old woman had once been very good-looking. Her complexion was pale. For a moment Ella had the absurd idea that they had shown her into the wrong room. Without makeup her mother looked the way a mother should, Ella realized gradually. Mollie Kovac had taken her profession very seriously. Her hair had always been dyed with henna, her face heavily made up, her lips scarlet, her skirts short, her heels high. Since her mother slept late in the mornings, Ella could not remember seeing her except when she was dressed for work. Yet this old lady in the bed had a rather sweet face. Ella could see her sitting in a rocking chair by the kitchen range, knitting for some beloved grandchild, ready with a fund of stories, advice, a helping hand. Ella shook her head as if trying to refocus the picture. Unable to do so, she sank down on the chair beside the bed and simply stared.

More from curiosity than anything else, Ella reached beneath the covers and took one of Mollie's hands in hers. It was a small hand with short, capable fingers—a warm, living thing. There was so much, Ella suddenly realized, that she wanted to ask her mother. Why, why had Mollie Kovac chosen her way of life? Did she enjoy it, or did she really have no choice? What had started her on the rocky road to ruin and degradation? What, too, of her father, Mollie's husband? Mollie had told her that her father had run off. He had been a tobacco worker, Mollie had said. They'd had a whirlwind romance and married, but he had gone off to another part of the state before the baby was born. As Ella grew older and wiser she no longer believed the story, imagining her father to have been one of her mother's clients. Not for the first time, Ella thought of the similarity between her own conception and Greg's. Like her own mother, she could not disclose the name of her child's father.

Time passed, and Ella did not hear the discreet knock on the door. She looked up, startled, when Aaron placed a hand on her shoulder. "Come on, sweetheart. You've been here long enough now."

Ella stared at him vaguely. "Have I? How long?"

"Nearly two hours."

"Jesus!" Ella looked confused. She ran a hand through her dark curls, her eyes glazed with fatigue and strain.

"Come on," said Aaron, "doctor's orders—I'm taking you home."

Ella stood up, stiffly. "I imagined she'd be all wired up to equipment."

"She isn't, at my request," said Aaron. "I hope you approve, but I felt there was no point in prolonging her life.

The damage caused by the stroke is profound. She's nearly seventy, and it didn't seem right."

"No, no, of course not," said Ella. "So what you are saying is that even if she regains consciousness she wouldn't be able to speak or understand?"

Aaron shook his head. "I very much doubt it." Ella felt tears spring into her eyes. "I know what you're feeling," Aaron said gently. "You want to talk to her one last time." Ella nodded. "Come on, honey, you'll feel better once you're back home."

The warmth and kindness of the Connors family did help. Ella had no appetite, but she drank the whiskey and strong coffee Doc Connors offered. Greg seemed perfectly at home, and over supper he regaled everyone with details of their stay at Wickham, which suddenly seemed a very long time ago to Ella. After Greg and the older folks had gone to bed, Aaron, Alice, and Ella continued to sit out on the front porch, enjoying the peace and quiet of the Kentucky night. "You know," said Ella, "I sometimes wonder what the hell we're doing living in New York."

Alice looked up and smiled. "I know what you mean. We're always complaining about what hell the city is, and yet there we stay. Why don't we give it all up and buy ourselves a ranch someplace? Raise the kids as kids should be raised—riding, swimming in the river, plenty of good fresh air day after day."

Ella looked at Alice affectionately and thought, not for the first time, how lucky she herself had been, as well as Aaron, in his choice of a bride. For Alice was without any form of jealousy, recognizing, understanding, and even enjoying the extraordinary closeness of Aaron and Ella's relationship. There could be few such generous-spirited people as Alice Connors, yet how would she react if she knew how his childhood friend really felt about Aaron, Ella wondered. Still, the Connorses' marriage was safe with her; she would never do anything to hurt either of them. She loved Aaron, loved them both, too much for that. "Well, I'm all for it," Ella said at last, "but we'd better ask the boss."

Aaron leaned forward and knocked his pipe thoughtfully on the railing. "We need a plan," he said. "How about us all retiring in, say, ten years? We should have made a few dollars between us, and we could then eke out the rest of our days as Alice suggests, playing farmers."

"But the kids will all be grown up and gone by then," protested Alice.

"Then they can bring our grandchildren back to see us."

"You're serious, aren't you?" asked Ella.

The question went unanswered as the telephone suddenly shrilled. "I'll get it," said Aaron. He was back in a moment, and even before he spoke Ella knew what he was going to say. "That was the hospital, Ella. I'm sorry, sweetheart, I'm afraid she's gone."

For a moment the breath seemed to be driven from Ella's body—she gasped at the air to fill her lungs. She felt nothing, so why was she sobbing as though her heart would break?

"Why didn't you let me come with you yesterday, why, why, why?" The normally easygoing Greg was lying face-down on the bed, thumping his fists into the pillow.

Ella was astounded by the apparent violence of his feelings. She had expected no more than a token reaction. "Greg, I don't understand why you're so upset. I know it's sad, but you never actually knew her."

"Don't you see"—Greg hiccuped—"don't you see that's what's wrong? I wanted to meet her so much. I want a family, Mom, a proper family. I wanted to ask her stuff, about my grandpa, things like that."

In an instant Ella understood she was witnessing a carbon copy of her own feelings of the previous evening—the lack of identity, the need to belong. Without thinking too hard for fear she would falter she said, "OK, sweetheart, this is what we'll do. I'll ask Aunt Irene if we can borrow the car today, and we'll take off with a picnic. There's a park near here—it's beautiful. We'll find a quiet spot and have a good long talk. I guess I owe you a few explanations, right?"

* * *

The Jenny Wiley State Resort Park was hugged by mountains and rimmed a huge lake. Its beauty was breathtaking, and neither Greg nor Ella felt the need for conversation as they drove along the outer perimeter road until they found a perfect picnic spot by the lake.

"You make a campfire," said Ella. "I'll unload the stuff from the car."

Irene had done them proud—there were sausages, chicken, bread, salad, homemade lemonade, and great chunks of cold apple pie. Ella poured them each a cold drink while Greg took charge of the cooking. They talked of inconsequential things—his school friends back home, his grades, his chances on the various teams come fall. At last, when the meal was finished, Ella embarked on the conversation she knew was long overdue. She told Greg quietly and unemotionally all about her life in Silver Springs, about what her mother did for a living and how much she owed the Connorses. Only when she came to the story of Greg's birth did she hesitate.

"OK," said Greg, "you've told me my father went away just like your father, but you must know who he is, Mom."

Ella shook her head and took a deep breath. "That's the awful thing, Greg—your birth was so very much like my own. I behaved like a very silly girl, though I was only fifteen, as you know. I went to a local party and danced a lot with this one boy. He was tall, dark, good-looking, just like you. We went for a walk by the river after the dance, and—well, I behaved very stupidly and let him make love to me. I was very young, and so was he. I don't think it occurred to either of us that I might get pregnant. The next day he left town. I was sad because I liked him very much. It wasn't until a month or so later I realized what had happened."

"You must have known his name, though," said Greg.

Ella shook her head. "I know this sounds crazy, but I didn't."

"But why was he in town?" Greg persisted. "He must

have been staying with somebody. Didn't the Connorses know who he was?"

Ella shook her head. "He was just a student on vacation passing through, I guess. But—but the thing is, Greg, never feel you've been abandoned by your father—he simply doesn't know you exist. If he did, he'd be very proud of you, and I'm very sorry that you've never had a father of your own."

"Why didn't you marry Aaron, Mom? You were such good friends as kids."

Ella smiled. "I couldn't do that. Aaron's like a brother," she said hurriedly, terrified her feelings would betray her. She smiled to lighten the atmosphere and was rewarded with a smile back. So she continued the story of her working for Andrew Connors, of her interest in the stock market and how she finally made it out of Silver Springs.

Greg poked at the fire distractedly. When at last he spoke his words cut her to the quick. "I guess you did the right thing, Mom, except that if you hadn't made all that money, we'd still be living in Silver Springs, and I kind of like that idea."

"But we'd be poor!" said Ella, horrified. "You'd have no fancy bike, no private schooling, no summer camp, no trips to Europe—"

"But we'd be living in the country," said Greg.

Holding on to what sanity she could muster, Ella recognized that despite his assumed maturity Greg was still a child and did not mean to be cruel. Yet when she thought of her years of struggle to give him a life away from Silver Springs, the knowledge that he would actually prefer to be there was almost too much to bear.

Later, when she was alone, she mulled over their conversation. Always anxious to be honest with herself, Ella could not help recognizing that her struggle to escape had not been purely for Greg but rather more for herself. The thought brought no comfort.

* * *

The crowd at the funeral was extraordinary. Aaron had warned Ella that there was likely to be a good turnout—not so much out of respect for Mollie Kovac as for the chance to glimpse Mollie Kovac's daughter. Ella was apprehensive and threatened not to attend at all, but the Connorses insisted she come. In fact, it was not the ordeal she had expected. Flanked by the Connorses, with Greg standing tall and solemn beside her, she felt among friends.

As Ella and Greg followed the coffin down the aisle of the church all eyes were on them. It suddenly occurred to Ella that both her father and Greg's could be in the congregation, unknowingly watching their son and daughter walk down the aisle. The thought made her raise her eyes and hurriedly search the sea of faces. There was no sign of her tormentors of fourteen years ago, although she was not sure now that she would even recognize them. The thought was unnerving.

As soon as the service was over she ran upstairs to her old bedroom in the Connors house and lay down on the bed, trying to keep her mind as blank as possible. After a while there was a knock on the door, and Greg entered. "Are you OK, Mom?"

She shook her head. "I'm sorry, sweetheart, but I just need some time alone."

He hesitated, something clearly still on his mind. "I'm sorry," he said at last.

"For what?" said Ella.

"I'm sorry for what I said yesterday. I do like our life in New York, really."

"I'm glad," said Ella. "You know something, Greg?" she said. "You're growing up so fast. I'm so proud of you, and I do love you very much."

"I love you, too, Mom." He looked at her awkwardly. "I'd better go downstairs now."

"OK."

After Greg had left her Ella swung her legs over the side of the bed and went to the window. The room looked out over the front of Doc Connors's house and gave a good view of the main street of Silver Springs. Ella stared with interest in both directions. Today the town had buried Mollie Kovac, the harlot, and with her mother's death Ella realized that she, too, was released—freed at last from the squalor of her childhood. Now it was time to look forward, to plan the future, released at last from the long shadow of the past.

Chapter 7

New York—*August 1977*

It felt good to be back in her office despite the scene that had just taken place with Henry Moss. It was not a question of choice, as far as Ella was concerned. She had to work with someone she trusted, and she knew that she no longer trusted Henry. The mistake with ADC's lease was too grave to simply brush under the carpet—he had to go, and go he had.

Ella's offices could not have been much more convenient, for they formed part of the ground floor of Gregory Buildings, the first property she had ever acquired. She and Greg lived in an apartment on the first floor, so commuting to work for Ella meant riding the elevator down just one floor.

Ella pressed the intercom, and moments later Jessie Lendle puffed into her office. Jessie had been with Ella since the very start of her business. She was middle-aged, black, and very large, but she had a heart to match her vast size, and to Ella she was indispensable. In the early days, when Greg was just a small child, Jessie had helped with everything—typing letters, taking Greg to and from school, cleaning the apartment, baby-sitting—whatever was needed to keep the business going. She was not, to be fair, a great typist, but she was blessed with something far more valuable—good, sound common sense and an absolute, unquestioning loyalty. "So you threw him out?" she asked as she sat down by Ella's desk.

"I had no choice, did I, Jess?"

"No," said Jessie, uncompromisingly, "though I blame myself."

"You?" said Ella, who had already spent most of the morning unraveling the affair. "You weren't even here, you were off sick."

"I know that," said Jessie, "but I had no business to be off sick when you were away in Europe. If I'd typed up that lease, I'd have noticed the mistake. You know that."

"Of course I know that," said Ella, "but your job, Jessie, is to type. His job was to think."

Jessie grinned. "I think I resent that, Miss Ella Kovac."

Ella returned the smile. "You know perfectly well what I mean."

"Yeah, I know what you mean." She tilted her head on one side and eyed Ella shrewdly. "I never liked him anyway."

Ella laughed out loud. As usual, Jessie went straight to the heart of the problem. "No, I didn't like him either."

The door burst open. "You two talking about me again, Jessie? Welcome home, Ella." Laurence Merman crossed the office and, bending over, kissed Ella on both cheeks.

"Hi, Laurence." She was at once pleased and irritated—pleased to see him and irritated by his way, as always, of bursting into her office as though he owned it.

"OK, OK," said Jessie, heaving herself out of the seat. "I'll leave you two lovebirds alone."

So far as Ella was aware, Jessie was the only person who knew of their affair, and this was by force of circumstances—it simply would not have been possible to keep it from her. The fact never worried Ella, but Laurence was always irritated by Jessie's references to the relationship—a fact which, no doubt, only encouraged Jessie's lack of discretion. Her words angered him now. "That woman really gets on my nerves," he said. "Why the hell don't you find yourself a decent secretary, Ella? She can't type, she can't mind her own business, and in the space she takes up you could have three secretaries, three typewriters, a copying machine, and a telex and still have room to spare."

"Without Jessie, Lexington Kovac Incorporated would grind to a halt," said Ella firmly. "Are you going to take me out to lunch, Laurence?"

"Why not? Where would you like to go?"

"Somewhere cheerful and quick. I want to be in the apartment by the time Greg comes back from the Connorses. We have a lot to organize before tomorrow."

It had been Alice Connors's suggestion that Ella return to London alone, for it was less than a week before Greg was due back at school, and the heavy negotiations Ella faced upon her return to Europe were hardly going to entertain a fourteen-year-old. Ella had agreed, and so Greg was to stay with Aaron and Alice.

"So how's this Paris deal coming along?" said Laurence as they sat over the remains of their wine.

"OK, I guess," said Ella. "The price has come down one hell of a lot." She explained the details. "Stephanie's pretty confident we can do a good deal on the funding, too—as she says, the bank has to be fairly desperate."

"She sounds like a bright woman, this Lady Stephanie," said Laurence.

"She is. You'd like her."

"So you're going ahead?" he persisted.

"I don't know. I suppose so."

"Forgive me for saying so, honey, but you're not exactly radiating enthusiasm."

"I guess I just don't want to be away from New York too much."

Laurence looked up at her sharply. "Not because of us?"

"No," said Ella gently, "not so much because of us,

although I will miss you, of course. It's mostly because of Greg. I'm all he's got. It doesn't seem right that I should be halfway across the world at this particular stage in his life."

"He has the Connorses," said Laurence. "And me," he added as an afterthought.

"And he's lucky for that," said Ella, "but it's still not family, not in the same way as he and I."

"You know I wish it could be," said Laurence quietly, his small, surprisingly delicate hand covering hers for a brief moment.

"Yes, I know," said Ella.

There was a time when she, too, would have wished to be a permanent part of Laurence's life, but no longer. She wondered if he sensed the change in their relationship and simply chose to ignore it. She still loved him, of course, and admired him tremendously. Like herself, Laurence Merman had come from nothing. Immediately after the war he had married a young French girl, Colette, who had been sent to New York with her mother to escape the Nazi invasion. Together Colette and Laurence had opened a tiny French restaurant in Greenwich Village named Café Colette. Colette's superb cooking soon became the talk of the town, and more Café Colettes followed, each on a grander scale, until the prefix "café" was almost laughable. Laurence had created a chain of top-class French restaurants. When Ella met him she was twenty-one and he forty-seven. He was not a particularly good-looking man—short, though taller than Ella, balding, and a little overweight—but his dynamism fascinated her. It was not long before what had begun as a business relationship promised to blossom into something more. Laurence had been straight with Ella from the beginning—he loved his wife and would never leave her. They had built an empire together, raised three children, and he looked forward to a long and happy retirement with his lifetime companion. But, Laurence explained, the physical side of their relationship was dead, and he was only human, after all. Haltingly, Ella had tried to explain that she, too, was not interested in sex, but for some reason this only enhanced Laurence's interest in her. Gently, with infinite patience, Laurence had eventually coaxed her into allowing him to make love to her, and after that first time Ella found her terror receding. Their relationship had never greatly roused Ella, but this did not worry her, for she suspected that her feelings toward men would always be tainted by her early experience. Laurence offered warmth, companionship, and love of a sort, and in the early days of their relationship Ella had occasionally fantasized about their being married one day. Now she recognized those early feelings toward Laurence for what they were. She could not have Aaron, the man she truly loved, and she had simply used Laurence as a substitute. Up to a point the delusion had been successful.

Thursday afternoon was taken up with shopping for Greg's return to school and Friday morning with putting her office to rights. "You know, Jessie," said Ella, "I can't help feeling that you should find my new assistant for me."

"Lord, Ella, I could do no such thing. What if I pick a dud?"

"Well, you can't do worse than I did," said Ella. "Besides, I just trust your intuition."

"Well, I'll try," said Jessie. "What kind of person do you want?"

"Well, somebody with some real estate experience, or at any rate some commercial experience of some sort, and—"

"No, no," said Jessie, "I mean do you want a male, a female, young, old, good-looking, ugly, with a sense of humor, with no sense of humor . . ."

"Jess, I'm not looking for a marriage partner," Ella said.

"Much the same thing," retorted Jessie. "You don't get much closer to someone than when you're working with them day in, day out. Look at you and me—I know what you're going to say even before you say it, before you've even thought of saying it—that saves us a lot of time and trouble, you have to own that."

"OK," said Ella, "let's put it another way—what sort of person do *you* think we need?"

"Someone just like me, with twice my brains and half my size."

"Done," said Ella, "but that won't be easy."

The cab that delivered Greg and his luggage to the Connors household took Ella on to the airport, so there was little time for a good-bye. "I wish I was coming with you, Mom." Greg suddenly looked very young.

"I won't be long," Ella promised, "a week at the most. You behave yourself now."

"Don't worry," Aaron promised. "I'll beat him regularly, every hour on the hour."

Mother and son embraced. He was too old to cry, but Ella could see his distress, and she realized with a shock that this was the longest that they had ever been apart. She wept in the cab at the thought of leaving her son, but once clear of Manhattan she pulled herself together. The new vigor that seemed to have come to her on the day of her mother's funeral had persisted. She was going to London to discuss a deal that could change her life. She was twenty-nine years old, independent, with a fine, healthy son and a good, profitable business. The future looked bright indeed.

Chapter 8

London—*August 1977*

"I don't believe this," said Stephanie, "I just don't believe what you're saying."

"It's true, I'm afraid," said Ella, "and having made the decision, I thought it was important to tell you as quickly as possible." She glanced at Margot. "I'm sorry to spoil your Sunday morning." The three women were sitting in a small conference room at the Meyer Hotel, London. Moments before the atmosphere had been pleasant and friendly; now it was thick with anger and accusation.

Stephanie jumped up and began pacing the room. "It's unbelievable! After all the work we've put in, you just coolly announce that it's over. I don't understand you, I don't understand you at all."

Margot's voice was quiet and calm by contrast. "There's no point in getting agitated, Stephanie. Ella, can you explain to us the reason for your decision—is it something to do with your mother's death?"

Ella shook her head. "No, not directly, except that it caused me to go back home and therefore step away from the negotiating table for a moment. I guess my reasons are twofold—one commercial, one personal. While I was in Europe my assistant, Henry, made a very serious mistake that over the next fifteen years is going to cost me thousands of dollars. It highlighted in my mind the fact that my business is a very personal one."

"So is mine," Stephanie burst out.

"I appreciate that, Stephanie," said Ella with studied patience, "but your business is based here in England—mine is five thousand miles away. In a practical sense, I cannot see how I can do justice to the Centre des Arts on the one hand and run my New York business efficiently on the other."

"You don't have to employ idiot staff," said Stephanie. "Just find yourself a good assistant."

"I'm in the process of doing just that," said Ella, "but however good my assistant, it's still my business, and I need to be around."

"You mentioned a personal reason," Margot said, attempting to deflect Stephanie's anger.

"Yes," said Ella, "and perhaps in a way it's the most important aspect to consider. My son, Greg, has no father, and up until now we have enjoyed a very close relationship.

Fourteen is not an easy age, and it's not fair to him for me to be on the other side of the Atlantic on a regular basis for what will be the better part of three years. By the time Centre des Arts is open Greg will be all grown up, and I will have missed what's left of his childhood."

Stephanie sat down heavily. "I think you're looking at this the wrong way, and because you're a single parent, you're in serious danger of stifling the boy. This is just the age when you should be letting go, teaching him to fly. I can see just what's going to happen—you'll give up this opportunity because you think Greg needs you, and sometime in the next six to twelve months you'll find out he doesn't. You'll regret your decision, Greg will be irritated by your over-protectiveness, and your relationship will develop into disaster."

"I'm sorry I don't agree," said Ella. "I'm not going to interfere with his life, but I want to be there if he needs me."

"It's strange," said Margot, "but here we are talking about the future of what is to become a multimillion-dollar venture, and we're having a discussion about bringing up children. If we were three men, the question of our children wouldn't even arise."

"Exactly," said Stephanie. "Either you're seriously in business, Ella, or you're not. Employ a good housekeeper, get your friends to rally round, ensure the time you do spend with Greg is quality time."

"No," Ella cut in, "I'm sorry, but my mind is made up. I'm pulling out of the Centre des Arts project. I don't feel it's right for my business, and I don't feel it's right for me. I'm very sorry, particularly as I asked for the deadline to be extended, but instinctively I know it's wrong for me." Ella appealed to Margot. "You know the extent of my business interests in New York and how much time they involve. Before this project came up I was already fairly well extended, both in workload and in a financial sense. There's another thing, too—I *know* about New York. I know how it works, I know instinctively whether a property is right for me or not. I know nothing about Europe. It's an unknown territory. The one thing my years in business have taught me is to deal in what you know." After this speech Ella was rewarded by a gleam of understanding in Margot's eyes.

No such argument was going to carry any weight with Stephanie, however. She pushed her chair back, ran a hand distractedly through her long fair hair, and flicked it over her shoulder. Her color was high, her eyes sparkling defiantly. "I can see we're not going to persuade you to think any differently," she said, "so I suggest we give up trying. However, I'm not prepared to let this project go, Margot."

Margot looked up from where she had been doodling on the pad in front of her. "You're not proposing to go ahead with it on your own, surely? There's no way you can, Stephanie."

"You mean you're not prepared to back me?"

"I mean the bank will not be prepared to back you. You're simply not large enough."

"Then I'll just have to find someone else to help me, won't I? The deadline is five o'clock tomorrow. I still have time."

Margot shook her head. "The price I was offering you was an exclusive price aimed at you and Ella. If Ella has pulled out, then as far as I'm concerned the deal's off."

"No," thundered Stephanie, "you gave us until five o'clock tomorrow afternoon—'us' by inference means jointly or severally. There's no way you can try and pull out now, Margot. If I can come up with the necessary backing by tomorrow afternoon, then you have to hold your price." She smiled slightly. "Either that or I'll go back to Sir Nicholas Goddard, who can act as arbitrator. I think you'll find he'll be none too happy if you persist in your unethical approach to this project."

For the first time since the meeting began Margot lost her composure. "I resent that remark," she said. "I have not behaved unethically. I was under no obligation to advise you as to who was backing the Slater/Balois venture."

"That's not what your chairman said."

Ella leaned forward in her chair. "Honestly, Margot, I don't see how you can withdraw your offer before the deadline is up. It may have been your intention that Stephanie and I should undertake the project together, but if one of us wishes to withdraw, I don't see how you can say the deal is off if Stephanie can find an alternative and acceptable partner."

"Well, thanks for something, anyway," said Stephanie.

"It's madness," said Margot, "absolute madness. I don't understand what you're trying to prove, Stephanie. You win some, you lose some, and this is one you've lost. Whatever we think of Ella's decision, it's clearly irreversible, so forget it. I'll offer Centre des Arts to the marketplace, and I'm sure we'll find someone to take it on."

"No," said Stephanie, "I want this project, and I'm sure I can find some . . ." She hesitated. She had been twirling a pencil in her fingers. Now she held it still and seemed to be staring at it intently.

"What is it, Stephanie?" Ella said.

"Meyer Hotels!" Stephanie said triumphantly, staring at the name engraved on the pencil. "Now that's the kind of organization that might be interested in Centre des Arts."

"They already have a Meyer Hotel in Paris," said Margot.

"Not on the South Bank. If Centre des Arts is going to be a prestigious tourist center as you would have us believe, then this should be just perfect for Meyer." She glanced up at Margot. "The European headquarters is in Geneva, isn't it?"

Margot nodded. "Yes, I think so, but the old man, Joseph Meyer, is normally based in New York. Still, he might be in Europe, I suppose."

Stephanie's expression was elated. "If you'll excuse me, ladies, I'll go and telephone." She pushed back her chair and walked to the door.

"Stephanie, you're clutching at straws," said Margot wearily.

"You concentrate on your business, Margot, and I'll concentrate on mine." Stephanie swept out of the room extravagantly, slamming the door behind her.

Margot smiled at Ella. "Coffee?"

Ella glanced at her watch. "Eleven o'clock. Shall we make it coffee and brandy, given the circumstances?"

"Why not?"

Ella lifted the telephone and ordered. "I suppose you're going to give me one hell of a lecture, right?" She stood up and wandered restlessly over to the window. Margot could not help but smile at the sight of her—she was dressed in jeans, espadrilles, and an old cotton T-shirt that looked like it belonged to her son. With her short, curly hair she could have passed easily for a teenager. She was so very different from Stephanie with her stylish designer clothes. Yet beneath the childlike appearance, Margot knew, Ella's astute business brain was always at work. "No," she said, affectionately, "I thought what you said made a lot of sense. Before offering you the project I have to admit I indulged in a fair amount of soul-searching on the wisdom of your becoming involved. However, I did decide it would work, provided you sold off some of your New York property, which I naturally assumed you would do."

"Sell my property!" Ella looked appalled.

"It's your one failing you know, your one blind spot," said Margot. "I just can't understand why you hang on to all these properties."

"The bank's not complaining," Ella said.

"Of course the bank's not complaining. It's making a fortune out of you, and a safe fortune at that—your collateral is excellent. Look, let me speak as a friend for a moment. The standard property development operation goes like this—the developer buys a run-down apartment block, does it over, leases it, and then sells on to an investment company, a pension fund, or whatever. That way he puts his money back in the bank and he has no requirement to continue servicing the property. He has gone in, made a tidy profit, and come out. By contrast the Lexington Kovac way is like a squirrel collecting nuts for the winter. You've bought some wonderful properties at wonderful prices, I don't deny it. You've also shown great flair and imagination in the way you have renovated them, and you've tied up some very fancy leases. So why hang on to them? Why not get out and move on?"

"Why sell them?" said Ella. "The price of real estate in New York is going up all the time."

"So's your interest bill, Ella. You're paying out a fortune in interest, not to mention the administrative hassles of looking after so many leases. What you need to do is sell off at least seventy-five percent of your property, put the money in the bank, and then start again—borrow, pay back, borrow again, pay back again. All right, I know you're operating a very profitable business, but the real profits are being made by Joshkers Bank."

"Do you remember Stephanie's parting shot?" Ella asked icily. Margot shook her head. "'You concentrate on your business and I'll concentrate on mine.' At least that's one thing Stephanie and I still agree on."

Tim Irvine lay back in the large sunken bath with Sunday newspapers scattered all over the bathroom floor. He heard his wife returning to their suite and knew he should get out of the bath and dress. However, the sound of the slamming door and Stephanie's strident voice on the telephone told him that things were not going well for her, and he recoiled from the inevitable dramatics that would ensue. It had been a hard week. The rain that had held off for most of August had decided to threaten this week, of all weeks, while he and his men were trying to get in the harvest. They had worked like dogs to beat the weather. They had managed it, but he was frankly exhausted. He was not sure why Stephanie had insisted that he come to London with her, following Ella's telephone call requesting an urgent Sunday meeting. He let out a sigh, pulled out the plug with his toe, and eased his aching body from the bath, stepping gingerly over the papers as he wrapped a towel around his hips. He padded into their sitting room just as Stephanie put down the phone. "What a bit of luck," she said triumphantly. "Joseph Meyer's in Geneva, and not only that, he'll see me for a breakfast meeting at eight o'clock tomorrow morning. All I have to do is to get myself there and plan my presentation. I'd better book a flight."

"Hold on a minute," said Tim, "you've lost me. Joseph Meyer, as in Meyer Hotels?"

"The same," said Stephanie, "the grand old man of the hotel business. It's quite an honor to get an interview—I mustn't blow it, I really mustn't."

"Am I being foolish, or is it not immediately apparent why you want to see the great Joseph Meyer?"

"Your friend Ella's pulled out."

"My friend?" said Tim.

"Well, you seemed to think she was so wonderful. After she stayed with us you talked about nothing else but Ella for days."

"Did I?" said Tim.

"Anyway, it seems your judgment of human nature went sadly astray in this case. She's let us down badly by refusing to go ahead with Centre des Arts."

"Why?" said Tim, collapsing in a chair before his aching legs gave out.

"Ridiculous reasons—she says she can't manage her New York business and a big project in Paris, and then she rambled on about Greg, saying it wasn't fair to him. Honestly, I think her relationship with that boy is positively unhealthy."

"I don't," said Tim.

"Well you wouldn't. Anyway, enough of Ella. I'm not letting Centre des Arts slip through my fingers. I want that project, Tim—Margot won't back me on my own, so I'm going to see if I can do some sort of deal with Meyer Hotels."

"Why don't you just let it drop, Stephanie?" Tim said heavily. "Goodness knows you have plenty to keep you occupied over here. There's your project in Derbyshire—"

"Oh that's nothing," Stephanie interrupted, "peanuts. I can do that in my spare time."

"What spare time?" said Tim. "You don't have any spare time now. If Centre des Arts goes ahead, you'll practically be living in Paris."

"Yes, I've been thinking about that," said Stephanie. "I think the best idea is to rent or buy an apartment." Tim said nothing. "Oh, for heaven's sake, you're not sulking, are you?" she said, clearly irritated.

"As a matter of fact, I think I am. Shouldn't this be a joint decision?"

"No, not really," said Stephanie. "I wouldn't dream of telling you how many cattle you should buy in a sale or what day you should start hay-making, so why should you interfere with what I do?"

"But this is not just business, is it?" said Tim. "This involves the whole family."

"Why?" said Stephanie.

"Well, if you're going to be away from home even more, the girls will see even less of you."

"They hardly notice me when I'm there anyway."

"Maybe not, but are you happy with that situation?" It was a well-worn argument, but the idea of Stephanie buying a Paris apartment suddenly seemed a real threat to family life.

"Look, Tim, it's no good trying to make me feel guilty, because you're simply not going to succeed. The girls have a wonderful life—they have each other, they have you, and they have everything money can buy. Their school reports are excellent, which suggests they have no real worries. They are happy, healthy, and very, very privileged. I really can't see why I should be expected to sacrifice myself on the altar of my children. I want this deal, Tim, I want it very much. I don't see that either you or the children have any right to stop me."

It was hopeless. "Well, if that's how you feel," said Tim, "there's really nothing else to be said, is there?"

Ella felt oddly deflated after she and Margot had parted. Yesterday had been a day for decisions, and, having geared herself up for the morning's meeting, she felt utterly exhausted. Yet there was a strange elation, too. She knew in her bones that she had made the right decision. She had used the long hours on the flight from New York to make up her mind, and she had no regrets, other than the severing of her embryonic relationship with Stephanie and Tim—particularly Tim, she guardedly admitted to herself.

The second decision of yesterday had been somewhat eccentric. The original reason she and Greg had been visiting Europe was to try and acquire a chateau in Provence for Laurence Merman. Laurence had long held a pipe dream that one day he would buy a piece of France for Colette. In the last few years that dream had come within his grasp—the cafés were making huge profits. Real estate was not his forté, Laurence insisted, and recognizing how much Ella and Greg needed a vacation, he had suggested that seeking the perfect holiday home for the Mermans provided the excuse for a trip to Europe. Margot's summons to Paris had cut short Ella's search, but she had loved Provence, and suddenly, realizing that no one was expecting her back in New York for a week, she decided to accomplish one thing on her trip. It was an irresponsible decision with so many commitments at home, but a call to a travel agent the previous day had secured a flight to Lyons. She intended to hire a car and explore the area for a few days. Her flight left Heathrow at eleven o'clock the following morning, so she had a whole afternoon and evening in London for sightseeing, but somehow, uncharacteristically, she could not summon up the energy to move outside the hotel. She ordered lunch in her room and spent the afternoon drifting in and out of consciousness, trying to read *Country Life,* which Stephanie had advised her was *the* real estate magazine in England. It was after six by the time Ella finally roused herself. She had a bath and decided that a meal in the restaurant downstairs would at least get her out of her room. She was just preparing to dress when there was a knock on the door. She opened it cautiously. "Tim!"

Tim looked affectionately at the diminutive figure,

swathed in a hotel terry cloth robe, her hair damp from the bath, her face shiny and well scrubbed—a child-woman, he thought. "Hello Ella. I hope you don't mind me seeking you out like this, only I thought after this morning's drama you might be feeling a bit down, and I wondered whether I could take you out to dinner."

"I'd love that," said Ella. "I didn't even know you were in London."

"I came up with Stephanie last night after we got your call. She's already left for Geneva, and I was planning to return to Wickham when I suddenly thought what the hell, they're not expecting me back until tomorrow."

"Give me half an hour," said Ella.

They met in the foyer. "There's a little restaurant I particularly like in Beauchamp Place," said Tim as he helped her into a cab. "It's very French, with wonderful food."

The restaurant was everything Tim had promised. "This is such a treat," said Ella. "I was feeling a bit bleak."

"Regretting your decision?"

"Oh, no," said Ella. "I've made the right decision, I'm sure of that."

"I'm well aware," said Tim, "that sorting out the priorities in your type of business is not easy, but you seem to manage it with such ease." The implied criticism of Stephanie was there, but he was not specific.

"It is difficult," Ella admitted, "because our business—mine and Stephanie's—is different from most in that there is no consistency."

"How do you mean?" said Tim.

"Well, take your business—the seasons come, the seasons go, some harvests are better than others, but the business runs on. Similarly, in manufacturing they have big orders, small orders, orders that go right, orders that go wrong, but the factory goes on producing the goods, and they go on getting sold."

"Surely that applies to your business, too," said Tim.

"Not really—our businesses are only as good as the next

deal. We could make a fortune on the last deal and lose it all on the next. Our business is all about making the right decision at the right time."

"Nerve-wracking," said Tim.

"Very," Ella agreed. They paused while Tim refilled their glasses. Ella could not help noticing his hands—strong, brown, the hairs at his wrist bleached white. "Enough of me," she said abruptly. "Tell me about you and your business."

And so he talked about his time at college and then about the early days of Wickham, how he and Stephanie had done it—the reform of chaos into order. "It was such a slow process because we had no money to speak of," he said. "The first few cottages we sold off. We couldn't even renovate them because we hadn't the money to do so. With the money we obtained from those sales we converted the next batch, for which we charged a much inflated price. That's how we progressed, one step at a time—only moving onto the next stage when we had the money to finance it." Tim gave a small dry laugh. "I have to admit I greatly regret the day I introduced Stephanie to Jeremy Colquhoun. He put her onto Margot, of course, and it was Margot who taught her that you don't have to wait until you have the money before you spend it."

They were well into their bottle of wine by now, and Ella was becoming bold. "How do you feel about Stephanie going ahead with the Centre des Arts, if she can get the backing from Meyer?"

"It appalls me," Tim admitted. "As far as I can see, it effectively means we will no longer be a family. Stephanie works a six-day week now. If she takes on Centre des Arts, she'll be spending a great deal of time in Paris. Just today she was talking about buying an apartment over there. We'll simply never see her."

"You can't enjoy the thought of that," said Ella.

"No, I don't, but it's the children I worry about most. They should have a mother. Mrs. Maggs is wonderful, but she's no substitute."

"You seem to be making a pretty good job of it, from what I saw."

"Thanks, but I suppose if I'm honest, there's also something else . . ." Tim hesitated.

"Go on," said Ella.

"Well, I think I'm a little jealous. Don't misunderstand me; the last thing I'd want to do is Stephanie's job—I can't think of anything worse—but it should be the man who travels around the world making exciting deals while the woman sits at home and looks after the children. We've completely reversed roles. I work hard, God knows. I think I run Wickham efficiently, and I make a decent profit out of the estate. Nonetheless, I deal in relatively small sums of money, while Stephanie deals in millions—it's an odd situation."

"You mean she's wearing the pants, and you don't like it?" said Ella.

"Something like that," said Tim. "She never defers to me over anything. She makes her own decisions, and I have to fit in accordingly. I'm sounding pathetic, aren't I?"

"Just a little sorry for yourself," Ella suggested.

"I'm sorry to complain. I suppose what I'm really saying is I get so damn lonely."

It was a surprising admission. "I know about loneliness," Ella said gently.

"But a woman like you . . . surely there must be men . . ." Ella shook her head, and Tim hesitated a moment. "Ella, don't answer this if you don't want to, but did your experience put you off men for good, or—"

Ella laughed. "Are you asking me whether there's a man in my life?"

"Yes," said Tim, "I suppose I am."

"I've had a long-term affair with a married man called Laurence. He's a colleague of mine—in fact, he has a stake in my business. He's much older than me. It's comfortable, safe, and undemanding."

Tim looked crestfallen. "It can't be very satisfactory."

"No, it's not—particularly since I like his wife and would

do nothing in the world to hurt her, but I guess it's better than being alone night after night."

Tim raised his glass. "Down with loneliness."

"I'll drink to that," said Ella.

It was after midnight by the time they got back to the hotel. "I should be tired, but I'm not," said Tim.

"Neither am I," said Ella.

"Why not come up to my room for a nightcap?" Tim suggested.

"No, come to mine," said Ella. The instinct to avoid seeing the room Tim had shared with Stephanie was very strong.

Tim searched her fridge and decided on champagne. "We haven't talked about your trip back to Kentucky, how you coped with Greg and how you felt when you saw your mother. Do you want to talk about it?" Tim asked, settling down on the sofa with bottle and glasses.

"It's extraordinary, isn't it?" said Ella. "Of all the people I have known, it's you I chose to share my secrets with."

"That's just because I was around when you received the call about your mother."

"Possibly, yet I've never even told Laurence anything about my past. Yes, I would like to talk about it—it was an odd experience. Do you mind?"

"Come here," said Tim. She sat down beside him, and he slipped an arm around her. "Put your head on my shoulder, relax, take a deep breath, and tell me all about it."

Ella did as she was asked, dimly aware of the strangeness of the situation, yet feeling it to be so natural that it could not be wrong. She began to speak, hesitantly at first, but with growing confidence.

"So what you're saying is that you're free from your past, at last?" Tim said when she had finished.

"Yes, in most respects, though of course my legacy is Greg—in a way he always links me back to my roots. Not that I'm complaining," she added hastily. "I wouldn't be without him for the world."

"Of course not," Tim said. There was a silence between

them, and in that moment, they both became aware of their closeness. Tim shifted uneasily, putting a little distance between them. "About men," he said awkwardly. "You said your relationship with Laurence was comfortable but nothing more. Do you feel your experiences may have—well, put you off the idea of sex permanently? I'm sorry, I shouldn't be asking, really . . ."

"It's OK," said Ella. "I guess it does some good to talk about it, but I don't know. You see, I have no other experience of men—only Laurence and the rape. I've always imagined, though, that I'm frigid. Certainly I've never . . ." Her voice trailed off as she saw the expression on Tim's face.

"You see, I have an ulterior motive for asking," he began, his voice unsteady, and leaning forward, he kissed her, at first gently, and then, as his arms tightened around her, with a burning intensity.

Somewhere in the recesses of her mind Ella knew she must not return his kisses and must pull herself away from his arms. What made her hesitate was the certainty that despite the mounting passion between them, at any time she could ask him to stop and he would. She felt safe in his arms, safe in a new, uncharted country, for the passion with which she responded to him was something she had never experienced before.

Lulled by this feeling of security, sometime later she found herself naked on the bed with Tim beside her. How long they had been like that she had no idea.

"I want you so much, but I'm frightened of hurting you," he whispered.

"I'm frightened, too," said Ella.

He took her then, tentatively at first, and was almost shocked by her reaction. She clung to him, urging him on, caught up in her own dark world. He concentrated on her pleasure, terrified of making the wrong move, but he felt his own control seeping away until they came together in a single exquisite moment, their tears mingling together on the pillow, their bodies straining together, completely at one.

When Tim woke he automatically assumed he was at Wickham. His first sensation was of the stiffness of his limbs, and then another feeling—lethargy, a sense of well-being, of fulfillment . . . and then he remembered. He opened his eyes abruptly. Through the closed curtains he could see it was already daylight. He turned to the woman beside him. Ella was still deeply asleep, one cupped hand supporting her head, her dark curls clustered haphazardly around her childlike face. It was incredible to Tim that the dramas of her life appeared to have had so little impact on her looks. After last night he knew he could not let her go. He could see no easy solution to a future together, but somehow they had to find a way. He shifted slightly in the bed to ease his stiffness, and his movement disturbed Ella. She began rubbing her eyes, and Tim cursed himself for waking her. He needed more time to plan what would happen next—everything was moving too swiftly, and he felt ill-prepared.

Ella eyed him a little ruefully with warm, sleepy eyes. "Did what I think happened last night really happen?" Tim nodded and, bending forward, kissed her. Ella's expression clouded. "It was wrong, Tim. What a terrible way to treat Stephanie—to pull out of a business deal and sleep with her husband all in the space of a few hours." Ella's voice trembled. He went to take her in his arms. "No," she said, "I must go to the bathroom."

While she was gone Tim's mind raced to find a solution to their predicament—to offer some form of comfort. He couldn't easily leave Wickham; he certainly couldn't leave the children. It would have been difficult before, but in view of Stephanie's determination to develop Centre des Arts he really had no choice but to claim one hundred percent responsibility for the girls. They were settled in school and happy in their life. He shook his head, hoping the effect would be like a kaleidoscope, rearranging the pieces into the picture he wanted. Supposing Ella was to give up her business in New York and come to live in England. He and Stephanie could divorce—he hardly imagined his wife would mind. They could make a home together with the three children, but not at Wickham—that was Stephanie's home.

"Tim." Ella slipped into the bed beside him. At the sight of her slender, naked body the hopeless grappling with future plans was forgotten. She came into his arms without protest. He held her close, kissing her, murmuring her name, aware of the warmth rising between them.

This time he was more sure. He teased her, tantalized her until she begged him to take her. She cried out his name again and again, her body taut as a bowstring, her nails raking his back. There was no one in the world but the two of them, nothing else mattered, until at last, utterly exhausted, they fell into a deep sleep in each other's arms.

Ella stirred first. Sitting up in bed, she stared at the alarm clock and then abruptly shook Tim awake. "It's after eight," she said, her face anguished. "This should never have happened. I'll have to get started or I'll miss my flight."

Tim had completely forgotten about her going to France, and it threw him into a panic. "Surely you don't have to go," he said, "not today, at any rate. Leave it for a couple of days. I can ring Mrs. Maggs and arrange that—"

"No, Tim." Ella shifted out of the circle of his arms. "There's no point in prolonging this, because there can be no future for us. Every moment we stay in each other's company is making things worse."

"There has to be a future for us," said Tim, "there has to be."

"What are you suggesting, then?" said Ella. "That you divorce Stephanie, give up the children and your life at Wickham, and come and live with me in New York? You'd never be happy, particularly not in a city, and especially being away from the kids."

"You could come to me," Tim said.

"Give up my business, disrupt Greg's schooling, move to a country I hardly know to live with a married man?"

"I don't think there'd be any problem about Stephanie giving me a divorce."

"OK, so living with you, married—but where? Surely not in Stephanie's family home. That really would be bizarre. So we set up a home together—you separated from your beloved Wickham, me from my business . . . we'd have nothing left of the lives we both love. That's hardly the best basis for starting a life together."

"But we have each other," said Tim. "I love you so much, Ella."

For a moment her expression softened. She reached out a hand and touched his cheek. "I love you, too, Tim, but it's not just a question of who you meet, is it? It's when you meet them. We met at the wrong time."

"I can't accept that," said Tim.

"Tim, you're going to have to. Hell, I have to get up, I have a plane to catch."

"Ella, please, please postpone your French trip. You don't have to go—not today. After last night we must talk. There has to be a solution, but we can't find it in this rushed way." For a moment it looked as though Ella was going to weaken, and Tim pressed home what he thought was his advantage. "We'll never have a better chance than this to talk, with Stephanie in Geneva."

Ella leapt from the bed as though she had been stung. "That just about sums up the situation, doesn't it?" she said. "We're talking about turning our lives upside down, and the only reason we're able to have such a discussion is that Stephanie is in Geneva." She turned and walked into the bathroom again, slamming the door behind her. If her words had been calculated to hurt, they had succeeded.

Tim was out of the bed in a trice, hammering on the bathroom door. "So why the hell did you spend last night with me?" Ella didn't reply. "What was I, just an acceptable stud to help you pass the time during an otherwise dull Sunday in London?"

The door flew open. "How dare you speak to me like that?" said Ella. "For some reason I can't understand, I've told you more about my life than I've told anyone else, ever. Knowing what you know, I don't know how you can make such a remark."

"I'm sorry," said Tim, "that was unforgivable."

An angry silence followed. Ella pulled a sweatshirt over her head and turned to face him. She was fully dressed now. Tim, suddenly conscious of his nakedness, felt stupid. He turned away from her and began to dress hurriedly, but she must have seen the expression on his face, for her voice softened a little. "Until last night, Tim, I didn't know what making love meant—please believe that, if nothing else."

Tim did not speak for several moments as he finished pulling on his clothes. Then he turned and, with a sigh, took Ella in his arms, pressing her close to him. "I believe you, because it was very special for me, too. Don't you see, that's why we simply can't lose one another? However long it takes, we have to find a way to be together."

"And what do we do in the meantime, live some sort of half life, five thousand miles apart, growing older?" Ella asked. "Besides, I'm no marriage breaker, and I suspect that without me, it would never have occurred to you to leave Stephanie."

"I don't know," said Tim, "I simply don't know the answer to that."

"Exactly—one night of loving doesn't justify breaking up years of partnership." Ella released herself from Tim's arms and began dashing around the room, throwing her belongings into her case in a haphazard manner as Tim watched helplessly. When she had finished she straightened up and went to him. "I'm sorry, Tim, but this is good-bye."

"Let me at least take you to the airport and see you onto the plane."

Ella shook her head. "I couldn't bear it—it would only be prolonging the agony."

"I'll come down to the foyer and help you find a cab." He

was desperate now to keep her in sight for a few more minutes.

"No, please don't make this more difficult than it already is." With a swift movement Ella reached up on tiptoes and kissed him lightly on the lips. Then, almost running, she seized her case and wrenched open the door.

"Don't leave me," Tim said, "please don't leave me."

"I have to," said Ella, "for both our sakes." In an instant she was gone, the door slamming shut behind her.

He went to the door, intending to open it and call after her. Instead he leaned his forehead against it, pounding at it with his fists. "Dammit. Oh, Ella, Ella." As he stood there, washed with despair, another sensation overtook him, a sudden ringing in his ears, getting louder, louder . . . lights flashed, and he closed his eyes to avoid the brightness but it was still there beneath his eyelids, blinding him. "Ella," he croaked as he slid to the floor, into unconsciousness.

Chapter 9

Geneva—*August 1977*

Joseph Meyer leaned back in his chair and gazed out of the window. It was a beautiful day, warm and sunny. From his office he had a clear view of the lake; the sun sparkling on the water was so bright he had to shield his eyes. The blue-green mountains at the far side of the lake were hazy, an early promise of the heat to come. He was pleased with his choice of Geneva as the European headquarters for Meyer Hotels. Everything about the city delighted him—its clean efficiency, its stylish good looks, the feeling that one was at the center of things. He watched with pleasure the progress of a small yacht scudding across the water, for small things pleased Joseph Meyer. Every day was a bonus, every bright summer's day a blessing to be counted.

"Well, don't you agree, Pop?"

His son's impatient voice cut into his consciousness. He knew he should have been concentrating, but the boy's persistence irritated him. "Don't call me Pop, you know how I detest it. *Father* is what I have asked you to call me. Is that too much to ask?"

Alex Meyer regarded him with disbelief. "You haven't been listening to a word I've been saying, have you?"

"I don't need to," said Joseph. "It's the same old argument, and I still don't agree."

"Are you ever going to give me a chance to do anything in this organization without being tied to your apron strings?"

Joseph regarded his son in silence for a moment. A good-looking boy. Well, hardly a boy—thirty-one—with the dark wavy hair he'd had himself once, and his mother's light, bright blue eyes. He was tall, nearly six feet, with a slightly aquiline nose, high cheekbones, and full, sensuous lips. He was such a success with women, but Joseph wished he would settle down. His heart ached at the thought of grandchildren, yet it appeared his son was not prepared to give him any. "You'll have control of this business soon enough when I'm dead," he snapped. "In the meantime we'll run it my way, at least while you persist in these goddam stupid ideas."

"Look, Father"—Alex put an insulting emphasis on the word—"the Arabs expect a show, they need wooing. I don't understand your objection. Our profits are spiraling, and it wouldn't matter a damn if the whole thing failed spectacularly. It wouldn't even be a flea bite in the side of Meyer Hotels—at least, however, you'd have given me a chance to prove myself."

"Alex, the problem is that it's not a question of *if* your scheme fails. It *will* fail. We don't need to woo the Arabs with a flashy PR show. One properly constructed, well-run, luxury Meyer Hotel will provide all the PR necessary. I don't mind spending money on any scheme you care to put to me if it makes sense, but this doesn't. I don't want to appear a laughingstock, and I believe your promotional ideas for the Middle East could actually have a detrimental effect on our launch out there."

"You're so old-fashioned, Father, you're not in touch anymore. Why can't you just bend a little and give me a chance to prove myself? Jesus Christ, I'm not a child."

"Then don't behave like one," said Joseph. Father and son glared at each other. The telephone on Joseph's desk rang. "Yes?"

"Lady Stephanie Bonham to see you," said his secretary.

"Hold on a moment. Alex, you ought to be in on this—it's Lady Stephanie Bonham. God knows what she wants, but it could be interesting. Remember, I told you about her."

"You can mess around with the English aristocracy if you wish, Father. I'm going to do some real work." Alex strode angrily to the door and opened it to find Stephanie standing on the threshold. She wore a pale apple-green silk dress with a prim little white collar. Her fair hair was simply brushed back from her forehead, hanging loose to her shoulders. Her clear green eyes regarded Alex's angry scowl with just a hint of amusement. "Er . . . Lady Stephanie?" he said, uncertain how to address her.

"Yes, indeed," said Stephanie in her clear English voice.

"Er . . . I'm Alex Meyer, and this is my father, Joseph."

Stephanie turned her attention from the handsome young man beside her and stepped into the room. A short, overweight, elderly man walked across the room toward her with surprising speed, shook her hand enthusiastically, and showed her to a chair. "Lady Bonham. How nice to meet you. Welcome to Geneva. Would you like a coffee?"

She nodded her head. The nervousness she felt was momentarily calmed by the avuncular greeting. Joseph sat down in the chair opposite her and regarded her in silence for a moment. The warmth of his greeting did not blind Stephanie to the power of the man she now faced. She noted the muted gray Italian silk suit, the Valentino tie, and through the glass top of his desk she caught sight of slim, elegant shoes, again Italian. Despite his small stature and bulky frame, the exquisite cut of his clothing did a lot for Joseph Meyer—as did the perfect shave, the beautifully cut hair, and his manicured hands with their surprisingly long fingers. All this Stephanie noted and stored away for the future.

Joseph Meyer was saying nothing. He leaned back in his chair, smiling sweetly, cigar in hand. The silence was in danger of becoming oppressive. "You may have found my call yesterday rather peculiar," Stephanie began, "but I have a proposal for you. I have the opportunity to finalize a deal at nearly half the asking price, and I have until five o'clock this afternoon to decide whether to commit myself to it."

"Then, my dear Lady Bonham, we had better not waste a moment," said Joseph Meyer.

On the conference table at the far end of Joseph Meyer's office Stephanie carefully laid out the plans for the Centre des Arts for father and son to study. Alex, who had been intending to leave the room, had remained, fascinated not so much by Stephanie's project as by the woman herself. He had never come across a woman so good-looking, so self-assured, and so obviously bright. With a series of artist's impressions Stephanie outlined the revised thinking on the Centre des Arts she and Ella had dreamed up. She produced estimates, building permits, and a schedule indicating the timing of the project as a whole. She told the story of the reduction in price following the discovery of the Joshkers involvement but carefully left out the contributions made by both Ella and Tim. When she had finished she was trembling with nervous exhaustion but desperate to appear calm. "Well, what do you think?"

"I think it's a fascinating scheme," said Joseph after a

tantalizing pause. He looked across at Alex. "What do you think? We already have a presence in Paris, of course. It's questionable whether we can justify another, and, of course, we've never been involved in this sort of complex before."

"I think it's a wonderful idea," said Alex decisively.

Joseph looked hard at his son. This uncompromising support for a proposition introduced by his father was quite out of character. Alex took the opposite viewpoint from his father as a matter of course. Surprised but pleased, Joseph continued. "I have the germ of an idea," he said with gathering enthusiasm. "I understand from what you've said, Lady Bonham, that you own a number of country clubs and small luxury hotels in the UK. How many have you?"

"Eight," said Stephanie. "Wickham was my first, the family home in Gloucestershire. I also have one in London, one in Wiltshire, one in Oxfordshire, one in Berkshire at Ascot, one in the Lake District, one in Bath, and one on the west coast of Scotland."

"Mmmmmm," said Joseph. "As you may be aware, I have four hotels in Europe presently—one here in Geneva, one in Paris, one in London, and then one in Amsterdam. It is my intention to expand in Europe, particularly in the UK, though first we are endeavoring to conquer the Middle East, which we feel has the biggest immediate growth potential. Supposing we were to buy out your hotels—don't let us worry about price at the moment, I am talking principle here. We could put your hotels together with ours, take on the Centre des Arts project, and put you in overall control as manager of the European operation. Although your country clubs and hotels obviously are not in the same league as Meyer, they could be upgraded, enlarged, or sold off, as necessary, and your pool of trained UK staff would be very useful. What do you say?" He smiled at her benevolently, as one would do to a child upon whom one had just bestowed an enormous and totally unexpected present.

"You have to be joking!" said Stephanie, her voice thick with anger.

"I'm not joking," said Joseph, "I'm perfectly serious, though I'm not quite sure why—I've never made such a generous offer to anyone before."

"A generous offer! You buy up my business, cash in on this Centre des Arts scheme, put me in overall charge as a *manager* . . . what sort of person do you think I am, Mr. Meyer? If I wanted to be a manager of a hotel group, do you think I'd have gone through what I have during the last eleven years? I may not run a business on your scale, but I do run a highly profitable one. I answer to no one. I run my business my way, and it works. Why on earth should I sell out to Meyer Hotels or anyone else? I see I've been wasting my time."

Joseph Meyer chuckled. "I like your style, Lady Bonham."

Stephanie flushed a brilliant scarlet. "I can't say I like yours, Mr. Meyer," she replied.

"Look, I have an idea," said Alex. "I know why you suggested what you did, Father. It's because we are very stretched in a management sense at the moment, trying to develop both in the Middle East and Europe," he explained for Stephanie's benefit. "Supposing we thought this through in a different way. It makes sense that if we are joining forces over Centre des Arts, we should join forces over everything else as well, but it also makes sense that Lady Bonham does not want to lose her independence. Supposing, Father, that we put all the hotels together as you suggest, including this new Centre des Arts project, and then we grant Lady Bonham a franchise on the whole European operation. This would have the joint effect of giving her the independence she requires and giving us the management backup we need. We would have to form a new subsidiary to achieve it, and I would like to suggest that you consider letting me run this new European operation while you concentrate on the Middle East." He smiled slightly. "It would keep us out of each other's hair."

"Look, wait a minute," said Stephanie, "I came here two

hours ago to present to you an idea for undertaking a single joint project. It certainly was not my intention that we should join forces altogether. I don't want to lose my independence, but I do need help with this scheme, which is why I'm here."

"The proposal that Alex has just put forward would maintain your independence," said Joseph. "It bears thinking about, of course, but essentially you would receive the revenue from all the hotels, including ours. You would have total management control and would simply account to us with a franchise fee plus an agreed percentage of the profits. Of course, either Alex or I would have to be on the board, and, as he suggests, it's probably better for him to handle Europe while I concentrate on the Middle East. I've studied your track record in some detail since your call—I do think we have a lot in common."

A germ of excitement was stirring in Stephanie. This was the big time, yet her excitement was seriously undermined by a feeling of caution. She had been her own boss for a long time, she enjoyed running her tight little ship her way, yet why was she here at all if not for the chance to expand? It seemed so improbable that in the space of a two-hour meeting the great Joseph Meyer was offering her an opportunity beyond her wildest dreams. "I just don't know what to say," she admitted. "A franchise operation is obviously attractive, but we hardly know each other. How can we possibly make this sort of decision about joining forces between now and five o'clock?" All three of them glanced at the clock on the wall—it was just after half past twelve.

"I have a proposal," said Joseph. "I think I should take you to lunch, Lady Bonham, while Alex runs through these Centre des Arts figures of yours with our accountant. Over lunch you and I need to concentrate on getting to know each other. If we're both satisfied by the end of it and the figures stack up, then I suggest we go ahead with the Centre des Arts project in any event, with no commitment to the bigger involvement until we see how we all get along."

Alex was furious. If anyone was taking Stephanie to lunch, it should be he, but a scene in front of Stephanie would look childish. He scooped up the figures and disappeared from the room without a word.

The Hotel Beau Rivage stood only a few paces from the head office of Meyer International Hotels. A maître d'hotel positively sprinted across the restaurant to greet Joseph Meyer and led him to what was clearly his usual table, in a quiet corner with a marvelous view of the lake. They were seated with a minimum of fuss, and two glasses of champagne followed almost immediately.

"My dear," said Joseph Meyer, "I'm afraid I have reached the stage in life where I have the same lunch every day: a little caviar followed by sole meunière, washed down with a glass or two of Pouilly Fumé. Does that sound appealing, or would you care to see the menu?"

Stephanie shook her head. "That sounds wonderful."

The maître d'hotel disappeared, and Joseph Meyer watched in silence as Stephanie examined her surroundings with obvious pleasure. She was a striking woman, Joseph thought, with an intriguing combination of charms. On the one hand, she was a typical English rose in appearance, with her pale blond hair, perfect complexion, vivid eyes that were such an unusual green color, and tall, slim figure. Yet he sensed beneath the cool exterior a volatile, perhaps even reckless streak that fascinated him.

"This is beautiful," said Stephanie.

So are you, Joseph Meyer thought, though he declined to say so. "Tell me how you built your business, Lady Bonham. I am fascinated that you have achieved so much in such a short time."

Stephanie launched into the story of her achievements, and Joseph listened attentively, asking the occasional, but always astute, question. The wine arrived; they raised their glasses in a silent toast and, as Stephanie talked on, she began to relax. The meal progressed with elegant ease; Stephanie learned that Joseph was a widower and had a son and a daughter. "Alex has come up the hard way," he said. "It's the only way to learn, but he's in such a hurry." He laughed, but there was an edge to his laughter.

"It can't be easy for him—you're a tough act to follow."

There was a moment's hesitation, and then Joseph smiled. They had reached the coffee stage. "Would you mind if I smoked?" he asked.

"Of course not," said Stephanie. She watched as he went through the preamble of lighting his cigar. She recognized it as Monte Cristo No. 3—her father had smoked them on special occasions. It appeared that Joseph Meyer enjoyed nothing but the best. Once he was settled with his cigar and coffee, she judged it was the right moment to start probing a little deeper to see what made the fascinating man tick. "You told me the basic facts about your life as it is now, but not how you built Meyer Hotels. My achievement, such as it is, pales into insignificance compared with yours. How on earth did *you* begin?"

Joseph Meyer drew on his cigar in silence for a moment. "You want the story of my life?" Stephanie nodded. The silence that followed was so long she wondered whether he had understood her. Then, quite suddenly and without preamble, he began. "I was born in Germany, in Bavaria," he said. "My father owned an inn, the equivalent of one of your English pubs. He did a good business, and I suppose it's where I formed my interest in catering. When I was twenty—young by today's standards—I married a girl from the village. I had loved her since she was a baby." His voice was warm. "Two years later we had a daughter, Freda. They were happy years. My father was semiretired after my marriage, and I ran the inn. I made many improvements. It was a good business. We were happy, had plenty of money, and then the war came." His voice hardened perceptibly. "I don't know whether a child like you knows about such things, but the Nazi movement began in Bavaria. We were Jews. It was a rough time, as history now acknowledges. I formed an underground movement. Looking back, it was a foolish thing to do with a family to consider, but I was young and impetuous. We used to meet at the inn and make desperate, futile plans to halt the direction of Nazi thinking. One afternoon the storm troopers burst into the inn. Myself, my wife Annetta, and Freda, we were having a picnic with the family dog. It was a beautiful day, I remember, in the spring. Spring in Bavaria is very beautiful." He hesitated, and Stephanie almost intervened to ask him to stop. It was obvious what was coming, and a sudden, unexpected feeling of compassion made her wish to spare him, though now that he had started, it seemed he wanted to go on. "They shot my parents, but first they tortured my father until he told them where I was. They found us by the riverbank. I was fishing. Annetta and Freda had built a little campfire. They dragged us away, but before they did so they shot the dog. I will never forget the look of surprise in his eyes and the sound of Freda screaming."

"Where . . . where did they take you?" said Stephanie, almost in tears.

"They sent us overland, by train mostly, sometimes by truck, to Poland, to Treblinka. The American 8th Army liberated us."

"You all survived?" Stephanie asked.

"After a fashion. Annetta and I, yes, but little Freda, she has been in a mental institution ever since the war. She"—he seemed to have to force the words out—"she was thirteen, you see, by the time we were liberated. They did things to little girls. Her mind couldn't cope." Stephanie reached out a hand and took Joseph's in her own; he turned over his wrist and pulled away the silk cuff. Stephanie saw the number printed there, T31027. Joseph smiled, a sad, tight smile. "The Great Joseph Meyer—that's all I was once—T31027."

"Why don't you have the number removed?" Stephanie asked. "A skin graft would do it, surely."

"I'll never do that," said Joseph, his voice suddenly rough and angry.

"Why?" Stephanie asked.

"Because it reminds me, always, of the depths to which human beings can stoop."

In the bright, sunny restaurant, amid every conceivable luxury, his words chilled Stephanie to the bone. There was nothing to say, no response that she or anyone could have made. After a moment Joseph shook his head. "I'm a foolish old man to worry your head with these stories. It is past, there is no value in dwelling on it."

"So what happened after Treblinka?" Stephanie said gently, anxious to move him on in the story.

"As to so many others, America beckoned," he said. "I'd managed to acquire visas, and once in the States I went to the Cornell Hotel School in New York. I spent four years there, working my way through college, supporting my family, perfecting my English."

"It must have been incredibly hard work."

"Yes," Joseph acknowledged, "but you see, I had an incentive, a reason, the best reason in the world."

Stephanie frowned. "What reason?"

"It was a miracle, really. There we were—my wife and I—suffering from malnutrition and God knows what else, and yet between us we managed to make a baby—a perfect, whole baby, untainted by war."

"Alex," said Stephanie softly.

"Yes, Alex. It was like . . . like a whole new beginning, like the world was starting over again. Can you understand that?"

"Yes," said Stephanie.

"They were hard years—there was the care of my daughter to pay for." He shrugged. "Anyway, I had some luck. While I was studying at Cornell I worked in a run-down hotel. It went bankrupt, and I managed to persuade some people to back me. I bought it, renovated it, improved it, hired the right people"—he laughed—"I make it sound easy, don't I? It wasn't, but then you know about that. The first hotel is always the hardest. Once you have a successful formula, all you have to do is repeat it. I have twenty-two hotels in America now. Then, four years ago, I said to myself, Joseph, you owe this country a lot, but you are a European. So I came to Europe, stumbled upon Geneva, fell in love with it, and decided to make it my base."

"And Germany?" Stephanie asked.

"I'll never go back to Germany," said Joseph. "I am German, but my country betrayed me. Yet we all see things differently. My Annetta, her life's ambition was to go back home to Bavaria, and for her I would have gone. But she died when Alex was five. She never really recovered from Treblinka." He smiled at Stephanie. "So there you have it, my life history, and what Meyer Hotels means to me—hard, grinding work and terrible risks. But after Treblinka it was so damn good to be alive, I felt I could conquer the world. On good days I still do." The other diners had long ago left the restaurant. Without turning in his seat Joseph shouted, "Two cognacs, large ones." In a moment the fussy little maître d'hotel delivered them with a flourish. "Well, Lady Stephanie Bonham," Joseph said, "may I call you Stephanie?"

"If I may call you Joseph," said Stephanie, smiling.

"Well, Stephanie, I know a little of you, and you know a little of me. What I see of you I like and admire. You are very young and have plenty of mistakes yet to make—maybe, just maybe, an old man like me has something to offer you."

"I'm sure that is true," said Stephanie, "but what have I to offer you?"

"Your youth, your beauty . . ." Seeing Stephanie's surprised expression, he laughed. "Don't misunderstand me, Stephanie. Sadly, I am past all that. You and Alex are the future. Alex told me this morning I am out of touch, and perhaps I am. If I am to go into partnership with anyone in Europe, then it should be someone young and ambitious like you. And why not a woman? Women are so much cleverer than men." He glanced at his watch. "Four o'clock. I suggest we go back to my office and telephone Joshkers Bank, but first let us drink to the future."

"The future," Stephanie said, again feeling tears prick her

eyelids. This extraordinary little man with his amazing charisma moved her in a way she found difficult to explain, and she instinctively felt she would be a better person for knowing him.

Chapter 10

New York—*October 1977*

Laurence Merman liked the fall. That first snap in the air, the changing colors of the trees in Central Park, a different smell in the air. It invigorated him, put a spring in his step, cleared the cobwebs from his mind. He turned the corner onto Lexington. Instead of waiting for the traffic lights to change, he sprinted across the avenue, causing a barrage of protests from passing cab drivers. He grinned, feeling like a kid again.

Laurence visited each of his restaurants for two or three hours every week, but never in the same order and never on the same day. His appearance was always unpredictable and ensured that his staff kept on its toes. He had a notorious reputation in the trade for being a tough boss, but he paid well, and as a result his staff was hardworking and loyal. This morning he was on his way to Café Colette on the corner of Lexington and 39th. It was no coincidence that Laurence had chosen this particular restaurant this morning, for it was part of Gregory Buildings, sharing the ground floor with Ella's office, and Ella would be home from Europe any time now.

Did Ella's return account for his mood? Laurence wondered. He had missed her, and the prospect of her extended vacation in Europe did not please him. "Selfish old shit," he said to himself under his breath as he pushed open the door of the restaurant. *"Bonjour,* Paul, how are bookings today?" In a moment he was immersed in the world of his restaurant, and for the time being Ella was forgotten. By midday, however, he was satisfied that the Lexington restaurant was running as smoothly as it should, and, accepting a glass of kir from the barman, he went and sat at a table near the window, with a view of the main entrance of Gregory Buildings. A call to Jessie had already established that Ella had not yet returned, and from his vantage point Laurence would be able to see her as she arrived.

It was only with Ella Kovac, Laurence mused, that he had come dangerously near jeopardizing his marriage. After the birth of their third child, his wife Colette, at only thirty-two, had lost all interest in sex. For a while Laurence had waited patiently, but eventually—always a practical man—he had begun a discreet affair with a young woman journalist who had come to interview him about the opening of a new restaurant. It had lasted for several months, until one day Christine had announced that she was going back to her boyfriend. It did not bother him; he simply transferred his affections to Christine's roommate, and so on and so on, seeking and acquiring sexual gratification with a minimum of fuss.

Everything changed on an October day much like this one. It had begun with a telephone call. "Laurence, it's Margot Haigh. How are you?"

Laurence smiled with pleasure at the sound of her voice. It was attractive, a little husky, and the clipped efficiency and economy of words only added to the attraction of this complex woman. Laurence was enormously attracted to Margot but recognized she was out of his league. "I'm fine, Margot, and how are things with you?"

"Oh, great. Listen, I know you've been looking for a property on Lexington in the mid-thirties. I've found the perfect place, and at the right price, too."

"A woman of many talents," said Laurence. "I guess when you get tired of banking you could always turn to real estate."

Idle banter did not amuse Margot. "I'm not prepared to tell you where it is unless you agree to a partnership deal, so far as developing the property is concerned."

"With you?" Laurence was surprised.

"No, of course not with me," said Margot, "with an extremely attractive young woman, just twenty-one."

"Oh, come on, Margot," said Laurence, "I'm too old to act as nursemaid to some kid."

"If you're not prepared to deal with her," said Margot, "I'm not prepared to disclose to you the identity of the property."

"I'll find it," said Laurence.

"You won't," said Margot, "because it's not on the market."

There was a long pause. "What's so special about this kid?"

For a moment Margot, normally so decisive, did not reply. Then she laughed, a crystal-clear sound, like a mountain stream—it made Laurence's heart skip a beat. "I don't know, Laurence. That's the strange thing. I'm honestly not quite sure why I'm insisting on you cutting her in on the action. I made up my mind as I lifted the phone—either you give her a break or I'll find someone else who can."

The property was wonderful, an eight-story apartment building, very run-down, owned by a property developer who was in deep trouble. The kid, it appeared, lived in one of the rental apartments but had gotten wind of the fact that her landlord was in a mess and had offered to buy the whole property from him.

"I guess it shows spunk," Laurence said to Margot grudgingly.

"She's been very thorough," said Margot. "It's no pie-in-the-sky plan. She calculates—and I'm sure she's right—that the apartments are far too big, and that the real requirement in this city is for small one- or two-bedroom apartments for young professional people. She's drawn up the plans, gotten the necessary permits—all she needs is the money."

"How much?" said Laurence.

"The total project, including conversion, will cost upwards of $500,000. My scheme is to split the cost three ways—she can put up ten percent of the stake money, I want you to put up twenty-five percent, and the bank will finance the balance. We've allowed additional costs for converting two thirds of the ground floor into a Café Colette. We'll set up a corporation in which she will have a seventy-five percent stake, and you'll have twenty-five. You'll pay a commercial rent for the restaurant, just like the other tenants, but, of course, you'll have a stake in the holding company."

"Why do I need the kid? Why can't I just do this on my own?"

"Because the kid found the property, the kid wants to go into real estate, and you're a restaurateur."

"OK," said Laurence, "suppose I go and look at the property. Where is it?"

"Do we have a deal?" said Margot suspiciously.

"OK, OK," said Laurence, "if the numbers work. Now where is it?"

"On the corner of Lexington and 39th. For the moment it's called Davidson Plaza, but Miss Kovac would like to change the name to Gregory Buildings."

"Gregory Buildings!" said Laurence. "Why, in God's name?"

"Gregory is the name of her son."

"Her son! Jesus, how old is he?"

"Six, I understand."

"Six! Jesus Christ!"

The future Gregory Buildings was everything Margot had promised, and so was Ella Kovac—and more. She looked like a child, yet there was a sensuous quality about her that attracted Laurence in a way that no other woman had ever done, not even Colette. When his tentative advances had been met first with a cold rebuff and then, when he persisted, with something very close to terror, he was totally hooked. He had to win this girl, and he had succeeded after many months of patience, by which time Laurence Merman was hopelessly and irrevocably in love. He still was today.

A cab drew to a screeching halt, and Laurence was snapped out of his daydreaming. Moments later he was rewarded by seeing Ella step out of the vehicle. She was casually dressed, as usual, in jeans, sneakers, and an expensive multicolored silk shirt. She had a nice tan, Laurence noted, but there was a strained look about her, and she seemed to have lost weight she could ill afford. The cab driver was fussing with her bags. Throwing back the remains of his kir, Laurence ran out to greet her.

Once inside her apartment, Ella collapsed on the sofa and allowed Laurence to fetch her a glass of wine. She glanced at her watch. "Jet lag, what a pain. Two hours until Greg comes out of school. I guess I'll go and collect him. How is he, Laurence, have you seen him?"

"Most days," said Laurence. "He's fine. He's getting to be a big boy—he's almost as tall as I am."

Ella looked at him affectionately. "Well, that's not awfully difficult, Laurence."

"No, I guess not." Laurence laughed and lowered his stocky frame onto the sofa beside Ella. "Are you going to give your old man a kiss?" She leaned forward and kissed his cheek. It was not what he had in mind, but she was tired, and he let it pass.

"Well, Laurence, I've found you your French château, except that it's not a château, it's a castle. It's inside your price range, with about forty acres of land, a small vineyard, two cottages, and a little farmhouse. The only problem is that you can't have the little farmhouse."

"Why not?" said Laurence, smiling at her. It was so good to have her back he was hardly taking in what she was saying.

"Because I'm going to have it. I'll buy it off you at the right price, of course. I just fell in love with it, though heaven knows when I'll get to stay there. It's for Greg, really, I guess. It's just his sort of place."

"Tell me more," said Laurence. "A castle—that sounds interesting."

"Here, wait, I've got some photographs and a map. The property is in the foothills of the Alps Maritime. The nearest town is Digne, and all the hot spots—Antibes, Nice, Cannes—are only a couple of hours' drive away. The castle is just out of another time, another world. Look at the photographs. I think they speak for themselves."

"What's it called?" Laurence asked.

"Castle de Challese. Look, there's the castle, and this is the view looking directly south. There's the vineyard, see, and the river below. It won't take more than a few thousand dollars to make it habitable, and the asking price is f360,000. It's a steal!" They pored over the photographs for some time.

"I love it," said Laurence, "it's dead right. I just hope nobody else gets it. You'd better call the agent right away and say to go ahead."

"I already have," said Ella. They both laughed.

Laurence raised his glass. "Well, here's to Castle Challese. Just wait until I show these pictures to Colette—she'll love it." There was an uncomfortable silence between them for a moment. "I'm sorry, Ella, that wasn't very tactful."

"It's OK," said Ella. Her voice sounded weary.

Laurence scrutinized her in silence for a moment. "You look peaked, kind of sad. What have you been up to, sweetheart?"

Expecting a negative response denying anything was wrong, Laurence was surprised when Ella stood up, reached for the wine bottle to refill her glass, and said, "We need to talk, Laurence, and I guess now is as good a time as any."

"Something's happened," said Laurence. "I'm right, aren't I?"

"Yes, something has happened." Ella collapsed back on the sofa and sipped her wine in silence for a moment.

Laurence tried to control a mounting sense of panic. "While I was in England"—Ella struggled with the words—"well, I guess I fell in love."

Laurence felt as though his world had collapsed. He recognized only too well that he was hardly a young girl's dream. Up until now he had been confident that he was the only man in her life. Indeed, the idea of her falling in love with someone else had simply never occurred to him. He forced himself to be generous—after all, he was married, and she was young, with her whole life ahead of her. "I can't pretend that this hasn't come as a shock, Ella, but I guess I'm really pleased for you. It is serious?"

"It's serious, for both of us," said Ella, "or rather, it was."

"Was! What do you mean *was?*"

"I mean it's all over, finished."

"But how can it be?" said Laurence. "You only just met the guy—how come you've had the time to fall in love and out again so fast?"

Ella gave a hollow laugh. "Because just my luck, yet again, I picked a married man."

His confidence came back. A married man had made a play for Ella. She had responded, and he had gone back to his wife. She would need him more than ever! Everything was all right. "I'm sorry, honey. It must have been rough on you. Still, you're home now, and you have Uncle Laurence to pick up the pieces."

"That's just it," said Ella, "that's what I'm trying to tell you—I'm afraid it means the end for us. After this experience, it wouldn't be right for us to continue. I mean, we'll go on being friends, of course, and partners . . ."

Laurence was suddenly angry. "OK, so you take a tumble with some guy, and then you find out the bastard's married. English, is he?" Ella nodded. "OK, it was a bad experience, but it's over. He's on the other side of the Atlantic, you're home, and I'm still here."

"It is over and I am home, but I am not the same, or rather I don't feel the same about you." Ella spoke slowly, as if to a child. "I do love you, Laurence, but more as a friend, a brother, a father. This other thing, it was different. Feeling as I do, I couldn't make love to anyone else, and that includes you."

"So what are you going to do?" said Laurence. "Turn into a nun, take holy orders?"

"Who knows?" said Ella. She looked exhausted, with dark shadows under her eyes.

Laurence suddenly felt defeated, his anger drained away. "This guy—does he want to leave his wife for you?"

"I think he would like to," said Ella, "but it's quite impossible. He has commitments at home, and his wife—well, she's not into kids. He's responsible for the children, and he has a business to run from home. His wife's away working most of the time, so you see he can't simply walk out."

"This isn't the guy . . . the people at Wickham, the husband of the woman Margot hooked you up with for the Paris project?" Laurence asked.

"Yes," said Ella, surprised. "How did you know?"

"An obvious guess. You don't know many people in England. This is going to make your Paris deal a little complicated, isn't it?"

"I'm not going ahead with the Paris deal—that's the other thing," said Ella.

"I can't keep up with all this. Are you saying you're pulling out of Paris because of this guy? This is most unlike you, Ella. You've never let your emotions rule your business decisions before."

"No, it's not because of Tim. I made the decision before . . . well, before I realized how I felt about Tim. I pulled out for a combination of reasons, Laurence, but primarily because I have the feeling that I can't do two jobs properly—look after things here and in Paris."

"So what happens next?" asked Laurence heavily.

"Nothing," said Ella. "I get on with my job, concentrate on looking after my son, and do my best to put Tim out of my mind."

Laurence brightened a little. "So we can still have dinner now and again, and lunch, maybe? You're going to need cheering up."

There were tears in Ella's eyes, threatening to overflow and run down her cheeks. She looked younger than ever, and it wrenched Laurence's heart.

"So long as you understand," Ella said, "that we can't turn the clock back and change things. You mustn't think that after a few weeks or months I'll forget all about Tim and we can go back to where we were. That will never happen, and as long as you understand that, we can meet as often as you like."

Laurence stood up and sighed. "Autumn's normally a good time for me."

Laurence left the apartment, rode the elevator, although it was for only one floor, and, avoiding his restaurant, stepped out onto the street. The early promise of the day had been fulfilled. The sky was a cloudless blue, the freshness of the air invigorating, but it meant nothing to Laurence Merman. He suddenly felt very old.

Chapter 11

Paris—*November 1977*

Stephanie replaced the receiver and stared out of the window in silence for a moment.

"Anything wrong?" Alex came to stand beside her, not touching, but close.

As always, Stephanie could feel his vitality flow through her as if they were joined by an electric current, but her feeling of guilt at the news she had just heard was by far the stronger emotion. She turned away so he could not see her face. "No," she said, "at least not with the business—the business is doing fine. In fact, that new manager I've appointed is unbelievably efficient. I think my absence is actually beneficial."

Alex studied her in silence, his pale blue eyes penetrating, inquiring. "All right, so there's nothing wrong with the business, but something *is* wrong."

Stephanie shrugged her shoulders. "It's just that Tim's not too well."

Alex raised an eyebrow. "Life-threateningly not too well?"

"Oh, no, nothing like that," said Stephanie with studied casualness. She was not ready to talk about Tim—especially not to Alex.

"What is it, then?" he persisted.

"Just a recurring childhood illness. The medics will sort it out."

"You mean you're not going to tell me?"

"No," said Stephanie, "but then, I don't think you really want to know."

"You're right, of course. Why should I want to spend time talking about your husband when here we are in your new Paris flat with the most enormous double bed I've ever seen, entirely unchristened."

Stephanie felt an instant warmth rush through her. She wanted to think through the news she had just heard from her office, but Alex's hands were on the nape of her neck, moving slowly, sensuously over her shoulders. It was extraordinary, the power he had over her—he could arouse her with a single caress, a look even . . . and he knew it.

Their affair had begun during their second meeting. At Joseph's suggestion, Alex had taken her out to dinner, and they had ended the evening in Alex's bed. It was not Stephanie's style—she enjoyed sex, and during her years in London, before meeting Tim, she'd had several lovers.

However, she had never been an easy conquest—at least not before Alex.

The situation worried her, for it seemed that her mind no longer had control over her body. Alex's reputation as an international playboy was well-known, and she did not want to fall into the trap of being simply another notch on his belt.

Yet her body betrayed her every time—like now. She wanted to think through the implications of Tim's sudden decline in health and its effect on the children. Instead she lay on the great double bed, her mind floating away while her body arched and tensed in ecstatic response to Alex's lovemaking.

She woke sometime later to find Alex hovering over her, carrying a wine cooler and two glasses. "Some champagne —yet another housewarming gift."

"What was the first?" Stephanie asked sleepily.

"Why, me, of course." She watched in silence as his delicate, artistic fingers, so like his father's, expertly opened the bottle and filled the two glasses. He handed one to Stephanie as he got back into the bed. "To the Centre des Arts," he said. They drank in silence.

"How long will you be staying in Paris?" Stephanie asked, snuggling up against his chest.

"As long as I'm needed," said Alex. "Now that we have the Centre des Arts up and rolling I think it's time we thought about the franchise."

"Do you and your father still want to go ahead with that?" Stephanie raised herself on one elbow.

"Yes," Alex said, smiling. "I think we work very well together, don't you?"

Stephanie sat upright in bed, tossed back the remains of her champagne, and refilled her glass. Alex, seeing her agitation, watched in silence. She was halfway through the second glass before she spoke. "How do you see the future, so far as we are concerned?"

"Once we've agreed on the nuts and bolts of this franchise

deal—once we have the structure right—Meyer has plenty of capital to invest in Europe. I see us expanding fast and furious, don't you?"

"That's not what I meant," said Stephanie. "I was talking about you and me."

Alex looked blank. "We enjoy each other's company"—he grinned, running a hand gently over her shoulder—"in and out of bed. We're both ambitious. The world is ours for the taking."

"There is one major difference between us," said Stephanie. "You're single, and I have a husband and two children."

Without a word Alex swung his long legs out of bed and disappeared into the bathroom, leaving Stephanie hurt and bewildered. She sat on the bed in silence, listening to the sounds of the shower. He was behaving like a spoiled child—not wishing to discuss anything other than the pursuit of pleasure. She was frightened. Despite her skill and experience, she knew that much of the success or failure of her growing relationship with Meyer Hotels depended upon her relationship with Alex. It was not why she had let herself become involved with him, but it was a factor. Her thoughts turned to Tim. If reports were correct, he'd had a reoccurrence of his condition, caused, she did not doubt, by stress. She had not told him of her affair with Alex, but he had to guess there was something more than business keeping her away from Wickham. How were the children coping, she wondered, with a sick father and an absent mother? When she thought of her daughters, she always thought of them as the babies she had loved and cherished, not as the children they were today, not far from puberty, strangers to her . . . Lying alone in the elegant but impersonal flat, at the emotional mercy of a man who was little more than a stranger, Stephanie had a sudden surge of longing for her home and family.

As abruptly as he had left Alex emerged from the bathroom, a tiny towel fastened around his waist. He looked sleekly handsome and very confident. "Sorry," he said, "I needed to think."

"And having thought?" Stephanie felt suddenly as nervous as she had been on the first occasion she had met the Meyers.

Alex sat down on the bed and took one of Stephanie's hands in his. "Look, I recognize that I've led a charmed life," he said seriously. "I've been denied nothing. I have been blessed with reasonable looks, a relatively adequate brain, and everything that money and power can buy—with one exception."

"What's that?" said Stephanie.

"I have no status of my own, no feeling of self-worth, no sense of achievement."

Stephanie could hardly believe her ears. This was Alex Meyer talking—heir to one of the most successful hotel groups in the world—always assured, always charming. His sudden admission was both disarming and disturbing. "I don't understand," she said. "Is this something to do with your father?"

"You admire my father very much, don't you?" said Alex. Stephanie nodded. "He is a truly remarkable man, I cannot deny that. His commercial achievements are amazing by any standards, particularly in the light of his early life. He has not made it to where he is today without being ruthless, yet there remains within the man—perhaps because of his experiences—a deep well of compassion that people at once find enchanting." Alex paused. "He's a great man, Stephanie, but a lousy father."

"Why?" Stephanie asked.

"He lets me do nothing, he treats me like a child. I have made no real decisions since I joined Meyer after college. He did the right thing—he started me off in the kitchens and had me work my way up through the ranks, learning all the jobs along the way. However, when eventually I made it to headquarters, he simply treated me as an office boy—that is, until now."

"What's changed things?" said Stephanie.

"You, apparently."

"Me? I don't see how."

"He's willing to grant you this franchise. It's a snap decision, like all his major decisions, and that in itself is not surprising—he took to you, recognizes your talents, and he always acts on impulse. However, because he doesn't know you, he's nervous, and for the first time I have a use. I am at least the devil he knows, and by allowing us to work as a team he feels confident enough at last to delegate a major responsibility. You may think this deal is important to you, Stephanie, but it's every bit as important to me."

"I accept that, Alex, and thank you for explaining it all to me," said Stephanie slowly. "It makes me feel more in partnership with you; it's actually comforting to know we both have a lot at stake." She smiled at him, radiating more confidence than she felt. "However, you have so far skillfully avoided answering my question—where do *we* go from here?"

"I was coming to that," said Alex. "I've never been in love, I guess. What I feel for you is good. I like you, I admire you, I enjoy working with you, and I adore going to bed with you. If that's love, then great."

"I feel the same," said Stephanie quietly.

"What I don't want," Alex continued, "are any complications. Not at the moment, not when there's so much riding on Meyer's expansion in Europe. What I need is a simple, straightforward personal life with no hassles."

Their eyes met. Alex's were steely with determination, Stephanie noted. "Because of Tim and the children?" she challenged.

"Of course," said Alex.

"Are you asking me to divorce Tim and stop seeing my children?"

"I don't mind what you do," said Alex, with horrifying candor, "as long as it doesn't affect me. You can divorce Tim or not, as you wish. You can see your children as often as you like, as far as I am concerned, as long as you don't expect me to play any role in their lives. I don't like kids; I have nothing to say to them. They make a mess, a noise—I don't want your children to be a part of my life."

"You're being very frank," said Stephanie coolly.

"Yes, I am," said Alex, "but is there anything wrong with that? You asked me a straightforward question, and I'm giving you a truthful answer. I don't know where we go from here, Stephanie, except that right now I want no other woman but you. However, I do know that I don't want to marry, I don't want kids of my own, and I don't want a part of your husband's kids. I may be a selfish bastard, but at least I'm a consistent one. I want to make Meyer Hotels, Europe, the most successful hotel group there is, and I'd like to do it with you at my side. I want you as a business partner, a friend, and a lover, but not at a price. In other words, whatever trouble this causes for you back home is your problem." He must have seen the dismay on Stephanie's face, for his manner softened a little. "Look, the last thing I want to do is put pressure on you. If you feel you can't cope, I'm sure we're adult enough to terminate the personal side of our relationship and concentrate on working together. Is that what you would prefer?"

Stephanie hesitated only for a split second. "No, no, that's not what I want."

"What do you want, then?" said Alex, smiling and relaxed now that his point was made.

"You," said Stephanie in a small voice.

Alex threw back his head and laughed, his white teeth gleaming against his dark skin. "And I want you, my love, so is there any reason why it should be more complicated than that?"

"No," said Stephanie, "no, I suppose not." Yet even as she came into Alex's arms she knew that it was. The ambitious, ruthless streak she recognized in Alex she knew she herself possessed—they were two of a kind.

It already seemed to Stephanie that she no longer belonged in the master bedroom at Wickham that she had shared with Tim for so many years. She had arrived home without warning to find Tim at work and the children at school. After a rather awkward cup of coffee with Mrs. Maggs, who clearly smelled trouble in the air, Stephanie decided to use the time before Tim returned for lunch to pack the bulk of her wardrobe to take with her back to Paris. For a moment she sat on the wide window seat looking at their large double bed, trying to understand what had occurred to make her feel so detached. Part of it was physical—the bedside table on her side was bare; it actually had a neglected look. On Tim's side the floor was littered with farming magazines and the table piled high with books. There was an alarm clock, his pills, a discarded handkerchief, a glass of water. And then there were the pillows—no longer lying side by side but piled up in a single column, indicating single occupancy of a double bed.

It was not just the physical changes in the room, however, that made Stephanie feel out of place. The long days with Alex, followed by the ecstatic nights, had somehow alienated her and made her feel a stranger in the one place in all the world she had always felt was home. This had been her parents' room—she could remember the happy days when she had bounced on their bed, opening presents on her birthday or on Christmas morning. It was the bed in which her mother had died, in which her two children had been conceived, and where Belinda, in what had been an unholy rush, had been born. Yet she felt nothing.

When would she be back here again? she wondered. Her mind closed, for contemplation of the future was pointless. In recent days she had come to realize that while Alex's declaration was admirable in its honesty, it was hardly comforting, and already she knew she was out of her depth in the relationship. Alex had laid down the terms, and she was so in love she was prepared to accept them at face value. She let out a sigh and stood up, wearily opened the first of four large suitcases, and began to pack.

"What the hell's going on?" Tim burst through the bedroom door.

Stephanie turned and studied him in silence for a moment before answering. He looked haggard and somehow pale beneath his tan. His eyes, normally so warm, were edged with pain. "You're back early," Stephanie said stupidly.

"Mrs. Maggs sent for me. She thought I should be here, and it seems she's right. Were you planning to pack and be out of the house before I got home for lunch?"

"No, of course not," said Stephanie. "I just thought I'd do this while I was waiting for you." Tim let out a weary sigh and sank down on the stool by the dressing table. "Are you all right?" said Stephanie.

"Yes, I'm all right," said Tim, "but I'd like an explanation."

"As you can see, I'm packing up most of my things to take to Paris, to the flat."

"By the size and quantity of suitcases it would seem you're moving all your things. Are you leaving permanently?"

"More or less," said Stephanie. "I think it's probably best."

"Best for whom?" said Tim. "For the children, for me, or perhaps for you?"

"For all of us," said Stephanie.

"Why?" There was a nervous tic hammering away at the side of Tim's right eye.

She took a deep breath. "I've become involved with someone else. I'm sorry, but it just happened."

"But it's serious?"

"Yes." Stephanie could not meet his eye.

"So you're leaving me. Do you want a divorce?"

"I—I don't know," said Stephanie.

"You mean he hasn't asked you to marry him?" Tim's voice was icily calm.

"No."

"Will he?"

"I don't know. Possibly not. Please don't go on with these questions, Tim."

"Does that mean he's married?" said Tim, ignoring her.

"No, he's not married."

"Then the man must be a bastard if he's prepared to take you away from your husband but not marry you himself."

"He's very different from you," said Stephanie defensively. "Certainly many of the standards you would consider essential for decent living, he would not. His upbringing's been so different."

"Am I permitted to know his name?"

"It's Alex Meyer," said Stephanie.

"The old man?" Tim looked appalled.

"No, the son."

"No wonder you've struck such a good deal with the Meyers. You're taking them to your bed."

Stephanie stepped forward and slapped him hard across the face. At the very moment she did so, she regretted it. "Tim, I'm sorry, I'm very sorry." He remained where he was seated, seemingly oblivious to the blow. Only the red welt appearing on one cheek indicated that she had not imagined what had happened. "Look, we're only upsetting each other by talking like this," she said shakily.

Still he said nothing; he simply stared at her as if she was a stranger to him. His face was so familiar—the laugh lines around his eyes, his rugged features—not, strictly speaking, handsome, but nonetheless a pleasing face, above all a good face—honest, caring. Suddenly, the enormity of what she was about to lose made Stephanie catch her breath. In response, she saw hope flare in Tim's face. "Don't do it, Steph," he said quietly. "Look, I know your business means everything to you, and presumably this man, this Alex Meyer, can do a lot for your career, but is it really worth giving up a marriage for?"

"Do we still have a marriage?" Stephanie asked quietly.

"I thought so," said Tim. He stood up and walked to the window. "Not a conventional marriage, perhaps. We see so little of each other, and when we do it's rushed and you're always exhausted, but we should be looking at this stage in our life together as just that . . . a stage." He turned to face her, his love for her plainly exposed in his eyes. "We were so happy in the beginning, and in the years that followed, when Millie and Belinda were small. I'm not imagining it, am I? Things were perfect, weren't they?"

Stephanie could not meet his eye. "They were good, certainly."

"So there has been a considerable deterioration since then, but it's not so much our relationship as the circumstances. Supposing I said to you—look, I won't fight your business aspirations anymore, you go your way, I'll go mine—wouldn't that help?"

"That's just what I'm suggesting we do," said Stephanie.

"Don't try to be so bloody clever," said Tim angrily. "I might be prepared to give and take on how much time you spend on your work, but I'm certainly not prepared to tolerate you being away from home in order to conduct an affair with Alex Meyer. You must take me for an absolute weakling. I usually let you have your own way without argument for the sake of family unity, but there is a limit, and this is it." He made an effort to control himself. "Will it help if I tell you I still love you as much as the day we first made love?"

Slowly Stephanie raised her eyes to meet his. "No, I don't think it will, Tim. You see, it's . . . it's too late."

The fight died in him, and he slumped back on the chair. Compassion welled up in Stephanie. She stepped forward, and, kneeling down, she slipped her arms around him. "I really am very sorry," she whispered against his chest. For a moment he responded to her, and she was aware, fleetingly, of a sense of warmth and security in his embrace, which, despite all the passion of their relationship, she never felt with Alex.

Almost as the thought came to her, Tim pushed her away abruptly. "I can stand just about anything except your pity," he said. "Let's talk about the practicalities, since clearly you're not going to change your mind."

She took her cue from him and stood up briskly. "You must stay on here, of course. It's your home as much as mine—you created it. As far as the children are concerned, perhaps I could arrange to see them sometimes."

"Whenever you like," said Tim mechanically. "At least that's one good thing."

"What's one good thing?" said Stephanie, frowning.

"At least they won't suffer from our marriage splitting up, as most poor little wretches do. Having a full-time mother would come as far more of a shock to their systems than having no mother at all."

"Do you have to rub it in?"

"Yes, I bloody well do," said Tim, suddenly standing up. The violence of his reaction made Stephanie step back, stumbling over a suitcase as she did so. "Look, just clear out. Get packed as quickly as you can, and please be gone by lunchtime. I don't want to have to sit through a meal trying to make small talk with you. Leave your address on my desk, and if there's anything wrong with the children, I'll let you know. No news is good news, all right?"

"All right," said Stephanie.

In an instant he was gone, not slamming the door but shutting it quietly behind him, as was his way. To her surprise, Stephanie found herself sitting on the bed with tears pouring down her face. It had been so much easier than she had expected—there had been few recriminations, the very minimum of explanation. So why was she crying?

Chapter 12

New York—*December 1977*

The bitter cold of early December in New York seemed to have penetrated every bone, Margot thought as she hurried on, head bent against the wind. It had been madness to walk through Central Park. The sky was so blue and the sun so bright that, from the safety of a centrally heated office, the prospect had seemed desirable; besides, she had wanted time to think, and she was early for her appointment. Having spent the first thirteen years of her life in Korea, British weather had been bad enough, but she would never get used to the New York winter. She was definitely a hothouse bloom, she thought. She quickened her pace at the sight of the Inn on the Park ahead. She was breaking all her normal personal codes of practice by having lunch with Ella Kovac today. She was not quite sure why she was doing it, except she felt instinctively that she understood Ella very well—an impoverished childhood followed by the phenomenal success of her venture into real estate had made her strangely vulnerable. If you have nothing, you have nothing to lose. However, once success has been achieved, then every decision you make could in theory throw you back to where you've come from. Ella, she felt, was in danger of becoming a prisoner of her own success.

Ella was already at the table by the time Margot had shed her coat and tidied herself in the ladies' room. She looked tired, Margot thought, and seemed to have lost even more weight. Man trouble, Margot wondered, or something wrong with the business? "Ella, how good to see you." The two women exchanged a perfunctory kiss.

"It's good to see you, too," said Ella, "and don't think I'm unaware of the great honor you are doing me—I know business lunches are not your style."

"I promised you a lunch when we last met in London. I don't forget my promises."

"I'm sure you don't," said Ella dryly.

They ordered salmon en croute and a bottle of Muscadet and then settled down to talk. It wasn't just Ella's appearance that had altered, Margot noted—it seemed she had lost her sparkle, her vitality. By contrast, as always, Ella was fascinated by Margot, as indeed the entire restaurant appeared to be. She was a spectacular sight with her dark auburn hair, her pale, oriental face, and eyes so dark that they appeared to be black rather than brown—almond-shaped but large, so that they dominated her face. Tall, slim, and dressed in a simple black silk Jean Muir jersey and skirt, she was all the more stunning because her appearance was so understated. Long red fingernails tapped the table, since there was no pen or paper with which to doodle. "So how's business, Ella?"

"OK," said Ella without apparent enthusiasm.

"You know, what you should be looking at is a fresh location where you can make a real killing for the same amount of effort—a real boom area where you can get in on the ground floor."

"If I wanted a project outside New York," said Ella, "I'd have gone for the Centre des Arts—surely we don't have to go through all that again."

"Ella, there are an awful lot of places nearer than Paris," said Margot, exasperated. "I was actually thinking North America."

"Like where?" said Ella.

"I don't know, it's not my job to know—this is your country, Ella, not mine, and it's your business. I just feel that you're in some kind of rut, sitting around waiting for the same old projects to come up."

"You make me sound as though I'm underemployed," said Ella ruefully. "I work damned hard, Margot. It's more than a full-time job looking after my properties, and I always have a new project on the go. I run a tight ship with the very minimum of staff—you know that."

"I'm not suggesting you're being lazy—of course I'm not—I'm just saying you're mentally stuck in a rut, and it can't be very stimulating."

"Thanks a bundle," said Ella.

"Come on," said Margot, "it's not often I see you minus your sense of humor. Is there anything wrong, have you any problems?"

"Nothing I can't handle," said Ella, anxious to steer the conversation away from herself. "The business is really running very smoothly at present."

They moved on to a wide range of topics as the meal progressed, until Ella could stand it no more and asked the question that had been foremost in her mind since Margot had joined her. "Tell me about Stephanie Bonham. How are things going?"

"Very well," said Margot, "in fact I have to admire her drive and enthusiasm—it's hard to keep up. Not only did she persuade old man Meyer to do the Centre des Arts project with her, she's sold all her hotels and leisure complexes to the Meyer organization and has taken up a franchise on them and all the Meyer units in Europe. It's worth an absolute fortune, but she acquired the license for a song, comparatively speaking. Mind you, I suppose it's not entirely surprising under the circumstances."

"What circumstances?" Ella asked.

"Haven't you heard the gossip?"

Ella shook her head. "I've had no dealings at all with Stephanie since that rather unfortunate meeting when I pulled out of the Centre des Arts project."

"She's started a well-publicized affair with Alex Meyer—Joseph Meyer's son and heir," Margot added with a grin. "They're seen everywhere together and frequently splashed all over the gossip columns. Stephanie's permanently based in Paris now, and Alex spends as much time in Paris as he can—it's all very cozy."

Ella was amazed by her own physical reaction—she felt at once sick and faint; her heart was beating a wild tattoo. "What about Tim?" she had to ask. "How has he reacted?"

"There's nothing much he can do, is there?" said Margot. "He and Stephanie have been leading separate lives for a long time. I gather he's doing what he always has done—keeping the home fires burning at Wickham."

"Are they getting divorced?" said Ella, aware that she was perhaps displaying too much interest.

"Who knows?" said Margot. "It probably depends on what Stephanie wants. He's always struck me as a little weak. On the other hand, he's an attractive man. I should imagine every unattached female in the country will be pushed in his direction." She laughed, blissfully unaware of the pain her words caused Ella.

Back at Gregory Buildings Ella found herself loath to go back into her office. Instead she took the elevator to the peace and quiet of her apartment—after all, she had her new assistant, Jackie, to fend off calls. Jackie Partridge was an odd choice by anyone's standards. Ella collapsed on her sofa, remembering her first meeting with Jackie. Jackie was the fifth would-be assistant Jessie had selected for Ella to inspect. She was also the last and, Ella suspected, Jessie's favorite. She was a large girl with wispy, pale brown hair to her shoulders that flew untidily in all directions. Her good features were her clear gray eyes and a pale, peachy complexion. She had a tendency to flush bright scarlet when she was embarrassed or unsure of herself.

Ella studied the résumé in front of her. Jacqueline Partridge had been in New York for nearly two years—she had begun working for a British publishing house and more recently had moved to an advertising agency, where she had only been for eight months. School had been Cheltenham Ladies College, followed by a secretarial college in Oxford. "You're English?" Ella asked.

"Oh, yes," said Jacqueline. She played nervously with the

handles of her handbag. She was conventionally dressed in a blue suit that was a little on the tight side for her.

"What are you doing in New York?" Ella asked, eager to put the girl at ease.

"Oh, I thought I'd like to see a bit of the world, travel around, you know," Jackie stammered.

"You must know New York pretty well by now, after two years. Forgive me for asking this, but if I am to take you on, I need to know what your long-term plans may be—in other words, are you intending to go back to England shortly? Whomever I employ, I want to feel he or she will be with me for a while."

"Oh, I shan't be going back to England," said Jacqueline emphatically.

"Why?" Ella asked pointedly.

"Because I like it here, and because . . ." She stopped in mid-sentence, looking flustered. "Oh, drat," she said, "it's no good. I'm going to have to tell you the truth."

"I'd appreciate it," said Ella dryly.

"I came over here originally because I was in love with my boss and he was transferred to New York. My parents were furious and said I was being very silly. It was awful—there were terrible scenes, but I came anyway." There was a note of defiance in her voice.

"I presume he was married," said Ella sagely.

"Y-yes, I'm afraid so." Jackie looked surprised.

"What went wrong?" Ella asked.

"He got fed up with me," said Jacqueline with commendable candor. "You see, I knew no one else in New York. I was lonely, and I smothered him, I think. With his wife still in England, I expected we would be seeing each other all the time." She shrugged her shoulders. "Anyway, he began an affair with an American girl. It was bad enough that he was married, but that was the last straw, so eventually I left."

"And clearly you're not very happy with the advertising agency where you're working now," said Ella.

"No, another disaster—I do seem to pick them. He was married, too, only the difference was he told me he wasn't.

When I found out, I felt such a fool. Everyone else in the office knew. They must have been laughing behind my back. Anyway, you can see why I can't go home—my parents would have a field day."

"Well," said Ella, "there's one good thing about Lexington Kovac: There are no men in this organization, except for a shareholder, Laurence Merman, whom we see fairly infrequently." Fleetingly, Ella wondered if Jacqueline Partridge could be Laurence Merman's type but dismissed the thought—Laurence liked his women small and dark.

There was something about the girl that appealed to Ella. She was not sure what it was—whether it was her candor, or whether her accent reminded her of Tim, or whether it was Jackie's obvious vulnerability. An English girl in New York, totally out of her depth, in some ways mirrored her own early experiences in New York.

Hiring Jackie was a snap decision and one Ella did not regret for a moment. If Jackie had a fault, it was that she was overanxious to please. She worked long hours, took her job very seriously, and seemed effortlessly to have won the affection and admiration of Jessie. Even Greg liked her.

Ella glanced at her watch; Greg would be home in half an hour. There was a desk full of work downstairs, so what was she doing sitting here in a solitary state? She knew, of course—Tim. Tim alone, without Stephanie—it was nearly four months since their one night together and their bitter parting, yet there seemed to have been barely a moment of her waking day when her thoughts had not strayed to Tim Irvine. Fumbling nervously, she opened her briefcase and pulled out an address book. She paused for a moment longer, then, lifting the phone, she dialed the Wickham number.

"Wickham 253." The comfortable, familiar voice of Mrs. Maggs was instantly identifiable.

"Hello," said Ella awkwardly. "Could I speak to Mr. Irvine, please?"

"I'm sorry," said Mrs. Maggs, "he's had his dinner, and he's out. He'll be back later, though—"

"OK, thanks. I'll phone back," said Ella.

"Should I say who's calling?"

"No, no message."

"All right then, good-bye."

"Bye," said Ella, replacing the receiver with a shaky hand. She had tried, and he was out—perhaps it was fate trying to tell her something. She cursed herself for not having left a message so that the decision as to whether to call again would not exist. Placing the responsibility on Tim to call her back if he wished would have been an immense relief. As it was, he would be none the wiser.

She stood up a little unsteadily, then, snapping shut her briefcase, strode purposefully toward the door. She was a fool—it had been madness to think of contacting him. Nothing had changed just because Stephanie had left him. Tim still could not move to New York, and she still could not move to England—those facts stood between them. Somehow she had to learn to forget him.

Chapter 13

"Ella, is that you?"

The practical side of Ella's mind recognized the voice, yet since it represented her wildest fantasies, she rejected it. "Yes," she said cautiously. "Who is this?"

"It's Tim, Ella, Tim Irvine. You do still remember me, don't you?"

She wanted to laugh and scream and shout, "I love you, I love you." Instead she said, "Yes, yes, of course. How are you, Tim?"

"I'm fine. Look, tell me to ring off if you like, and I'll understand. It's just that Mrs. Maggs took a call yesterday morning, and she swears it was from you. She says she recognized your voice. When you or whoever it was didn't ring back, I tried to resist ringing you, but I just couldn't. Was it you, Ella?"

"Yes," said Ella in a quiet voice.

"Oh, good. I have to admit I thought I might be making an idiot of myself."

"No, you weren't doing that, Tim."

"It's lovely to hear your voice," said Tim. "How have you been?"

"A bit low," Ella said.

"Me, too," said Tim. "I don't know whether you've heard . . ."

"Yes," said Ella. "That was one of the reasons I was calling you—the main reason, I suppose—to say I'm sorry about Stephanie. You must be very upset."

"Not as upset as I thought I would be," said Tim. "My pride has been hurt, of course. Taking second place to her business interests was one thing—recognizing that she is involved with another man introduces a whole new set of emotions. Strangely, though, I find it an odd relief."

"Why?" said Ella.

"We've been separated for years, really—several years, at any rate. We kept pretending we had a normal marriage, but of course we didn't, and now at least the position is clarified. Stephanie's free to get on with her life, me with mine, and I think the children are better for it, too. I was quite open with them and told them exactly what had happened, but without being too judgmental as far as Stephanie was concerned. They seem much more relaxed now that everything has settled down. Anyway, enough of me. How's Greg?"

"Greg's fine," said Ella, "enormous, good grades at school, happy and healthy."

There was a brief pause while both reflected on how easy it seemed to be to communicate. "Ella"—Tim hesitated—"you may think this is a ridiculous suggestion, but I just wondered . . . I wondered if you and Greg were doing anything for Christmas."

"We always spend Christmas with Aaron and his family."

"Why not break the rules and spend Christmas with me and the girls? Stephanie's not coming home. She's spending Christmas in New York with the Meyers."

There was no rancor in his voice, Ella noticed with surprise and admiration—it was simply a statement of fact. "Oh, Tim, I just couldn't come to Stephanie's home and take her place, so to speak—it wouldn't feel right. I know it's your home, too," she said hurriedly, "but I'd feel very uncomfortable and awkward."

"Then why don't we meet somewhere else—at a hotel? I know Christmas in a hotel isn't the same as at home, but the children are at an age when they might enjoy it. You could come here with Greg, or we could fly out to you."

As he was speaking a thought flashed into Ella's mind. She tried to reject it, but it sat there, persistent, demanding—it was the obvious solution.

"Ella, are you still there?"

"Yes."

"Look, I'm sorry if I'm embarrassing you. Does the whole idea appall you?"

"No," said Ella, "no, it doesn't appall me at all, it sounds wonderful. I was just thinking . . . Tim, I have this farmhouse in Provence—I've never stayed there, I just bought it on a whim. There are a few sticks of furniture, an old kitchen range, running water and electricity, but that's about it. We could go there, I suppose."

"Ella, could we, can we?" The enthusiasm in Tim's voice made Ella smile.

"Hell, why not?" she said. "It's crazy, but let's do it."

They made hurried arrangements. Tim insisted that it should be he and his daughters who were the advance party, to stock up with food and the equipment they would need.

"It's not fair," said Ella. "You're supposed to be my guests. I should be doing all that."

"You and Greg have a long way to come. We can be out there on the seventeenth."

"Greg and I couldn't make it before the twenty-third," said Ella, leafing through her diary, "and then we'd need to be back by January fourth—sorry, business commitments."

"That's OK," said Tim. "It still gives us two weeks." The thought of two weeks in each other's company silenced them both. "It's so simple," said Tim, "I can't believe it—it must be more difficult than this."

"It isn't," said Ella. "In fact, there's only one thing left to do."

"What's that?"

"I just have to mail you the key."

They followed a bend in the road. The village of Challese was laid out before them, the valley sloping away to the left before climbing again to form the foothills of the Alps Maritime. Ella slowed the car on the brow of the hill. "Look, there's Uncle Laurence's castle."

"Wow," said Greg, "that is impressive. Why aren't we staying there?"

"Because it's Laurence's, not ours. Anyway, who needs a castle? It's a bit much, don't you think?"

"Yes," said Greg, laughing. "Yes, it is, but it's typical Uncle Laurence."

A knot suddenly formed in the base of Ella's stomach as she swung the little Renault around the last few bends. "Here we are," she said in a small, strangled voice.

"It's wonderful, wonderful," said Greg, leaping out of the car before she had finished parking.

It was indeed perfect. The gray stone farmhouse was built in the fold of two hills. It was five miles from the village, and its isolation had troubled Ella slightly on her first visit. Now, though, it seemed appropriate. A watery sun warmed the brickwork, lights blazed from all the windows, and a reassuringly thick column of smoke was rising from both chimneys.

"Tim, Millie, Belinda, we're here!" Greg ran ahead of her, pushing open the stable door that led into the kitchen.

Wearily Ella pressed her hands into the small of her back, trying to straighten up after the hours of traveling, and then self-consciously she followed her son. Tim was out of the back door before she had reached it. She formed no immediate impression of him—they simply reached blindly for each other and embraced fleetingly, aware of the children. "How are you?" Tim said huskily.

"Tired," Ella managed before they were swamped with greetings from the children.

The Irvines had worked hard, very hard indeed. Ella walked into the kitchen and stopped, amazed—it was transformed. A lovely old scrubbed wooden table dominated the room, already set for a meal. Two Windsor chairs were pulled up in front of the range, highly colored rugs were spread over the stone flags of the floor, and plates and glasses gleamed in the firelight. She turned spontaneously, slipping her arms around the shoulders of the two girls. "You've done wonders. I can't believe this—you must have worked so hard."

"Daddy did most of it," said Belinda, "but come see, there's lots more."

In the sitting room a huge log fire crackled in the grate. There were more rugs and easy chairs, and an enormous Christmas tree filled a whole corner of the room.

"This is unbelievable," said Ella. "Greg, can you believe it?"

"It's great. Can we see upstairs?" Greg's face was bright with excitement.

There were four bedrooms—the girls already occupied one, one was for Greg, and one each for Tim and Ella, divided from the rest of the house by an intervening bathroom.

"Sort yourselves out and then come down for drinks in the sitting room," said Tim. "You two are not allowed to do anything tonight but let yourselves be spoiled."

The warmth, the good food, and the wine made Ella and Greg very drowsy, and when it was time for the girls' bedtime Greg went, too, without protest, leaving Tim and Ella alone for the first time.

"This is the most wonderful place, Ella. It was a brilliant find. I know it's cold outside, but come to the back door for a moment." Tim took Ella's hand, pulling her from one of the Windsor chairs and leading her to the stable door. He threw open the top part and let the cold night air rush in. "Listen," said Tim. They leaned over the half door, the cold air reviving Ella, and the silence enveloped them. There was not a sound to be heard except for the music of the stream that ran through the grounds a few feet from the back door. "It beats New York," Tim said.

"It certainly does," Ella whispered.

Instinctively they turned to each other, and a moment later they were in each other's arms, kissing as though they would never stop. Tears sprang into Ella's eyes and began flowing down her cheeks. Normally embarrassed by any show of emotion, she made no effort to brush them away and then realized that the wetness on Tim's face was not from her own tears but from his. Without speaking they crept upstairs and into Ella's room. They undressed quickly because of the cold and fell into bed. "I'll set the alarm," said Tim. "I'd better be back in my own room before the children wake."

It was not as good as the last time; it was better—much, much better. They'd now had time to adjust to their feelings. Stephanie no longer cast a shadow of guilt, and, perhaps most important of all, they were not in a hurry—two glorious weeks stretched ahead of them.

"It's been awful the last few months," Tim whispered when at last they lay sated in each other's arms.

"Yes, every day was an effort," Ella admitted.

"If that's how we both feel, then there has to be a way to be together . . . and we'll find it," Tim murmured as they drifted off to sleep.

The days followed much the same pattern, which seemed

to please them all. At times both Ella and Tim were aware of being a little over-demonstrative with each other, and on several occasions Ella caught Millie watching her with Stephanie's eyes and wondered what was going on in the child's head.

On Christmas Eve Tim and Ella filled stockings for the children and for each other, and on Christmas morning, when they were awoken early by Belinda rampaging through the house, it was actually snowing. They ate a huge Christmas lunch and afterwards exchanged presents. Ella had struggled hard trying to think of a suitable present for Tim and in the end had bought a watch from Tiffany's, engraved simply with the date and his initials. For Millie and Belinda she had spent a fortune on dresses she had found at Macy's. She'd had to guess at styles and sizes, but they seemed appropriate presents. She rightly assumed that clothes were never high on their priority list, without a mother to help them choose. Judging by the squeals of delight, her decision had been the right one, and they insisted on wearing the dresses for the rest of the day.

Tim had bought Ella an antique pearl necklace, which, once it was fixed around her neck, she could never imagine taking off again. He had bought Greg an air rifle. "I hope you don't mind," he said, looking at Ella apprehensively. "It's just that since he enjoys country life, I thought he would probably like to learn to shoot, and this is the right way to start."

"It's brilliant, great," said Greg. "I can't believe it. When can we try it out?"

"This afternoon, if you like," said Tim. "I've brought my gun with me, and I have already spoken to Jean Valois at the farm, who says we may shoot over his land."

On Christmas night they went to Mass. It was a beautiful little church lit entirely by candles, and as they stood together in the pew, Tim's hand in her own, it already seemed to Ella that they were one family—had always been and would always be. On Boxing Day it had snowed some more, and they went tobogganing on kitchen trays. And so the days passed, each one a new delight, until the New Year had come and gone and time was running out.

On the evening of New Year's Day, when the children were in bed, Tim finally raised the question that they had both been avoiding. "So where do we go from here?" he asked gently.

They were in the sitting room, drinking brandy in front of the fire. "I don't know," Ella answered truthfully.

"Let's look at the really important issues," said Tim. "We have each other and our relationship, we have the children and theirs. What flaws do you see—not in the practicalities of living together, for a moment, but purely in how we get along as people?"

Ella considered the question for a moment. "We're lucky because you have girls and I have a boy, so there is no direct competition. The children seem to get along incredibly well. I wonder about Millie, though—she is always very polite and helpful, but I wouldn't dare be demonstrative with her in the way I am with Belinda."

"That may be her age. Twelve-year-olds are very independent, and in Millie's case, she's had to be."

"Yes, I guess so, but I think she's more aware of our relationship even than Greg, and I don't honestly think she's very pleased about it."

"If you're right, I'm sure she'll come around," said Tim gently. "How do you think Greg and I are doing?"

"That's an unnecessary question and you know it," said Ella, grinning. "He thinks the world of you, it's as simple as that."

"And us?" They kissed, and it was some time before they drew apart.

"There's really nothing to say about us, is there?" said Ella.

"Other than it's perfect?" Tim suggested. Ella nodded. "All right," he said, his voice anxious despite his efforts to be practical. "Having looked at our various relationships, would you agree that there is nothing to stop us being together, and that we can't possibly live apart? It would be a crime." Ella nodded. "So all we have to do," said Tim, "is to decide how and where"—he ruffled Ella's curls—"but I don't think we should start that tonight, sleepyhead. We'll pack the children off to bed early tomorrow night and try to make some plans then. Let's think about it during the day, and tomorrow evening we can have an in-depth discussion."

Chapter 14

South of France—*January 1978*

The next day, in one of the outbuildings of the farmhouse, Greg found an old television. Despite the attractions of farm life, the children had been raised on a diet of television and were missing it. Greg, who considered himself something of an electronics expert, set to work to mend it. By lunchtime he had managed to produce a shaky black and white picture that steadily improved, so that by midafternoon, when a cold east wind had set in and a snow-laden sky had already made it nearly dark, the whole family was able to settle down and watch an appallingly sentimental French film—so predictable was the plot that even the children understood it without the benefit of much French.

Belinda and Ella had baked a cake of which they were exceedingly proud. They made tea and sat near the fire, watching the film in perfect, cozy harmony. Ella had almost drifted off to sleep when suddenly she heard Millie's voice, shrill with alarm. "Daddy, Daddy, are you all right?" Her eyes snapped open to find Tim lurching to his feet, his teacup going in one direction, his plate in the other. He seemed quite oblivious to both as they crashed to the floor, and although he had his back to her, Ella saw immediately that his limbs seemed to be twitching spasmodically.

"Tim, Tim, what's the matter?" She stood up and went toward him.

"Don't touch him," Millie shrieked, "clear some space," and as she spoke Tim suddenly pitched forward and crashed to the floor.

The noise and vibration of a grown man apparently hurling himself to the floor trapped them all in a paralyzed silence for a moment, while the television droned on in the background. Then from the body there began a low gurgling noise that grew rapidly in strength. "Tim!" Ella screamed, and she dropped to her knees beside him. She reached out for him and then stopped, horrified at what she saw. His face was contorted and twitching, his cheeks flecked with spittle, his top lip drawn back, baring his teeth like the snarl of an animal. His eyes were wide open but glazed and unseeing.

"It's all right, he's having an epileptic seizure," said the small, cool voice of Millie above her. "I know what to do."

Ella watched, helpless, as the little girl knelt down by her father and began loosening his tie—how could she touch him like that? Ella turned her face away and caught sight of Greg and Belinda, both white-faced and staring at Tim. "Go into the kitchen, you two, and wait for us there," she managed. They went immediately, without argument.

Shaking from head to foot, Ella stood up and turned off the television. "What shall I do?" she asked Millie helplessly.

The child looked up at her; there was no mistaking the look of triumph in her eyes. "There's nothing to do. We just have to wait until it stops."

At last it was over. Ella sat numb and hunched in a corner of the sofa, watching Millie wipe her father's face clean every few minutes as foam gathered at the corners of his mouth. The violent twitching began to ease, and then it stopped altogether. His head lolled sideways, exposing a large bruise on his temple. The man was returning; the foaming, grimacing animal had gone. It was Tim lying there once more. He was ill and hurt, but Ella could not move toward him. She cleared her throat and tried to speak. Her voice sounded strange even to her. "I'd better fetch a doctor, Millie."

"There's no need," said Millie. "He'll sleep now for several hours, and when he wakes up he won't remember anything that's happened. He'll realize he's had a seizure, of course, when he finds he's on the floor, but he never remembers this bit, and he'll be quite well."

"What . . . what about the bruise on his head? He may have knocked himself out."

"I don't think so," said Millie, completely self-assured. "This was one of his more violent ones, but I don't think he'd have been able to throw himself about if he was unconscious. Once he knocked himself out in the stable—he hit his head on the corner of a beam as he fell. The fit didn't happen at all that time. He just lay there, twitching a bit."

"Does it happen often?" Ella managed.

"No. At least, he hadn't had a seizure in ages until a few months ago, but just recently he's had quite a lot. It was the television that started him off. It was silly of him to watch it, but I suppose he didn't want you and Greg to think there was anything wrong with him."

"He should have told me," Ella said, more to herself than to the child.

"I think he wants to marry you," said Millie, her cold little voice very self-important. "He probably thought you wouldn't want to marry him if you knew he was an epileptic."

Millie's words galvanized Ella into activity. She and the child put more wood on the fire, and Millie put some cushions under Tim's head. To her mounting horror, Ella found she still couldn't touch him. When Millie went in search of blankets, Ella found she had to leave the room, too—she could not stay alone with Tim's inert body. She found Greg and Belinda sitting huddled together in front of the kitchen range. "It's all right," she said. "Tim's going to be fine."

"What was it, Mom? What happened? Belinda said he does this sometimes, she says it frightens her. I'm not surprised—it frightened me. He's not going to die, is he?"

At Greg's words Belinda burst into sobs. Ella scooped the child into her arms and sat down beside Greg. "No, of course he's not going to die. He has epilepsy. You must have heard of that, Greg. It's when people have fits called seizures—something goes wrong with their brain for a moment. He's sleeping now. Millie's just fetching a blanket for him, and she says he will be awake in a little while and quite OK." She hugged Belinda tight to her. "By the time you wake up in the morning he'll be completely his old self."

Supper was a subdued affair, and no one was hungry. Greg and Belinda seemed anxious to go to bed, but Millie hovered. "I'll stay with him if you like," she said. "I'm not really tired."

"No, it's OK," said Ella, "you go off to bed." She hesitated. "Millie, I thought you were great the way you coped with him. It put me to shame, I'm afraid—I'm sorry I didn't behave better, but I've never . . . well, I've never come across anything like it."

If she'd hoped for some understanding from the little girl, she was disappointed. "He won't have any more tonight, if that's what you're worried about."

"No, it's not," Ella lied. "I just wanted you to know that I think you did wonderfully well."

"It's no problem," said Millie, "it's just a part of our lives." With that she turned away and began climbing the stairs toward her bed.

Ella wanted to go after her, to kiss her good night, to comfort her, but the barrier between them seemed insurmountable. Wearily, nervously, Ella went into the sitting room and closed the door.

Tim was sleeping deeply. Ella sat down on the sofa, in the furthest corner away from him, tucking her legs up in an effort to make herself warm and comfortable, but there was no comfort in the room. She stared at Tim. This was the face that had lain on her pillow last night—this was the face she loved, she told herself. She tried to identify her emotions—fear was certainly one, and revulsion, she realized. Tim's epilepsy seemed to have changed her whole view of him, standing between them now as an insuperable barrier. There were questions, too. Why hadn't he told her of his condition? Why had he allowed her to witness the seizure without any preparation? How could he have talked of the future when this fundamental fact remained a secret? Suddenly it seemed to her that they were strangers. What did they really know of each other? How long had he imagined he could have kept his condition from her? Her thoughts, quite unexpectedly, turned to Aaron. Sometimes she felt she was betraying her love for Aaron by loving Tim. It was ridiculous; Aaron was happily married and would remain so. Yet now the thought returned unbidden—perhaps this was the punishment for her betrayal, perhaps the problem lay in trying to deny her destiny—to love Aaron hopelessly from afar. Her tired mind tried to rationalize, to understand her feelings, but gradually her eyelids drooped, and she slept.

Tim realized what had happened within seconds of waking. The cold hardness of the floor had stiffened his joints. He sat up, rubbing the sleep from his eyes, and looked around him. Ella was asleep, propped up on the sofa. He watched her in silence for a moment, wondering, with mounting apprehension, what she had seen. Instinct told him it had been a bad seizure. Why the hell had he watched television? It was a stupid thing to do. Yet as always, between fits, he was able to convince himself that he was cured. He simply could not accept his condition and really made little effort to try. He stood up stiffly and crept from the room to the bathroom. When he returned to the room, washed and changed, he felt more confident. He sat down carefully on the sofa beside Ella and gently shook her awake.

As she stretched and came out of sleep Ella turned her face toward him. Her eyes flicked open and, seeing his face above hers, she smiled, the happy, sensual smile of a woman in love. Then suddenly memory flooded back, and she literally recoiled from him, her face a mask of fear. The change in her was so horrific that it left Tim no doubt that whatever he said or did, this moment marked the end of their relationship.

Chapter 15

The seeds that were to change Tim Irvine's life were sown on a cold, crisp night in December 1961, when he was seventeen years old. At home for the holidays from Marlborough, where he was in his final year at school, he was presented with an early Christmas present in the form of a motorcycle. The gift was unexpected and absolutely perfect—a Yamaha 250 in silver with blue trim. Tim had spent the evening at a pub in Cirencester with a group of local friends. Because he was driving he didn't drink, and although he was somewhat exhilarated by the twin pleasures of the Christmas holidays and the avid attention of the prettiest girl in their group, he left the pub just before eleven, sober and alone. He knew the roads back to Monkswell Farm, where the Irvines had farmed for three generations, like the back of his hand. The crisp air invigorated him. The recent acquisition of his bike had opened up his mind to the possibility of being responsible for his own destiny. There were so many places to see and people to meet. He was looking forward to going on to Cirencester Agricultural College the following autumn and promised himself exotic holidays during the coming summers.

He took the final bend before Monkswell Farm at a perfectly acceptable speed. What he could not know was that the old oak, whose bows formed a canopy across the lane at this point, had been steadily dripping water on the lane all day, which had now turned to black ice. Tim hit the patch of ice at thirty miles an hour. Instinctively he braked, and the bike slid sideways and mounted the bank. The impact pitched Tim over the handlebars and catapulted him headfirst into the base of the tree with some force. It was all over in a split second. He felt no sense of fear; there was no time.

At shortly after one A.M. Charles Irvine finally gave in to his wife's increasingly worried pleading and telephoned the Cirencester police. There was no trace of their son, the police reported slightly less than an hour later—he was probably staying with friends, they suggested. It was a rough night—the lad had clearly made a sensible decision not to risk the roads.

Embarrassed and annoyed, Charles Irvine telephoned the three or four families Tim might have stayed with, waking them to no purpose—for he was not there. Finally, putting a heavy overcoat over his pajamas, he got in his car and drove the familiar route from the farm to Cirencester and back. There was no sign of Tim or his motorcycle, though he frightened himself on the return journey when he nearly lost control of the car on the final bend before the farm. Frustrated, exhausted, and secretly worried, he insisted that he and Christine should go to bed, as the boy was bound to call in the morning. They finally slept while, six hundred yards away, their unconscious son lay exposed to the freezing night air in a pool of blood.

At eleven-fifty the next morning Trevor Baines negotiated the narrow lane to Monkswell Farm, cursing the weather conditions. There was no letup in his job—the milk had to be collected, regardless of how icy the roads. As he made the final turn before straightening out into the driveway of Monkswell Farm he thought he saw something in the ditch from his high vantage point in the tanker cab. He tried to stop, but when he applied the brakes nothing happened, and he had to accelerate swiftly to avoid losing control altogether. At the farm he was rewarded with a hot cup of tea while the milk was being loaded. "A bit of a fuss up at the house," Nevil the dairyman informed him. "Young Tim Irvine has gone missing—on his new motorcycle, too."

Trevor laughed. "I expect he found himself a girl last night."

"That's what I told the boss," said Nevil. "He thinks so, too, but Mrs. Irvine, she'll have none of it."

Milk loaded, Trevor began the journey back to the depot. At the bend he again glanced in the direction of the ditch and this time could see, without doubt, the wheel of what looked like a motorcycle. His tired mind began to race—the missing boy, the motorcycle. Cautiously he applied the brakes and in a few yards managed to pull up the tanker. Cursing the cold and the snow, he ran back up the lane and climbed the bank. It was a bike, all right, and there beside it, partially covered by snow, was a body. Frightened now, his heart pounding, he turned the body over on its back. It was the boy without a doubt, but to Trevor it seemed that he had arrived too late.

Trevor Baines was mercifully wrong. Tim was suffering from a concussion and severe hypothermia. In the ambulance on the way to hospital in Swindon his heart stopped twice. The doctor later informed his parents that another twenty minutes of exposure would have been twenty minutes too long for them to have saved him. As it was, Tim remained in a coma, hanging on to life with the help of machines, for five terrible days while his mother, father, and sister took turns sitting by his bed, making futile conversation to his inert body. On the fifth day, when they had all but given up, he opened his eyes, saw his sister, and said, "Hi, Jen, you look ghastly. What's up?"

The road to recovery was a slow one, but he was young and strong and healed fast. By halfway through the Easter term he was ready to go back to school, and more than happy to do so, but for the slight embarrassment of his closely cropped hair where his head had been shaved for the operation. To be self-conscious about something so trivial was an emotion he would look back on with contempt.

The rest of the term progressed without incident. When school ended he went to stay for a few days with John McKenzie, a friend from school. John lived in London, and staying with him involved one long social riot—dances, parties, balls. On the second night in London, after a particularly heavy evening that had begun with a pub session at five-thirty P.M. and finished with breakfast at five-thirty A.M. Tim went to bed and woke several hours later to find himself on the floor. Cold and embarrassed, he climbed back into bed and thought no more about it, assuming that his fairly drunken state had been responsible. When the same thing happened two weeks later at home, it was again after a heavy night, and again he was able to dismiss it. However, on the third occasion it was the beginning of the summer term, and it was John, coming to wake him up for an early-morning game of tennis, who found him. "What the bloody hell are you up to, Irvine?" he said, shaking him awake.

Tim stared around him and sat up feeling cold and stiff. He shook his head. "I don't know. I must have fallen out of bed."

"You can't have done," said John. "It would have woken you up."

"Well, I don't know, do I?" said Tim irritably. "I must have been sleepwalking or something. What bloody time is it, anyway?"

"OK, OK," said John, "don't get angry. Do you still want to play tennis or not?"

Tim felt oddly lightheaded and tired. "I—I'll leave it, if you wouldn't mind, this morning." John gave him an odd look but said nothing.

Three nights before the end of term a dance had been

arranged with a local girls' school. Tim and John were less than enthusiastic, maintaining that the girls were all squares and the whole affair was an embarrassment. Nonetheless they went along and were rewarded, if by nothing else, with extremely good music.

Tim was dancing with an exceptionally plain girl with pale, thin, mousy hair and a mouth full of vicious-looking braces. The music, though, was great, the lights flashed—and in three days his school years would be over. He threw himself into the dancing, but as he danced he found himself more and more attracted to the flashing lights. Soon he found he was staring fixedly at them, and he realized dimly that he had stopped dancing.

"Tim, are you all right?" The girl was shaking his arm; he could feel her touch, but he could not respond to it.

He tried to speak, but no words came out. He tried to step away from her, but his movements were jerky and uncontrolled. Moments later he seemed to be hurling himself to the floor. When he came around he was being supported by two people who were half carrying him, half dragging him through an open door into the school sanitorium. He tried to speak, but he still seemed unable to do so. He felt oddly detached, and when, seconds later, he was laid on the bed he felt no sense of curiosity as people came and went. He must have slept, for the next thing he saw was his mother and father leaning over the bed, and they lived a good hour's drive away from the school. "What's happening?" he asked.

"You had a—a little accident," said his mother.

"Accident! I didn't. I was dancing, and something happened."

"You sort of fainted," his father said. "Don't worry, son, you're going to be all right. Tomorrow morning we'll get you into hospital so they can have a look at you."

A consultant spelled it out to the shocked family the following day. "It seems you had an epileptic seizure, Tim. I don't know if it will happen again, and I'm not absolutely certain why it happened, but I suspect it's connected to your motorcycle accident. But I shouldn't worry. These days it's possible to control seizures very well with the right medication."

The next few months were a nightmare for Tim. The drugs made him feel lazy and lethargic—totally out of character with his normal temperament. Not only that, but they did not seem to be doing any good. The next seizure took place in the pub on a Sunday morning, when he was surrounded by all his friends. When he came around, his parents took him home. He could remember nothing, but he could tell by the reaction of his friends that however he'd behaved, it had both embarrassed and shocked them.

The next seizure happened just a week later, at a summer charity ball. This time the embarrassment he caused was actually palpable. John McKenzie was staying for the weekend. On the following morning, as they tramped across the fields for a walk before lunch, Tim asked the inevitable question. "What happens to me, John? What do I do?"

"Oh, nothing much. You roll around a bit, grunt, and so on. Don't worry about it."

They stopped at a stile. "How long have we known each other, John?" Tim asked.

"From prep school onwards—nine, ten years, I suppose. Why?"

"I think you owe it to me to tell me exactly what happens to me when I have one of these fits. I have to know, you must see that. I'd do the same for you."

So John told him, with no details spared—the foaming at the mouth, the grotesque movements of his facial muscles, the frightening way he threw himself about, and the gurgling noise he made in his throat. From that day on Tim Irvine became a recluse. At his request, Cirencester Agricultural College was postponed for a year. At the time it seemed sensible, for his seizures were bad, happening four or five times a month. Experimenting with the anticonvulsant drugs gradually improved his condition, and he began to learn what he could and could not do. He discovered that alcohol—or at least a heavy dose of it—tended to encourage a seizure. Flashing lights and television also provoked them. The number-one enemy was fatigue. If he went without sleep and became even slightly overtired, then he was asking for trouble.

His family was marvelous, treating his seizures as just a normal part of life, as did the men with whom he worked on the family farm. All had been counseled on what to do and taught to minimize the importance of what had happened. Only Jenny, at sixteen, seemed to find it difficult to cope. One of the things Tim began to be most painfully aware of was that, in his view, the family of an epileptic suffered most.

As the year came to an end Tim's future became the subject of heated family debate. Both his parents were adamant that he should still go to Cirencester. "Why do I need to?" said Tim. "One day I will inherit the farm, and I can learn everything I need to know about farming these acres right here."

"Farming's changed," his father insisted. "The techniques I employ are very different from my father's, and hugely different from my grandfather's. Yours, too, will be different—besides which, if you are to spend your life here, you need some time away first, with people of your own age."

"I'm rather a liability to people of my own age. I think you will agree with that," said Tim.

"And that's another thing, darling," said his mother. "You've simply got to come to terms with your illness. It's no good hiding away. People who really care about you, the friends that matter, won't mind about it."

"Of course they mind. I'm a grotesque, grunting, spitting creature." He stormed out of the room and slammed the door.

In the end, Charles Irvine took what he knew was an appalling gamble. He called his son to his study one morning and announced there would be no further work for Tim on the farm for the next three years, nor would there be a roof over his head, unless he went to agricultural college as planned. He added that if he failed to go to college, not only would he have to go into the world and make his own living, but his family would be deeply ashamed of his cowardice.

Tim went to college. He rented an apartment from a landlady who understood and felt she could cope with his condition. He worked hard and made a few friends, but essentially he kept to himself. Girls he found particularly difficult, for while he felt able to explain to his male friends the nature of his condition, he always sidestepped the issue when it came to women, convinced that it would put them off him instantly. As a result, he was always afraid to make a date with a girl, just in case he might have a seizure without her being forewarned.

The three years at Cirencester passed quickly enough, despite the restrictions on his social life. His seizures had been reduced to two or three a year, and while this meant he still could not drive, in all other respects he led a normal life.

Having coped with the obvious difficulties of college life, Tim was enthusiastically welcomed by his father into the farm as a partner, after he had failed to persuade him to take a job elsewhere first. "I can't drive farm machinery, and I can't be relied upon. Who would want me?" said Tim. "There are more people than jobs, anyway. Why take on a farm manager with epilepsy when there are plenty of able-bodied people to choose from?"

His defeatist attitude upset his parents, but there was little they could do about it. The condition, the doctor was absolutely certain, had been caused by Tim's motorcycle accident. It was not hereditary, so there was no reason he should not marry and have children. The doctor was reasonably confident that his condition would improve rather than deteriorate as better drugs became available. Yet Tim was changed irrevocably—the outgoing, happy-go-lucky young man had gone forever. Instead he was a serious-minded, hesitant, shy individual, old beyond his years.

Towards the end of the summer of 1966 the Irvines held a big party at Monkswell Farm to celebrate Jenny's twenty-first birthday. It was a sumptuous affair. Invitations were issued to 250 guests, and it was the one social event that Tim realized he could not avoid. He went on a regime of early nights and decided not to risk even a drop of alcohol during the party, so determined was he not to spoil Jenny's evening. Since he also had to keep away from the disco and his parents had employed catering staff to serve all the food and drink, there was little for him to do, and while he wished Jenny well, he longed for the party to be over.

It was shortly after midnight—after Jenny's health had been drunk to, speeches made, and the cake cut—that Tim was accosted by an exceptionally pretty fair-haired girl. She wore a long, pale blue dress that exposed her shoulders, which were slightly suntanned. The dress added bluc tone to the green of her eyes. "Hello, Tim. How are you?"

"Fine, thank you." He looked at her and frowned, struggling to remember who she was and wondering how on earth he could forget a girl who instantly attracted him so much.

She laughed at his obvious discomfort. "Stephanie Bonham. You haven't seen me since I was about eleven, maybe ten. We used to ride together, do you remember?"

He did. Lady Stephanie Bonham, daughter of the Marquis of Burford. They had taken riding lessons for a while and had attended the same pony club. She had been pretty and vivacious even then, and that early promise had been more than fulfilled. His mind struggled—the Marquis of Burford, hadn't he . . . yes, he'd been killed in a hunting accident last season. "I—I'm sorry about your father," he said somewhat lamely. "It must have been awful for you. I should have written. I'm sorry."

"Of course you shouldn't have written," said Stephanie. "We barely know each other. And yes, it was awful." Her eyes clouded over for a moment. "There's only me left, you see."

"Of course," said Tim, suddenly remembering, "your mother died when you were young."

"Eleven," said Stephanie.

"Any brothers or sisters?"

"I had a brother, but he's dead, too."

"Poor you," said Tim. "I'm very sorry. I had no idea."

Stephanie smiled. "Well, we all have a cross to bear, don't we? You should know that. I'm really sorry about your epilepsy, Tim. I heard about it quite recently. It must be a frightful bore for you."

Two things struck Tim instantly. First, Stephanie was the only person who had ever mentioned his epilepsy before he did. Secondly, she spoke about it entirely unself-consciously, and the glorious understatement of describing it as a bore had Tim laughing out loud.

"What have I said?" she said, smiling back. "Did I say something wrong?"

"No, no, you didn't. Quite the contrary. No one ever talks about it, you see."

"Don't they?" said Stephanie. "How extraordinary! Hey, shall we go and dance?"

"I'd rather not, if you wouldn't mind," said Tim. "I'm really sorry, but the lights . . . they sometimes cause seizures."

"OK, I don't mind. Why don't we go for a walk instead? It's a lovely night."

They spent the rest of the evening together and learned a great deal about each other. From Stephanie Tim learned that following her father's death there had been a tremendous fight over the will between herself and her stepmother. The result was that Stephanie had been left with the bulk of the estate of Wickham, but no money nor means to run it. "So I'll just have to sell it," she said. "It seems awful—the family home and all that. There have been Bonhams at Wickham, you know, for nearly four hundred years. That's pretty much a record, even for Gloucestershire."

Stephanie learned a great deal about Tim, too—not so much from what he said as from what he didn't say. She sensed the loneliness and isolation caused by his condition and the feeling of self-revulsion. It was after four by the time they realized the party was all but over.

"I can't even offer to run you home," said Tim, characteristically frustrated.

"It's OK," said Stephanie, "I've got my car anyway. Hey, look, I know this is rather forward, but would you mind handing out some free advice?"

Tim would have handed Stephanie the world by this time, if it had been his to give. "Of course. What sort of advice?" he asked.

"I was thinking you must have learned a lot at Cirencester, and then, of course, growing up here on your father's farm. You wouldn't come over to Wickham and give me some advice, would you? Daddy never employed a farm manager, you see—he did it all himself—so apart from a couple of old laborers, no one knows anything about the land. I really would appreciate it."

"Of course," said Tim. "When shall I come?"

"Tomorrow?"

"Yes, all right . . ." He hesitated.

"Oh, don't worry about transport, I'll come and fetch you."

"I'm sorry," he said helplessly.

"It's no problem, we're only quarter of an hour down the road." She glanced at her watch. "Well, it's this morning, really. Shall we say eleven o'clock?"

They spent the whole of the following day touring Wickham, which consisted of a beautiful old house, one thousand acres, and a village. By evening they were both tired, and while Tim sat in the garden with a beer and a set of plans, Stephanie cooked some supper.

"This is an awful responsibility for you," Tim said, looking up from the plans. "Isn't there anybody who can advise you?"

"My father's lawyer," said Stephanie, "but he's such an old fuddy-duddy. In any case, he lives and works in London, and he has no idea about the country. He just thinks I should put the whole thing on the market and not worry my pretty little head about it. Direct quote," she said with a grin. She was dressed in an old T-shirt and jeans, her fair hair loose around her shoulders and not a trace of makeup. Tim found her even more enchanting than he had the previous evening.

"I do have an idea," said Tim. "The land immediately around the house is by far the best quality. I think you should sell off this piece here and here"—he indicated on the plan—"about four hundred and fifty acres, all of the poorer quality land. I think you might find one or two local landowners interested. Then there are these acres here around this farmhouse—it might well be worthwhile renovating the farmhouse and selling it as a working farm—one hundred and fifty acres should be enough to make it viable—and that still leaves you with four hundred acres, which, bearing in mind the quality of the land, could be worked up to be very profitable indeed."

"I was thinking along the same lines," said Stephanie, "but not in such detail. Some of the cottages would convert beautifully—the trouble is, I have no money with which to improve them."

"One step at a time," said Tim. "If we start by selling off this land and some of the cottages as they stand, we can use the money we receive to renovate the farmhouse. Then we can sell the farm and use that money to start on the remaining cottages. If the home farm is meanwhile properly managed, then—" His voice was full of enthusiasm.

"You said 'we,'" said Stephanie.

"A slip of the tongue. What I mean is that anyone could do it, with a little experience."

"If I paid you the proper rate for the job—no messing about, no favors—could you help me get this place sorted out, Tim? I can't tell you how much it means to me. The thought of selling up completely, giving up the house—I just can't bear it."

"I'll certainly help," said Tim, "but there's no need for wages."

"If you won't enter into a proper commercial relationship, then we won't do it at all," said Stephanie. There was a stubborn set to her chin, and it was clear she meant what she said.

"All right," said Tim, "but you must only pay what you can afford. It would be wonderful to be involved in a project like this."

"What about your father?" said Stephanie. "Won't he mind? I think you'd need to be full-time here for a year or so, at any rate."

Tim shook his head. "He's been plaguing the life out of me to do something else before taking over Monkswell."

"Do we have a deal?"

Tim looked at Stephanie. "We have a deal," he said.

Tim couldn't travel to Wickham each day, so despite the criticism and innuendo, Tim moved into an apartment in a wing of Wickham a week later. When it became clear that their intentions were to work hard and make a success of the estate, the gossip ceased. Their plans went well, although money was very tight, and the gradual success of their enterprise fueled their ambition. The village pub became a hotel, and they obtained planning permission to convert the barns as well as the farmhouses and cottages. The Cotswolds were becoming a very desirable area in which to live, and as Stephanie and Tim worked they found themselves building a new community, which was both lucrative and satisfying.

The close working relationship with Stephanie and the rewarding nature of his work had a miraculous effect on Tim. Not only did he grow in confidence, but his seizures ceased altogether. He was building something, something good and useful, and his feeling of self-worth was restored. After eleven months' work, on the advice of Stephanie's attorney, they formed a limited company called Wickham Estates Limited into which they paid all their proceeds and from which they each drew a salary. Stephanie was the major shareholder, but she gave Tim a small stake, and they were both directors. It gave Tim the feeling of being in partnership, which was not lost on Stephanie, who encouraged his increasing confidence.

One November evening, when they had been together for over a year, they had returned home late from London, where they had been choosing tiles and bathroom fittings for the stable block they were converting into four houses. They were both very tired. Tim went out to check the stock while Stephanie made some sandwiches. She piled a tray with fruit and a bottle of wine and heard Tim shuffling around in the study, lighting the fire. She entered the room, tray in hand, just in time to see him stagger back and fall to the ground in what was his first seizure in nearly two years. She sat with him while the fit ran its course, put a pillow under his head, and she cleaned him while he slept. When he woke she was sitting beside him, holding his hand. "W-what happened?" he began. "Oh my God, I had a seizure, didn't I?"

"It's my fault," said Stephanie. "I'm so sorry. You've been doing too much recently, you need to take things more slowly." Tim pulled himself into a sitting position and studied her face carefully. There was no obvious sign of revulsion, although he searched for one—certain it must be there. "Go and have a bath," she said gently, "and then tuck yourself into bed. I'll bring you a drink in a little while."

They rarely entered each other's parts of the house. When they were together they used communal rooms—the kitchen, dining room, and study. Tim's bedroom was cozy, much cozier than her own, Stephanie realized as she knocked and entered, carrying a cup of coffee and freshly made sandwiches. He had a desk by the window looking out over the fields he had come to love. He had built bookshelves on two of the walls, and a couple of comfortable chairs were pulled up to the fireplace, where a fire burned merrily.

"You self-indulgent old thing," said Stephanie. "I didn't know you lit the fire in your bedroom."

"I don't always," said Tim with a grin. "Only when I have company." He was sitting up in bed. His hair, freshly washed, was brushed back, which made him look very young. His pajama top was casually buttoned, and Stephanie could not help but notice his strong, deep chest.

Slightly confused, she laid down the tray by his bedside table and retreated to the fire.

"I'm really sorry about what happened," Tim said after a moment.

"Sorry about what?" said Stephanie, genuinely bewildered.

"About my seizure," said Tim.

"Tim, you never have to worry about having an epileptic fit in front of me," said Stephanie.

"But it's horrible," said Tim. "I know what happens, I know how ghastly it is."

Stephanie came and sat on the side of the bed and took Tim's hand in hers. "Tim, I've seen cancer slowly eat away my mother, and I've watched my father drink himself to death. I was here when they brought my father's body in off the hunting field." Tim winced. "I'm no stranger to the unpleasant aspects of life. I'm tough, Tim, and I can honestly look you in the eye and say that without a shred of doubt, your epilepsy worries me not even slightly. It doesn't disgust me or frighten me. It's simply one aspect of you, something one accepts about you, like the fact that you never take off your muddy boots when you come into the kitchen. Do you understand what I am saying?"

Tim stared at her. "You really mean it, don't you?"

"Of course I mean it. You know me—I never say anything I don't mean."

"Do you know," said Tim hoarsely, "that is the nicest thing that anybody has ever said to me?"

Moments later they were in each other's arms, and from there it seemed quite natural that Stephanie should end up in his bed. When next morning Tim asked her to marry him, she did not hesitate before saying yes.

Chapter 16

New York—*March 1978*

It was warm for March. The long, cold winter was at last over, and New York seemed determined to show its new season's face. The sky was blue and the sun really warming for the first time. Ella had just finished a breakfast meeting with her architect, Ross Campbell, at his studio—a crazy apartment on top of an old brownstone on 71st and Park.

She decided to walk home. With the smell of spring in the air, for the first time in what seemed like forever she felt a slight lifting of the black despair that had gripped her ever since she had left France and Tim. She had failed him, she knew, in the worst of all possible ways—by rejecting him, not for anything he had done, but for what he was. A thousand times she had asked herself why she had reacted so violently, and when she had not asked herself the question, Greg had. With the resilience of youth he could not understand why Tim's seizure should have shocked and horrified her so much. The sad, strained parting of the two families, which Greg had instinctively recognized was forever, seemed to have hurt him as much as it had hurt her. He adored Tim. In many ways he represented the father Greg had never had, and Ella was only too aware that in rejecting Tim she was causing deep distress not only to him but to her son as well. She had tried again and again to analyze her feelings. She recognized that much of the revulsion was a physical rather than an emotional reaction. The intimacy of her lovemaking with Tim was without restraint. She had given herself to him completely in a way that she would never have believed herself capable of doing. To find there was a part of him she knew nothing about made her feel betrayed in some way. She could no longer see him as the same person he had been before the seizure.

What had made the situation so terrible was that Ella did not have to explain any of these feelings to Tim—he had understood them all without words. He kept saying she must not blame herself, that he would feel the same in her position. It was heartbreaking. If he had been angry, it would have been easier. She could have retaliated by accusing him of deceiving her. As it was, she was aware only of a deep-seated sense of failure and loss. They'd had so much to offer each other and their children, and now their future was in ruins, and there was simply no road back.

On a corner ahead of her Ella spied a new shop. A window full of bright new spring clothes attracted her, and on an impulse she went in. She emerged an hour and a half later, nearly $2,000 poorer, with a complete new wardrobe. It was not the end of the world losing Tim Irvine, she told herself firmly—it just felt like it.

She turned the corner into 59th Street and glanced at her watch. Five to twelve already, and she had a million things to do in the office. She hurried on, laden down with parcels. A group of men staggered out onto the pavement in front of her from Helen's Bar, a seedy but popular basement haunt for most of the local drunks. Restricted by her piles of parcels, Ella tried to step around them.

"Look, you guys, the little lady's been shopping. Happy St. Patrick's Day, sweetheart. How about a kiss from those cherry-red lips?"

St. Patrick's Day, of course. She had forgotten. The streets would be full of drunks later in the day, but Helen's Bar never closed—this bunch had probably been celebrating since last night. "Let me through!" she demanded.

"After a kiss, lady, after a kiss."

They were all around her, and suddenly the familiar sense of panic rose and overtook her. Any group of men, threatening or otherwise, sent her reeling back in time to that August night when she was fifteen years old. "Let me through, let me through." Her voice was shrill with desperation.

"Oh, come on, lady, it's St. Patrick's Day—you wouldn't leave a poor Irish boy without a kiss, now would you?" The spokesman for the group lunged at her, but despite the parcels she managed to sidestep him. Then, in her agitation, she tripped, and half her parcels went scattering across the pavement. "Will you look at that now, throwing her shopping around."

Ella was almost in tears. "Leave me alone, leave me alone." She bent down to try to gather her bags.

"We'll help you, won't we, lads?"

"No, no, leave me," she shouted at the top of her voice, tears now starting to cascade down her face. The feeling of panic was stifling—she could barely breathe. A conversation began above her. Ella heard the words, but they had no meaning. She was plunged into her own personal world of terror.

"You heard the lady, boys. Beat it."

"Who says so?"

"I say so."

"You and who else?"

"Just do it, will you? Can't you see you've upset her? Come on, now. Here, have a drink on me."

"Hey, thank you. You're a gentleman, sir. Happy St. Patrick's Day."

"And to you, boys."

Strong hands helped her to her feet. She hurriedly wiped her eyes before looking up and confronting one of the handsomest men she had ever seen. He was tall and broad-shouldered with a spectacular suntan, extraordinary jet-black hair, and bright blue eyes. He looked about forty, but he could have been younger or older; it was difficult to tell. He gave a roguish grin. "Michael Gresham, at your service. Here, let me help you with those bags. They didn't touch you, did they—harm you in any way?"

"No," said Ella. "I feel so stupid."

"You're not being stupid at all. You must have felt very threatened."

"I was attacked . . . once, when I was fifteen, by a group of men, and it has left me extra nervous, I guess." Why on earth had she said that? She never referred to the incident, never.

"Look," he said, "on St. Patrick's Day the streets are full of guys like those. Please let me escort you to where you're going."

"Oh, no, it's not far," Ella protested. "You can almost see my office from here, on the corner of Lexington."

"Nonetheless," said Michael Gresham, "I'll feel happier if I see you safely there. You're not going to send me away, are you?"

"No," said Ella, smiling.

In the short walk to her office Ella learned that Michael Gresham was a lawyer, that his home was in Houston, and that he was in New York on business for a week. "Actually," said Michael, "now that I have persuaded you to trust me, I have to admit to being something of a fraud."

"Oh?" said Ella.

"I'm an Irishman myself, second generation. My father was born and brought up in County Clare. So you see, Miss Kovac, you find yourself in the dangerous position of being escorted through the streets of New York by an Irishman on St. Patrick's Day—very unwise."

They had reached Gregory Buildings by now. Ella realized she would have to go up to her apartment first to unburden herself of her shopping bags, and suddenly, on an impulse quite out of character, she heard herself say, "I live above my office. Would you like to come up to my apartment for a glass of wine, as a thank-you for rescuing me?" Michael Gresham didn't need asking twice. While Ella poured the wine Michael wandered around the sitting room. Within the confines of her apartment she was aware of what a big man he was—tall, handsome, flamboyant, confident, not the sort of man who appealed to her normally, and certainly very different from Tim. She wondered what on earth had possessed her to invite him into her home.

"I love the apartment," he said. "It's big, isn't it, by New York standards? It must cost you some in rent."

"No rent," said Ella with a grin.

"No rent!" She watched his face. Clearly he was desperate to ask why not, presumably imagining she was a kept woman, the mistress of some rich man. Curiosity got the better of him. "How come?" he asked with studied casualness.

"I own the building."

"You what?"

It was clearly the last thing he had expected to hear, and Ella chuckled with amusement at his obvious surprise. "I own the building. I'm in real estate—that's my business."

"This I can hardly believe. You don't look old enough."

"I'm older than I look," said Ella. She laughed—a throaty chuckle that Michael Gresham found very attractive.

"Jesus, this is amazing. Do you own much else in New York?"

"My whole business is based in New York," said Ella, "although my banker is always trying to persuade me to diversify. I currently have about twenty, twenty-five projects total."

"A lady tycoon. I am impressed." It was clear that he was.

They drank their wine in silence for a moment. "The other apartments in this building are much smaller," Ella said, encouraged by Michael's admiration. "When I bought the building there were just four apartments on each floor. There are seven floors altogether. Initially we lived in the ground-floor apartment, which is now my office, while all the other apartments except this one were carved up into three units. It's what people wanted at the time—small, medium-priced accommodations. I've got sixty apartments where there had been twenty-eight before, and I've never had any trouble renting them."

"You said 'we,'" said Michael. "Are you married, then?" He was not able to disguise the note of disappointment in his voice.

Ella shook her head. "No, I live with my son, Greg. He's almost fifteen."

Michael's eyes widened. "Greg as in Gregory Buildings?"

"That's right," said Ella. "This was my first project, so naturally I named it after him. Do you have any kids?"

Michael grinned. "No, nor am I married. I've managed to avoid the whole scene to date, but I guess one of these days I should settle down. Time marches on. It'll be the big four-oh for me in a couple of years." He drained his glass. "Hey, I can't hang around—I expect you have a lot to do, and so do I. Why don't I take you out for dinner later, though, to celebrate St. Patrick's Day?"

Ella hesitated. She had not been out with a man since leaving Tim in France. "Well, I'm not sure," she began. Then she remembered that Greg was staying the night with a school friend. It would be another long, lonely evening she would try to fill with work while her thoughts strayed to Tim. Why not have dinner with this charming, handsome man—what harm could it do? "All right," she said suddenly. "Thank you, I'd like that."

"Great," said Michael. "Cocktails at the Rainbow Room, and then I know this great little Italian place . . . do you like Italian?"

"Love it," said Ella.

"Good. I'll pick you up at six."

From their vantage point in the Rainbow Room, at the top of the RCA Building, they had a wonderful view of sunset over Manhattan. They lingered over their cocktails, reluctant to leave the scene. Michael talked of his life in Houston. "It's a great city—so fast-paced. The average age is no more than thirty—it's a young town, and that means there's one hell of a lot going on."

"I've never been there," Ella said, "but I think I have a New Yorker's prejudice against Texas—a lot of guys walking around looking foolish in their Stetsons, shooting their mouths off about the millions they've made from their oil wells."

"It's all those things," said Michael, "but so much more. I have a tiny bachelor apartment in Houston—it's near where I work—but my real home is a ranch about thirty miles outside the city. I spend as much time there as I can. I breed horses in a small way and aim to make as much money as quickly as I can and then retire to my ranch."

"It sounds great as ambitions go," said Ella.

"What's yours?" Michael asked.

Ella thought for a moment. "You know, I don't have one."

"That's crazy. You must have."

Ella shook her head. "My driving force has been to give Greg a good life. I think I've done that. In a few years he'll be all grown up and have no need of me anymore. What I'll do then, I'm not sure."

"You need dreams of your own," said Michael, clearly appalled. "It's great that you want to do the best for your boy, but you need to want to do the best for yourself as well. What do you want out of life—a yacht, a private jet . . . what grabs you?"

"None of those things," said Ella, "not material things." She hesitated. "I had a very tough childhood with no money and no security. My sole ambition, I suppose, has been to ensure that I never have to go back to where I started. Money for money's sake holds very little appeal for me." As she spoke the words she realized how true they were.

"And power?" Michael asked.

"Power, I don't know." Ella shrugged her shoulders. "I enjoy the thrill of the chase, doing the deal. I like to feel I'm on top of the situation—I can't bear wasted money or wasted opportunity. Whatever I do, I like to do well, but power—hell, I certainly don't want to be first woman president. Does that make sense?"

"I guess so," said Michael, "but you know something, Ella? You could really take the world by storm if you wanted."

He left the subject until they were drinking coffee at the

end of their meal. The little Italian restaurant in Greenwich Village had been everything he had promised. Ella felt relaxed in a way she did not normally feel with men—at least men she did not know well.

"I've been thinking about you a lot today," said Michael.

"I'm flattered." Ella grinned.

"You know what you ought to do? You ought to extend your interests to Houston."

Ella frowned. "Oh, no, it's too far away."

"Of course it's not—the flight's only two and a half hours. It's the ideal location for you to expand your activities."

"Why?" Ella asked.

"Because like I said, it's a boom town. With the rise in oil prices more and more people are crowding into the city—young people requiring singles' accommodations today and family accommodations tomorrow. They need shopping arcades, they need office complexes. There simply aren't enough property developers in Houston to meet the demand, which way outstrips what's available at the moment. Honestly, Ella, I'm not kidding you."

"Is this really true?" Ella could not conceal her interest.

"You bet your life it is. I spend a hell of a lot of time trying to find my clients suitable accommodations and office space."

"Well, maybe I should check it out sometime," said Ella.

"Maybe you should," said Michael, "and the sooner the better."

Over the next few days Michael Gresham showered Ella with invitations—to lunch, to dinner, to the theater, to a concert—his excuse being that he was returning to Houston and wanted to see her as much as possible. He was a difficult man to resist. He had just the right balance of apparently sincere flattery and enthusiasm and joy for living; it was hard to resist. Ella spent three more evenings with him, against her better judgment, during which she grew increasingly relaxed and confident in his company, loving his jokes and his happy-go-lucky ways. She missed him when he left, and although he promised to come and see her the next time he was in New York, Ella felt she needed to recognize that she might well never see him again. Michael Gresham was no more than a brief, happy interlude.

During the week before Easter it was Greg's fifteenth birthday. In a moment of weakness Ella had agreed to give him a stereo, and by seven o'clock on his birthday morning the level of rock and roll in the apartment was deafening. There were presents, too, from the Connors family and from Laurence, and when the postman arrived there was a mountain of mail, including a parcel with a clear Gloucestershire postmark. "It's from the Irvines!" said Greg.

"That's nice," said Ella warily.

"At least they haven't forgotten us," said Greg, and, ignoring all his other presents, he settled down to open the one from England while Ella sat watching him, filled with remorse. His present was four prints of English hunting scenes showing a pheasant shoot, fishing for salmon, fox hunting in full cry, and beagling. They were clearly very old, and Greg was thrilled. "These are wonderful, just wonderful. I'm so glad they haven't forgotten us, Mom. Look, there are letters." There was a letter from Millie and Belinda and a short note from Tim, just wishing Greg a happy birthday and sending his love to Ella. "See, he still likes us," Greg said accusingly. "I'm going to call him and thank him."

"Not now," said Ella hurriedly. "You're already late for school."

"When I get back from school, then."

Ella hoped that he would forget during the school day, but as soon as he returned home he went straight to the telephone. "I'm going to call England, Mom. Do you want to speak to them?"

"No, no, it's all right," said Ella. She tried to busy herself in the kitchen while her son spoke on the phone. There was a lot of talk and laughter, and all Ella's instincts cried out to her to run to the phone and speak to Tim. Instead she sat down shakily at the kitchen table, clasping and unclasping her hands. She heard Greg's footsteps come across the hall. It was over.

"Mom!" he called, "Tim would like to speak to you." His cheerful face appeared around the kitchen door. "He sounds great—the girls are asleep, but Tim and I had a good talk. Come on quick."

"I told you I didn't want to speak to him," said Ella.

"But what could I say? He asked if you were in, and when I said yes he said he'd like to say hi to you. I couldn't say you wouldn't talk to him. Come on, Mom."

"Hello," said Ella tentatively.

"Hello, Ella," said Tim, his voice warm, deep, so well remembered. "How are you?"

"I'm fine," said Ella, "and you?"

"Much the same."

"And the children?"

"They're fine, too. Greg sounds very grown up—his voice is so deep now."

"Yes," said Ella.

There was a moment's silence. "Would it be in order for me to say I miss you?" said Tim. There was an edge to his voice.

"I miss you, too," said Ella.

"But you don't think we should meet again." Tim's voice shook a little.

"No," said Ella, "I don't think so." The moment she spoke she regretted the words, but she did not know how to retract them.

"Well, you never know—perhaps our paths will cross again one day. I'd better go—your telephone bill will be horrendous. Give my love to Greg." The phone went dead, and Ella stood poised, the receiver still in her hand.

"What happened? Did you get cut off?" said Greg.

"No." She made an effort to sound cheerful. "They seem fine, don't they?"

"Yes, they do," said Greg. "I just hope we can go and visit them this summer. I really miss them."

"We'll have to see," said Ella with a sinking heart.

Her feeling of depression and unhappiness persisted during the rest of the evening. Greg went to his room to watch television, and Ella sat at her desk, pretending to work. It was about nine o'clock when the telephone rang. "Ella?" She recognized the voice immediately.

"Hello, Michael. Are you back in New York?"

"No, I'm not, I'm calling from Houston. Look, I was wondering whether you and your kid would like to come and stay on my ranch over the Easter break. It would be a nice change for you both, and then I could show you around the Houston real estate scene."

"It's very kind of you, Michael," Ella began.

"It's not kind, it's what I'd really like, Ella. I don't know why I didn't think of it before. Come on, say yes."

"I'll have to go and discuss it with Greg," said Ella. "I could call you back."

"Why do you have to discuss it with Greg? He's just a kid. You decide what happens, and he can go along with it."

Ella was vaguely irritated. "We don't have that sort of relationship," she said somewhat tartly. "I'll call you back."

Greg was not particularly enthusiastic. "I've got plans for the Easter break," he said.

"Like what?" said Ella.

"Oh, meeting people—you know, the usual stuff."

"Well, if it's the usual stuff," said Ella, "it won't do you any harm to miss it for once. Some fresh country air will do you good—it's a ranch, with horses. You'll love it."

"Is this a new boyfriend?" Greg asked with heavy irony.

"Well, no, not exactly," said Ella, a little sheepish.

"Whatever's he's like, he won't be as nice as Tim," said Greg, twisting the knife in the wound.

Chapter 17

The journey from Houston Airport to Michael's ranch northwest of the city passed quickly enough, mainly because Michael did not stop talking for an instant.

Ella simply sat back and smiled, letting his enthusiasm wash over her. She was surprised by Houston, by the vast mirror buildings and its attractive lushness. There was an enormous amount of greenery, whereas she had expected it to be dry and arid.

Greg sat silent and morose in the back of the truck. The initial meeting between him and Michael had not gone well. Michael had simply said, "Hi, kid," and then ignored him completely. Greg had given Michael a single look of hostility and remained monosyllabic ever since. They'll settle down, Ella thought.

They took the main freeway out of Houston and then turned onto a country road. Lush grass and trees ran for unspoiled mile after mile on either side of the road; there was an occasional pond and a continuous creek running beside the road. After about half an hour Michael suddenly veered off to the left down what was no more than a dirt track. "Not far now," he said. "What do you think of the countryside?"

"I think it's wonderful," said Ella genuinely.

"This is nothing," said Michael. "I have two thousand acres of the best land in the county."

They turned a corner and the trees on either side of the road thinned out and all but disappeared. Ahead of them was a vast meadow in the center of which sat a strange but enormous one-story building. "It's not a great architectural triumph," Michael said, laughing. "In fact, it's three mobile homes bolted together with a deck built around it, but we've got hot water and electricity. One of these days I guess I'll build a proper home here, but in the meantime this is comfortable." It was difficult to find anything favorable to say about the building, so Ella kept quiet.

The door opened at the sound of their car, and a young couple emerged. They were an attractive pair with huge dark eyes and olive skins. "Hi, boss," they called.

"Hi to you. Everything OK?" Michael said.

"Yes, fine."

"That is Jesus and Juanita," Michael whispered as they began unloading the back of the truck. "They're illegal immigrants from Mexico. They live here and look after the place while I'm away. Jesus is handy with horses, and Juanita keeps the place tidy. They have a little shack at the back."

Ella and Greg followed Michael up the steps and through the front door. As they entered the house both of them gasped aloud. The ugly prefabricated exterior stood out in total contrast to the interior. They went straight into a huge sitting room, traditionally furnished with what looked like English antiques. There were old prints on the walls and a Persian rug on the floor. It was the height of traditional luxury and totally at odds with what either of them had expected.

"What do you think?" said Michael.

"Amazing," said Ella. "Such a contrast."

"Yeah, well, it's not what the outside of a house looks like that counts, is it? Come on, I'll show you to your rooms."

Ella's and Greg's rooms were virtually at opposite ends of the house, which Ella immediately hoped was not significant. Hers was a massive double room with a private bathroom, lavishly decorated with heavy slubbed silk drapes and a carpet with pile so thick her feet seemed to disappear into it altogether. The overall color scheme was cream and blue. The effect was cool and restful, but far too ostentatious for Ella's tastes.

Greg's room was a little study with a divan in it. It suited him well enough, particularly since the room included a large TV. Some of his sulkiness seemed to be disappearing —he was clearly impressed and intrigued by Michael's somewhat eccentric home.

"Come out on the deck when you're ready," said Michael, "and we'll have drinks and then a barbecue."

It was a beautiful evening. The back of the house faced west, and the setting sun was truly spectacular. An enormous barbecue pit glowed, and Juanita was expertly turning steaks and sausages.

"We just have wine or beer here," said Michael. "Wine for you?" he asked Ella.

"Yes, please."

"And some Coke for you?" he asked Greg.

"I've been wondering, whether I could go and see the horses," said Greg.

"Of course," said Michael. "Jesus!" The Mexican appeared miraculously from the shadows. "Can you take the boy to see the horses?" The Mexican nodded silently and beckoned to Greg.

Ella watched in silence as the two of them strode across the paddock toward the stables. Greg had done a lot of growing in the last year. He was head and shoulders taller than his mother and the little Mexican walking beside him. She was enormously proud of him, she realized with a rush of maternal satisfaction. Her thoughts were interrupted by Michael handing her a glass of wine.

"It's wonderful to have you here, Ella." He bent forward and kissed her gently on the lips. "Welcome to Texas."

The barbecue was a gargantuan affair—venison, sausages, enormous steaks, corn, beans, potato salad, and coleslaw. Greg, with a typical fifteen-year-old's appetite, ate everything with enthusiasm. The atmosphere seemed to have lightened a little between him and Michael, particularly when he showed a very real interest in Michael's horses.

When the meal was finished Juanita served coffee on the deck. It was now quite dark, except for a single beam of pale moonlight cutting a path across the paddock in front of them. "It's beautiful," said Ella.

"It is," said Michael, reaching for her hand and squeezing it. "Greg, I reckon it's your bedtime," he said firmly.

Greg looked amazed. "It can't be, it's only ten o'clock."

"Ten o'clock—that late? Then it's definitely your bedtime."

"He doesn't normally go to bed this early," Ella ventured.

"Well, here in Texas kids do as they're told. You run along, boy. I need a little time with your mother on her own." Greg, clearly very angry, left them without a word.

"Was that necessary?" said Ella as soon as her son was out of earshot.

"Yes, it was," said Michael. "Hell, Ella, the boy's had a fine day. He's here in Texas for the first time, he's seen the horses, he's had a good meal, and he can watch TV if he's not tired. Right now he's overstayed his welcome—you know, you should be firmer with him."

"Exactly what experience do you have with children?" Ella asked, her anger mounting.

"You don't have to have kids of your own to know something about them," said Michael. "Plenty of my friends have kids, and I have to tell you, Ella, your boy is spoiled."

Michael Gresham had gone too far. Like a lioness protecting her cub, Ella was instantly on the attack. "I resent that remark very much," she said. "I've had to bring him up entirely on my own. He's had to cope without a father, a normal family life, brothers, or sisters, and as a result we're very close. From a very early age I've had to treat him much more as an adult than a child. From as young as six or seven he's been the man of the house."

"And has it occurred to you," said Michael, "that all this time he might have been holding you back? He resents me—I can see that—and I suspect that he sees me, and probably all men, as a threat to his relationship with you."

The arrogance of the man took Ella's breath away. For a moment her thoughts strayed to Tim. Never for one moment had Greg resented Tim—quite the reverse. "If he resents you," she said, "it's because of the way you're treating him. If we're going to enjoy this weekend, Michael, it would help a great deal if you treated him as an adult rather than as some little brat. I'm sorry, but I simply won't take any more criticism of him."

"OK," said Michael, clearly already bored with the discussion, "if that's what you want, then I'll do whatever you say." His handsome face broke into a smile. "I want you to have a really good weekend, have fun, and relax, because on Monday I'm going to put you to work."

"Doing what?"

"Looking at real estate possibilities in Houston. I'm dead serious—it's the most wonderful opportunity for you, just sitting here for the taking."

"I've thought about what you said," replied Ella, "and really I don't think it's sensible for me to diversify to this extent."

"Just keep an open mind," said Michael. "At least until Monday."

"You're very persuasive," Ella ventured.

Michael grinned. "I aim to be."

Despite having had a very heavy week, Ella did not sleep well that night. The heat was oppressive compared with spring in New York, and her thoughts disturbed her. She had to admit she was very attracted to Michael. There was a distinct physical reaction when he touched her; but, far from giving pleasure, her feelings horrified her. How could she love one man and be attracted to another? It made her no better than her mother had been. Perhaps that was it—perhaps her heritage was coming to the surface at last. After all, here she was, carelessly ricocheting from the ruins of her relationship with Tim into this new and infinitely more dangerous liaison with Michael. He had not so much as hinted that they should sleep together that night, despite the obvious positioning of their rooms, but sometime he would make his move, and what terrified Ella was her uncertainty as to how to react. Michael's views on Greg had disturbed her greatly but had not diminished her physical attraction to him, and when at last she fell into an exhausted sleep it was with the fervent hope that the following day would see Michael and Greg more reconciled to each other.

But the next day was no better. They spent most of it riding over Michael's ranch, getting a feel for the countryside. It should have been idyllic, but it wasn't. They picnicked by a secluded pond surrounded by trees while the horses grazed contentedly. Greg was sulky and silent—quite out of character—and his morose presence clearly irritated Michael.

When they returned to the ranch Greg went straight to his room, and Ella followed him. He came out of the shower in response to his mother's call. "What do you want?" he asked insolently, standing in the middle of the room, dripping, a towel draped around him.

"I want to know why the hell you're being so rude to Michael."

"He's a jerk, Mom. He treats me like some sort of snotty-nosed kid."

"Only because you're behaving like a snotty-nosed kid."

"That's not fair." Greg paled—a sure sign that his temper was mounting. "I tried to be nice to the guy when we arrived, but he's impossible. He's so sure of himself. I can't see why you like him, Mom, and I sure hope we don't ever have to come back here again."

"That depends," said Ella coolly. "Look, Greg, I don't tell you who you should or should not have as friends. Why should you start criticizing my friendships?"

"My friendships don't affect you," said Greg practically. "You forced this Michael on me—you know I didn't want to come."

There was a certain logic in his argument that Ella could

not refute. "Nonetheless, you're here," she said, a little lamely, "and while you're in Michael's house you are to be polite to him. Is that clear?"

"Yes, Mother," Greg said pointedly. He turned his back and returned to the bathroom, slamming the door behind him.

Shaken by their exchange, Ella returned to her room, showered, and then joined Michael on the deck, where he had waited for her.

"A glass of champagne?"

"Thank you, that would be lovely."

Michael removed the bottle from the ice bucket and deftly shot the cork high into the evening sky. "Best sound in the world." He filled their glasses. "To you, Ella, and your big brown eyes."

Ella laughed and sipped her drink. She let out a sigh. "You have a good life, don't you, Michael?"

"Not bad."

"Tell me something about yourself—tell me about your family." She was not sure that expressing such a personal interest in him was the right tactic, but she wanted to turn her weary thoughts away from her son.

"Nothing much to tell," said Michael. "My father emigrated to America as a young man—only nineteen. He was one of eleven children, and I guess life was pretty tough in Ireland then. He worked on ranches in Texas for a while and then married the boss's daughter. He fell in love and ran off with the sixteen-year-old daughter of the guy he was working for on a ranch just north of Galveston. My ma died a couple of years back, and the drink got my father about ten years ago."

"Are you an only child?" asked Ella.

"No," said Michael. "I have two sisters—Betsy is married to a doctor and lives in Washington, and Annie's married to a Canadian and lives in Banff in the Rocky Mountains. I visit them sometimes. They're a really nice couple, but they keep having kids—five now, or is it six?" He laughed and drained his glass.

"Don't you like children?" said Ella.

Michael hesitated. "I don't know. I guess I'm not wild about other people's. I'd probably be different if I had some of my own. Then again, perhaps not. I'm a selfish bastard at heart. Are you going to tell me about Greg's father?"

The unexpected nature of the question threw her for a moment. "No," said Ella. "No, I don't think so."

"Were you married to him?" Ella shook her head. "As I thought," said Michael. "I've recognized that in you."

"Recognized what?"

"The independence—you're a free spirit, sweetheart, like me. So many people tie themselves up in complicated relationships as a security net. So they don't die alone, I guess."

"That's a very cynical view of love and life," said Ella.

"Is it so cynical? How many truly happy marriages do you know?"

"Several," said Ella.

"Really? Well, maybe you're lucky with your friends, but mine . . . Jesus, most of their marriages are a living hell. The moment they've gotten themselves into it, they're trying to find a way out of it again, and along the way they pass the time by cheating. It's not my idea of fun. Maybe when I'm about seventy and a dirty old man I'll find myself a young bride to see me out of this world in comfort."

"If she'll have you," said Ella.

"Oh, she'll have me."

Again his arrogance irritated Ella, but in spite of it she found herself laughing. He was a rogue, but he did not pretend to be anything else. She liked his honesty.

"What time's your flight?" Michael asked over breakfast the following morning.

"Four-thirty," said Ella.

"Do you have to leave that early?"

"I do, really. There's a lot of work waiting for me at home, and although Greg doesn't have school in the morning, he has all sorts of commitments connected with ball games, parties, and—"

"Girls?" Michael asked. "Are you into girls yet, Greg?"

Greg was embarrassed. "Not really," he said, glancing awkwardly at his mother.

"Then it's time you got a move on, boy." It was a remark calculated to humiliate, and it succeeded. Greg pushed his chair back from the table and left the room without a word.

Ella and Michael watched him in silence as he walked off across the paddock toward the stables. "Was that really necessary, Michael?"

"Hell, I'm sorry," said Michael, "only your boy really gets to me with his long, sulky silences. I was hoping for some sort of reaction from him. I'd have been happier if he'd bonked me on the nose rather than just walking away."

"I haven't brought up my son to go around hitting people," said Ella hotly. "Normally he's a very charming person, but for some reason he just doesn't find it easy to be charming to you. Look, Michael, I've really enjoyed this weekend, and it was kind of you to ask us, but it's no good you trying to turn me against my son. He and I get along just fine, and if you don't like him, perhaps it's better we don't see each other anymore."

"Why—don't you like me? I thought we were getting along real well." Michael looked genuinely hurt, and never more attractive.

"I like you very much. I don't like this unpleasantness between you and Greg."

"Jesus!" Michael stood up and began pacing the deck. "You have to be crazy, Ella. You're making yourself a slave to this boy. It's not only stupid, it's unhealthy. If you don't like me, if you don't want us to develop this thing we've started, fair enough, but I know that's not true." His blue eyes bored into hers. "When we touch, something happens to us both. You recognize it, so do I. It's only a spark at present, but I reckon it could grow to be a forest fire given a chance. We have a lot in common, you and I. The boy has no right to stand in our way."

"He has rights," said Ella, "and my first loyalty is to him."

"Your first loyalty should be to yourself."

"You've never had a child to bring up. You don't know what you're talking about."

"You've done all right for him," said Michael. "He's clearly got everything a boy could want. When do you see it ending—when you're a wizened old woman to whom he pays a courtesy call four times a year?"

"That's cruel," said Ella.

"Is it? Get on with your own life, Ella. Let Greg get on with his. If one of you doesn't like the way the other is developing, well, that's just life."

"I can't believe I'm hearing this—" Ella began.

There was a sound of footsteps on the deck. Greg had returned without either of them being aware. "Are we going riding this morning?" he asked, innocently enough.

Ella looked at his face. It was carefully blank, but, knowing him as she did, she saw a look of triumph in his eyes, and for the first time in her life she doubted her son. Was Michael right? The thought horrified her.

The rest of the day was strained, and it was a relief when Michael suggested that they leave early for the airport so he could show Ella some of the new development going on around Houston.

"This really is the place for you," he said as they drove. "It's all here waiting. Condominiums are what you should concentrate on—small units for working people, one or two bedrooms, luxurious, with plenty of recreation facilities. These guys in the city may be young, but they've got money to burn. They want swimming pools, workout rooms, and tennis courts. They want somewhere to park their car, someone to bring in their groceries, someone to empty their garbage and clean up after them."

"Sounds more like a hotel than an apartment," commented Ella.

"That's it exactly," said Michael, swerving dangerously with elation as he thumped the wheel. "When these guys aren't earning bucks they want to be having fun. They don't want any of the hassle of domestic life."

Something stirred in Ella. Meeting the requirements for accommodating working people was how she had started out. She had followed her instincts, and she had been right. She had the same feeling now. She was listening to what Michael had to say, but she felt as though she knew it already, as though he was only confirming her own views. "I thought Texans liked big open spaces," she said, challenging her own feelings as much as Michael's.

"There's no bigger open space than the sky," said Michael. "High-rise condominiums preserve the Texan's love of space. You can have offices on the ground floors, then the facilities, and not even start on apartments until, say, the sixth floor. If you look at Houston from high up, it looks like jungle, it's so green."

"So you're suggesting I build from scratch?" said Ella.

"Surely."

"I've never done that. My only experience is in converting existing property."

"So why shouldn't you start something new?" Michael challenged.

"OK, we're coming out into Post Oak now. This is the area I recommend. It's got everything—shops, restaurants, classy bars—but there's nowhere to live and just look at the space around you. Acquiring a site is no problem. The city will fall over itself to give you a permit, as many permits as you want. They're as aware of the problem as anyone else."

"And money?"

"You'll have your own sources, of course, but money's no problem here in Houston. I can introduce you to any number of bankers, if that's what you want. In fact, I can give you all the contacts—the right contractors, designers, realtors to sell your condominiums when complete, business contacts to take your offices . . ."

Ella gave him a shrewd look. "And what do *you* want from all this, Michael?"

They were waiting at the traffic light. Michael turned and gave her one of his lightning smiles. "Nothing, sweetheart. I'll charge you a few legal fees if you'd like me to represent you down here, because that would only be fair to my partners. As for the rest, I'll be delighted to help. You can't start a business in Houston without visiting the place now and again. That, honey, will be my just reward."

They smiled at each other, and the exchange was a warm and amused one. The moment would have been very special but for a crushing silence from the back of the car, where Greg sat silently and listened.

Chapter 18

New York—*March 1978*

Ella said nothing to Greg until they were back in the privacy of their apartment. She watched him as he helped himself to a soda from the fridge. He had grown so much just recently, her son—tall and broad for his age, almost a man. Perhaps that was where the problem lay.

"In all the years of your life, Greg," she said, "we've been able to communicate. I want you to tell me now what's going on, what turned you from being your normal, charming self into a sulky, bad-mannered brat this weekend."

Greg sighed heavily. "There's no point in talking about it, Mom. You're not prepared to listen to my point of view, so it's a waste of time. Let's just drop it."

"We will not drop it," Ella thundered. "You were extremely rude to one of my friends. It's out of character, and I want to know what prompted it."

"I told you, Mom, when we were down there. I don't like the guy, and I can't see why you do. I think he's creepy, and I don't understand why he wants you to start buying real estate in Houston. What's wrong with your business here in New York? We have a good life, Mom. Why do you want to go and wreck it?"

"I'm not going to wreck it," said Ella, "and it is time I diversified. Margot's always telling me I should, and this could be a great opportunity."

"How do you know it's a great opportunity?" said Greg. "Just because the guy says so? Houston is a long way from New York, and it'll mean you'll be away all the time." He suddenly sounded very young and vulnerable.

"I won't be away all the time, I promise. And I'm not going to go on just one man's view of the market. There's a lot of research needed."

"Are you going to marry him?" Greg challenged suddenly.

"He's not the marrying sort," said Ella. "He's already made that quite clear."

"I just don't understand you," he said, standing up so abruptly that his chair fell to the floor. "If you must have some guy in your life, why couldn't you have married Tim? Then we could all have settled down like a proper family, instead of you carrying on with that . . ." Words failed him; he was close to tears. Red-faced, he stormed out of the kitchen, slamming the door as he went.

The following morning she found a hasty note placed underneath a jar of peanut butter on the kitchen table: "Gone to stay with the Connorses for a while."

After two days of uncertainty Ella invited Aaron and Alice out to dinner. They met, as usual, at a little Italian restaurant midway between their respective homes. Ella, who had been building herself into a state of tense worry, relaxed a little in the familiar surroundings with these two people who knew her so well. They sat regarding her thoughtfully. They were her rock, the background security to her life—for her and Greg. The Connorses had always been there and always would be. "Where have I gone wrong?" she asked as soon as the waiter had poured the wine.

"I don't think you have, sweetheart," said Aaron. "It's just that Greg's growing up. When William gets out of line it's always *one* of us he's angry with—not both. If he's giving his mother a hard time, then I move in and sort things out, and vice versa. Kids are meant to have two parents operating as a team. It's not easy coping with growing children—you need emotional backup, someone to keep telling you you're doing the right thing."

"I suppose what you're saying should be comforting," said Ella, "but it's not, because I can't provide Greg with a father."

"Men are so bad at expressing themselves," said Alice impatiently, nonetheless smiling at her husband. "What he's trying to say, Ella, is that you mustn't feel inadequate because you're finding it difficult to communicate with Greg. Aaron and I often have periods when we can't get through to the kids, but it usually only applies to one of us, so the channels of communication are at least fifty percent open. That's what you were trying to say, wasn't it, honey?"

"That's what I *did* say," said Aaron without rancor.

"Has Greg talked about what's bothering him?" Ella asked anxiously.

"A little," said Aaron. "I know he doesn't approve of the new man in your life, and apparently he did approve of the old one." Aaron grinned. "You've been keeping a lot to yourself recently, Ella—I didn't realize you were being besieged with suitors."

"Hardly that," said Ella hurriedly, "but it's true he doesn't like Michael."

"What he's saying, I think, is that you have to choose between him and Michael," said Aaron.

"But that's ridiculous," said Ella. "I've only just met the

guy. I had dinner with him a few times when he was on business in New York, and then he invited Greg and me to Texas for Easter."

"Do you really like him, this Michael—could it be a serious relationship for you?" Alice asked.

"I do like him," said Ella. "He amuses me. He's also very bright. He has this idea that I should expand my interests to Houston. The oil boom has made it an up-and-coming area at the moment, and my bankers are always hassling me to expand." Ella shrugged her shoulders. "I've had so many years on my own, I don't actually need anyone. I don't want to marry Michael, and he's already made it clear that marriage isn't what he has in mind. As to the future of our relationship . . . I don't know, though we do seem to have a lot in common."

"Greg's jealous," said Alice, "and it's very understandable, but he'll get over it. What does Michael think of Greg, by the way?"

"Not much," said Ella. "That's another problem. Greg behaved pretty badly over the weekend, although, to be fair, Michael did provoke him. Michael thinks I spoil him, you know, because of the circumstances. Now I think maybe he's right." Ella, her big brown eyes filled with pain, gazed from one to the other, desperately seeking reassurance.

"There is such a thing, Ella, as loving someone too much," said Aaron gently. "Perhaps this is the moment you should search your heart and ask yourself a few straight questions. Is this Michael really the rogue Greg imagines him to be? If not, then what right has Greg to dictate the terms of your friendship? Greg can't have everything his own way, Ella, and you can't ease his passage through life forever. That's what good parenting is all about—teaching your children to be independent of you." Ella nodded dumbly. "In the meantime, Greg can stay with us as long as he likes. If he asks us for our views, then we'll tell him what we honestly feel—that he's out of line about this. In the meantime, you can agree to differ, but you must communicate."

"I'll try," said Ella.

Four days later Greg Kovac returned home to his mother. He was tight-lipped, monosyllabic, and, worst of all, horrifyingly polite. Whenever Michael Gresham called from Texas, he simply left the room. When Michael again invited them to Texas for the weekend, Greg declined and said he would go and stay with the Connors family instead. Ella tried to get through to him, to understand how he felt, but failed. They were living as polite strangers who just happened to share the same apartment. Judging by his report card, Greg was continuing to work well at school; he had plenty of friends, and the Connorses seemed to have taken over the role of family in his life. It was as though Ella had become suddenly superfluous to his requirements. She was unspeakably hurt, but pride kept her from telling him just how miserable she felt.

What Greg was too young to understand, however, was that his rejection of her was inevitably pushing her into Michael Gresham's arms.

Chapter 19

London—*March 1981*

The last few years had changed Stephanie Bonham, Margot noted, watching her surreptitiously as she sketched a pattern on the pad in front of her and listened with half an ear to Stephanie's chatter. Formerly very much the typical young Englishwoman, Stephanie had become positively continental. Her long fair hair had been replaced with a smooth, stylish bob that capped her head, bright and glossy. She was much thinner—too thin, Margot thought, but undeniably chic. Her clothes, so obviously Parisian, she wore with a style she had not possessed before. The influence of Alex Meyer, perhaps? Margot wondered idly. She pulled herself out of her reverie. "So, Stephanie, how's business?"

"Very good—in fact, excellent. We seem to be going from strength to strength. The old man's very pleased."

"And how's Alex?"

The question was loaded, and Stephanie knew it. She smiled. "He's fine, or to answer your question more fully, we're fine. People may find our relationship odd, but we don't."

"I don't find it odd at all," said Margot.

"Ah, yes," said Stephanie, "but you're an exception because you're not married yourself. Alex and I have been living together now for nearly four years, and most people think it's time we settled down into a state of married respectability."

"Do you miss marriage?" Margot asked.

"No, I don't," said Stephanie. "I honestly don't think it suited me."

Margot shifted in her seat. "Anyway, you didn't come here to talk about relationships. What can I do for you?"

"There's a warehouse coming up for sale on the Thames—it's a four-, maybe five-acre site in Fulham, and it's currently owned by a firm of haulage contractors. They have no intention of selling it at the moment, but a little bird tells me they are in trouble and that their major customer is not going to renew his contract next year. When this customer pulls out, the haulage firm will be forced to sell the site or go bust. I would like it, and I'd like to develop it as a small-scale Centre des Arts."

"It sounds like a good idea," said Margot, "but what's it to do with me? Surely it's Joseph Meyer you should be talking to."

Stephanie gazed out of the window in silence for a moment. "I was thinking of not involving Meyer in this one."

"Whyever not?" said Margot.

"I suppose you could call it a need to establish some sort of independence," said Stephanie. "There's nothing wrong, truly," she said, seeing the query in Margot's eyes. "I just feel the need to have a little insurance. Up until now I haven't had time to consider any outside interests, but I have this job very well buttoned up, and we're not expanding any more this year, so there are no new units to worry about."

"Are you allowed to diversify under the terms of your contract with Meyer?"

"Yes, amazingly, I am." Stephanie grinned. "I think in the rush to produce the contract it was something that was simply overlooked, and I certainly wasn't going to remind them."

"How much money is involved?"

"Something up to a million pounds to acquire the site. Development should be possible inside a ten-million-pound note."

"And who's going to fund all this?" said Margot.

"Well, I'd rather hoped you might," said Stephanie.

They spent an hour going through the figures. At last Margot pushed back her chair and stood up. "I'm sorry, Stephanie, I just can't see this one. I know your Meyer franchise is worth a great deal of money, as are your Meyer shares, but basically you haven't enough capital. OK, so you can raise a million of your own, but you should be thinking of putting two, three, or even four million into the pot in order to attract a loan from the bank. There's a high risk factor attached."

"Oh, come off it," said Stephanie. "Look at Centre des Arts—it is a monumental success."

"Yes, I agree, but how much of that is due to Meyer?"

"Precious little," said Stephanie. "It was my scheme. I masterminded it."

"With unlimited money," said Margot. "Centre des Arts worked so well because you weren't counting the pennies. Meyer could afford to take a long-term view about the investment, and they were prepared to give you access to a bottomless purse. This project in Fulham you'll have to budget down to the last paper clip. You can't afford any mistakes. There is no provision for anything going wrong. More important than either of those two factors, you can't afford to service a loan of this size. I like the idea, Stephanie, but what you need is a partner."

"You know I can't work with partners," said Stephanie.

"You work with Alex Meyer."

"That's different," said Stephanie.

"Maybe, maybe not," said Margot, "but either way, I'm not prepared to fund you to this extent."

"Even with my track record?"

"Even with your track record. You'll have to find someone else if you won't involve Meyer." There was a moment of silence between the two women. "There is Ella, of course," Margot said suddenly.

"Ella! You mean Ella Kovac?" Margot nodded. Stephanie threw back her head and gave a hollow laugh. "You have to be joking, Margot. I could never go into partnership with her."

"Because of how she let you down in Paris?"

"That's reason enough, surely, and then there's the fact that she used to screw around with Tim."

"You're joking," said Margot, genuinely surprised.

"You mean you didn't know?" said Stephanie.

"When did all this happen?"

Stephanie shrugged her shoulders. "I don't know exactly. It started sometime around the period when the Paris deal collapsed, and it drifted on after that for a year or so." She was feigning vague disinterest, but Margot could see the hurt in her eyes.

"How do you know all this?" Margot was fascinated.

"Millie told me." Margot looked blank. "My elder daughter, Millie."

"Of course," said Margot.

"Tim took the girls on holiday to France. They shared a house with Ella and her son. It was obvious Tim and Ella were having an affair, but it all went wrong."

"How come?" Margot asked.

"I don't know whether I've ever mentioned to you that Tim is an epileptic." Margot shook her head. "Anyway, he had a seizure, and apparently Ella couldn't take it."

"You'd be surprised how she's changed," Margot said. "She's loosened her grip on her boy and has hooked up with a lawyer from Texas. Nice guy. I've met him a couple of times—very good-looking and oozing Irish charm."

Stephanie leaned back in her chair. "She certainly seems to know how to pull in the men. To be honest, at the time it never occurred to me that Tim would get involved with someone else—he just isn't the type. Between you and me, his affair with Ella came as rather a blow to the ego. As for Ella herself, pulling out of our partnership was bad enough without her seducing my husband as well."

"I don't think you're being very fair," said Margot. "You and Tim were all washed up by then—you were even involved with Alex. Anyway, think about it. She's making a lot of money currently and expanding fast, and I think this project might be of interest to her."

"I don't know why you're so eager to throw us together," said Stephanie, "particularly after the last fiasco. I'm sorry, Margot, but honestly, if Ella Kovac was the last person on earth with cash to spare, I think I'd still rather let this deal go."

Chapter 20

Houston—*April 1981*

"How about iced coffee while you're waiting, Miss Kovac?" Jack Smith's pretty secretary smiled at Ella.

"You know my vices," Ella admitted. "Will he be long?"

"He's been on the telephone for twenty minutes already."

They smiled at each other, both aware of their fondness for James N. Smith III, president and founder of Sunbelt Industrial Bank, Houston. Jack Smith had been a good friend to Ella over the last two years—a good friend and an enthusiastic backer, although not without a degree of initial reluctance.

"You want *what?"* he had said, his heavy frame shaking with laughter.

"Three million dollars to build a high-rise condominium just around the corner from here."

"Little lady, you have to be joking." He had three chins, each of which seemed to have an independent life of its own, for they did not move in unison. Ella tried not to stare at them.

"I don't joke about business," said Ella. "I've bought the site, I'm putting in over a million dollars of my own capital, and my collateral is excellent."

"If I wanted to back a property speculator, which I don't, there are plenty of Texans here I could lend a helping hand to, not a little lady from New York I've never met before."

"I've already explained to you," said Ella impatiently, "I've banked for many years with Joshkers, which, I understand, owns ten percent of your bank. You may not know me personally, but I have no secrets from Joshkers. They'll tell you everything you need to know about me and more."

"Sorry, little lady, it's just not my scene. I run a tight little bank here, and I have to protect my investors' money. Property speculators I don't need."

"I'm not a speculator," said Ella, "I'm a developer. This town needs rental housing—you know that . . ." she continued, but she had been unable to convince him and had left disappointed.

It came as an enormous surprise, therefore, when, on returning to Michael's apartment, she heard the phone ring. She instantly recognized Jack Smith's deep voice. "Meet me at the Houston Yacht Club in half an hour," he said. "I've had a change of heart."

It was only in recent months that Ella had learned the truth about this U-turn. Within minutes of her leaving his office, Jack Smith had received a telephone call from Sir Nicholas Goddard, chairman of Joshkers Bank, informing him that Joshkers would consider it a great favor if he could advance funds to a certain Ella Kovac, who had a big future. Sir Nicholas Goddard, a legendary figure in banking circles, was not someone easily ignored. Margot had instigated the call, of course, and had rightly gauged its impact upon Jack.

"Little lady, come along in." Jack Smith had waddled to the door of his office, which he flung open, revealing his enormous form resplendent in an appallingly loud checked suit that actually made Ella wince. "How are you, sweetheart, and how's that good friend of yours and mine?"

"I'm fine," said Ella, "and so's Michael. He has a big case on at the moment, though, so I hardly see him."

"There's no such thing as too much business, you know that. Is this a social visit, or have you come to twist my arm on some new project?"

"Business, I'm afraid," said Ella. "How does the idea of my building a shopping mall grab you?"

"Where?"

"In Tanglewood."

"It'll be a big project, Ella—do you think you can handle it?"

"I reckon so. I feel I'm ready for a challenge."

She looked as if she was ready for a challenge, too, Jack Smith thought. There was a sparkle in her eye, her glossy curls shone, her skin was a light tan. She wore a cool, pretty summer dress in pale apricot, which enhanced her brown eyes. "OK, so you're going to sell some property to fund it, is that right?"

"No," said Ella. "I'd rather borrow the money."

Jack eyed her in silence for a moment. "Is that wise?"

"From your point of view, there's no risk. You have my Houston properties as collateral. The net revenue I receive from them, I've calculated, will cover the interest payments on the new money I need to borrow two and a half times over."

"I see the logic in what you're saying, but don't you feel you're overextending yourself?"

Ella shook her head. "No, it's too soon to sell my Houston properties. The market's still rising. It would be crazy to pull out now."

"All right," said Jack Smith after a pause. "Shoot me some figures."

Two hours later Ella let herself into Michael's apartment in Tanglewood. As always, Ella looked around fondly at the place Michael Gresham called home. In the three years they had known each other Ella had made no mark on the place; with its book-lined walls, heavy leather armchairs, and constant, faint background smell of Michael's cigars, it was entirely a bachelor's apartment. When Ella was staying in Houston for a few days and spread her clothes and makeup about, she always felt it was an intrusion, and she suspected Michael did, too. Despite it, though, their relationship was a good one. They made no demands on each other, yet what little time they did have to offer was surprisingly emotionally satisfying, and in bed they seemed to operate as one person. It surprised Ella, this development of the sensual side of her nature, which for so many years she had imagined had been killed off in Silver Springs.

Occasionally Ella allowed herself to fantasize about the idea of her and Michael marrying, settling down, and having children, but she could not quite see it—it was simply not practical. Their lives did not allow for domesticity.

Ella knew she would be eternally grateful to Michael for the introduction to Houston, though. Business had boomed beyond her wildest dreams. Everything she touched seemed to turn to gold. In the last three years she had put up five condominium complexes. Some she had sold off, others she had rented, some a mixture of the two, but whatever she did, the demand seemed insatiable. Now, as she had told Jack Smith, she was ready for the ultimate challenge of a shopping mall, which she saw as the showpiece of her work in Houston.

Going to the bar, Ella helped herself to a whiskey and collapsed in one of Michael's big, comfortable armchairs. She sipped her drink and glanced at her watch—Michael should be home any moment, and there was a lot to tell him tonight. It was good having someone to talk to at the end of the day. She found she had come to rely on this aspect of their relationship and missed it hugely when she was in New York. New York made her think of Greg, and with the thought came the customary stab of guilt. Greg was eighteen now, and the relationship between mother and son had never recovered from the arrival of Michael Gresham in their lives. Ella was beginning to doubt that it ever would. Somewhere they had taken a wrong turn—the little boy with whom she had shared all her hopes and dreams was gone forever. The tall, handsome stranger he had become did not seem to need her in his life.

The telephone rang abruptly, making Ella jump. It was probably Michael calling to say he'd be late. She picked it up casually. "Hi."

There was a moment's pause. "Mom? Is that you, Mom?"

She recognized Greg's voice immediately, though his manner startled her. It was a long time since he had called her Mom—it was either Mother or Ella these days, or more often nothing at all. "Greg, is that you? Is something wrong?"

"Yes. Oh, Mom." His voice broke.

She realized suddenly that he was crying. "Oh, my God, Greg, what's happened? Are you all right? Are you hurt?"

"No, no, I'm OK."

"Well, what is it? Tell me!"

"Oh, Mom, it's Alice, Alice and Joan." Joan was the Connorses' younger child. "They've . . . oh, Mom, they've been in a terrible accident on the highway. Alice . . . Alice is dead, and Joan's in the hospital, but they don't think she's going to make it."

"Alice . . . dead?" Ella's voice was barely above a whisper.

"Mom, are you there? Did you hear me?"

Ella tried to pull herself together. "Greg, did you say Alice was dead?"

"Yes," said Greg brokenly.

"And Aaron and William?"

"They weren't in the car. Alice had just picked up Joan from a ballet lesson. They were on the way back here. We were all waiting for them, to have some lunch together . . ." He seemed unable to go on.

"Where's Aaron now?" Ella asked.

"He's at the hospital with Joan. William and I are here on our own, and Mom—Mom, we need you."

His words were the trigger; tears began pouring down Ella's face. It was only later, sitting numb and shaken on the first flight she had been able to catch back to New York, that Ella had realized in a single moment of horrifying clarity that Alice Connors' death had given her back her son.

Chapter 21

New York—*April 1981*

He knew it was vital to keep a grip on reality. To reject everything that had happened during this long and terrible day, even for a moment, would be very dangerous. Yet there seemed to be no resources within him to face the truth head on. Why couldn't he, of all people—a practical man—simply get up, leave the room, and go home to comfort his son? He realized suddenly that much of it had to do with the familiarity of the surroundings. He knew every inch of the hospital. This little room was exactly the same as so many others where he had treated patients over the years. How many children had he delivered, he wondered. How many had he lost? How many had he saved? He had never counted—each new human being was an individual. His job was to ensure that every new baby took its first breath, and then it became the responsibility of others to help it begin its journey through life. Yes, it was the familiarity of the room, the color of the curtains, the tile on the floor, the bed, the bedside table, the IVs, now disconnected . . .

Only the patient was different. This time the patient was his daughter, Joan, and the patient was dead.

Aaron stared at the little head on the pillow. Her face and the floppy fair bangs were unmarked, and from where he was sitting he could not see the great gash in the back of her skull. He reminded himself it was a blessing she had died—had she lived, the brain damage would have rendered her little more than a vegetable. Her life had ended the moment the car had somersaulted—that had to be the way to look at it. Eight years old and dead, cut off when her life had barely begun. Despite the evidence lying there before him, he could not believe it.

And Alice . . . he had seen her, but she had been such a mess, crushed beneath the front wheel of the jackknifed tractor-trailer, that the mangled body of the woman he had been shown bore no relation to his wife. Alice was whole; Alice would be back later today. Alice would calm his fears, hold him in her arms, tell him that everything was all right. Yes, that was it. It was awful seeing Joan lying here, but Alice would make everything OK.

He heard the door open behind him, and the sound angered him. He had asked to be left alone. He swung around in his chair. "What the hell . . . ?" He saw the image of a crumpled little face beneath a riot of brown curls, eyes red-ringed from crying, arms outstretched. He knew she wasn't Alice, but he knew she was his only salvation. He half rose and almost fell into the outstretched arms. "Ella." As he said her name the dam burst, and the tears began.

The four of them naturally closed ranks, as if a true family. Greg and Ella fielded visitors and phone calls, well-wishers, the press, the curious, and the devastated patients who looked on Aaron as a personal friend. Mother and son moved into the Connorses' apartment, and Ella told Jackie she would not be in the office for several weeks. Aaron was kept mercifully busy—women went on having babies despite his own personal tragedy; they were his patients, and he could not let them down. William could not face school; exams were over, and so Ella kept both boys at home.

Within a few days of the terrible joint funeral life took on a semblance of normality, and they all had routines and responsibilities. Irene Connors had died suddenly the year before, and Doc was now so frail he could not cope with a journey to New York. With no other close relatives, the full responsibility for Aaron and William rested on Ella. She slept in Joan's room, and little by little she packed the child's possessions into boxes, stowing away everything in the basement when William and Aaron were out of the house. After a week the room resembled nothing more than an impersonal guest room. In the room Aaron and Alice had shared Ella clearly could do nothing that would not be an intrusion. Aaron had to work that out for himself, but it seemed a long way off. Except for the moment when he had first seen Ella by his daughter's bedside, Aaron had shown no visible emotion at all. He had been kind and supportive to his son, efficient at work, but he seemed on some sort of autopilot, which worried Ella greatly. Sometime the truth would have to be faced, and the longer he pushed it away, the harder it would be to accept.

William cried a great deal, mostly at night in bed. For this reason Greg slept on the sofa in the sitting room to give him privacy, and night after night Ella would creep into the boy's room and hold him in her arms until he slept. William's grief was terrible to watch, but there was something positive about it—you could see and touch it and therefore deal with it.

Greg and Ella had stayed with the Connorses for four and a half weeks. Eventually, uncertain of what was best, Ella suggested to Aaron one night that perhaps it was time to leave him and William alone.

"You've been wonderful," said Aaron, "but yes, it is time you got back to your own life."

"That's not what I meant at all," said Ella. "Greg and I just feel you're probably ready for some privacy now—you and William."

"I suppose you're right," said Aaron.

He still had a vacant look, and it seemed to Ella that he was barely listening to her. Yet what could she do? At some stage he had to face up to what had happened, and while she was there to cope with his son and shield him from the practicalities of life he was never going to come to terms with the tragedy.

"Look, we'll leave you guys alone this weekend and see

how things go. If you feel like some company again next week, then we'll come back. Would that be OK?"

"Yes, thanks," said Aaron distractedly.

Jackie had worked wonders in her absence. Ella's desk was virtually clear, and everything in New York seemed to be running smoothly; but then, she had come to expect nothing less from Jackie. Over the three years she had been establishing the Houston development Ella had left New York almost entirely to Jackie, who had taken up the challenge and made an excellent job of it.

"That's all the good news," Jackie said, clearing away the last of the papers that had needed Ella's attention. "The bad news is that there seem to be all sorts of crises brewing down in Houston. Someone's put in a counterbid for the shopping mall site that is higher than yours, and there's some trouble with one of your tenants—Rogers International Computers—in the office complex in Post Oak."

"I think I might travel down to Houston over the weekend," said Ella. "It's kind of hard on Greg since we've only just gotten home, but it can't be helped." She hesitated. "Has Michael called?" she asked with studied casualness. Jackie shook her head. "Oh, it doesn't matter. I'll see him when I'm down there."

Ella, in fact, had not heard from Michael for over a week. He had called regularly immediately after Alice's death, but the calls had become less frequent, and though Ella had tried to contact him he seemed never to be at home in the evening. The situation did not worry her, Ella told herself. After all, their relationship was a relaxed one.

For some reason Ella tried hard not to analyze, she did not call Michael before catching her plane for Houston. He had probably gone to the ranch for the weekend, she told herself. She would not have time to join him, and it would be a shame to wreck his break by putting him under an obligation to stay in the city with her.

It was ten-thirty P.M. when she caught the cab from the airport. On her arrival, the apartment was in complete darkness, and Ella felt a stab of disappointment. It would have been good to find him there, she realized suddenly. She let herself in with her key and turned on the living-room light. The place was a mess—discarded glasses, the remnants of a meal, an empty champagne bottle, and clothes . . . Michael's and . . . her eyes followed the trail of discarded clothing leading to the bedroom door. She did not stop to think; she simply walked to the door, threw it open, and snapped on the light.

"What the . . . ?" Michael turned over in bed. His hair flopped attractively over his eyes. He raised himself on one elbow and hurriedly flapped the sheet over the long, lithe, naked body of a very beautiful, very young girl.

Chapter 22

New York—*April 1981*

Aaron looked dreadful. He sat at the kitchen table in an old bathrobe, sipping black coffee and wincing with apparent pain as he swallowed. There were deep, dark circles under his eyes, and his face played host to a well-established stubble. It was just after eleven-thirty on Saturday morning. He looked up without interest as Ella burst through the kitchen door. "Hi," he said. "Do you want some coffee?" Ella said nothing, and the silence eventually penetrated Aaron's mind sufficiently that he raised his eyes to look at her. She was crying—standing in the middle of his kitchen crying her eyes out soundlessly. "What's up?" he asked. He realized vaguely that he was sorry she was crying, but he wasn't particularly interested in why.

"The bastard," she burst out.

"Bastard! Who, me?"

"No, of course not, sweetheart." She bent over him and kissed his forehead; tears splattered onto his face.

"Who, then?" he asked slowly.

"Michael Gresham, that's who."

Aaron struggled with the name. "Michael from Houston?"

"Of course Michael from Houston."

"OK, so what's he done?"

"I've just found him in bed with a young girl."

Her outrage brought a small smile to Aaron's face. "Does it make it worse because she's young?"

"No, of course not," said Ella defensively. "She was just so . . . so . . ."

"Pretty?" Aaron asked.

"Very pretty," Ella conceded.

"What did you do?"

"I stormed out, caught the next plane home, and here I am." She brushed the tears away with the back of her hand, like a child. "Did you say something about coffee?"

"On the stove, help yourself. You'd better fill up mine, too." He made an effort to concentrate. "Look, I'm sorry, Ella. You must be very upset."

Ella poured the coffee in silence and then came and sat down at the kitchen table beside Aaron. "I should be upset, I should be devastated—we've been together now for nearly three years—but all I seem to be is mad. I'm angry as hell he cheated on me like that, but it doesn't seem to have touched me emotionally."

Aaron frowned; he was finding everything difficult this morning. "I don't follow you."

"Well, it goes to show what a waste the last few years have been. Clearly I never loved him, which makes our affair squalid, trivial, and utterly pointless. In other words, Greg was right all along. To think I put my relationship with my son on the line for that . . . shit."

"So," said Aaron, "no harm done. Now drink up your coffee like a good girl."

Ella lifted her coffee to her lips and then burst into tears again.

"Now what?" said Aaron wearily.

"I just feel so . . . so sordid. To think I've messed around with the guy for so long, and now I find I don't give a damn that I've lost him. It's so cheap—when I compare it with you and Alice, it makes me shudder." The words were out before she could stop them. Alice had been a taboo subject since the funeral.

There was a heavy silence. "There isn't a me and Alice any longer, so that kind of comparison's pretty pointless, isn't it?" The despair in Aaron's voice was an agony to hear.

Ella studied him properly for the first time that morning. He did look terrible. "You and Alice made each other very happy," she said gently. "No one can ever take that away from you."

"But someone did," said Aaron, anguished and close to tears. "That damned truck driver. I keep thinking about him. Suppose he'd forgotten the key to his truck and had to go back for it. Suppose the telephone had rung and he'd stayed to answer it. Suppose it had taken him ten seconds longer to shave, five seconds longer to respond to his alarm clock—anything, anything—and Alice and Joan would be alive." His head sank forward onto his hands, and Ella watched as, from somewhere deep inside him, great, heaving sobs began, gaining in strength until they wracked his whole body. She did not touch him or speak to him. From time to time he spoke disjointed sentences. "How can there be a God to let this happen . . . they nearly didn't go out that morning . . . Joan, she'd cut her knee in the playground the day before . . . there was a big bruise on it. She didn't want to go to ballet, you know that . . . perhaps she sensed something. Little kids are strange, they understand things adults don't sometimes. I think about that a lot. Suppose deep down she knew she mustn't go to that ballet lesson . . .

we talked her into it, didn't force her but said she was being a big baby, it was only a little bruise. Perhaps she knew, Ella. I can't bear that. Perhaps she knew." The sobs grew in strength.

Ella left him and went into the sitting room. An empty whiskey bottle lay by Aaron's chair—clearly that accounted for how he looked this morning. She hunted in the liquor cabinet and found a bottle of brandy, poured two hefty measures, added ice and soda, and carried the drinks back to the kitchen table.

Aaron seemed a little calmer. "Drink this," she said.

"I can't, I'll be sick."

"You won't."

He tried a tentative sip. "You're right, it's good."

"Where's William?"

Aaron's eyes clouded as he struggled to think. "He stayed over with Greg last night. They were going somewhere—a party."

"Have you two talked yet?" Ella asked.

Aaron shook his head. "No, I can't."

"But Aaron, you have to. You're a family."

"No, we're not!" He shouted the words aggressively.

"Yes, you are. OK, half the family you were, but a family nonetheless."

"No, no," said Aaron, shaking his head, tears starting in his eyes again. "William's nearly grown, he'll be eighteen next month. He'll be off to college to new friends, a new life. That's what I want for him—I want him to put this tragedy behind him."

"This is ridiculous," said Ella. "You must stop thinking like that, Aaron—you must. That boy needs you desperately. He lost his mother and his sister just over a month ago, and to all intents and purposes he's lost his father, too. He needs to talk, you need to talk. Between you, you need to plan a future. It's painful, but life goes on. What do you think Alice would have wanted you to do?"

"Oh, don't start that old line about how Alice would have wanted me to be happy. I loved Alice. Alice was my wife, and now that she's gone, I'm finished. I have nothing to offer William. I have nothing to offer anyone."

"You're selfish and cruel, and so self-centered that you can't think of anyone but yourself." Ella spat out the words.

Aaron banged his glass down on the table and stood up. "How dare you say that? Get out, get out of my sight—I never want to see you again."

"If you want me out of this house, you'll have to throw me out," Ella said quietly. She continued to sit at the kitchen table, not daring to stand up for fear her trembling knees wouldn't carry her weight. She was taking a terrible gamble with their relationship, and the thought of life without Aaron terrified her. When she spoke again it surprised her that her voice was steady and strong. "I'm your friend, Aaron—the most loyal friend you'll ever have. For most of the time we've known each other it's been you looking after me, but now the roles are reversed. It's my turn to help, and you must let me. William is going to get over this tragedy in a way that you probably never will. On the other hand, you have known what it is to have a happy marriage, to raise kids, and to build a successful career—William hasn't, not yet. So you've had some good years, and if you want to mess up the rest of your life that's fair enough, but what right do you have to ruin your son's? Five weeks ago two wonderful people died on the highway out there. A casualty list of two out of a family is enough, but the way you're behaving, you're going to make it four."

The fight went out of Aaron. He looked at Ella helplessly, like a small child. "God help me, Ella, I know you're right, but I haven't the strength."

She went to him then, slipping her arms around his waist, resting her head on his chest, for she was a foot smaller than he. They held each other in silence. Fleetingly Ella thought how good it felt to be in his arms, and then she thrust the thought away. "You may not have the strength, but I have, and so has Greg. Between us we can help you and William through this, but only if you want to be helped. We can give you the strength, but we can't give you the will."

"I think the trouble is I feel kind of disloyal."

Ella drew away a little. "Disloyal! How do you mean?"

"I feel it's wrong to try and put the pieces together again. It's as though I'm being unfaithful to Alice by trying to build a life without her."

Ella sighed and, leaving him, walked over to the window and gazed out across the park. "I've never been as lucky as you in having a really close relationship with someone. I suppose I really mean marriage—a true partnership, anyway. Perhaps because of that, I may have a rather romantic and idealistic view of marriage, but it seems to me that if you really love someone, you must know how they would want you to react in every situation." Aaron nodded. "Well, that being the case, you must know how Alice would want you to react now. If I were able to hold a conversation with her right now, surely she'd say, 'Ella, I want Aaron to build a new life for himself, I want him to look out for William, and I want him to look forward, not backward. I want him to remember Joan and me always, but he must realize the past is finished. He and William must build a future together. They must laugh and be happy and one day, perhaps, love again'—you know she'd say that, Aaron, don't you?"

"Yes . . ." Aaron's voice was barely above a whisper. He was crying again, and for a long time they held each other in silence.

"OK," said Ella after a while, "that's enough heart searching for one day—your new attitude starts as of now. Go shave and shower and get dressed. I'm going to take you out to lunch."

Aaron looked at her quizzically. "When did you sleep last?"

Ella shrugged her shoulders. "I didn't sleep last night—I was traveling. But then neither did you, much, from the look of it." Aaron nodded. "Look, I'll tell you what we'll do. We'll have a long, very alcoholic lunch followed by an early night, and tomorrow we'll take the boys out into the country for the day. What do you say?"

"You're wonderful." Aaron smiled, tipping his head to one side. "Will that do?"

"For now," said Ella.

He walked toward the kitchen door and then stopped. "You came here to talk about your problems with Michael, but we've spent the whole time talking about me."

"Michael?" said Ella with a smile, her big brown eyes wide and innocent. "Michael who?"

Chapter 23

New York—*August 1981*

The shrill sound of the telephone invaded Margot's consciousness. Squinting through sleep-filled eyes, she grappled with the receiver. "Yes?"

"Your wake-up call, Miss Haigh. It's six-fifteen."

"Oh, thanks." She replaced the receiver quietly, and, resisting the temptation to lie there a little longer, she slipped quietly out of bed and padded into the bathroom. She ran a deep, hot bath. She could never understand the American devotion to the shower. Functional it might be, but a bath was so much more than simply a method of keeping oneself clean. Most of Margot's major decisions were made in the bath—she read reports, plotted and schemed—there was a solution to everything from the vantage point of a bathtub. Now she pinned up her long, thick auburn hair, creamed her face and, with a deep sigh of satisfaction, climbed into the fragrant foam.

Half an hour later she emerged from the bathroom sparkling clean and good-tempered. She dressed in an impeccably tailored Armani coatdress, grabbed her briefcase and the *Wall Street Journal,* and called for her car.

Margot made it to Joshkers' New York branch on Wall Street at eight-twenty. She sat down at her desk, ordered coffee, and eyed the pile of untouched work. It was not worth trying to tackle it before her first appointment—better simply to sit and compose herself for the day. When the coffee arrived she took a sip and then, taking her cup, went and stood by the window. A few minutes later there was a discreet knock at her door.

"Ella, how nice to see you." Margot turned from the window, and the two women kissed warmly. "Would you like some coffee?"

"Love some," said Ella. "Boy, is it hot out there, even at this hour. I feel frazzled."

"I was about to say you looked a little frazzled," said Margot.

"Thanks a bunch. A fine friend you turned out to be, and I was going to say I thought you looked rather"—Ella searched for the word—"sleek, contented, pleased with yourself—like a cat after a bowl of cream. Business must be good."

"It is," said Margot. "And how are things with you?"

"Well, commercially I don't seem to be able to do anything wrong at present, which terrifies me. Personally, though, I've been having a rough ride."

"What's been happening to you?" Margot asked.

"One of my best friends has died, killed in an automobile accident. Greg and I have been looking after her husband and son. Her little girl was killed in the accident, too."

"That's really awful," said Margot. "I'm sorry."

"Yes," said Ella. She sipped her coffee thoughtfully. "You know, Margot, when something like that happens it really puts life into perspective."

"How do you mean?" said Margot.

"Oh, I stumbled across Michael in bed with someone else. A classic case—I traveled down to Houston unannounced, and there he was—hardly missing me at all, from the looks of things. What a naïve idiot I've been."

"Are you very upset?" Margot asked.

"No, that's just the point. Compared with Aaron's loss it's nothing, is it?"

"Is it going to affect your plans in Houston?"

"No, not at all." Ella's brown eyes sparkled. She grinned at Margot defiantly, and Margot threw back her head and laughed. "I get it. You're going to take the city by storm just to show the bastard what he's missing."

"Something like that," Ella admitted. "Seriously, Margot, business is business, as you well know. I'd be crazy to pull out. I've got a few problems with the shopping mall, but none that can't be ironed out."

"It sounds great," said Margot. "You know, Ella, you've come a long way in the last two or three years."

"Don't I know it," said Ella. "I hate to admit it, but you were right to make me diversify out of New York."

"Well, I never," said Margot. "An admission—will wonders never cease? You're still hanging on to too many properties, though, but that's a failing of yours I can see we're never going to alter."

"Jack says the same," said Ella.

"There you go, then. I'm not a voice in the wilderness."

"Over that particular issue you won't change me," said Ella. "The business works, right?"

"OK, OK, I give in," said Margot. She glanced at her watch, a gesture Ella spotted. The time allotted to personal chatter was over. Margot, if nothing else, was predictable. Ella forestalled her. "You wanted to see me—have you a new project in mind?"

"Yes, but you're going to be less than crazy about the idea when I suggest it to you."

"So why are you suggesting it to me?"

"I don't know, a hunch." Margot stood up and wandered over to the window where she had stood earlier. The sidewalk had been deserted then; now it was teeming with people. "You remember Stephanie Bonham?"

The smile left Ella's face. "Yes, of course," she said coolly.

"There's a new project coming up, a big one, in London. She needs a partner, and I thought of you."

"Me!" said Ella. "You have to be joking!"

"Why?" Margot asked.

"Oh, hell, come on, Margot—after the Centre des Arts fiasco, Stephanie would laugh herself stupid at the idea of involving me in any project of hers. In any event, while I'm happy to expand into Houston, I'm still operating in North America, which is a far cry from London. The reasons I didn't want to become involved in the Centre des Arts are still valid today."

"Are they?" said Margot. "Are you sure? Four years have passed, Ella. Greg's grown up; he can't need you as much as he did, and your ideas and experience have greatly broadened, not to mention your financial standing. You have a highly successful business, Ella. You're a very rich woman, and you have a unique experience of the trade. Why rest on your laurels? What you need is a new challenge."

"I need no such thing," said Ella. "We've been through all this before, Margot."

"Look, I wouldn't be trying to involve you in small potatoes. This project really has enormous potential. I had a look at the site before coming to the States."

"Hey, wait a minute," said Ella, "I thought Stephanie was all bound up with Meyer Hotels."

"She is, but she wants to do something on her own. I can understand the feeling—she's a born entrepreneur. Although her relationship with Meyer is set up so that she owns the franchise and in theory operates as an independent, most of the time it must feel like she's on the payroll. She was offered this site and decided she would like to do something in her own right again. Apparently the contract with Meyer does not preclude her from doing her own thing."

"What sort of project is it?" Ella asked.

"Ironically, it's another riverside site, this time on the banks of the Thames at Fulham. It's just under five acres, absolutely prime land, and the company that owns it—a big haulage firm—is going under in about six months' time."

"You sound very definite about that," said Ella with a laugh. "How come you know?"

"I'm only working on hearsay, but I did some checking."

"Tell me more."

"Well," said Margot, "it seems that the profitability of the entire firm depends on one large contract. It's this contract that keeps them afloat; the rest of their business is worthless."

"So?" said Ella.

"According to Stephanie, their major customer is pulling out at the end of the current contract."

"And how would Stephanie know?" Ella asked.

"Can't you guess?" said Margot.

Ella hesitated. "The major customer's Meyer, right?"

"That's right," said Margot.

"Shit, Margot, that's not very nice, is it?"

"I did suggest to Stephanie that perhaps it wasn't quite legitimate to bankrupt a company in order to acquire its biggest asset. She tells me, though, that old Joseph Meyer made the decision based on the fact that the firm is inefficient. Stephanie only came to know about it because Joseph asked her to look for an alternate firm."

"Does the firm know it's being fired yet?" Ella asked.

"Apparently not, or they'd stop performing."

"It's all a bit cutthroat, isn't it?"

"Come on, Ella," said Margot. "Would you like me to start quoting some of your past deals at you?"

Ella smirked. "OK, point taken. What does Stephanie want to do with the site?"

"Shops, restaurants, offices, and luxury apartments."

"And why does she need a partner?"

"She hasn't enough money, nor has she enough time to run the project alone. She doesn't agree with me, but I'm not prepared to back her unless she has some help. She's your opposite, Ella—you're overcautious, but she isn't cautious enough. I think it's why I've always wanted to get you two together. Her ideas tend to be a little extreme, and she needs someone to put the brakes on. On the other hand, she has a visionary flair you lack. You two were meant for each other."

Ella laughed. "You make it sound like marriage."

"Which is how most of the big business partnerships operate, isn't it?"

"I don't know," said Ella, "I've never had a partner."

"What about Laurence?"

Ella's voice was flat. "Laurence and I get along by not interfering with each other." Her voice was casual, but it was difficult for her to hide the sense of hurt she felt. Since she had stopped being Laurence Merman's mistress the friendship that she'd assumed would always be there seemed to have vanished. They met from time to time to approve accounts or deal with some matter of business that required his signature. Other than that, he did not even send her so much as a Christmas card. "Anyway," she said, "you can't honestly tell me that Stephanie's happy about the idea of us joining forces, can you?"

"No," Margot admitted with a smile, "she's not, but she's mad to do the deal, and she won't get the backing from anyone but me; I've seen to that. I've issued her an ultimatum—deal with Ella Kovac or no deal at all."

"No," said Ella firmly.

"Just because the last project went wrong, there's no reason for this one to go the same way."

"Maybe not," said Ella, "but I still don't want to get involved."

"Because you had an affair with Tim Irvine?"

Ella stared at Margot. "How the hell did you know about that?"

"Stephanie told me."

"Stephanie told you? You mean she knows I had an affair with her husband, and yet you're still suggesting we work together?"

"Oh, come on, Ella, don't be such a wimp," said Margot. "What right has Stephanie to resent your having an affair with her husband when she's living with another man? I don't know why she and Tim are not divorced, but it's not because they have any marriage left. She's Alex Meyer's woman, and that's the end of it."

"Still," said Ella, "she can't be too happy about what happened between Tim and me."

"If that's what's worrying you, I'd forget it. Anyway, give the idea some thought. I'm here in New York for another"—she glanced at the calendar—"another couple of weeks. Give me a call if you'd like to talk about it some more, and don't close your mind to it—all right?"

Ella got up and smiled. "You've got a one-track mind, Margot."

"On this occasion I'm also right. So think about it, Ella Kovac—this could be a big opportunity for you."

Chapter 24

"Are you sure you guys have everything?"

"Mom, quit worrying. We're ready for anything," said Greg.

"Yeah," William confirmed with a grin. He was a nice-looking boy, tall, fair, and slender, like his parents.

Ella regarded them both in silence for a moment. "I'm not sure it's fair to let you two loose on the female population of Canada."

"They'll be waiting, Mom, you can be sure of that," said Greg. "Is that the cab?"

William crossed to the window and looked down to the sidewalk below. "Yep."

"Come on, then. We'd better get going."

Aaron and Ella went down together to the waiting cab to see their sons off on their vacation. It had been Greg's idea that the two of them should take off for part of the summer, and both Aaron and Ella agreed it was a good idea.

"Will they be all right?" Ella asked a little tearfully as they waved the cab out of sight.

Aaron put an arm around her shoulders. "Come on, honey, those boys were raised in New York City—they're streetwise."

"I guess so. It's just that—"

"Stop it," said Aaron. "You're clucking away like an old mother hen. They'll be fine—now how about me buying you some lunch?"

Ella shook her head. "I've got a hell of a lot of work to do today."

"But it's Sunday."

"I know, but I've spent the last few days getting the boys' things together, and I've been neglecting my work."

"You're very good to us—William and me," Aaron said. "I don't know what we'd have done without you in the last few months."

"You'd have coped," said Ella gently, but she was pleased with the compliment. All during her youth Ella had fantasized about her and Aaron having some sort of future together. With Alice dead, she now recognized she was the most important person in Aaron's life, but her fantasies had died with Alice. Ella's affection for Alice had been deep and genuine—the idea of taking advantage of her tragic death was abhorrent. Nonetheless, Aaron's obvious dependence on her brought a warm glow.

Aaron grinned at her. "Look, I'll make a deal with you: I'll let you off lunch if you'll have dinner with me."

Ella hesitated. "I really do have a lot of work."

"Look, this is blackmail, I know, but today is Alice's and my wedding anniversary, and I could really use the company."

"I know," said Ella gently. "I was thinking about the date this morning. Of course I'll have dinner with you, Aaron."

They dined in Greenwich Village in a delightful little French restaurant. The food was excellent, but neither of them was terribly hungry; it was a hot night, and thoughts of the anniversary hung over them both. They drank a great deal of Chablis in an effort to keep their mood light and the conversation flowing. Inevitably, though, over coffee and brandy, the conversation drifted toward Alice.

"I'll never marry again," said Aaron, "never."

"You can't say that," said Ella. "You're not fifty yet. You've years and years ahead, and I know you don't like living alone."

"I don't—you're right, of course—but the thought of another woman quite literally repels me. One or two of my colleagues have come on hot and strong in the last few months, but the idea of kissing another woman, never mind sleeping with her—I guess that side of my life is finished."

Ella was shocked. "I can understand your not being interested in women at the moment, but don't you think you're overreacting, Aaron?"

"Maybe, maybe not, but I can't help it—it's how I feel."

"It still hasn't been that long," said Ella. "Things will get better."

"I don't particularly want them to get better," said Aaron. "I'm quite reconciled, in a strange way, to my funny bachelor existence. I'm sure now I was right not to move us out of the apartment—it's home for William and me—but the idea of another woman living there is appalling." He grinned. "Your good self excepted, of course." He called for more brandy and coffee. "Anyway, enough of me. What about you, Ella? How's your love life?"

"Nonexistent," said Ella.

"Truly?"

"Yes."

"Any particular reason?"

"Same as yours, I suppose. I feel I can't cope with anyone

in my life at the moment. My work's very fulfilling, I have Greg, and after the fiasco with Michael Gresham, my natural inclination is to leave men strictly alone."

"A dreadful waste," said Aaron, shaking his head sagely.

"You're a fine one to talk," said Ella. "I bet the female members of the hospital staff are panting with frustration at not being able to get their hands on you."

The brandy arrived. "Perhaps we should raise our glasses to celibacy," Aaron suggested.

"Perhaps we should," said Ella.

They drank in silence for a moment. "Do you remember, Ella, when we were kids and we used to talk about what we would do when we grew up? I guess we'd be surprised if we could see ourselves now." Aaron gazed thoughtfully into his brandy glass.

"Two corrections to that statement," said Ella brusquely. "We were never kids together—I was the kid, you were all but grown up—and we never talked of what *we* would do when we grew up, only what *you* would do."

"Only because you never said what you wanted. All you would ever say when I asked you what you wanted to do was that you had to get away from Silver Springs as soon as possible. I used to think it was strange, but now, of course, it makes sense. Still, you never seemed to have dreams like other little girls."

"I only had one dream," said Ella quietly, "and that was not to follow in my ma's footsteps."

"Yes," said Aaron quietly, "I can see that now, but I should have understood you better then."

Ella looked at him, amazed. "You made my life possible, bearable, Aaron. You were the one bright spot in my whole childhood, and then, later, after . . . after Greg was born, your family was my rock, my salvation."

"You know," said Aaron with a grin, "when you were very young, I suppose about the time we first met, I decided I'd marry you when you grew up."

"Did you?" Ella stared at him with incredulity. It seemed

impossible, yet at the same time miraculous, that he should have shared the dream that had dominated her life for so long.

"Yes. You were a pretty little kid even then, though too skinny, of course. I used to think when we both grew up I'd marry you and take care of you, but I guess I bargained without the difference in our ages." He looked at her almost shyly. "Did you ever think about me like that?"

Ella hesitated and then shook her head. "No," she answered unsteadily. There was a strangely tense silence between them. Did he know she was lying? Ella wondered. She tried to justify herself. "You see, you moved in a completely different world from mine." Still the silence. Ella continued nervously, circling nearer to the truth, "The only thing I do remember is being very jealous when you first brought Alice home. I was pregnant at the time, and I know I behaved badly toward her, yet she was so sweet. She talked to me a lot that first time she came to Silver Springs, and by the end of the weekend I just adored her."

"She adored you, too, you know," Aaron said. The bill arrived, and he put some cash down on the table.

Ella was almost grateful the subject had turned to Alice. Just for a moment she had been tempted to tell Aaron that she had loved him always, despite the other men in her life and the passage of years.

"Come on," said Aaron, suddenly standing up and swaying slightly. "We're going home—we can talk some more there."

The fresh air made them realize they were both very drunk indeed. They giggled their way into a cab and out at the other end, holding each other unsteadily. In the elevator they pressed the wrong button and ended up on the wrong floor, which for some reason seemed hilarious. Once inside Aaron's apartment they stood and surveyed each other.

"Do I look as bad as I feel?" Ella asked.

"A little disheveled, but very sweet. Now, we have a decision to make . . . we could be sensible and have some coffee, or we could continue with brandy. Somehow it doesn't feel like a night for being sober—shall I get the bottle and to hell with it?"

"Definitely," said Ella.

They sat on the sofa by the window in silence for a while, sipping their drinks and watching the night sky.

"I suppose I should go home," said Ella at last.

"No, not yet." Aaron shifted slightly, drawing her closer to him. "If you go, I'll start to think about Alice. This time last year we had dinner together and took in a show. In some ways it seems like just the other day—in others, it seems forever since I had Alice beside me."

"Of course I'll stay for a while," said Ella gently. "I'm not really tired, strangely enough, though heaven knows I should be."

"Have some more brandy." Still keeping his arm around Ella, Aaron leaned forward and refilled their glasses. As he lay back on the sofa a shaft of moonlight streaming through the window illuminated Ella's upturned face. The short tangle of curls, the huge brown eyes, the overgenerous mouth, the turned-up nose—everything about her was at once familiar and comforting, and in the moonlight she was suddenly beautiful.

Aaron stared at her in silence for a moment. Everything was the same, but different. The twist in his stomach told him suddenly that here was a woman he greatly desired, but it was crazy—it was just Ella. Ella was his friend, his sister. If he had been sober, it might have been different, but the drink had blunted his caution. "Ella," he murmured, and, leaning forward, he kissed her on the lips.

At first the kiss held no significance for Ella. They had always been demonstrative with each other. When his hands moved to the buttons of her shirt a sense of shock thrilled through her, but she did not attempt to draw away. Ella had drunk a great deal less than Aaron, but still enough to blur her senses—to enable her to believe that what was happening between them was normal. Only when his lips found her bare nipple did she recognize what was happening, and by then it was too late. She thrilled to his touch, arching her body toward his. She knew it was Aaron, yet the man who was making violent, desperate love to her was a stranger. He was at once heartbreakingly familiar and yet completely unknown.

When at last their passion for each other was spent, they slept on the sofa in each other's arms, their discarded clothes scattered around them. At some point during the night they woke again, and, murmuring her name, Aaron fell upon her once more, taking them both to dizzy heights, and so on to another exhausted slumber.

There was no time to consider the implications of what they were doing, the rights and wrongs. They were acting instinctively, fulfilling a desperate mutual need; reason had no part to play that particular night.

Ella was already in the kitchen when Aaron surfaced the following morning. He was in terrible shape, but how he looked paled into insignificance compared to the turmoil in his mind. Ella had her back to him; she was making coffee. "Are you all right?" he asked. She did not reply.

"Would you like some coffee?" she said after a moment, her voice small and strained.

"I could certainly use some," said Aaron. He hesitated. "Look, Ella, I'm really sorry about last night."

She turned to face him, and he was shocked by what he saw. Her face in the morning light was pale with dark circles under the eyes. The smiling, sunny girl of yesterday had gone. Had he done that to her? His mind recoiled from what had happened between them. He had behaved no better than an animal—he had betrayed Ella, and he had betrayed Alice . . . Alice. God, she had not been in her grave five months before he had allowed himself to make love to another woman. And how he had loved—his desire for Ella had been insatiable. It sickened him to think of it—what would Alice have thought? She was always so protective of

Ella. He tried to put his thoughts into words. "To have behaved like that, to you of all people—I just can't believe it. I feel so ashamed. You must hate me."

"No, no, of course not." Ella could hear the desperation in her own voice, but Aaron seemed oblivious to it.

He took the coffee she offered him and sat down heavily at the kitchen table. "I guess it would be sensible if we didn't see each other for a while—while the boys are away, at any rate. What do you think?"

"Is that what you want?" said Ella dully.

"Hell, I don't know what I want." Aaron brushed the hair out of his eyes and brought his fist down on the table, making his mug jump and spilling the coffee. "Oh, God, Ella, I'm a fool. Will I ever be able to look you in the eye again? Will I? Will I?"

"I hope so."

"It's going to take some time to get back to where we were, if we ever do." Ella said nothing. "Hell. Look, Ella, I'm all jumbled up right now. I think it would be better if you went home. I'll call you sometime. When are the boys due back?"

"In about five weeks," said Ella. "In late September."

"I'll call you when the kids come home—perhaps we'll find it easier with them around. I just can't handle this right now."

"OK," Ella managed.

She opened the door to her apartment and realized with astonishment that she had no idea how she had reached it. She remembered leaving Aaron's apartment, but nothing in between. She fumbled with the lock, at last opening the door, and then she slammed it behind her with such force that it seemed to shake the whole building. She ran straight into her bedroom, slamming that door, too, and she threw herself onto the bed. Only then did she give way to a storm of tears.

Her sense of isolation was complete—there was no one for her now. Laurence Merman had been a fair-weather friend. When she was his mistress he was interested in her, but when she no longer offered him what he wanted he simply faded away. She had let Tim down; he would never forgive her. Michael? He didn't seem to count at all. Greg, who was almost grown, would be off to college in the fall. Her mother—even her mother was dead.

The tears poured down her face, and she pounded her fists into the pillow. "No, no," she wept. She knew she must try to make sense of the conflict in her mind, yet her thoughts shrank from facing reality. To Ella, Aaron Connors had been a man set apart. She had begun life by hating men; men had made her mother what she was, men had raped and humiliated her. She remembered crying hot, angry tears when she was told her newborn baby was a boy—she had yearned for a daughter. That her subsequent relationships had ended in disaster was no surprise to Ella—in fact, it seemed to her almost inevitable. Men were not destined to make her happy; indeed, it never really occurred to her that they could.

Yet Aaron had been different. Despite her fantasies, she had never considered Aaron as a possible lover. He was her friend, her brother, sometimes the father she had never known, always her mentor . . . until last night. Last night she had seen a different Aaron, his face a mask as his lips, his body, devoured hers. At the thought she felt the heat of passion rise in her again, and the sensation horrified her. Alice had been dead only a few months; Aaron had needed friendship last night, nothing more, and she had betrayed him—betrayed them both—by letting her secret desires get the better of her. Yet at the time it had seemed so right, so natural, as though it was always meant to be.

Forcing her mind to concentrate, Ella thought over their conversation of that morning. Clearly, the night before had meant nothing to Aaron. He had momentarily given in to his desires because he was drunk, and now he was appalled by what had happened. He must despise her utterly. How could she throw away a lifetime of friendship for one night of passion? It seemed likely that there would be no way back into Aaron Connors's heart. Get away, that's what she must do. Living in the same city as Aaron without being able to see him was impossible . . . Still half-blinded by tears, she sat up in bed, reached for the telephone, and dialed the number. "Could I speak to Margot Haigh, please? It's Ella Kovac."

"Ella. How are you?" Margot's voice sounded warm, cheerful, and reassuringly normal in a world gone mad.

"I'm fine. Listen, I've been thinking about that warehouse deal of Stephanie Bonham's."

"Yes?" said Margot expectantly.

"Well, I wouldn't mind taking a look at it."

Chapter 25

Houston—*October 1981*

"What do you think?" said Ella. "Doesn't it look great?"

Greg lounged in the doorway of the new guest suite and smiled indulgently at his mother. "I guess so—a little fancy, though, isn't it?"

"I wanted to make things nice for her—it's not every day one's banker comes to stay, and for a vacation, too."

The big room was predominantly cream and apricot. A huge picture window looked out over Houston, and there was a bathroom and dressing room. It was relaxing and spacious, and Ella hoped fervently that Margot would like it.

It had been a scramble to get ready. Greg had returned from Canada just ten days before, and Ella had spirited him down to Houston to select an apartment suitable as both a home and an office. They had chosen an apartment on the fourteenth floor of the first building Ella had built in Post Oak. While perhaps it was not ideal as an office, it had spectacular views of the city. When looking out of the windows Ella was always reminded of Michael describing Houston as a jungle when viewed from above. It was true; below them was a sea of green. The apartment was a large one, with four bedrooms and bathrooms, a big reception area ideal for entertaining, and a separate kitchen and dining room. The largest of the bedrooms Ella had turned into an office. She had already hired a secretary from Dallas—a girl in her early twenties named Tessa Decker, who looked promising—and decorators had been working on the apartment all week. Ella would not have been in such a hurry but for Margot's call the previous week. It had been out of character, Ella thought. Margot had said she was going to be in New York for a few days and expressed interest in coming down to see the Houston developments. Ella, though surprised, had insisted Margot stay with her and Greg, although there were times over the last week when she had regretted the offer—certainly all the hassle was starting to irritate Greg.

"I know you want to impress her," he grumbled as they crossed the hall to the kitchen, "but honestly, I don't know what all the fuss is about. So she's the lady who hands out the dollars . . . but Jesus, her bank has to be real pleased with you. You're the customer—shouldn't she be rolling out the red carpet for you, not the other way around?"

"Yes, I suppose you're right," said Ella. "Coffee?"

"Thanks," said Greg. "Anyway, I'm not looking forward to her visit. You're going to spend the whole time talking business, I just know it."

"You're probably right," Ella admitted. "I'm sorry, Greg, about dragging you down here so soon after your return. It's just that I wanted to see something of you before you go off to college—it's been a long, lonely summer without you."

"You had Aaron," Greg said.

"That's true," Ella lied. She and Aaron had not been in contact once during the period their sons had been away. When the boys returned they had met for a celebration supper, but Greg and William had been so full of their adventures that neither of them had noticed that their parents barely spoke to each other. Following that evening, it was Ella's feeling of despair at losing Aaron that had prompted this dash to Houston during the last two weeks of Greg's vacation.

"I don't mind coming to Houston, Mom. I like the city now that we don't have to spend time with . . ." He looked awkward, suddenly very much the child.

"It's OK," said Ella, laughing. "You were right, I was wrong. Michael Gresham is a loser where women are concerned—that's official, OK?"

Greg laughed. "What time's her plane?"

"She should be getting in about an hour from now. I had thought about having lunch out, but I guess she'll be tired, so I thought I'd fix something here."

"I tell you what," said Greg, "why don't I pick her up from the airport while you fix us lunch?"

"Would you?" said Ella. "That would be kind. You'll be careful on the highway, though, won't you?"

Greg laughed. "Come on, Mom."

"OK, I know," said Ella. "It just takes some getting used to—you being old enough to drive."

"Just think of the advantages. You can lounge around here while I sweat it out at the airport. Now how will I recognize your lady banker—does she have dollar signs for eyeballs?"

"No, she doesn't, Greg. Actually, she's an extremely attractive woman."

"Tell me more," said Greg, leering.

"She's about five-foot-ten. She has long auburn hair, which she normally puts up. She usually wears black, and she has a wonderful face—big brown eyes, high oriental cheekbones—she's half Korean. She'll probably travel light, because she's very efficient. Why not hold up a card with her name on it?"

"After a description like that," said Greg, "I shouldn't have any problem recognizing her. Why didn't you ask this lady to come and stay before?"

"Oh, where's my little boy gone?" Ella mourned.

"Aw, come on, Mom. Let's have the car keys."

With Greg gone, Ella had time to turn her thoughts to Margot's proposed visit. The possible motive bothered her, but she suspected it might be in some way connected to the Fulham warehouse project. Margot was still unhappy about the financing. It was a big scheme, and she and Stephanie would be very stretched to cope. Perhaps that explained the visit; Margot probably wanted to check up on her collateral. Ella had scheduled lunch with Jack Smith the following day, and she certainly felt confident that Jack could reassure Margot on the success of her Houston projects.

The sound of Margot's laughter in the hall surprised Ella, and she left the kitchen to greet her. From Margot's own description of her general state, Ella had expected to be greeting a pale and weary creature. Instead, Margot was laughing in response to something Greg had just said, and the unaccustomed vivacity lit her face and made her look years younger than her age. Ella was pleased. Margot was always something of an unknown quantity, but if she was in good spirits, she would be easier to handle.

The three of them had a relaxed and friendly lunch—steak and salad washed down with two bottles of Beaujolais. Margot was full of praise for the apartment and what she had seen so far of the city. Like everyone visiting Houston for the first time, Margot had been surprised by its greenness. Greg had promised her a guided tour the following day. It was a tremendous relief to Ella to see how well the two of them got along. Ella had imagined that the moment Margot arrived she would begin firing questions at her concerning the business, which was normally her way. Instead, she seemed eager to talk about almost any subject except real estate.

"Mom says you're half Korean," Greg said as they sat over coffee. "Did you grow up in Korea?"

Ella blanched. It was an unwritten law that one never asked Margot anything about her personal life—a few short rebuffs had seen to that.

"Yes, I did," said Margot, "until I was thirteen."

"And then you went to England?" Margot nodded. "Why was that?"

Greg's persistence was embarrassing Ella, but Margot did not seem to mind. "Well, it's a strange story, really," said Margot, "though I don't know if you'd be interested."

"Fascinated," Ella had to admit.

"Well, my mother was Korean, my father English. He was managing director of a chemical plant. It was an American company with branches scattered around the Middle and Far East. He married late in life. I suspect he was really a confirmed bachelor, but my mother was the daughter of a valued customer of his, and marriage was probably a political move. At the time of their marriage he was forty-seven and she eighteen."

"Was the marriage happy?" Greg asked.

"I think so, fairly. I was born about a year after they married. We had a nice house in Seoul, and we enjoyed the best of both worlds, mixing with both British families and Koreans. My father was very well paid. I went to a British school but was more or less bilingual. They were happy, tranquil years—in fact, so much so that I remember very little about them."

"So what happened?" Ella asked.

"The Korean War." She took a sip of wine thoughtfully. "When the communists invaded, our world was turned upside down. I was at school when the bombs hit Seoul. My parents were both killed outright. The whole city was in chaos. I wandered around for some days, but I had nowhere to go. Eventually I was taken pity on by the good old British Army—the Duke of Wellington's regiment. Because I was an orphan, I was sent over to England on a troop ship and adopted by the family of one of the soldiers I met. I spent the rest of my childhood in Reading, Berkshire, and then on to university, of course."

"It must have been an extraordinary contrast for you," said Ella.

"In a way, yes," said Margot, "although I'd always wanted

to come to England. My father, like most expatriates, had a rose-colored view of English life. I expect"—she hesitated—"no, I won't say that."

"What?" Greg asked, intrigued.

Margot looked slightly embarrassed—something Ella had never seen in her before. "Well, I suspect my father's family came from a rather different social background than that of the family with whom I lived. It sounds very snobbish to say this, but my father talked a great deal about his upbringing, and it bore very little resemblance to the life I lived in Reading."

"Still," said Greg, "you've made up for it since."

Margot laughed. "Yes, I suppose I have."

That evening the three of them had dinner at one of the top Mexican restaurants in Houston, then showed Margot around downtown. The following morning was taken up with business. Greg stayed in the apartment while Ella and Margot had lunch with Jack Smith and spent the rest of the day viewing Ella's various properties.

Over cocktails that evening Margot gave her verdict. "I like this town," she said. "It's crazy, but it's got something —there's a feeling of excitement and dynamism about the place. I can quite see its appeal from your point of view—to find yourself a part of its development, its growth, must be very stimulating."

"Yes, it is," said Ella. "I've been lucky."

"And clever. You must be proud of your mother, Greg."

Greg nodded. "I am, though I guess I take it all for granted—all the deals, all the millions of dollars. It's not like real life, is it?"

"I disagree," said Margot. "I think it's very much a part of the real world—there is nothing more tangible than property."

"Ah," said Ella, "now you're talking like a banker."

"You two are going to start talking business again if I'm not careful," said Greg. "What are our plans for tomorrow? Why don't we take Margot down to Galveston for a peek at the Gulf?"

"That's a good idea," said Ella. "Would you like that, Margot?"

"I'd love it," said Margot, "but don't feel you have to entertain me. I can look after myself."

"We'd like to," said Ella. "I'm only working part-time at the moment because I want to see something of Greg before he goes off to college."

"Then I'm intruding," said Margot.

"No, you're not. You stay as long as you wish."

A very different Margot was unfolding, Ella thought as she prepared supper that evening. Greg and Margot had embarked on another round of cocktails and were watching the sunset over Houston. She was softer, altogether less brittle, and while not exactly forthcoming, she was certainly more prepared to talk about her private life than she had been at any time during the years Ella had known her. How long was it now? Twelve, thirteen years of association—it was extraordinary to have known someone that long and yet to know so little about her.

Ella was almost ready to serve the seafood pasta she had prepared when the telephone rang. "Get it, would you, Greg?" she called. "I expect it's Jackie with an update on New York. Tell her I'll call back after supper."

Greg appeared in the kitchen doorway moments later. "No, it's not Jackie. It's Stephanie Bonham, and she sounds pretty upset."

"Stephanie!" Ella glanced anxiously at the dish of pasta—if she left it in the oven it would overcook. "Did you say I was in?"

"Yes, I'm afraid I did," said Greg.

"I'd better take it, then." Ella was aware that her relationship with Stephanie was still precarious. They each wanted the Fulham project for a different reason, and the price they had to pay for having it was getting along with each other, but there was no point in pretending it was easy. "Hi, Stephanie."

"Oh, Ella, I'm so glad to get you. I've got a problem—a big one—and I need your help."

Stephanie Bonham never needed anyone's help. Ella was astounded. "How come?" she asked.

"Joseph Meyer has found out about our Fulham deal, and he's absolutely furious. He's threatening to throw the book at me and says he doesn't care what it costs him, he'll stop us from going ahead."

"I don't understand," said Ella. "I thought your contract didn't preclude you from doing deals on your own."

"It doesn't," said Stephanie, "but Joseph says I used privileged information, because I knew the haulage company was going bust. He's been ringing me on and off all afternoon, shouting about business ethics and so on. He's already called in his lawyer. I just don't know what to do about it. I can't afford to fall out with him irrevocably, but at the same time I'm damned if I'll be forced to give up this venture. The trouble is, he's big—so big he could really ruin us. I can foresee mysterious difficulties with planning permission, builders not being prepared to work for us—that sort of thing."

"He has that much power—even in the UK?" Ella asked.

"Oh, yes," said Stephanie, "without a doubt, and he won't be afraid to use it, either. Joseph Meyer's a good man, but he's absolutely ruthless when he's crossed."

"Won't Alex help?" Ella asked.

Stephanie gave a hollow little laugh. "Alex agrees with his father."

"Did he know about the project?"

"Good heavens, no," said Stephanie. "As I explained to you and Margot, it was something I wanted to do on my own, separate from the Meyers, father and son. They're being so unreasonable, Ella—it's not as though we are including a hotel in the complex and going into competition with Meyer. I tried to play it down, to put the whole scheme across to them as a sort of lucrative hobby, but they just won't have it. Look, I was wondering whether you could come over to London and help me persuade them that the project isn't going to hurt them. We could change our story a little—say *you* approached *me* to find a project for us both in London—something like that. It would make it seem less premeditated on my part. I'm sorry to ask you, Ella, but they're only in London for a couple more days, and I really am desperate." She sounded it.

Ella sighed. "It's difficult to get away at the moment—Greg's just about to start college, and I have Margot staying with me."

"Margot! So that's where she is—I've been trying to reach her all day," said Stephanie. "The bank kept telling me she was on holiday, but I didn't believe it—Margot never has a holiday. What's she doing with you?"

"Taking a vacation, at last," said Ella. "It's part business, of course, being Margot. She's looking at my Houston operation, but she's planning a few days off as well. Anyway, I'm sure you appreciate that I can't very well walk out and leave her."

"Quite the reverse," said Stephanie. "She's the one person who really will understand. After all, it's her project, too—she's funding us. She just has to spare you for thirty-six hours—it shouldn't be longer—honestly, Ella. You can fly straight into London and straight out again. I just need a few hours of your time—I'll fix up a meeting with Joseph for whenever you arrive."

"I can't make it this week," said Ella. "Next week, certainly—"

"Next week will be too late. It has to be resolved now—we can't let it fester, or by next week we'll be in court."

"Hang on a moment," said Ella. "I'll talk to Margot."

Ella quickly explained the position, and Margot was at once efficient and very much back to her old self. "I think you have to go, Ella," she said, "if you want to save the project. My guess is that Stephanie and Joseph need someone to intervene and find a compromise." She smiled at Ella. "I can't think of anyone better for the job."

"But what about your vacation?" said Ella.

"Oh, to hell with my vacation," said Margot. "This is much more important. I can always fly back up to New

York. God knows, there's a desk full of stuff waiting for me there."

"Why don't you stay here until Mom gets back?" said Greg. Both women turned to him, surprised. He shrugged his shoulders, looking slightly self-conscious. "Well, you're not going to be away long, Mom, are you?"

"No," said Ella, "no, I suppose not. Hell, we'd better talk about it in a moment. I still have Stephanie waiting on the line."

"Tell her you'll catch the first flight out," said Margot, "and then we'll work out what to do."

The relief in Stephanie's voice only served to emphasize the seriousness of the situation, as did her gratitude. "I really don't know how to thank you, Ella."

"It's no problem," said Ella. "I'll try and catch an overnight flight tonight, and I'll ask Greg to call you with the flight details. Could you possibly arrange for someone to pick me up?"

"Of course—and Ella, thanks again."

When Ella returned to the sitting room Greg and Margot were deep in conversation. "I've talked her into it," Greg said triumphantly. "She says if you don't mind, she'll stay on for a couple of days while you're away, and then the three of us can take some day trips on your return. I thought we could go to NASA, and if you hurry back, Mom, we might have time to go down to Mexico."

Ella looked at Margot uncertainly. "Are you sure this is what you want to do, Margot?"

Margot seemed equally unsure. "I'd love to stay, but I don't want to be in the way. I needn't take up any of Greg's time—I have a lot of reading to do, and to be honest, it's just so nice to be out of a hotel and in an apartment for once."

"If you're sure you don't mind, I know Greg would welcome the company."

"I would," said Greg emphatically.

"Well"—Ella hesitated—"I will only be gone for a few

days . . . oh my God, supper!" She ran through to the kitchen. "Oh, yuck, it's congealed—completely ruined. I could kill Stephanie. It was going to be so good!"

Greg and Margot joined her. "Can't you heat it up?" said Greg.

"No, the pasta's all soggy, and . . . oh, shit."

"Look," said Margot, "I can start making myself useful right away. You go and pack, I'll fix your flight, and then Greg and I will run you to the airport via a suitable restaurant. What do you say?"

"It sounds like a great idea," said Ella. "Oh, hell!" She picked up the bowl of pasta and began scraping it into the garbage, wondering as she did so whether she would be disposing of the Fulham project the same way in a few hours' time. She wanted that deal, wanted it badly. She was also aware that being able to help Stephanie out of the hole into which she had dug herself boded well for their future relationship. There had to be a way to salvage the project, and if there was, she felt confident she could find it.

Chapter 26

London—*October 1981*

It was one-thirty by the time Ella's car drew to a halt outside the Meyer Hotel in Park Lane. Stephanie was waiting for her at reception in a state of obvious agitation. She embraced Ella warmly, as though none of the former animosity had ever existed. "Thank you for coming, Ella. They're already up in the boardroom waiting for us, but I lied and said I didn't think you'd be in until two. Come up to my room. It will give us a chance to talk strategy." In Stephanie's room a pile of sandwiches was waiting for Ella. "A glass of wine?" Stephanie asked.

"Coffee, I think," said Ella. "A combination of jet lag and booze could be a little dulling on the wits, and it looks like we're going to need ours about us."

Stephanie ordered coffee from room service and then came and sat down opposite Ella. She looked chic and sophisticated—very European, Ella thought—but terribly thin and pale. There was a strained look about her face that had not been there before, and she plucked nervously at the skirt of her dress as she talked. "I suppose I should have told Alex about the scheme from the beginning," she said. "Then at least I would have stood a chance of having him on my side. As it is, he seems to feel as let down as the old man, if not more so. I know this is a dreadful thing to say, Ella, having dragged you all the way across the Atlantic, but I honestly think we're going to have to pull out."

"We're not pulling out," said Ella. "Joseph Meyer can make as much noise as he likes, but if your contract with the Meyers is watertight, then there's nothing he can do."

"Don't be so naïve, Ella," said Stephanie desperately. "There's one hell of a lot he can do. To start with, he can make my life unbearable within the Meyer organization. My franchise comes up for renewal in ten months—that gives him plenty of time to prepare a case as to why he shouldn't renew it. And then, as I said to you on the phone, I'm perfectly certain he can pull strings to such an extent that we'll never get Fulham off the ground."

"I think you're overreacting," said Ella. "These bullying tactics go on all the time in New York, and my experience is that most of them amount to no more than bluff."

"And what about when they don't?" Stephanie asked.

Ella smiled. "The way I've always handled bully boys is to threaten them with the press. Just imagine how the Meyer organization would look if it could be proved they were trying to put us out of business. You're English, born and bred—if anybody has a right to develop real estate in this country, it's you. A story detailing how Meyer, a German-

American, is trying to stop you could ruin his reputation in this country."

"I suppose so," said Stephanie reluctantly, "though I certainly wouldn't like to be the one to threaten Joseph Meyer along those lines."

"I don't think we'll have to," said Ella. "I'm sure we'll find a compromise. But whatever way we have to play it, just remember: We're not letting him stop us from going ahead with this project."

The telephone rang, making them both jump. Stephanie picked it up. "I gather Miss Kovac has arrived." Joseph Meyer's voice was clipped and formal. "Perhaps you would be good enough to join us in the boardroom right away—we've waited more than long enough for you as it is."

Stephanie put down the phone, white-faced. "The old bastard knows you're here. He must have his spies everywhere."

"Calm down," said Ella. "Let me use your bathroom to refresh the war paint, and then it's off to do battle."

The boardroom was impressive—a large room with big picture windows looking out over Hyde Park, dominated by a round mahogany table. Ella, who had seen Joseph Meyer only in press photographs, was immediately struck by the contrast between his diminutive stature and the power of his presence. There were three men sitting at the table when Ella and Stephanie entered. Joseph, with a courtesy that was obviously inbred regardless of the circumstances, rose and came to greet them. He shook Ella's hand warmly but made no attempt to greet Stephanie other than with a curt nod. From the moment Ella took his hand and met the appraising gaze of his deep-set eyes, she recognized for the first time the substance of their adversary. No wonder Stephanie was nervous. This man would make a wonderful friend and a terrible enemy. His grip was firm, his hands dry and soft. Taking Ella by the elbow, he steered her to the table. "I'd like to introduce you to my son, Alex, and this gentleman is our lawyer, Jacob St. Clare."

That a lawyer was present was disconcerting, but not

enough to distract Ella from a fascinated appraisal of Alex Meyer. He was not her sort of man—he was too obviously sure of himself, too sophisticated. However, there was no use denying that he was extremely attractive. With his dark curly hair and smooth, aquiline good looks he had an almost feline grace. Instantly, though, there was something about him she did not like—there was a petulant curve to his mouth, and, yes, he was clearly enjoying the situation. The realization appalled Ella. He was supposed to be in love with Stephanie, and in Ella's mind he should have been either leaping to her defense or looking hurt and angry. Alex Meyer was reacting in neither manner—he looked as though he was about to relish watching Stephanie squirm.

The situation made Ella very angry. She glanced at Stephanie, who was sitting beside her, pale and nervous, and suddenly felt very protective toward her. It was a strange reversal of a relationship that had begun with Ella most definitely feeling the inferior.

Her thoughts were interrupted by Joseph Meyer's deep, melodious voice. "Thank you for joining us, ladies. I think I should make it quite clear before this meeting opens that neither my son nor I have any argument with you, Miss Kovac. Clearly, if you wish to extend your business interests into the UK, that is up to you, and you are free to bid for any UK property, should you feel it appropriate for your business expansion."

"Thank you very much indeed," said Ella with heavy irony. She met Joseph's eye as she spoke.

"However, I do query your choice of partner. My experience would suggest that *Lady* Stephanie Bonham"—he emphasized the title—"is far from an ideal partner, since you can be assured she will put her own interests before those of the partnership."

"That's untrue!" Stephanie's complexion had turned from white to pink; her eyes were overly bright.

"Mr. Meyer," Ella cut in, "I can see absolutely no point in having a meeting if all we're going to do is to exchange insults. I've known Stephanie Bonham longer than you have. I consider her to be an honorable and trustworthy person, and I have decided to go into partnership with her in this venture as a direct result of the recommendation of our mutual banker."

"Ah, the indomitable Margot Haigh," Alex said with a sneer. "She's always keen on promoting women's projects, I notice. I should watch yourself, Steph—she's probably a dyke." The venom in his voice was shocking in its intensity.

Ella rose to her feet. "I've just flown in from Houston because you requested a meeting, Mr. Meyer, but I can only repeat that I am not prepared to sit at this table in order to bandy insults. If you have anything to say, then please say it. Otherwise, I'm catching the next plane home."

"Please sit down, Miss Kovac," said Joseph Meyer. "I apologize for my son's outburst. It was rude and unnecessary." Alex glared at his father, and Ella returned to her seat. "I'll stick to the facts. If you and Stephanie persist with this Fulham project, I will finish you. It's as simple as that." He looked directly at Stephanie. "I suppose you think you've been very clever, Stephanie. Technically, under the terms of the contract, you are free to develop other sites independently from us, but you used privileged information as a director of Meyer Hotels in order to acquire the site at a below-market price. It was a breach of trust of the most serious kind, and you, Miss Kovac, should not be a party to it. I must warn you that Jacob has instructions to serve an immediate injunction upon you both if you decide to proceed."

"I cannot see your objection—" Stephanie began.

"Can't you?" Joseph Meyer roared. He was truly terrifying when he was angry. "The most fundamental requirement of any successful business is that the principals involved trust and respect one another totally. For some reason I cannot now understand, from the first moment I met you I believed you to be a person of integrity. I suppose I mistakenly based that assumption on your background. That you deceived not only me but also Alex is utterly incomprehensible to me."

"The Meyers don't own me," Stephanie said.

"That, Stephanie, is where you are wrong," said Joseph. "The Meyers own you from the pretty shoes you are wearing to those little pearl earrings of yours. I made you, and I can destroy you."

"I made myself," said Stephanie, "and it's your high-handed attitude that made me feel the need to branch out on my own again. I was my own person with my own business when I first approached you. Yes, I've learned a lot from you, and I'm grateful. You put a great deal of trust in me, and I'm grateful for that, too, but when all is said and done, I am little more than an overpaid office boy. There is no decision, major or minor, that can be made without your blessing. I feel stifled, claustrophobic, and that's why I need to do something on my own." Stephanie looked directly at Alex. "Surely you understand that, Alex."

"Even if I do," he said coldly, "there are still ways and ways of doing things. My father and I don't always see eye to eye—you know that better than anyone—but it doesn't mean I'd go behind his back, or he behind mine. Whatever the ups and downs of our personal relationship, to the world we present a united front. It's the only way to survive."

"That's right," said Joseph. His voice was slightly choked, and Ella realized his son's words had moved him—he was vulnerable after all. It was a question of timing, of choosing the right moment, and now was as good a time as any, while tempers were momentarily cool.

Stephanie beat her to it. "I don't believe you can serve an injunction. I've done absolutely nothing wrong," she burst out. It was the worst thing she could have said.

"Oh, can't I?" roared Joseph. "Well, why don't you just sit back and watch me? Jacob, go prepare the papers. I'm sorry you're being involved in this, Miss Kovac, but if you persist in joining Stephanie in this project, my argument is with you as much as with her. You're dealing in privileged information, too."

"One moment," said Ella. "I've sat here and listened to you all screaming at one another like kids in a playground, and I find it hard to believe my own ears." She had their attention. She stood up and wandered over to the window, taking her time. At the window she turned to face them. "Look, whether we proceed with the deal or not is of no importance to me. As far as I'm concerned, there are other deals in other towns, in other countries. What does concern me, however, is the apparent tragic breakdown of your relationship. Your partnership has become legendary in the hotel business; you know that. You're an unlikely trio, God knows, but together you make sweet music. The flair and imagination you have brought to the new Meyer hotels around Europe has left the other hotel groups gasping with admiration. Speaking personally, I'd never stay anywhere now but at a Meyer Hotel, and I like to flatter myself that I'm showing good sense and an appreciation of style." She had them eating out of her hand now. She was talking about their baby, their creation—all three of them were flattered, seduced by pride in what she was saying, their differences momentarily forgotten. "So," said Ella, "we're talking about one crummy site in Fulham. How can you be serious about letting it be responsible for breaking up a partnership that up to this moment has been one of the greats in the hotel industry? The tragedy is that if either of you wins at this stage, you both lose." She looked directly at Joseph. "If you win, Mr. Meyer, and force Stephanie to withdraw from this project, you will lose the best franchisee you are ever likely to have. If you win, Stephanie, and proceed with this project against the wishes of Mr. Meyer, you will lose out on your relationship with the Meyers. You will have to quit or else wait for your current franchise agreement to finish—needless to say, it won't be renewed. Maybe, Stephanie, you were a little imprudent in going ahead with this project without discussing it with the Meyers. Maybe, Mr. Meyer, you have forgotten what it's like to be young and impetuous. I guess if I could take you back, stage by stage, through your amazing career, we could highlight several occasions where your behavior would bear some startling similarities to Stephanie's. You are both entrepreneurs; you are both used to, and indeed thrive on, taking risks. We didn't get to where we are now by always playing it straight down the line."

"What are you suggesting, Miss Kovac?" Joseph said quietly.

"I'm suggesting a compromise. Let's go ahead with this Fulham project, but let's go ahead with it on a fifty-fifty basis. By that I mean fifty percent Meyer, fifty percent Stephanie and me. At the moment the project is not intended to include a hotel. Let's change that. Let's build a Meyer Hotel as part of the complex. Let's run the whole scheme under the Meyer banner, but Stephanie and I will only put up half the capital and receive fifty percent of the action for seeing the opportunity and masterminding the plan."

There was a long silence. Joseph stood up, too, and came to join Ella by the window. His expression was unreadable. She retained her relaxed pose, leaning nonchalantly against the windowsill, but her heart was hammering. "You know something, Miss Kovac? I now understand completely why you are so successful. You're a very sensible, intelligent young woman. I like you, and I like your scheme. We'll go with it." He swung around to Stephanie. "Do you agree?"

"I suppose so," said Stephanie.

"You *suppose* so, you *suppose* so!" Joseph strode across the room toward her. "I've just let you off the hook, dropped proceedings, and I've given you fifty percent of the action."

"Correction—*we* have given *you* fifty percent of the action," Stephanie said.

For a moment there was a horrible silence, during which Ella was convinced that all the progress she had just made was about to be blown apart. Suddenly, without any warning, Joseph Meyer threw back his head and roared with laughter. "OK, OK, so *you'll* give *me* fifty percent of *your* project. I accept, gratefully, thankfully—Lady Bonham, you are too good to me." He swept a low, theatrical bow. "Have you ever heard anything like it, Alex?"

Alex made no reply, and none seemed to be required. In that fleeting moment Ella began to understand Alex's predicament. Although when the meeting had begun it had seemed that the Meyers were the predators and Stephanie the victim, it was clear that, despite all their differences, she and Joseph had a lot in common. They had started with very little and made it through their own drive and initiative. Alex had started with everything, and yet he had nothing.

"OK, you guys," said Ella, "can we shake hands on it? I have to get some sleep—I'm bushed."

"You must be," said Joseph.

The four of them shook hands formally. Ella noticed that when Stephanie shook hands with Alex neither looked at the other. They sat together for a few minutes more, talking through the details necessary to set the project in motion, and Ella agreed to return to London in two weeks, when Greg was settled in college, to start work on the site in earnest.

Five minutes later the two women found themselves outside the boardroom door, only half an hour after their meeting had begun. "Phew!" said Stephanie. She put a hand on Ella's arm and squeezed it. "I'm grateful, truly. We were really riding for a fall there, and without you the meeting would have collapsed."

"You and Joseph certainly seem to have the knack of getting under each other's skin." Ella grinned. "Boy, he packs a punch, doesn't he?"

Stephanie nodded. "I still wish it hadn't been necessary to give him fifty percent of Fulham. Effectively it means I'm still tied to Meyer."

"I don't think you should lose any sleep over that," said Ella as they went into the elevator. "Margot's been very reticent about the financing of this project, you know. She thinks we're undercapitalized and that we're both stretching our personal resources too far. I happen to think she's right. With Meyer's name and money behind us the project is assured of success, and that, after all, is what we are both aiming for, isn't it?"

"Yes, but at what price?" said Stephanie. "Hell. Look, I'm

sorry, Ella. I'm sounding ungrateful, and I'm not, truly. You handled the meeting brilliantly, and I won't forget it."

"Good," said Ella. She leaned back against the wall of the elevator and closed her eyes for a moment.

"God, I'm a selfish bitch," said Stephanie. "You must be dying to get horizontal. I've got the key to your room here. Let me take you to it." Inside Ella's room, without discussion, they poured themselves large brandies from the minibar. "To us," said Stephanie.

"To us," Ella echoed.

"Have you decided what flight you're catching back to Houston?"

Ella consulted her watch. "Jesus, it's only three o'clock. That's wonderful! I'm booked on a flight from Heathrow that leaves at eleven o'clock tomorrow morning, so I guess I'll do some catching up on sleep between now and then."

"I tell you what," said Stephanie. "I have an idea. Why don't you and I have dinner together later? You have a good sleep now, and I'll come and collect you at—what, eight o'clock?"

Ella studied Stephanie in silence for a moment. "I have an even better idea. Tell me to mind my own business, but if I were you, I'd relax in a hot bath for an hour with another of these brandies, and then I'd go and find Alex and sort yourselves out. It's clear there's a lot of ill feeling still running between you two, and it needs sorting—for the sake of the project, yes, but much more important, for the sake of your own happiness."

"I shouldn't think he'd want to see me," said Stephanie.

"Well, try. You've nothing to lose."

"You know, you're a very nice person, Ella," said Stephanie. "I hadn't realized just how nice until now. At the time of the Centre des Arts project everything was so rushed I never really had a chance to get to know you. Tim kept telling me what a wonderful person you were, but I didn't appreciate it." At the mention of Tim's name Ella visibly blanched. Stephanie smiled. "It's OK," she said. "I know about you and Tim, and I don't mind. I'm sorry it didn't work out for you both."

"You *must* mind," said Ella.

Stephanie shook her head. "Truly, no. At the time, a little. You must admit that pulling out of the project and stealing my husband all at the same time was a bit rich."

"I'm not disagreeing," said Ella ruefully.

"Realistically, though," said Stephanie, "Tim and I were already leading separate lives, as you well knew. I had no right to be resentful."

"How is he?" Ella felt compelled to ask.

"Oh, Tim's fine. I don't see him very often—the girls are old enough now that they come up to London or over to Paris to see me on their own. As far as I know, there isn't anyone else in his life. I wish there was, but who knows—perhaps he's still pining for you. I will say this, though, Ella: Now that you're going to be in England a lot more, if you feel like renewing your friendship with Tim, I'll be genuinely delighted. You need have no fear it will cause any trouble between us."

The words spoken were warm and apparently genuine, yet there was an undercurrent Ella detected but could not identify. "What tangled lives we lead," she said with a laugh, in an effort to ease the tension.

"Yes, indeed," Stephanie agreed. "Hey, I must let you sleep." She looked slightly embarrassed. "If I don't see you again tonight, I'd really like to drive you to the airport tomorrow."

"There's no need—" Ella began.

"Yes, there is. We have a lot to talk about."

Ella grinned at her. "OK. Now, don't take this wrong, but I hope I don't see you until the morning." The women exchanged a conspiratorial smile as Stephanie stepped out of the door.

Left alone, Ella undressed wearily. Too tired even for a shower, she slipped between the cool sheets and rested her head on the pillow. She was pleased with herself. The meeting had been a success, and not only that, she was a great deal happier about the project now that she knew Meyer was contributing to it. Her enthusiasm for Fulham had been a means of escaping from Aaron. She had been desperate to get away from New York, and for that reason she had been prepared to become involved on almost any terms.

In the last moments before sleep Stephanie's words about Tim came back to her, and in that instant she recognized what had troubled her about Stephanie's little speech of reassurance. It was insincere . . . there was no doubt in Ella's mind about that. Stephanie had simply been testing the water, hoping to elicit a response from Ella as to her true feelings for Tim. What did it mean? That Stephanie still cared for Tim, or simply that she did not like the idea of his finding happiness with someone else? And what of Tim—was it possible he still loved her? She doubted it after the way she had behaved. She must tread carefully. She could not afford to upset Stephanie and jeopardize their deal. There was another factor, too. Her wish to spend more time in London was all about running away from one man—she had to be very careful not to run straight into the arms of another.

Chapter 27

Houston—*October 1981*

It was three o'clock Houston time when Ella staggered out of the elevator and into her apartment. The wonders of modern air travel were all very good, but they certainly took their toll.

"Margot, Greg, I'm home!" There was no reply, so Ella

walked into the office to find Tessa hard at work at the typewriter. "Hi." Ella collapsed in a chair opposite her.

"Ella! That was quick—we didn't expect you back until tomorrow. How did it go?"

"Fine. How are things here?"

"OK." Tessa consulted her pad. "There were a few calls, but nothing that can't wait." She pushed her long, straight dark hair back behind her ear. She was an attractive girl, and she took her job very seriously. "I have a couple of leases here for you to sign."

"I'll see to them in the morning. Where are Margot and Greg?"

Tessa gave her a slightly strange look. "They're out to lunch, although I thought they'd be back by now."

Ella stood up. "I think I'll take a shower and lie down for a while. When they get back, tell Greg to come and wake me."

"OK," said Tessa. "Have a good sleep."

Her son sitting down heavily on the end of her bed woke Ella some hours later. With the curtains drawn, the room was in semidarkness. "Is that you, Greg?" Ella asked.

"It certainly is, Mom. Why, were you expecting someone else?"

"No, idiot."

"How was the trip? Did it go OK?"

"It went fine." Ella struggled up in the bed and switched on the light. Greg was grinning at her, a little foolishly, she thought. Something was not quite right with him, and her tired mind tried to analyze what it was.

"We've had fun, too. We've just had the most brilliant lunch—you should have been there." His eyes were overbright, his cheeks flushed.

"You've been drinking, Greg," said Ella sternly. "In fact, if I'm not mistaken, you're drunk out of your mind."

"Hardly that, Mom, but we did manage a couple of bottles of champagne between us."

"A couple of bottles!" said Ella. "What were you celebrating?"

"I don't know, really," said Greg, "just life, I guess." He giggled a little self-consciously.

"So if this is the shape you're in, how's Margot doing?"

"Much the same, I guess. She's making us coffee right now. Would you like some?"

Ella consulted her watch. "Six o'clock," she said, "I think I'd do better with a cocktail."

"Good idea. We'll have one, too."

"No, you won't," said Ella, "you'll stick to the coffee. Tell Margot I'll be up in a moment."

"OK, Mom."

The sound of their laughter penetrated even through her closed bedroom door, and for a moment Ella was irritated. She tried to consider why this was as she brushed her hair. Establishing any sort of personal relationship with Margot Haigh was extremely difficult. That her son had succeeded so effortlessly should please her—after all, leaving them alone could have been a disaster. She slipped on her bathrobe. Perhaps I'm jealous, she thought, but the idea appalled her, and she strode out into the hall determined to cover her irritation.

They were in the kitchen. Margot was pouring out mugs of coffee, and Greg was attempting, somewhat clumsily, to fix his mother a dry martini. It was Margot, though, who riveted Ella's attention. She was dressed in a pair of designer jeans, loafers, and what was clearly recognizable as an old workshirt of Greg's. Her hair hung down onto her shoulders like a young girl's instead of being caught up in the severe chignon she so often wore. At first glance she almost looked to be a contemporary of Greg's. Ella was dumbstruck.

"Ella! How did it go?"

"OK," said Ella a little warily. "I think you'll be pleased with the outcome."

"Great, you must tell me all about it. I'm sorry we weren't here when you got back. This wretched son of yours took me out to lunch and got me drunk."

"So I gather," said Ella, "though you do seem to be in slightly better shape than he is."

"Years of experience," said Margot with a smile.

"One dry martini, just as you like it, complete with olive." Greg handed the glass to Ella with a flourish, spilling some on the kitchen floor as he did so.

"Oh, Greg, you're a wreck."

"Hey, come on Mom, where's your sense of humor?"

"Somewhere over the Atlantic, I expect," said Ella wearily.

"You must be absolutely exhausted," said Margot. "Let's go and sit down."

They took their drinks to the living room to catch the sunset, and Ella explained the deal she had struck with Joseph Meyer. As she had anticipated, Margot appeared to be very pleased but, in some strange way, oddly detached. Normally Ella would have expected Margot to fire questions at her—she was a stickler for detail and liked to understand precisely what was involved. But not this evening. She asked a few perfunctory questions, confirmed her approval, and then started talking about Galveston, which she and Greg had visited the day before.

"I had forgotten how much I loved the sea," Margot said dreamily. "My father used to take me sailing every weekend. Greg rented a little sailboat, and I realized I had not been sailing in all those intervening years. Strange, really, when it was so much a part of my life."

"You went sailing!" Ella was surprised. "I didn't know you could sail, Greg."

"I learned when we were in Canada, though Margot's much more experienced than I am—she was great."

"Hardly," said Margot, laughing.

Ella managed to limp through supper without falling asleep, though she found Margot's and Greg's high spirits grating on her tired mind. Shortly after ten she excused herself, and it was a relief to be back in the privacy of her bedroom. What was wrong with her, she wondered. She should be pleased to see Margot so relaxed, yet somehow she found herself resenting it. There was a stack of work waiting for her on her desk, she knew, despite Tessa's reassurances, and there was a message to phone Jackie in New York, which always meant trouble. Jackie never bothered her unless something was seriously wrong. Then there was the planning of the Fulham project to consider. Suddenly it all seemed too much, and Ella found herself wondering whether she had really taken on too much this time. Jet lag, she told herself firmly—in the morning you'll feel better.

Initially she slept well, but by half past twelve she found herself awake again, restless in mind and body. She decided a drink of milk might help her and was on her way out of the bedroom when she heard Greg coming out of his room. She was about to go out and greet him when something stopped her, and she realized it was the stealth with which he was apparently creeping down the corridor. What was he doing? Where was he going, she wondered. And then in an instant, with a terrible sinking feeling, *she knew.* She waited until she heard the bedroom door click and then, carefully opening her own door, crept along the passage to Margot's room. A dim light showed under the door. Pressing her ear to it, she could hear the sound of whispered voices, punctuated by Margot's crystal-clear laugh.

Ella did not sleep again that night. Her initial reaction was to storm into the bedroom and demand to know what was going on. But she knew what was going on—it had been staring her in the face—and she could not endure the embarrassment and humiliation of confronting her son in Margot's bed. As she lay far from sleep her mind tried to recoil from the obvious facts, but there was no escape. Her eighteen-year-old son was having an affair with a woman Ella knew to be well into her forties. It was inconceivable and disgusting, and above all, Ella felt a deep sense of betrayal. Margot had known of Greg since he was five years old, and she knew only too well how much the boy meant to Ella. To seduce him in his own home while Ella looked on was unforgivable. In calmer moments during that long night Ella tried to reason the other side of the story. Was it such a bad thing, after all? Greg had to learn about women from someone, and Margot was probably very experienced. However, there was no way she could reconcile herself to the relationship, and by morning, hollow-eyed through lack of sleep, Ella was determined to confront them with her knowledge.

Ella was first in the kitchen the following morning. She made coffee and laid the breakfast table, just like on any other morning. Margot appeared next, her hair newly washed, still wearing the casual clothes of yesterday, belying her age. Ella found it difficult to speak at all without her voice sounding waspish, but Margot seemed oblivious.

"Shall I give Greg a call?" she asked.

"No, I'll do it," said Ella sharply.

She had heard Greg return to his bedroom shortly after five o'clock in the morning, and therefore she was not at all surprised to find she had quite a job waking him. In the innocence of sleep, with his dark curls falling into his eyes and his cheeks flushed, he looked little different from the child he had once been. The image fueled Ella's anger so that she was only just able to contain herself long enough for Greg to stagger into breakfast in his robe before she turned on them both. "I know what's going on," she burst out. "You must take me for one hell of a fool to have imagined I wouldn't find out."

"What do you mean—you know what's going on?" Greg said defiantly.

Margot said nothing, but she paled slightly, Ella noticed. "Don't be ridiculous, Greg. You and Margot . . ." She searched for the right words. "I heard you go to her bedroom last night, and I heard what time you came back. Don't tell me you were reading her a bedtime story."

The smile vanished from Greg's face. He glanced apprehensively at Margot, clearly seeking her guidance as to what to say next.

"I'm sorry, Ella," said Margot, "we should have told you about it last night, but you seemed so tired and preoccupied. We weren't going to keep it from you, though, were we, Greg?" Greg shook his head.

"Keep what from me?" Ella said.

"Margot and I are in love," Greg said.

"Oh, don't be ridiculous," said Ella. "There must be nearly thirty year's difference in your ages—it's absolutely revolting."

"Is it?" said Margot quietly. "Why?"

Ella turned her full venom on Margot. "I just don't understand how you could have done this, Margot. I leave you alone with my son for no more than forty-eight hours, and I come back to find that in my own home you have seen fit to seduce him. I may have said 'make yourself at home,' but I didn't mean for you to go this far. I want you to leave, to leave now, and I don't want to see you again."

"As you wish," said Margot. She stood up.

"No, wait," said Greg. "How dare you speak to Margot like this, Mom? She didn't seduce me. If anything, it was the other way around—not that it's any of your damned business."

Ella struck Greg across the cheek. "You're my son, and that makes it my business."

"I don't have to listen to this," said Greg.

"Fine, then—get out," Ella screamed, "get out of here, both of you." Margot moved uncertainly toward the door. "Go," Ella spat out. "Now."

They went, Greg shutting the kitchen door behind him. For a moment Ella stood in stunned silence, and then she collapsed at the kitchen table and burst into tears. She half rose and then returned to sink once more into her chair. She must stay calm and think. Margot was leaving; that was good. When Margot had gone, she would try to explain to Greg why she had reacted as she did. Besides, there was no point in pursuing their relationship—Margot spent most of her working life in London, and Greg would be off to college in five days. Perhaps she had overreacted—yet no; the feeling of outrage was justified. She dried her eyes and poured herself a fresh cup of coffee with shaking hands.

There was a light tap on the kitchen door; it was Greg.

The anger had left him, and his face seemed calm and composed. "I thought I'd better let you know we're going, Mom."

"What do you mean, *we're* going?" Ella said, rising out of her seat.

"Like I said, I'm going with Margot."

For a moment Ella was too stunned to react. "Where?" she said at last, when her strength returned.

"New York—not to Gregory Buildings. I'll be staying with Margot."

"Margot doesn't have an apartment in New York," said Ella.

"No matter. I'll be staying with her."

"Greg, this is madness."

"Mom, don't start again, or we'll both say things we'll regret."

"Where is Margot?" Ella asked.

"She's gone down in the elevator. She felt you and I might want a few moments alone."

"Then let her go, Greg. The sooner she's out of both our lives, the better."

"No," said Greg. "I've already told you I'm going with her."

"What about college? You start college next week," said Ella.

"I can't think about college at the moment, or about the future at all. I just know I don't want to stay here with you, and I do want to go with Margot—that's as far as my thinking takes me."

"Greg, three days ago you hadn't even met her." Ella tried desperately to stay calm.

"So?" said Greg. "Now I have met her, and she's without doubt the most wonderful woman I have ever met and am ever likely to meet."

"You're talking like a child," said Ella. "What can you possibly know about anybody in three days?"

"Exactly," said Greg cheerfully, "that's why I'm aiming to learn a whole lot more. I'll call you." Before Ella could protest further, he had gone across the hall and out the front door.

Ella was too stunned to follow. She picked up her coffee and went to stand by the kitchen window. Her legs felt weak, almost too weak to hold her. She clung to the windowsill for support. Of all the women she knew, it seemed to Ella that Margot Haigh was the most unlikely candidate to be having an affair with her son. She was so cool, so remote, so confident and self-assured as to where she was going, so certain that right was on her side. Throughout their association it had seemed to Ella that Margot was her rock, the yardstick against which she judged the rights and wrongs of the commercial world. That was a laugh. How could Margot have just walked out of the apartment, taking her teenage son with her without even a word? But Margot Haigh was a woman who knew what she wanted—and always got it. With a sinking heart Ella realized that, at the moment, Margot wanted her son.

Chapter 28

Ella replaced the receiver and sat down at her desk, glad that Tessa was not there to witness the call she had just received. It had been Greg, calling to tell her the astonishing news that he and Margot were now in London and that he was living at her house in Chelsea.

While Ella had viewed her son's encounter with Margot as likely to have an unsettling effect on him, it had never occurred to her that he would go to London with her. For one thing, there was the practical difficulty—he did not have the money, so clearly Margot must have paid for his airline ticket. The thought distressed Ella still further. Margot was treating her son quite literally like a toy and wrecking his life in the process. But it was the speed with which her son had walked out of the life they had mapped out together so carefully that astonished her. Ten days before, Greg had just been a normal boy like any other, humoring his doting mother with a few days at home before going off to college—confident, happy about his future, and generally at peace with the world. Now he had thrown it all aside—for what? An affair with a woman older than his own mother. The stupidity and the waste of it was upsetting enough, but in the brief telephone call from Greg, Ella felt sure she had sensed his own bewilderment. He did not seem to know what had hit him either. How could Margot have done this? For a moment Ella considered telephoning her, but there seemed little point. Margot was not going to relinquish her hold on Greg in response to an impassioned telephone plea from his mother. It would take more, a lot more, to shake him free of Margot's clutches.

Slowly, as Ella sat there, her mind cleared, and a plan emerged. She studied it from all angles and considered the pros and cons with steely detachment. In business, despite her childlike appearance, Ella could be as ruthless as anyone, particularly if she felt threatened. But no one had ever threatened her son, and she recognized at that moment that there was nothing she would not do in order to protect him.

"Who?" said an astounded voice.

"Ella, Ella Kovac. Surely you haven't forgotten me already."

"Ella!" Michael Gresham's voice sounded stunned and totally disbelieving, but he rallied quickly, his Irish charm rising to the occasion. "I knew this morning when I got out of bed that it was going to be a good day. It's really great to hear from you, Ella. You're doing real well in this town—

the mall's taking shape, isn't it? I pass it every day on the way to work."

Ella let him ramble on for a few moments. "Michael, I need a favor. Could you join me for lunch so we can discuss it?"

"I never expected to hear from you again," Michael said as they settled down in a corner of the restaurant. "What can I do for you?"

"I need someone to keep an eye on the Houston operation for me while I'm in London for the next few weeks."

Michael smiled. "Is that all?"

"It's enough," said Ella. "I wouldn't ask you, but I don't know who else I can rely upon in Houston. I have a good girl working for me down here named Tessa, who operates from my apartment, but she only has the experience to deal with the more mundane problems at the moment. Jackie is fully occupied keeping New York going, and it's not the kind of responsibility I can hand over to just anyone. Do you see my problem?"

"How long do you expect to be away?" Michael asked.

"I need to stay for about three weeks total, but it wouldn't be worthwhile coming back to Houston in between appointments unless there's a real crisis. I'm not intending this to be a favor—I expect you to charge me the right rate for the job," said Ella firmly.

"If that's the case," said Michael, "then I will charge you fees. I'll put one of my clerks quite specifically in charge of your business, and we'll set the whole thing up as a proper commercial relationship. If we do that, you won't find it difficult to call on me whenever you need me. What do you say?"

"It's a good idea," said Ella. "I am grateful, Michael, truly."

He grinned. "It's what friends and lawyers are for."

They spent the rest of the afternoon running through Ella's various Houston projects with Tessa in the office.

Tessa and Michael got along right away, and Ella made a mental note to warn her of the dangers of Michael Gresham's charms. By six o'clock that evening Ella knew her business was in good hands.

"How about dinner?" Michael suggested. "Just to seal the agreement."

Ella shook her head. "Thanks but no thanks. I don't want to start all that again."

"OK, it was just a thought. You'll call just as soon as you reach London?"

"Yes, of course," said Ella. "I'm flying up to New York tomorrow morning. I'll spend a couple of days there, and I aim to be in London by the weekend." And I'm going to find out all there is to know about Margot Haigh, she added silently. There's something odd about that woman, about her past. I'm sure of it, I feel it. I'm going to find out what it is, and when I find it I'm going to use it to break her hold on Greg.

Her thoughts were venomous, but she smiled warmly at Michael as she said good-bye.

Alone in her apartment, Ella went through the motions of packing up for her return to New York. She sat on the edge of her bed, going over and over in her mind the alternative ways of handling the Greg/Margot affair. Yet all her instincts told her it was a relationship she must break, and fast; and if that was the case, then she recognized pleading with Greg was pointless. It was Margot she had to get to, Margot she had to destroy, if necessary, for the sake of her son.

Sitting there alone, she was suddenly filled with longing for Aaron. The last time there had been trouble between herself and Greg, Alice and Aaron had been there to help, to act as a buffer, to give them security and reassurance against which to act out their difficulties. The more she thought about it, the more the idea grew. Why not once again turn to Aaron for help? After all, wasn't he Greg's godfather? Wasn't William Greg's best friend? They would be able to counsel and advise her as to whether she was doing the right thing. Indeed, they might well have some influence over

Greg in a way she had not. It occurred to Ella that they might already know about Margot. After all, Greg had spent some days with her in New York, and it would seem unlikely that he had failed to tell his best friend he would not be going to college after all. Relief flooded through her. She would call Aaron now and meet him, perhaps tomorrow, for lunch maybe, in a restaurant—somewhere safe and neutral. Talking about Greg's problems would help them to start communicating again, help them to reestablish their relationship on its old footing, or perhaps—she hardly dared form the thought—perhaps there might be a future for them after all. She found herself smiling as she lifted the receiver and dialed the familiar number.

The phone rang for some time, and she was on the point of putting it down when a female voice answered, unmistakably young, girlish almost. "Hello, Dr. Connors' apartment. How may I help you?" The voice was mocking and amused.

Ella stumbled over the words. "Could I speak to Dr. Connors, please?"

"I'm sorry, but he's in the bathtub right now. Can I ask him to call you back?" There was definite laughter in her voice.

Ella was stunned. "No, no, it's all right."

"Whatever you say. Bye." The phone went dead.

Ella replaced the receiver slowly. So Aaron had a new woman in his life. The thought brought a pain so sharp it momentarily took her breath away. How could he? She forgot all about Alice; all she could think was how Aaron had betrayed her love, her caring over all the long years they had known each other. So . . . he did not love her and clearly saw no future for them. At least she now knew his position, and in a way it was a kind of release. She was free to concentrate on Greg now, and certainly she could manage without Aaron Connors' help. This fight was a personal one to save her son. She did not need anybody to tell her she was doing the right thing; she knew she was. It was a battle she had to win, and instinctively she knew she could.

Chapter 29

London—*November 1981*

To Ella, seated with some distaste on the only decent chair in the scruffy, dirty, little office, Toby Paradise, standing by the window, hands in pockets, seemed quite at ease. Yet all his concentration was aimed at avoiding the betrayal of his pounding headache—the legacy of last night's session at the local pub. Toby winced at the light coming in from the window but remained standing in front of it for a few more seconds to collect his thoughts before attempting to deal with this wretched woman and her apparently wayward son.

"OK," he said, "what do you want?" His voice was gravelly and deep, the result of too many cigarettes, too many late nights, and too much booze. He stared at Ella aggressively, and her heart sank. She had acted on a whim, asking Stephanie's advice as to whether she could recommend a private investigator. She did not know whom else to ask, and she had been surprised when Stephanie instantly gave her a name and a recommendation. "I use him when I need commercial information," Stephanie had said. "He's not a particularly savory character, but he's good." Ella had been anxious not to prolong the conversation, in case Stephanie asked her why she wanted the help of a private investigator, and so this was the extent of the information she had on the man who was to set her plans in motion.

Now she cleared her throat, suddenly reluctant to begin. "M-my eighteen-year-old son was due to start college last week," she said. "I left him in my apartment in Houston briefly while I came over to London on business. On my return I found that he was having an affair with a colleague of mine—a merchant banker. She's half English, half Korean, and she's in her mid-forties." Toby Paradise showed no surprise whatsoever, so Ella continued, slightly encouraged. "When I made an attempt to break up the relationship, my son simply left home. He's now living in London, with the woman. He's lost his chance to go to college this year, and I'm worried about him, both on moral grounds and because he's clearly thrown away his future."

"If he's eighteen," said Toby, "I suppose the law can't help you."

"No," said Ella, "that's not the way I want to handle it. The only way I can split them up is to get at the woman. Her name is Margot Haigh, she's a director of Joshkers Bank, she's single, and she's something of an enigma. I've known her for twelve, thirteen years. She handles most of my commercial banking, but I don't know much about her. I have a feeling that the reason she is so private about her personal life is that she has something to hide. I want you to find out what that something is, and then I can confront her with it."

"Blackmail, you mean?" said Toby Paradise.

Ella was instantly on the defensive. "I'm not asking you to make a moral judgment, Mr. Paradise, I'm simply asking whether you want the job or not."

"Yes, I know." He flipped open a pack of cigarettes and offered one to Ella. She shook her head. "I just like to get my facts straight. You want me to dig up some dirt on Miss Haigh, something sufficiently juicy that you can threaten to disclose unless she gets the hell out of your son's life. Am I right?"

"Yes," said Ella. She looked at him doubtfully. "Will you take the job?"

"Tell me, why the hell don't you just let your boy have his fling? Sounds to me like he's having a great time."

"It's not that simple," said Ella.

"Isn't it?" Toby Paradise drew heavily on his cigarette. "Far be it from me to talk myself out of a job, but it seems to me you're getting a little uptight here. Kids grow up, they make their own mistakes. Sometimes overprotection rebounds. It's you who may get hurt—hell, if he finds out about this, he may never speak to you again."

"Do you have any children, Mr. Paradise?" There was an edge to Ella's voice.

"Yes, I have two. I'm divorced from their mother, so I don't see them that much, but I know for sure that when my son's eighteen I'm not going to start telling him who he should be sleeping with."

Ella stood up brusquely. "Perhaps I'd better find somebody else to handle this case."

For a moment Toby was tempted to let her go, but the woman intrigued him. She was his sort of woman—small, petite, and absurdly young-looking to have a child of eighteen. "You can go somewhere else if you wish," he said, "but I'll get the information you want, and I'm cheap." He looked around his tiny office. "As you can see, my overhead is low."

For a moment Ella hesitated, and then she smiled. There was something oddly appealing about the man—his total honesty, perhaps. As she watched him, he put his hand on the back of the chair in which she had been sitting as if to steady himself. "Are you feeling OK, Mr. Paradise?"

He grinned at her. "Actually, no, I feel dreadful. I had an affair with a whiskey bottle last night. Black coffee and a run around the park is probably what I need. What I *want* is some more of the same. How about you and me adjourning to the pub around the corner? You can tell me all you know about this Margot Haigh while I sort out the demands of my liver. What do you say?"

"It sounds like a sensible plan," said Ella.

St. Annes Road, Reading, depressed Toby Paradise beyond belief. It had seen better days—the Victorian terraced houses must have been attractive once, and they could be again, but currently they were trapped in lower-middle-class respectability. He was disappointed. Although Ella Kovac had been unable to provide him with a photograph of Margot Haigh, he saw her as an exotic bloom. He envisaged a willowy, exotic creature with pale olive skin—an image very much at odds with the environment in which he found himself. Heaving a sigh, he threw a cigarette butt into the gutter and walked up the impossibly neat path to number nine.

The bell, when he rang it, had the chime of an ice-cream van and made him shudder. There was a long pause, followed at last by hurrying footsteps, accompanied by the distant sound of a wailing baby. A girl opened the door. "I was looking for Mrs. Haigh," he said reproachfully.

She looked blank for a moment, and then her brow cleared. "Oh, Mrs. Haigh. She died a year back. We bought the house from her estate." The baby's howls in the background grew to a fever pitch. She glanced over her shoulder.

"Do you know anything about the Haigh family? I'm trying to trace them."

The girl shook her head. "No," she said. "I knew of them, of course—I've lived around here all my life. Mrs. Haigh just had the one son. His name's Terry. He lives in London somewhere, but I don't have the address."

"And a daughter?"

"You mean the girl from Korea?"

"Yes, that's the one."

"I don't know anything about her. She was very clever. I think she left these parts a long time ago. You might have a word with Dick Simpson. He should be able to help."

"Dick?" Toby queried, his spirits rising slightly.

"He was a friend of Terry's. Well, still is. They were at school together, and then in the army. They were both stationed in Korea, I'm sure, and it was there, you know, that Terry came across Margot and brought her back for his mum to adopt. I bet Dick will be able to help."

"Where can I find him?" Toby asked.

"Well, he's a boozer. He can never keep a job because of the drink. He'll be down the Coach and Horses in a quarter of an hour, and then you'll have difficulty getting any sense out of him for the rest of the day. That's how I know about him, really—my uncle runs the Coach and Horses."

Toby brightened visibly. Clearly, this Dick Simpson had potential. "Can you tell me where I can find him now?"

The street in which Dick Simpson lived was depressingly like St. Annes Road, except that it was not as well maintained. The gate leading to Dick Simpson's house was hanging off its hinges, and there was a broken pane in the window of the front room. When Toby pressed the bell nothing happened. He attacked a rather dilapidated door knocker instead.

Dick Simpson was a big man; he towered over Toby. He had a hefty frame that once must have been very powerful but had now gone to seed. His paunch lapped well over his belt, and his expansive face was purple and puffy. Nonetheless, the clear blue eyes that gazed out from between the folds of flesh were friendly and amused. This man might be going to seed, but he knew what he was doing and was enjoying the process. Toby warmed to him instantly. "Dick Simpson?"

"Yeah, that's right."

"Look, I was given your name because I need some information on Margot Haigh."

"Margot, really? Why?" The eyes were shrewd, and instantly Toby sensed that his prepared story would be not so easily accepted by this man. He needed to stall for time and blunt Dick's perceptions with a few drinks before he explained the situation. "Look," said Toby, "it's a long, complicated story, but I gather you're the man I should be talking to. Is there a local pub around here where we could have a few drinks and discuss it?"

Dick's face lit up. "A man after my own heart—wait there, I'll fetch my coat."

Two pints of beer and two rum chasers later, Toby judged Dick Simpson was ready to talk without demanding a lot of explanations.

"Tell me about the first time you met Margot," Toby said. "No, wait, let me get in another round of drinks."

Settled in at a corner of the bar, Dick Simpson began. "It was a bastard of a war—before your time, I should think."

"I was a kid," Toby said, "but I remember reading about it."

"There were dreadful atrocities—the commies, they were bastards, worse than the Japanese in World War II. The things they did to people. The North Koreans poured into South Korea, and we—that is, the United Nations Force—moved in to sort out the mess. Everyone suffered."

"I take it you didn't enjoy your time in Korea?"

"Not bloody likely," said Dick. "It's a terrible country. Boiling hot in summer—move so much as a muscle and you broke out in a sweat—and freezing in winter. The water supplies were always short, and if you were lucky enough to avoid a communist bullet, you caught every sort of goddam awful disease known to man. It was hell." He took a long swig of beer. "Terry and I were lucky. We were with the Royal Engineers. We saw plenty of action, but a lot of our work involved building bridges and so on. It was late in the war when we met Margot—three months before the end, perhaps four. We found her when we were on patrol one day, four or five miles from Seoul. She was terrified, poor child, starving and in rags. She did not know whether we were friends or enemies. In fact, Terry had quite a job catching her. She tried to run away from us."

"How old was she?"

Dick hesitated. "Twelve, as it turned out, but she was so tall she looked older. That was because she was only half Korean, of course—her father was English."

"How come she was in such a state?"

"Her parents had been killed in a bombing raid of Seoul, and she had nowhere to go. There were thousands of kids like that who were lost. Our job was to repair a road that particular day, and we hadn't time to mess around with kids, but she was in such a pitiful state we took her along. She stayed with us for nearly a week, eating what we ate, living as we lived. We dressed her in some spare army uniform. Terry got to be very protective toward her. Of course, she was different from the local girls, because she spoke perfect English. She was actually quite helpful to us with her knowledge of the area. After about a week, as I say, we went back to base, and we handed her over to the WVS, reckoning it was the safest place for her."

Toby looked blank. "The WVS?"

"Women's Voluntary Service. They were nice girls, wonderful girls. They were literally responsible for the army's welfare. They wrote letters home for some of the boys who couldn't write, listened to our problems, advised on girlfriends, ran the canteen, and organized entertainment for us . . . bloody good they were at it, too. Anyway, Margot stayed on with them. The war ended, but Terry and I didn't feel ready to go home, so we spent our leave in Japan, returning to Korea for a few months to join the United Nations Peacekeeping Force."

"Stop there," said Toby. "I'll get another round of drinks."

"You know something? You're a real gentleman," Dick insisted.

"So when you came back from leave, after the war, you obviously met up with Margot again?" Toby continued his questioning as he set down two more pints.

"Oh, yeah. Well, when we came back from Japan the war was over. We had more time on our hands, of course, and so we went to see how she was getting on. She was still with the WVS. Anyway, we took her out a few times, and then she told us her one idea was to go to England. She said Korea was finished for her now her parents were dead, and her father had always told her so much about England, she thought she would like to go there. I thought it was just a kid's pipe dream, but Terry took it very seriously. Anyway, eventually he fixed it up, and she came over to England in a troop ship and was adopted by his mother. They soon found out at school what a bright kid she was—she had only been in England five years when she went to Oxford University. She had a lot of determination, that one."

"Do you see her much now?"

"No, I'm not in her league anymore. She sees Terry, though, regular enough. She goes to visit his wife and family—takes the kids presents, that sort of thing."

"You must give me Terry's address. I'd like to go and talk to him." It took some minutes to extract the address from Dick Simpson. His hand was shaking too much to write now, and his eyes seemed barely to focus.

It was time to go—there was clearly nothing more he was going to get out of Dick Simpson. The guy was almost asleep, lolling back in his chair. Toby stood up and then hesitated as a thought struck him. "Dick, there's one thing I don't understand. How come she calls herself Margot Haigh? I would have thought she'd have kept her father's name. After all, she was twelve when he died—it wasn't like she was adopted as a little kid."

Dick's eyes opened. "Well, that *was* her name, wasn't it? Having married Terry, his name became hers."

"Married Terry!" Toby said. "When did she do that?"

"While we were still in Korea. She left the WVS, and she and Terry married. They lived in a little flat—a nice little place on the outskirts of Seoul."

Toby sat down again. "But I thought you said she was twelve when you found her—at that rate, she couldn't have been much more than thirteen when she got married." Clearly in his drunken state Dick had gotten his facts wrong.

Dick Simpson's eyes suddenly snapped into focus. "I'm not supposed to talk about the marriage," he said, like a small child who's been caught doing something wrong. "Forget what I said about the marriage."

Toby put a hand on Dick's arm. "Look, we're pals, right? I'm not going to tell anybody anything you tell me."

"No, no, that's right, we're pals."

"Would you like another drink, Dick?"

"Yeah, I would."

On Toby's return from the bar Dick was asleep, and it took some time to wake him up. "About this marriage," Toby said, carefully. "How come it happened if she was so young?"

"She lied about her age," said Dick. "She had no papers, of course—they'd all been destroyed in the bombing. She said she was seventeen, and she looked it, too. It was only when we got back to England that the truth of her age came out. Terry's mum saw through the girl at once—realized how young she was—and of course she was terrified her boy would end up in prison for—well, you know . . . with an underage girl. Mrs. Haigh kept the girl with her, made her son leave home, and legally adopted Margot."

"So the marriage was never annulled?"

"I don't know," said Dick. "I shouldn't think so. No one knew about it in this country, you see, except me, and I wasn't telling."

"Oh, no, of course not," said Toby. Dick was drifting off to sleep, and Toby judged it was time to leave before he was asked to make any promises of silence. "See you around, Dick," he said, and then he made a fast exit out of the door.

In the car on the M4 on the way back up to London Toby Paradise's mind was racing. If Terry Haigh had married Margot in Korea, was the marriage valid in England? If Terry Haigh had not acknowledged the existence of a Korean marriage in Britain and had subsequently remarried, that marriage might well be bigamous. Margot Haigh had never married, so there was no hope of bringing pressure to bear there. However, the fact was that Terry Haigh had. This in itself did not give Ella Kovac the ammunition she wanted, unless Margot was particularly fond of Terry and wished to protect him and his wife from any scandal. Yes, there was the possible weakness—Margot might well have a great feeling of affection for Terry. After all, he had saved her life, and he had made it possible for her to come to England; when the truth of her age had come out into the open, he had even left home to give her the benefit of his mother's care. The next stage in his investigation was clear—first he had to find out the validity of a Korean marriage in England. Second, he had to visit Terry Haigh.

* * *

It took Toby Paradise a week to obtain the information he needed, a week during which Ella rang him daily, sometimes twice daily, for a progress report. His patience began to wear thin. "Look, if I try and push the Korean Embassy anymore, they'll shut up like a clam. They're already deeply suspicious of me. They wouldn't tell me a damned thing until I'd given them my life story."

A week to the day from when he had first approached the Korean Embassy, Toby had the information he wanted—a marriage had indeed taken place between Terry Haigh and Margot Stephenson on July 15, 1954. It was a formal, civil service, properly registered, and a marriage certificate had been issued. Margot and Terry, it appeared, had been legally married and were still legally married today.

Toby had been sitting in his car outside Terry Haigh's house in Forest Hills since seven o'clock that morning. He had seen what had to be Terry go off to work, dutifully kissed and waved good-bye to by his wife. He had then seen the wife take their two children to school, returning with a basket of shopping shortly before ten—coffee time, he gauged. He allowed her a quarter of an hour to unpack her shopping on returning home and then crossed the street and rang the doorbell.

June Haigh was a pleasant-looking woman with a gentle and homely face. "I wonder if I could talk to you about Margot Haigh for a few minutes. I'm from Joshkers Bank," Toby began.

"Margot! Is something wrong? Is she ill, has she been hurt?"

"No, no, nothing like that. As a matter of fact, I was rather hoping for your help, because we want to make her a special presentation." It was gratifying to see that June Haigh was completely taken in.

"Why don't you come in and have some coffee?" she said. "I'm just making some." They sat comfortably at the kitchen table. "Of course, it's Terry you should be talking to, really. Margot's his sister, you know—well, at least she was adopted by his mother. Terry rescued her from Korea."

"So I understand," said Toby. "I expect they're very close."

"Oh, yes, Terry thinks the world of Margot," the woman confided, without a trace of jealousy in her voice. "Actually, I'm very proud of what he did for her—rescuing her from that terrible place. Just look what she's become . . . and you say she's going to be made a partner in the bank?" Toby nodded. "That's wonderful. Mind you, she's earned it—it's not just that she's clever. She's always worked hard, too."

"It's a shame she's never married," said Toby conversationally.

"Yes, that's what I always say to Terry, that she ought to settle down. He says she's not the marrying kind, but I think every woman is underneath, don't you?"

"I wouldn't know," said Toby.

The woman's conversation drifted along as she racked her brain for a suitable gift for Margot. "The trouble is, you see, she's got everything. I don't know what she earns at that bank, but it must be a lot of money. She's always giving the kids wonderful presents."

"Does she visit you often?" Toby asked.

"Oh, yes. On the first Sunday in every month she comes down for lunch, and at Christmas, and on her birthday. I often say to Terry I can't understand why she bothers with us. That always makes him angry. He says it's because she's very fond of us, because we're the only family she's got."

"Don't you think he's right?"

"I suppose so," said June Haigh.

It was clear to Toby that as far as June was concerned, Margot might just as well be a Martian—they moved in totally different worlds.

Toby watched Ella over the rim of his wine glass. They were sitting in a wine bar just off Sloane Street. Ella did not look as pleased with his news as Toby had expected. To him, the case was all wrapped up. She was silent for some time. "Are you sure this is enough?" she said at last.

"Absolutely," said Toby. "In my view, Margot will do anything to protect Terry. All you have to say to her is that unless she leaves your son alone, you'll tell June Haigh the true nature of her relationship with Terry. They are a very respectable little family, Miss Kovac. I know the social structure is different in America, but here in England there is a class of people to whom being respectable is of the ultimate importance, and the Haighs fall into that category. If June Haigh was to find out that not only was her husband's sister his former wife, but also that her own marriage is bigamous and her children illegitimate, it would finish her—and Terry, too, come to that."

"But he already *knows,*" Ella protested.

"Yes," said Toby, "he knows, and it's probably the one guilty secret of his life. I haven't met the guy, but he sounds to me like a pillar of the establishment. He works in a local bank, he's a good husband and father—a rather dull, not very intelligent man who had just one moment of glory when he married an exotic thirteen-year-old thirty-odd years ago. I don't have any doubt that it's something that makes him feel quite proud—at any rate, it gives him a thrill in private—but at the same time, the thought of his wife ever finding out must horrify him. Am I getting through?"

"Frankly, it sounds very condescending to me," said Ella.

"Maybe it does, but those are the facts. June Haigh's world and that of her husband would be completely destroyed by the knowledge you now have. While you may not have the imagination to see it, Miss Kovac, I bet my reputation and my fees on the fact that Margot Haigh does."

Chapter 30

She recognized she must be very nervous, for she never drank at lunchtime. Yet here she was helping herself to a gin and tonic, and the hand that held the glass was none too steady. Margot, drink in hand, walked to the sitting room window and checked yet again for a sight of Ella coming up the street. It was stupid; she was not due for another ten minutes, and there were plenty of things she could be doing while she waited.

It had surprised Margot that Ella was willing to come to her home, where she must know Greg was now living. She could not guess what Ella had to say but imagined her preference would have been for neutral ground for their talk. As it happened, Greg was away for the day. Now that her holiday was over, Margot had welcomed his suggestion that he visit the Irvines for the day while she was working, which had made it possible to meet Ella here in Flood Street. Perhaps Ella was right; perhaps it was better to talk of Greg in private.

Greg. Margot turned the image of him over in her mind—the dark, curly hair, the strong, square jaw, the youthful, muscular frame. Greg's youthful demands on her body, which left her weak and shaken, represented an entirely new experience—indeed, he was already master in the bedroom. Yet outside it he had a vulnerability that she found almost unbearably touching. It surprised her. Being a strong person herself, Margot had always respected strength in others, yet she reveled in Greg's dependence upon her.

She had been late for work this morning on two counts. Greg had forced her back to bed from the breakfast table when she had been all ready to leave. Then, seconds before she tried to leave for a second time, he had admitted he was nervous about getting lost at Paddington Station—which train should he catch, how would he find out, where would he get his ticket? Margot could not understand why this had not irritated her. Instead it had pleased her to the point where she had taken a taxi with him to Paddington and seen him onto the right train, thus making herself later for work than she had ever been in her life.

So what was Greg Kovac in her life—her lover or her son? In an effort to try to bring some sort of realism to the situation, at times she tried to equate the man in whose arms she lay with the little boy who had so dominated Ella Kovac's early working life and who Margot had always thought of as a tiresome waste of Ella's undoubted talents and energies. As hard as she tried, she could not force the two separate personalities to become one in her mind, although she knew they were so. She wondered now, standing by the window, what she should say to his mother. This woman who over the years had become, if not exactly a friend, certainly more than just a bank customer. What could she say to Ella—I love your son? No, it was not possible; it was not possible because Margot herself could not yet face the truth of her emotions.

The doorbell rang, making her jump. Ella must have come up the garden path without her even noticing. She must have seen her standing in the window, drink in hand—it was not a promising start. Taking a hefty swig, Margot went to the door and opened it.

Margot had not known what to expect, but certainly Ella's appearance took her by surprise. She seemed neither dragged down nor depressed by the apparent loss of her only child. Indeed, it was impossible to look at Ella and envisage her as Greg's mother. She was dressed casually, as usual, in tight jeans, a big, baggy sweater, and sneakers. The curls framing her face were shiny and bright. She wore little makeup, and apart from a slight tiredness around the eyes, she looked like a healthy college kid. Her appearance only served to heighten in Margot's mind the ludicrous nature of the situation. She had lost count of the times over the years that she and Ella had met. In the past she had always enjoyed the upper hand because she had something Ella wanted. Now the roles were reversed—or were they?

"Would you like a drink?" Margot asked. "I was just having one."

"No, thanks," said Ella.

Margot looked longingly at the gin, discarded on the mantelpiece. "Won't you sit down?" she said.

"No," said Ella, "this won't take long."

"I assume you've come about Greg?"

"You bet I've come about Greg," said Ella. "I'm here because I want you to give him up. At the moment he's unlikely to listen to reason from me or anyone else. The only way your relationship is going to end is if you tell him that it's over, that you don't care for him anymore, that you've had your fling, and that he's about as exciting as yesterday's news."

"You don't seriously expect me to do that," said Margot.

"I most certainly do, but not because I'm relying on your sweet nature." Ella's voice was cold with loathing, and Margot shivered involuntarily. "I know the sort of person you are, Margot. I don't know why you chose to pick on my son, but I recognize that for some reason he has an attraction for you right now. This is just another case of your wanting something and just taking it. Are you aware that you're ruining his life?"

"I don't see it that way," said Margot. "You'd mapped out his future for him, as you saw it. You've never been prepared to listen to him."

"I don't want to hear all this crap," Ella said caustically. "You're not interested in Greg's welfare, and I'm not going to make any attempt to appeal to you as a mother, because it's pointless. My feelings, Greg's feelings, are not relevant to you."

"Then why are you here?"

"To fight you—to fight dirty, if I have to—in order to get my boy back."

"You're talking in riddles, Ella," said Margot. "I don't understand what you're saying."

"Let me spell it out," said Ella. "I've had a private investigator working on you and your past, and what he has told me is enough to ensure that in order for me to keep my mouth shut, you're going to have to agree to my demands and kiss Greg good-bye."

She felt a tightening in her chest; her mouth went dry. She turned away so that Ella could not see her expression and walked over to the window. "So I gather we're talking about blackmail. Is that right, Ella?"

"I can't think of another word for it," said Ella.

"Then you'd better tell me what skeleton in my closet you wish to parade for public scrutiny."

"Not public scrutiny exactly," said Ella. "What I have discovered is that Terry Haigh's marriage is bigamous—is bigamous because he married a thirteen-year-old girl in Korea named Margot Stephenson. I know the marriage was hushed up as soon as you arrived in this country, but I also know that the marriage was never annulled, and that technically you and Terry are still married."

So that was it. For a moment, all Margot could feel was relief. "I can't see that your information is of any interest to anyone. Neither Terry nor I are exactly celebrities, and I can hardly imagine the *News of the World* getting very worked up about the story." Her voice was full of contempt.

"I wasn't thinking of the *News of the World,*" said Ella, "I was thinking about June Haigh, Terry's so-called wife, and of their kids. How do you think June's going to feel when she learns that Terry's sister is not his sister after all, that she herself is not his wife, and that their kids are illegitimate? Think about it for a moment, Margot, put yourself in June's shoes, in her little world. How do you think she's going to feel?"

Margot stared at Ella in astonishment. "You mean to say

that you are prepared to tell June all you know about my past in order to persuade me to leave your son alone?"

"That's about it," said Ella.

"I honestly think you've judged this wrong, Ella. OK, so it would come as a shock to June, but she and Terry love each other, and they'd soon adjust. After all, my marriage to Terry was only a marriage of convenience to get me into the country—she has no reason to feel threatened by it."

"That's not what Dick Simpson says," said Ella. "He says you and Terry were shacked up in a little flat on the outskirts of Seoul, all very cozy. June and Terry's daughter is thirteen now, I believe. Try telling June that her husband used to have sex with a girl the same age his own daughter is now. I think that's pushing her understanding a little far, don't you? In fact, Margot, I'd go further—I guess the truth would destroy their lives."

Margot slowly raised her eyes and met Ella's. They were steely and determined; there was no room for negotiation. "How will I know that you won't use this information you have again?"

"You have my word," said Ella. Margot waved her hand dismissively and turned away. "Come on," said Ella. "In all the years we've known each other, I've never let you down, have I? I have never misled you in any way, bullshitted you around. I've always been straight."

"I'd like to think about your proposal," said Margot coldly. "I'll call you later tonight or tomorrow morning."

"You've got twenty-four hours," said Ella. "If we can wrap this up by the weekend, I can still get Greg back for college. I'll wait for your call. I'm staying at the Meyer Hotel."

Margot shut the front door and leaned a burning forehead against it. "Would you understand if I told you I loved your son, if I told you just what you were asking me to give up?" she said to the empty room.

When Greg burst through the front door the cold night air had whipped color into his cheeks, and he seemed more alive and vibrant than anyone Margot had ever met. "Wow, what a great day," he said, kissing her soundly on the lips, then walking past her into the kitchen. "They haven't changed a bit," he shouted. "The Irvines, I mean. Well, Tim hasn't—he's exactly the same. The girls . . . they're all grown up. Millie is incredibly sophisticated, and Belinda, she's just as sweet as ever." He came into the sitting room carrying a beer. "Tim has done a great deal to the farm. He's even bought back some of the land they sold years ago, and . . . is something wrong?"

The carefree expression died on his face, and Margot mourned its passing with an almost physical pain. She knew she would not see it again, for she was just about to murder his youthful exuberance. "Yes," she said.

He put down his beer instantly and tried to slip his arms around her. She pushed him away, and instantly he looked hurt and bewildered. "What's wrong?"

"I have something rather unpleasant to say, and frankly, I'm not looking forward to it."

"What is it?" said Greg.

"You and I are finished." Margot met his eye. Inside she was screaming, but on the outside she was icy cold.

"You're kidding." He smiled a little tremulously. "Is this some sort of joke?"

"No joke. It was a mistake, your coming to London. You were so keen on it I didn't want to disappoint you, but you don't fit into my world, Greg—you're too young, too unsophisticated. For example, I should be at a dinner with some customers tonight, but I couldn't take you along—it wouldn't be right."

"Why not?" Greg challenged. "Because of our age difference?"

"It's not as simple as our age difference. Look, I—I don't know how to put this . . ."

"Try me," said Greg.

"Well, you want to make a career out of life in the country—on a farm, something like that."

"Yes," said Greg. "Is that wrong?"

"No, it's not wrong—in fact, I think you'd be well suited to it. I suppose what I—I'm really saying, Greg, is that you have rather a country hick mentality already, and I guess—well, I'd be ashamed to have you meet my colleagues. You're so naïve."

"Ashamed!" Color suffused his face. "You weren't ashamed of me last night in the sack."

"That's different. You're great in bed, Greg—it's outside of bed that things are not so good."

Greg stared at her, one hand plucking at the edge of his jacket. "I don't get this, Margot, I don't understand. Everything was so great between us this morning."

"Great for you, maybe, but not for me. I want you out of my life, Greg, and I want you out now. It so happens that your mother's in London. I suggest that you call her and sort out a passage home."

"My mother! So Mom put you up to this?"

"No, your mother and I aren't speaking at the moment. I only happen to know she's in London because she rang a colleague of mine today about a business matter, and he mentioned it in passing. She's staying at the Meyer Hotel."

"I'm not going to Mom—no way."

"Greg, you have no choice," said Margot with forced weariness. "You have no money, no means of supporting yourself, and no home here in England. Mothers are a pain in the neck, but she'll welcome you back with open arms, you know that. She warned you I was a shit—all you have to do is tell her she was right."

"I want a full explanation, I want to understand what's made you react like this. Somebody somewhere must have put pressure on you."

"Nobody's putting any pressure on me, Greg. I'm forty-two years old, I make my own decisions, and I've made one just now." She got up and walked purposefully into the bedroom. "I've packed your things." She picked up his luggage and carried it out into the sitting room. "I'll call you a cab."

"No." Greg seized her arm.

"Yes," she thundered back. "You go without a fuss or I'll call the police."

His face went from red to deathly white. "You mean it," he said incredulously.

"I mean it," said Margot. She shook herself free from him and walked to the telephone. Greg watched in a stunned silence as she dialed the number. When she had finished the call she turned to him. "It'll be here in two or three minutes."

"Did I do something stupid?" he asked. "Did I upset you in some way, did I say the wrong thing? For Christ's sake, Margot, tell me—you owe that much to me."

"You said or did nothing wrong, Greg, it's simply what you are—a kid straight out of school. We had some fun, but the party's over. Call it a holiday romance—that's how you should look on it."

"But I love you," said Greg simply.

Just for a moment Margot nearly weakened. All her instincts cried out to throw her arms around him and tell him how much she loved him. "Love!" she scoffed. "What the hell do you know about love at eighteen years old? I'm the first woman you ever had, remember? All you're suffering from is a severe case of lust."

"Stop it, stop it," said Greg, "I won't have you talk about us like this. It wasn't like that, it wasn't." There were tears in his eyes now, childish tears, and she could not bear to watch them. They stood on opposite sides of the room, each locked in an individual world of misery. They were released by the sound of the taxi outside.

Margot went to the door and opened it. "She's at the Meyer Hotel," she repeated. "Have you enough money for the taxi fare?" It was the final insult, as it was intended to be.

"You bitch, you heartless bitch," Greg said as he stumbled out into the darkness.

"Miss Kovac, please."

Ella answered the phone before it had barely rung—she must have been sitting over it, willing it to ring, Margot thought. "Your son is on his way over," she said, her voice completely devoid of emotion.

"Back for good?"

"I don't know about for good. You'll have to sort out your own relationship, but he's finished with me."

"What did you tell him?" Ella asked.

"It's none of your goddam business," said Margot, "but I didn't mention you, as we agreed. All I said was that I knew you were in London because you rang a colleague of mine at the bank today about a business matter, but he's not thinking straight at the moment, so I doubt you'll be cross-examined."

"I don't see that I need to say thank you," said Ella, "but thank you anyway."

"Go easy on him, Ella," Margot managed before she slammed down the phone.

Ella stared at the receiver in her hand. Margot had sounded quite choked, but it had to be because she couldn't cope with failing to get her own way, Ella reasoned. Still, this was not the time to think about Margot—Greg was coming back, Greg was on his way home.

Chapter 31

Paris—*Christmas Eve, 1984*

The scene was the very model of elegance and romance; it could have been lifted straight from a glossy magazine. The table was set for two in the little dining alcove where cut glass glistened, the family silver gleamed, the plates were of Crown Derby, and the napkins of pure snowy-white damask. In the sitting room Stephanie reclined gracefully on the sofa in pale gray satin pants and an evening top, a glass of champagne in her hand. Opposite her sat Alex—handsome, dark, debonair. Candles flickered around the room, a Christmas tree sparkled in one corner, exquisite notes of a Beethoven piano concerto contributed the background music. It should have been perfect, but it was far from that—the air was heavy with anger, resentment, and suspicion.

"OK," said Alex, "are you going to tell me what's bugging you, or do I have to guess? It's been a long, hard week, and I could do without the guessing games."

"You know very well what's wrong," said Stephanie.

"You mean our arrangements for Christmas Day?"

"Of course I mean our arrangements for Christmas Day."

"Look," said Alex, "I don't see that I have to justify to you why I want to spend Christmas Day with the old man. Anyone with even the slightest degree of sensitivity would understand. He's all alone, he's not very well, and every Christmas could be his last."

"Of course I understand that," said Stephanie. "I just wish you'd told me earlier."

"How the hell was I supposed to know you were going to cancel Christmas with your family?"

"Because," said Stephanie with studied patience, "when we discussed it earlier in the year we agreed that we would spend this Christmas together, and I went ahead on that basis."

"Fine," said Alex. "So I had a change of heart. I'm sorry, but if you hadn't fallen out with Father, the three of us could have enjoyed Christmas together."

"I think that's what I resent most," said Stephanie. "The way you always side with your father against me, as though our differences are all my fault."

"I'm not siding with him against you," said Alex, "I just understand why he's never forgiven you for the Fulham business. He has a lot of faults, but he always plays things straight—you know that. He felt terribly let down by you, and since he's old and intractable, he's not going to change his mind."

"He would if you pleaded my case," said Stephanie. Alex stood up and went to refill his champagne glass. His expression was bored. I'm overdoing this and spoiling the evening, Stephanie thought, but there was nothing she could do to stop herself.

"I don't think anybody's ever persuaded my father to do anything he didn't want to," said Alex after a pause. "I just don't understand your sudden desire to play happy families —we've spent several Christmases apart in the past."

"I don't want to play happy families," said Stephanie irritably, "it's just that thanks to you I'm not spending Christmas with my family, I can't spend Christmas with yours, and I'm going to be alone."

Alex sat down wearily. "Why don't you tell your family you've changed your mind? I'm sure the long-suffering Tim will be more than happy to welcome you back into the fold for the festive season."

"I can't do that. Tim's made other plans."

There was an odd note in her voice that quickened Alex's interest. "What sort of other plans? Don't tell me Tim has found a woman at last."

"No, no, not exactly. Ella and her son are spending Christmas at Wickham with Tim and the girls."

"And you're jealous!" said Alex triumphantly.

"No, I'm not. It's just that when Ella asked me if I would mind them going, as it is, after all, my home, I said I wouldn't because at that time I thought I was spending Christmas with you. Now it seems I have nowhere to go."

"It's just a day," said Alex, "like any other."

"You're an absolute brute sometimes, Alex," said Stephanie. "Come on, we'd better eat or it will be ruined."

She placed before them plates of smoked salmon and poured a glass of Muscadet. The setting was wonderful, but the evening had lost its sparkle, like so many evenings between them in recent months. In her heart of hearts Stephanie knew she was losing Alex—it was only a question of time. All this would have been easier to bear if only . . . She glanced up at him. She had to tell him now. Every day during the last week she had promised herself to raise the subject and then had lost courage at the last moment. It had to be now.

He glanced up at her, sensing her scrutiny. "Come on," he said, "you're not eating your smoked salmon."

"Alex, there's something I have to tell you."

He looked at her mockingly. "This sounds serious. Another man, is it? Am I getting my marching orders?" He grinned, superbly confident that this was not the case.

For a wild moment Stephanie contemplated telling him how wrong he was, just to see the expression on his face. "No," she said, "nothing like that, as you well know. It is a problem, but one I hope we can sort out between us."

Alex's face was suddenly serious, to match her own. "Well, go on then, spit it out. What is it?"

"I'm pregnant, Alex."

"You're what?"

"You heard," Stephanie said wearily. "Seven weeks pregnant."

"Is the child mine?" Alex said, his voice suddenly very cold.

Stephanie wanted to hit him. "How dare you! Of course the child is yours. You know damned well there hasn't been another man in my life since the moment you first made love to me."

"How could you have let this happen?"

"I didn't do it on purpose, Alex," said Stephanie.

"Didn't you? Are you sure it wasn't some kind of plot to ensnare me, to force my hand? Is it marriage you want?"

"You're so bloody sure of yourself, aren't you?" said Stephanie. She pushed back her chair, leaving her meal uneaten, and refilled her wine glass. "What makes you think I want to marry you any more than you want to marry me?

And why should you automatically assume that my getting pregnant is some sort of contrived act? It's insulting and wholly inaccurate."

"In which case I assume you're getting rid of it." He spoke without emotion.

She had known his reaction to the news would be disturbing, but not this bad. "Alex, we're talking about a human life, about your son or daughter, your precious father's only grandchild."

"Oh, don't start all that," said Alex. "You know very well I've never wanted kids—*never*. Just because you have made a silly mistake, there's no reason I should change my view. Anyway, you haven't got time for a baby."

"I could make time," said Stephanie.

"Not you. You're the woman who abandoned her last family without a qualm—remember?"

His words stung her—more and more Stephanie found she valued the time she spent with her daughters, and she had begun to miss them dreadfully when they were apart. "I left them to be with you," she said defensively.

"Maybe, maybe not. Either way, I'll say this, Stephanie—if you go ahead with this pregnancy, you do so without my blessing. I will not acknowledge the child as my own, you may not give it the Meyer name, and as far as I'm concerned, our relationship will be at an end."

Anger momentarily rescued Stephanie from the depths of her misery. "You're talking as though I had leprosy. What's so wrong with having a baby, your baby?"

"If for any reason I ever change my mind and decide I would like children," said Alex, "it will be a joint decision between myself and my partner. I will not have a child—any child—thrust upon me."

In silence Stephanie cleared away the plates, hers still untouched, and in the kitchen she began dishing up the main course. Hot tears splashed down her cheeks, some falling into the steaming casserole in front of her. Why was she standing there serving a meal to a man who did not want either her or their baby? She was a little drunk, she knew. If she was sober she would not have reacted as she did. She tossed back the rest of the wine in her glass and, slamming the lid back on the casserole, walked out into the dining area.

"There doesn't seem to be much point in continuing with this meal, does there, since neither of us is having a good time? I suggest you go." Her voice was surprisingly steady.

He remained unmoved. "I was planning to stay the night here, as you know."

"You'll just have to find yourself a room somewhere else in Paris for the night. This is my flat, if you remember, and I don't want you here."

"As you wish." He got to his feet and started toward the door.

Stephanie had expected some show of resistance. She panicked. "When . . . when are you going skiing?"

He stopped and turned to face her. "I wouldn't have thought you'd be interested."

Her mind raced. "I need to know for business purposes."

"I leave on the seventh, and I'll be away for two weeks." His manner softened slightly. "Look, Stephanie, be realistic about this baby. Parenthood is not for us. Why not arrange an abortion for immediately after Christmas, and then come skiing with me to recuperate—you haven't had a holiday in a long time."

His sudden kindness brought tears to her eyes. Just for a moment his suggestion was tempting. "No," she thundered, as much to frighten off her own thoughts as to make the point to Alex. "I'm going to have this baby, with or without your blessing. I'm not sure being excluded from the Meyer empire isn't the best thing that could happen to the child. Certainly I wouldn't want a child of mine to turn out like you, playing to your father's tune, another Joseph Meyer clone."

For a moment she thought he was going to hit her. She saw the sudden fury in his eyes, the clenching of his fists, but the moment passed. The expression that replaced it, though, was almost more chilling—a cold, dispassionate look that suggested he might just as well be addressing a complete stranger. "I'll be back on January twenty-first. Either get rid of the baby by then or we're finished. Have I made myself clear?"

"Perfectly," said Stephanie.

Her heart was still thudding uncomfortably against her ribs long after he had left the flat. She made no attempt to clear up the discarded debris of supper. Instead she poured herself another glass of wine and then remembered the baby. Tipping the wine down the sink, she walked slowly, deliberately to the fridge and helped herself to a glass of milk instead. It was a deliberate act of defiance and sealed forever in her mind the decision she had already made. This baby would have a chance at life.

Chapter 32

New York—*Christmas Eve, 1984*

The tall figure of his son stood framed in the doorway. Aaron smiled with pleasure as he looked up from his desk, where he had been sitting and staring into space for some time.

"You were so quiet in here, Pop, I thought you were out."

"No, no, not tonight. I've given up the high life, particularly now that you're home from college."

"Don't give it up on my account," said William.

Aaron grinned ruefully at him. "It's about time I did, at my age. Did you have a good evening?"

"The best. I'm sorry I left you alone, though, on Christmas Eve. I shouldn't have done that."

"William, I don't need a nursemaid." Aaron's tone was belligerent.

"Is something wrong?" William asked anxiously.

"No, nothing more than usual. I'm just getting to be a morose old man."

"And lonely?" William suggested.

"That, too."

"So why don't you stop sulking in your study and come have a drink in the living room before we hit the sack?"

They smiled at each other in mutual appreciation and wandered into the living room.

It was after one when William finally went to bed. For Aaron, sleep was still a long way off. Pouring himself another whiskey, which he justified on the grounds that it was, after all, the festive season, he went back into his study and looked down at the piece of notepaper on which were written just two words—"Dearest Ella." Although he had sat at the desk for most of the evening, he had gotten no further than that. He slumped back tiredly into his chair, slopping his whiskey as he did so. There was so much he wanted to say to her, so much he should have said before. It was three years since Alice had died. Not only had he behaved badly during that period, but he was no nearer coming to terms with the grief of losing his wife. To cap it all, in the process he had lost his best friend.

When he thought about his life-style during the last two years, it sickened him. Following that one night he had spent with Ella he had gone a little crazy and pretty much gone after every woman in sight. As a handsome, revered doctor working in a hospital full of adoring women, he had behaved like a child let loose in a candy store. Over and over again he tried to analyze why he had behaved so stupidly. Part of it, he knew, was a desperate attempt to drive Alice from his mind, to seek relief from the all-consuming grief. It was not as simple as that, though. Ella, in a single night, had changed all that he had known about a physical relationship, awakening something in him that he had thought long dead, if it had ever existed. Yet the stream of faceless women he had used and discarded had brought him no nearer coming to terms with his life as a widower. Now at last he knew why. The key to his future happiness was Ella—whether as a friend or a lover, he needed her, needed her desperately—and it was this that he had to tell her.

At last, his eyes aching with tiredness, Aaron picked up the pen and began to write. Not making any attempt to hide or excuse his behavior, he simply poured out his soul onto paper, and the more he wrote, the more the words flew from his pen.

Across town, in the cramped little apartment Jackie Partridge called home, Michael Gresham stretched with a groan and squinted at the clock beside the bed. "You know something, sweetheart? You really ought to get a double bed."

"I know I should," said Jackie anxiously. She looked up at him adoringly from under a thatch of tousled hair.

"I've got to get going. I have to catch a flight."

Jackie sat up in bed and stared at him, round-eyed. "A flight! When?"

Michael glanced at the bedside table again. "In about two, two and a half hours. I'm getting the five-twenty out of New York to Houston."

"But you didn't tell me," Jackie wailed.

Michael frowned and slid gracefully from the bed. He stood before her naked, magnificent; she could not take her eyes off him. "We made no plans to spend Christmas Day together, sweetheart, and I have to get back to Houston—there's a whole bunch of friends dropping by for a party this evening at my place."

Jackie said nothing but watched with growing misery his retreating figure as he padded across the bedroom toward the shower. She supposed it did not occur to him to invite her to come along to meet some of his friends. No, she was being stupid. She knew what he was. This was the man who had two-timed Ella—Ella, a million times more attractive and desirable than she herself. If Ella had not been able to hold him, how could Jackie expect to do so? Hearing Michael turn off the shower, she hurriedly reached for her robe.

She was sitting at the dressing table again, frantically brushing at her hair, when Michael reappeared. It was hard to believe he had managed no more than a couple of hours' sleep. Showered and shaved, he looked refreshed, invigorated, and ready for anything. He dressed hurriedly, seeming anxious to leave. "Would you like some coffee, or can I fix you some breakfast?" Jackie fussed.

"No, no, I'm fine."

"You have plenty of time."

"I said no . . . thanks." She sat miserably watching him.

"Now, you *will* remember to call Ella," he said. "I don't know where the hell she's gone to this Christmas. I've tried calling her from home, but she hasn't even bothered to put on the answering machine." Jackie looked at him blankly. "Jackie, you do remember what I said?" He sounded impatient.

"About the oil market?" Jackie said dully.

"Yes. Now pay attention—this is important—there's something going wrong, I just feel it in my bones. Everyone knows the oil market is in for a slump, but I think it could be very serious, and I think it could be long-term. The vibes I'm getting are bad, and if I'm right, one of the first things to be hit will be real estate."

"I'll tell her."

Michael sighed. "I don't think I'm getting across to you the importance of it, am I?"

Jackie pulled herself together. "Yes, you are. Sorry, it's just that it's rather late, and I'm sad that you're going."

"Yes, yes." Michael dismissed her explanation. "The problem is, the case I'm working on will be taking me to Toronto after Christmas, which means I'll be out of town for three, maybe four weeks. Ella knows this, of course, and there are plenty of people geared up to see that her business runs smoothly while I'm away. However, what I'd like her to do is to come to Houston as soon as possible and take a look around herself—see what she thinks about the market. Maybe I'm overreacting, but since she's made me custodian of her Houston business, I want to do the right thing by her."

"I understand," said Jackie distractedly.

"Just make sure you tell her."

Jackie hesitated. "About your business trip . . . will I see you before you go?"

"Not a chance," said Michael. He was concentrating on straightening his tie in the mirror. "I don't expect I'll be up in New York for a couple of months, probably three. There'll be a pile of work waiting for me when I get back to Houston, and if I'm right about the oil market, what's bad business for Ella is good business for me."

"It's Christmas now," said Jackie, half to herself, "so I may not see you again until nearly Easter."

Michael swung around smiling, bestowing on her the full force of his charm. "Cheer up. There must be plenty of young men in New York pining for your charms. Perhaps it's time you gave them some consideration."

Jackie looked at him, appalled. "Are you saying you don't want to see me again?"

Michael looked at her with a smile. "You're such a serious little thing, aren't you?" He seized her shoulders and kissed her warmly on both cheeks. "What I'm saying," he said, keeping an arm around her, "is that the problems in Houston will require Ella's personal attention for some months. It's my view that when she knows what's going on, she'll be anxious to stick around. There's no one like Ella for making a good deal, and if she's to dispose of some of her assets, I reckon she'll want to do it personally."

"Yes, yes, of course," said Jackie, looking confused.

"You're not following me, are you, sweetheart?" Jackie shook her head. "You know Ella and I had a relationship for some time, right?"

"Yes," said Jackie in a strangled voice.

"Well, it would be pretty tactless for me to be seen having

an affair with you, her right-hand woman, behind her back. I don't want to upset her by rubbing her nose in the fact that she and I are no longer together."

"I've got feelings, too," said Jackie in a small voice.

Michael hugged her some more. "Yes, I'm sure you have, but you and I—well, it's just been a casual thing, hasn't it? With Ella it was more serious, and I'm aware I upset her a lot at the time. I just don't think it would be very considerate, do you?"

He caught a glimpse of her crestfallen face, at the tears welling from under her eyelids. This was proving more difficult than he had anticipated. He had been a damned fool to get involved in the first place. "Look, Jackie, Ella's done a lot for you, hasn't she?" Jackie nodded. "Well, this would be a pretty dumb way to repay her, wouldn't it? I'm not saying we won't ever get back together again—of course we may—but not while Ella is in the States. You understand, don't you, honey?" He was rewarded by Jackie nodding miserably. "OK, I'd better get going."

"Your plane's not for an hour and a half—it will only take you half an hour to get to the airport."

"I know, I know," said Michael, impatiently, "but I have some calls to make."

"On Christmas morning?"

"On Christmas morning," he said, his voice suddenly hard and determined. Jackie knew better than to argue.

After he had gone Jackie turned on the television—anything to dispel the sense of isolation and loneliness—and sat down in front of it with unseeing eyes. She was crying again, but it didn't matter now—it didn't matter how she looked, because no one was going to see her. For a moment she thought longingly of her parents in their neat little terraced home in Harrow and then dismissed the thought. She had chosen the life of a career girl in New York; she had to expect some knocks—you win some, you lose some. She knew she had been foolish to put so much store by her relationship with Michael Gresham, but she kept remembering her mother saying how attractive men often married plain girls—to boost the ego or some such nonsense. Her mother had cited several examples among her friends, and it had seemed true at the time. Now her hopes were shattered—and why? Because of Ella. Ella wasn't even interested in Michael anymore. She had told Jackie as much. So why was it necessary to be so cautious? It wasn't fair. Ella had everything—wealth, good looks, a child, a jet-setting life-style . . . Jackie buried her head in her hands. At that moment she hated Ella Kovac.

Chapter 33

Gloucestershire—*Christmas Eve, 1984*

"Bye, Tim. Thanks for a wonderful party, as usual." The crystal-clear voice of Babs Cunningham, notorious, aging libertine and impressive drunk, was accentuated by the cold, hard frost of the night as her car roared off down the drive.

"Thank God she's gone," said Tim wearily. "She shouldn't be driving in her condition, but if I'd said anything along those lines, she'd have taken it as an invitation to stay the night. She's a dear, but the thought of Babs with a crashing hangover on Christmas morning is just too much."

"You sound tired," said Ella, standing by his side. She shivered. "And it's cold out here—let's go inside."

Tim let out a sigh, closed and bolted the great front door of Wickham, and followed Ella into the study, where Greg and Belinda were sprawled on the sofa with a bottle of champagne. "Millie's gone to bed already," Greg said. "Why don't you two help us finish this off?"

Tim and Ella pulled up two chairs, and the four chatted companionably about the various party guests until both Greg and Belinda said good night and drifted off upstairs.

After they had gone Ella gave Tim a quizzical look. "There's something going on between those two, isn't there?"

"I don't know," said Tim. "They're good friends, certainly."

"More than that," said Ella, "I'm sure of it."

Tim smiled. "Women's intuition. You could be right. It's a strange thought, though."

"You mean because of what happened between us?"

"Yes, I suppose so," said Tim.

"You seem very . . . down tonight." Ella probed gently. "Is there something wrong?"

"No, not really," said Tim. "I'm just tired. I'm afraid I'm not very good company. You go off to bed, and I promise tomorrow to be full of joie de vivre. How will that do?"

"And you don't want to discuss it, whatever it is that's bugging you?" Tim shook his head. "OK, I guess I'll do as you suggest."

He could see the look of hurt on her face. He felt sorry for her suddenly, but all he wanted her to do was to go and leave him alone.

"What about the cleaning up?" Ella said.

"I'll stack a few glasses and leave the rest for the morning," said Tim. "Mrs. Maggs will be in early. She's wonderful, that woman. Even on Christmas Day she insists on working."

"Then let me help you," said Ella.

"No," said Tim, too quickly. "No, thanks. I won't do much, honestly."

Ella hurried across the hall, shivering with cold. She ran up the stairs, hurried across the landing, and, with relief, opened the door of her bedroom to a blast of warm air. Hurriedly, she stripped off her clothes, removed her make-up, and climbed thankfully into bed, absurdly grateful for the warmth that greeted her there—an electric blanket had been an essential ingredient of staying at Wickham. She turned off the light and lay in the darkness, thinking of Tim.

During the last few years they had established a good, solid platonic friendship, yet underneath it there was always a tension—they had been lovers once; perhaps they could be again. Tim had never so much as hinted that this was the case, but Ella always felt that even the slightest encouragement from her would bring him back to her bed, if that was what she wanted. Now, suddenly, she was not so sure. He seemed preoccupied and distant. Was there perhaps someone else? Had he gotten tired of waiting for her, if indeed that was what he had been doing? She tried to marshal her thoughts. After all the years of loving, her relationship with Aaron was clearly over. She supposed this meant she needed a man in her life, and if this was the case, what better person could there be than Tim? But as always, she could not think of Tim without thinking of his epilepsy, and her fear of it was not something she could hide from herself—nor, it appeared, from him. It was ridiculous. He would never harm her while having a fit; neither was the condition catching or terminal. Yet still the very thought of it horrified her, and while it did, she knew there was no hope of a future with Tim. Should she tell him? she wondered. No, for in her heart she felt certain he already knew.

It took Tim less than twenty minutes to clear the glasses from the three main rooms. He worked his way systematically around each room. God, people were messy—cigarettes, half-eaten sausages, all piled in ashtrays; glasses knocked over, peanuts scattered across the carpet. The smell of champagne and cigarettes was abhorrent to him. What's wrong with me, he thought, as he worked—a regular Scrooge. It had been a successful party; it always was. Anyone who was anyone in Gloucestershire came to the Wickham party on Christmas Eve. It was a tradition that had been begun by Stephanie's father, and which Tim felt compelled to continue. Not *compelled;* that was the wrong word . . . he wanted to continue it. He believed in traditions.

The job finally completed, he turned out the lights in the house, but the thought of bed and sleep had no appeal. Instead he drifted back to the study, threw another couple of logs on the fire, and poured himself a whiskey. He had not drunk during the party; he never did. His doctor allowed him one whiskey a night, and this evening he made it a little larger than normal and took it to his desk, where he sat down and stared at the papers in front of him with unseeing eyes.

There was no future for him and Ella. In reality, he supposed he had known it ever since France, but somehow seeing her here at Christmas only served to highlight the problems of their relationship. It was not simply a question of her being afraid of his epilepsy, though God knows that was enough; the fact remained that she didn't fit. Perhaps he was not being fair. She'd been a good co-hostess at the party and had done her best to find something in common with his guests. But the landed gentry of England were a race apart; he recognized that. How could he expect an American with Ella's background to fit into his way of life—indeed, why should she? Yet strangely her son did—Greg had been at home in the English countryside from the very first day he had set foot in it. It was as if he had come home, Tim thought fancifully, with affection. He was inordinately fond of Greg—the son he had never had, perhaps, he thought. There was a warmth about the boy, an instinctive gentleness, whether he was dealing with people or animals. He would make a good farmer—the best—and if Ella was right and there was something between him and Belinda, it would make him very happy, Tim realized. So why the depression? He took a sip of his whiskey, and as he did so his eyes caught the photograph in front of him. It showed a youthful Stephanie, the girls hanging around her neck—babies almost, two and four perhaps, not more. They were all laughing. It was spring, and Stephanie had an apple blossom tucked behind her ear. The picture clutched at his heart, making him draw in his breath sharply. It never failed to surprise him that after everything that had happened he should still be as much in love with his wife as he had ever been. At last he could admit it to himself, but the knowledge brought him no comfort—just a feeling of emptiness, bitterness, and jealousy, too, thinking of her in the arms of Alex Meyer.

"Stephanie." He said the word aloud and, raising his glass toward the photograph, whispered, "Happy Christmas, darling." That was what was wrong with tonight—there was no Stephanie. Without her at his side this party, like all parties, held no joy for him. They had spoken early in the day. Stephanie had called to wish them all a happy Christmas. Her voice had sounded small, sad, and ridiculously far away. That was what had affected him, he knew. At least when she was happy, even if it was with another man, he could convince himself that their parting had been for the best. But when she sounded as she had today, vulnerable and forlorn, he could not bear it. He wanted to run to her, wherever she was, and take her in his arms, and make whatever the hurt was better.

He looked again at the photograph. He had been so proud to have her as his wife, so proud and grateful. Perhaps it was this gratitude that had adversely affected their marriage. Her obsession with her business, to the detriment of himself and his children, he had accepted because he felt he owed her so much. A different man, a more confident man, would have stopped her. Yet could anyone stop Stephanie Bonham from pursuing something she wanted? He doubted it. He drained his whiskey glass and stood up. A smile suddenly flitted across his face at the irony of the situation. Here he had under his roof a charming, desirable woman who had loved him once and who might, with careful wooing, love him again. Yet there was no way he could pursue the relationship honestly, because he was still in love with his wife, who clearly never gave him a thought.

Chapter 34

London—*January 1985*

Ella glanced at her watch impatiently. It was almost twelve-twenty, and Stephanie had been due at twelve. It was not like her to be late, certainly not this late. She had a light lunch already laid out and, on impulse, had put a bottle of champagne in the cooler. After all, they were discussing the grand opening of their joint project—they deserved a celebration.

Unable to settle down to any more work, Ella wandered into the conservatory and gazed out on the bare January bleakness to the patch of garden beyond. She loved this little house—her own home in London. It was in a quiet mews off Holland Park—not nearly as fashionable as Stephanie's headquarters, nor as flamboyant, but it suited her well. The house had a cottage atmosphere, and Greg loved it as much as she did—indeed, he had helped her choose it. Greg . . . they had come a long way since his moment of madness with Margot. He was now in his third year at Cirencester Agricultural College and was having a wonderful time. He had tons of friends and tended to go to Wickham on the weekends, taking loads of Cirencester students with him, which always pleased the Irvine girls. During the holidays, though, he spent most of the time with his mother. All trace of their former difficulties had gone, and Ella recognized the reason for this. At last Greg was leading the sort of life he had always wanted. A childhood spent in the concrete jungle of New York had been all wrong for him, and though he had tried to tell her so repeatedly over the years, she had not been prepared to listen. Still, that was all behind them. Thanks to Tim and his encouragement, Greg was set on the right path. She doubted if she would ever get him back to America, but did it matter? He loved England and the English way of life. Once the Fulham project was launched, she would look for other work in England, which would keep her in touch with her son.

The doorbell rang, and Ella went swiftly to open it. Stephanie looked quite unlike her normal self. She wore an old duffel coat over a tweed skirt. Her hair was untidy almost to the point of being unkempt, and her face was deathly pale, with dark circles under her eyes. "I'm sorry I'm late," she said. "It's been one of those mornings."

"Not to worry," said Ella lightly. "Come on in, I have some champagne on ice."

"Champagne! What on earth for?"

"To celebrate our opening, since that's what we're here to talk about."

"Oh, that!" said Stephanie. "It's hardly a cause for celebration."

"Why not?" said Ella. "We're both making a great deal of money out of the development personally, and, wearing your Meyer hat, you're going to continue to reap the rewards into the sunset. Where's the problem?"

Stephanie relented a little. "You're right, of course. I'm sorry, I'm just irritable. Perhaps a glass of your champagne would help."

Ella began opening the bottle. "Is anything wrong?" she asked.

"No, no, nothing. Did you have a good Christmas?" Her voice was sharp.

So that's it, Ella thought—even after all this time she still minds me seeing Tim. "Yes, we did have a good time, the children especially." She handed Stephanie a glass and looked at her shrewdly. "It's bugging you, isn't it—Greg and I being at Wickham for Christmas? I'm sorry, but I did ask you first, and I honestly never thought you would mind or I wouldn't have gone at all."

"No, no, of course it hasn't upset me," said Stephanie irritably. "At least, I'm not upset that you were there, but perhaps just a little that I wasn't."

"There's nothing between Tim and me now," said Ella hesitantly.

Stephanie rounded on her. "Oh, so you think that's what is upsetting me, do you—you think I'm jealous of you because of your relationship with my ex-husband? I'm sick to death of telling you how wrong you are. Tim and I were washed up years ago, and I have no feelings for him at all other than the fact that he is the father of my children. I don't know why you persist in thinking that whatever you and Tim get up to is any concern of mine."

Her words irritated Ella, but she did not attempt to retaliate. She could see that Stephanie was currently a deeply unhappy woman, and for some reason her denial of still caring for Tim was wholly unconvincing. Not for the first time Ella thanked God she had not been tempted to become involved with Tim again. Quickly she turned the conversation toward business, and soon they were poring over their files, discussing final arrangements for the opening of the West London Meyer Centre. It was nearly three by the time they sat down to lunch.

"I noticed from the guest list," said Ella, "that you've included Margot Haigh. I deliberately excluded her."

Stephanie hesitated, fork poised in midair. "We have to ask her, Ella, whatever your personal feelings. She put together the financing for this project and, through me, dealt with it on a day-to-day basis."

"I simply thought we could ask her chairman instead. I've never met John Shepherd, and I thought perhaps it's time I did."

"By all means ask the chairman," said Stephanie, "but we have to ask Margot as well."

"I don't see why," said Ella stubbornly.

"Oh, really," said Stephanie, exasperated. "It's been quite ridiculous the way I've had to be responsible for all contact with the bank over this project just so that you two did not have to deal with each other personally. I've bridged the gap temporarily, but you can't keep this feud up forever. You're two mature women."

"But Greg's coming, along with Tim and the girls."

"OK, so Greg and Margot and two or three thousand other people are all going to be at the Meyer Centre together on the same day. Big deal. Are you frightened they might get back together again?"

"I suppose I am," Ella admitted.

"In which case," said Stephanie, "I think your fears are groundless."

"I just hope you're right," said Ella.

"Always the mother hen," said Stephanie. "You worry too much. Children are much better left to get on with it. How are my two, incidentally? You've seen more of them recently than I have." Again there was the sharp note in her voice.

"They're fine, very well. They asked after you, of course."

"Of course," said Stephanie sarcastically.

"Look, I know you may not have a conventional relationship with either of them," Ella said, eager to comfort, "but they're both enormously proud of you, you know that."

"I don't need you to tell me what my daughters think of me," said Stephanie.

"I wasn't," said Ella patiently, "I'm just trying to say you needn't feel bad about how little you see them, because they expect their relationship with you to be like that."

"I don't need your reassurance, Ella," said Stephanie.

I should have kept my big mouth shut, Ella thought. For whatever reason, Tim and the girls are clearly a taboo subject. "I'm sorry, I wasn't trying to interfere," she said gently. "Would you like some coffee?"

Stephanie glanced at her watch. "No, I think I'd better be getting back. I said I'd be in the office again at three. We've covered just about everything, haven't we?"

"I guess so," said Ella. The two women got up and walked to the front door. "I was thinking," said Ella, "that I would like to do another project in England."

"What sort of project have you in mind?"

"I don't know, really—that's what I wanted to ask you. Would you be interested in our joining forces on something else?"

Stephanie shook her head. "I don't think I could stand the hassle with the Meyers."

"But surely," said Ella, "if we did another project together, you wouldn't have any hassle. The reason Joseph was so uptight last time was because you used what he saw to be confidential information. If we found an interesting site with no Meyer connection—"

"The answer's no," Stephanie interrupted.

"I thought we worked well together," Ella persisted.

"Look, can you leave it alone, Ella? I'm late, I don't have time to discuss this now, and in any event I've given you an answer."

There was clearly nothing more to say. The telephone rang. "Hold on," Ella said, "I'll just answer that."

"I won't wait," said Stephanie. "No doubt we'll meet again before the opening. See you around."

For a moment Ella stood rooted to the spot watching Stephanie cross the street toward her car, both confused and dismayed by her behavior. At last the persistence of the telephone dragged her away.

"Hello, Miss Kovac?"

"Yes," said Ella. It was a female voice she did not recognize.

"This is Joseph Meyer's secretary. Is Stephanie Bonham with you, by any chance?"

"She's just left," said Ella.

"Oh, no." The woman sounded distraught.

"I might be able to catch her," said Ella. "Hang on."

"Thank you, it is terribly urgent."

Ella dropped the telephone and ran out into the street. It was virtually dark. Stephanie was just easing her BMW out of the parking space, and Ella ran across the road waving her arms.

"What is it?" said Stephanie, opening the window, clearly annoyed.

"It's Joseph Meyer's secretary on the telephone. She says it's urgent."

"I'll ring her when I get back to the office."

"Honestly, Stephanie, I think you ought to take the call—she sounded sort of frantic."

"Oh, drat," said Stephanie. "All right. What does he want now, I wonder." She reparked the car and followed Ella across the street.

To be tactful, Ella started to leave the room, but the tone of Stephanie's voice stopped her. "No," she heard her say, "no. Are you absolutely sure? Is there really no . . . no mistake?" There was a pause. "I see." Her voice was barely above a whisper. "Yes, thank you for letting me know."

"What is it? What's happened?" said Ella.

Stephanie was standing, receiver in hand, her face ashen. Slowly she sank into the chair beside her and raised a tortured face to Ella. "It's Alex. He's been involved in a skiing accident—an avalanche—he's dead."

Chapter 35

New York—*January 1985*

Joseph Meyer stood at attention as they lowered the body of his son into the open grave. The snow fell relentlessly, like tears, but much to his own surprise, he remained dry-eyed. There would be years of tears ahead, as long as he lived, but at this moment he felt a strange numbness, as though he was watching a film of someone else's grief and bereavement. He had chosen to bury his son in New York so that he could be beside his mother. That left just two of them—Joseph, as he felt now, at the end of a long and fruitless life, and his daughter Freda, eking out a nothing life in a body that would not set her free. It was all over except for . . . across the gaping wound in the earth he could see Stephanie standing, head bowed, beside Ella Kovac. Both women were standing under an umbrella, and it was impossible to see the expression on either face. Was she grieving? he wondered. Had she really loved his son, or was it his position she loved? For above everything else, Joseph judged that Stephanie was motivated by a desire to succeed. Try as he might, Joseph could not feel sorry for her.

The group of people around the grave were starting to move away. The rabbi came to his side. "Are you going home now, Mr. Meyer? Would you like me to come with you, to talk?"

Over his shoulder Joseph could see Stephanie and Ella hurrying away. "No, no. Excuse me, I have to see someone. I'm sorry to be rude." He caught them by the line of cars waiting to take the mourners away. "Stephanie?" She turned. Her appearance shocked him profoundly—she had lost a great deal of weight, her face was very pale, and her eyes were red-ringed. She looked very different from the golden girl he had met so long ago. "Stephanie, we need to talk."

"Not now," she ventured.

"Yes, now. The car's just here, we'll go back to the hotel."

"I can't," she said.

Joseph took her arm. "You owe me," he said.

They did not speak at all on the journey to the Meyer Hotel, each locked in a silent world of grief. It occurred to Joseph that they were the two people who knew Alex best in the world, yet somehow he did not feel he would ever be able to discuss his son with this woman.

The flags on top of the Meyer building were flying at half-mast. A doorman leapt forward, recognizing the car, and ushered them inside. "Come up to my apartment," said Joseph. It was an order rather than an invitation. Stephanie followed numbly to the presidential suite on the top floor.

Once inside the sumptuous apartment, and alone, the

silence between them seemed to paralyze them both. They stared at each other helplessly. "Do you want anything?" Joseph asked. "A drink?"

"No, thank you."

Joseph motioned her to a chair and sat down across from her. "I'm sorry it's necessary to talk to you at this moment, Stephanie. Whatever our differences, I appreciate that it is not an easy time for you." Joseph avoided her eye. "I imagine you can guess what I want to talk to you about."

Stephanie shook her head. "I have no idea."

"I want to talk to you about the child you're carrying."

Stephanie gasped. "How do you know about that? Nobody knows."

"Alex told his friend Peter Barlow, the man who survived the avalanche. Peter came to see me a couple of days ago to tell me details of . . . well . . . how Alex died. He asked me if I knew about the child. I didn't, of course—Alex did not often confide in me, as you know. What horrified me most was that Alex apparently wanted you to get rid of it." Stephanie nodded dumbly. "H-have you done so?" The old man tried to keep the emotion from his voice, but it was tremulous, and there were tears in his eyes.

"No, I haven't."

"Thank God. I will do everything, everything I can for you, you know that. Please let me help you, Stephanie, in whatever way I can—and the child, of course the child."

"No," said Stephanie quietly, without any visible emotion.

"You mean . . . you're going ahead with an abortion?" Joseph Meyer was hunched forward now, quite literally wringing his hands in his anguish.

"No," said Stephanie. "I'd already told Alex, even though he didn't want the child, that I was not prepared to have an abortion for his convenience, but I am not prepared to have my child brought up as a Meyer product either."

"I understand that," said Joseph, relaxing a little.

"I don't think you do," said Stephanie. "I'm sorry if this hurts you, but I need to explain. I realize that this child I am carrying represents your one hope for the future, but I have to tell you that, boy or girl, this child will be no Meyer. This child will have a normal childhood—he or she will grow up not under your shadow, but a free spirit. If nothing else, I owe that to Alex."

"Don't you think you also owe Alex the chance for his son or daughter to benefit from who I am and what I have to give?"

"No," said Stephanie. "Alex did not want this child. Alex told me that if I persisted in carrying it, he would disown both me and it. He told me that the child would never bear your name and that he would never acknowledge it as his own. The Meyers have already rejected this child, Joseph."

"Alex in his foolishness may have rejected it. I haven't."

"It was Alex's right to do so," said Stephanie, "not yours."

It seemed to Stephanie that Joseph Meyer was aging before her eyes. She knew she was responsible, knew she should feel a sense of compassion, bearing in mind the long, long road this old man had traveled and knowing that today he had buried his only and much-loved son. Yet there was no room for compromise, and there was no point in leaving ajar a door she intended firmly to shut.

"Are you saying I may never see the child?" There was a pleading note in Joseph's voice.

"I think it would be best for you both."

"How can you do this to me?" Joseph burst out. "To deprive me of my dead son's child. How can you do it?"

"I can do it because I believe it is right."

"What do you want?" said Joseph. "You can have anything—the whole damned group, for all I care. Anything, anything—however much power, money you want—you can have it all."

Stephanie shook her head. "I have the franchise, and I will continue to run that as I have always done, efficiently and to your satisfaction."

"You cannot be a good mother and continue in this business. The child will never see you."

"That's up to me," said Stephanie. "I will make arrangements so that the child is well looked after, you can be sure of that."

"Is this revenge?" Joseph said after a pause. "Is this your way of getting back at me?"

"No," said Stephanie, "it's not revenge. I can only repeat that I'm doing what I believe is best for the child." She stood up. It was time to go now, quickly, while she still had the strength. "I'll go now, shall I?"

Joseph Meyer suddenly slumped into his chair, a little old man finally broken by life. Stephanie felt remorse, but not enough to change her mind. He would rally in a few days, she reasoned. Joseph Meyer was a survivor; she need not waste her sympathy on him. Yet as she crossed the room to the door she looked back. He sat, small and almost frail-looking, like a helpless baby, and for a fleeting moment the desire to run to him, to throw her arms around him, to weep out her misery was almost overwhelming. This man had fathered Alex. Could it be right to tear herself away from the one close tie she had with the man she had just lost? She carried the seed of Alex within her; it was Joseph's, too. For a moment she hesitated. Then she turned abruptly and left the room.

Chapter 36

Something had happened to Jackie. Ella recognized it immediately, despite her preoccupation with the mound of work on her desk. The girl was polite, as efficient as ever, but oddly detached. The morning's work included the need for some leases to be delivered to a publishing company two blocks away. Using the excuse that Jackie looked like she needed a breath of fresh air, Ella managed to get her out of the office and immediately summoned Jessie.

"England suits you," Jessie said without preamble, "but I miss you, and I miss that boy of yours. Tell me about him—every last detail."

Wasting precious moments, Ella gave Jessie a quick update on Greg and his life and then turned the conversation to Jackie. "What's wrong with Jackie? Do you know, Jessie?"

"Man trouble," said Jessie promptly.

"Again? That girl doesn't have much luck with men, does she?"

"Nor will she, I guess," said Jessie philosophically. "She's a born loser where men are concerned."

"I think you're right," said Ella. "Any idea who's causing the trouble this time?"

"I was hoping you weren't going to ask me that," said Jessie.

"I'm asking," said Ella firmly.

"Your Michael Gresham."

"Michael? Surely not! She's not his type at all, Jessie."

"I agree with you," said Jessie, "and maybe I'm wrong, but he took her out to dinner once, oh, six or seven months back, and, of course, they normally call each other two or three times a week. I don't know, maybe I'm losing my touch." She grinned hugely, displaying wonderful white teeth. "Want me to do a little detective work for you?"

"I'd appreciate it," said Ella. "I have to get back to London in the next couple of days, and I don't really have the time to sort out Jackie's love life."

"Leave it to me, boss," said Jessie with a grin.

It was a decision Ella was to regret . . . regret very much indeed.

Ella worked in the office until after nine that evening and then went upstairs to her apartment. It was strange—the apartment had been home for so many years. Greg had grown up there; it was the base from which everything had flowed; and yet somehow it no longer seemed like home. The little mews house in London was home now. Home is where Greg is, Ella realized, and she found the thought disturbing. Greg had been her life, her raison d'être, but now he was moving away from her, forming his own life, and the void created sometimes seemed unbearable.

Ella helped herself to a whiskey, sat down on the sofa, and eyed the telephone thoughtfully. It was two weeks since she had received the letter from Aaron. It had come as an extraordinary shock, for it was the first proper communication she had received from him in nearly three years. His rambling, disjointed epistle had nonetheless made his feelings plain—he wanted her. In what capacity he did not know, but he needed her back in his life. On receiving the letter she had been tempted to abandon everything and take the next flight to New York, but caution had prevailed. There seemed so much at stake with Aaron. Having loved him all her life, she had felt agony over their estrangement, but she knew they could not simply pick up the threads of their old relationship as if nothing had happened. Somehow she had built a life for herself without Aaron, but she knew instinctively that if she let him into her life again it would make her vulnerable in a way she had not been before. His letter suggested that he felt as uncertain as she, but he had not attempted to disguise his need for her. It was a cry for help, and she could not but respond. She drained her whiskey glass and, taking a deep breath, lifted the telephone.

"Aaron, it's Ella."

"Ella!" He sounded both pleased and apprehensive. "You got my letter?"

"Yes, I did," said Ella.

"I thought maybe you were angry about it, since I hadn't heard from you. Were you?"

"Of course I wasn't," said Ella. "I'm sorry I haven't been in touch, but I . . . well, I needed to think about it."

"And?" said Aaron.

"We need to talk," said Ella.

"I agree. I was thinking—I have some vacation time due. Why don't I come over to England for a couple of weeks?"

"There's no need for that," said Ella. "I'm here in New York."

"In New York! Now? At this moment?" The obvious joy in his voice warmed her heart.

"Yes, right now," said Ella. "I came over to attend the funeral of Alex Meyer. You probably saw the press coverage."

"Yes, I did, poor devil. I didn't know you were friendly with the Meyers."

"Business," said Ella. "I didn't know him well."

"Oh, I see. Ella, can we meet?"

"That's why I'm calling," said Ella. "We could go out to dinner, perhaps."

"Are you at your apartment?" Aaron asked.

"Yes."

"I'll be there in ten minutes, and then we can decide what we want to do."

She just had time to change and fix her makeup before the buzzer rang. She forced herself to stay calm and walk slowly and steadily to the apartment door. Aaron stood there, taller, fairer, better-looking than her memories of him, and at the same time so infinitely dear and familiar. She did not think, she did not even wait for him to come into the apartment, she simply hurled herself into his arms. He held her close and then, scooping her up, carried her into the apartment, to the sofa, where he held her tight and kissed her—lover's kisses, but gentle, controlled. She felt safe in his arms.

At last he drew away a little, his face very serious. "I didn't realize it until this moment," he said, "but that night—the night we spent together—has changed our relationship irrevocably, hasn't it? We can't ever go back to just being brother and sister."

Ella's face fell. "Can't we?" she asked in a small voice.

"I—I don't think so." He still held her in the circle of his arms, gently, but he trembled a little as he spoke, his face troubled. "I never realized how much I was attracted to you. I—I suppose because of Alice the whole thing was unthinkable, and therefore it never crossed my mind. Since that night I've tried so hard to see you as I used to, as my funny little tomboy friend." He smiled a little. "Yet the image I have of you now is that of a highly desirable woman, a woman who's made me feel as I haven't felt in years, if ever."

Ella studied his face in silence for a moment, her heart beating. "You mean that night together was . . ." She struggled for words.

"For me . . . it was wonderful," said Aaron, "like nothing that has ever been before, like a new experience."

Ella stared at him. "But that's how I felt, too."

"Oh, darling, darling Ella." He drew her into his arms and kissed her.

It was some moments before they drew apart. "I thought you hated the whole thing," Ella said in a shaky voice. "The next morning you seemed so . . . so angry, so upset about what had happened."

"Only because I felt I'd betrayed our friendship," said Aaron. "We were both drunk, and I felt I'd taken advantage of you and our relationship. I suppose I felt guilty, too, about Alice—it was so soon after her death."

"Yes, it was," said Ella.

"I felt sure you must hate me, and I thought it was probably best that we parted, because I simply couldn't face you."

"We've been very stupid," said Ella, "very, very stupid—you and I of all people, who have never had a moment's difficulty in communicating with each other, letting this happen—it's crazy."

"We can put it right," said Aaron gently. "How long will you be in New York?"

"Only for a couple of days," said Ella. "I have to get back to London because the Fulham opening is at the beginning of next month." She averted her eyes. "And then, well, I . . . I think I'll look for another project in London. Real estate's going crazy over there at the moment."

"But why?" said Aaron. He moved away from her. "I don't understand you. You have your Houston business, and you have your business here . . . surely they can't run themselves indefinitely. Sooner or later something will go drastically wrong if you continue to spend all your time in London." A thought struck him. "Is there . . . someone over there? Tim? Have you seen him again?"

"Yes," said Ella, "but there's no future for Tim and me."

"Because of his condition?"

"Partly," said Ella.

"And what are the other reasons?" Aaron persisted.

"Because of you," said Ella simply.

He moved closer; his arms were tight around her. "Then why, why do you have to find another project in London?"

"I like London, I feel at home there. The pace is much slower than in New York, and it suits me—it's old age, I guess." She tried a bright smile, but Aaron did not respond.

"It's Greg, isn't it?" he said.

"I suppose so," Ella admitted. "I know he's making his own life over there and doing very well, but he's still very young. I like to be around, and also . . ." She hesitated.

"Go on," said Aaron.

"I guess he's going to stay in England permanently. He hasn't said so, but I think that's his intention."

"So you want to stay in England, too?"

"Not all the time," said Ella defensively, "but if I have the odd project going on, I could at least spend part of each year there."

"During the last few years you've spent practically all your time in London," said Aaron. "Why should the future be any different?" His voice sounded bitter.

"Is it so wrong for me to want to be near my child?"

"No, no, of course not," said Aaron. "It's just that I don't see what future there is for us."

"Is there an 'us,' then?" Ella asked.

"I want to marry you," said Aaron abruptly, as though suddenly making the decision. "I don't want you as my little sister anymore, or my lover, I want you as my wife."

"Oh, Aaron," Ella whispered. They kissed.

"Let me show you how much I love you," Aaron said hoarsely, "properly this time. I love you so much, Ella."

He took her hand and led her into her bedroom. They were both nervous and unsure. Before, drink had blunted their senses, enabling them to take the giant step from lifelong friendship to becoming lovers. Ella drew the curtains, and Aaron switched on the bedside light. They undressed quickly, turning away from each other, embarrassed, self-conscious. They slipped between the sheets. Aaron held out his arms, and the moment Ella came into them, the moment their bodies touched, they both let out great sighs of relief. They clung to each other, skin on skin, savoring each other's warmth.

"I can't begin to tell you how often I've longed for this," Aaron whispered.

"I tried not to think about us at all—I guess I was afraid," said Ella.

"Afraid of what?" Aaron asked.

"Of daring to think there might be any future for us,

because I thought you regretted what had happened between us. What took you so long to write, Aaron?"

"I don't know. Perhaps I felt we weren't ready until now."

He kissed her, and they began caressing each other, both aware of the extraordinary contrast between knowing each other so well as people but so little as lovers. They made love swiftly then, each sensing the desperate need in the other. It seemed to Ella as they climaxed together, shouting out in triumph, that they had attained the impossible—the perfect union of mind and body. The thought made her cry, and when she reached up to caress Aaron's cheek she found his face, too, was wet with tears.

It was two o'clock in the morning when Ella woke to the chimes of the grandfather clock in the hall. Aaron slumbered by her side; she drew closer to him, seeking comfort and reassurance. She tried to think of the future—the irony of the situation was not lost on her. Years before, when she had loved Tim and thought she would marry him, the fact that she lived and worked in America had stood between them. Now the reverse applied with Aaron. Of course, she did not have to stay in London, but until this evening that had been the course she had set for herself. It would not be easy to change direction.

Although Ella was lying perfectly still, the turmoil in her mind was considerable, and perhaps it was this that made Aaron stir beside her. "What are you thinking about?" he asked softly.

"About us."

She could sense him smiling as he spoke. "You never answered my question. Will you marry me? You will, won't you, Ella?"

"I—I don't know," said Ella.

Aaron propped himself up on one elbow. She could see the silhouette of his angular features in the darkness. "But how can you hesitate after this, after tonight?" His voice sounded anguished.

"It's not that I don't love you, Aaron, and it's not that I don't want to be with you. It's just that before I received your letter I'd worked out what was going to happen to me next. I'd decided to base myself in London, I had my whole life mapped out. Now, suddenly, you've turned it upside down."

"I'm sorry, truly," said Aaron, "but we have to be together always—surely you can see that. We can't conduct a relationship worth anything from opposite sides of the Atlantic."

"I know and understand why you want a conventional marriage, but I'm not the same sort of person Alice was," Ella said carefully. "I can't be the sort of wife to you that she was—always being there, attending your medical dinners, being kind to junior doctors . . . I can't be like that, Aaron. I must have a life of my own."

"I know, and it doesn't matter," said Aaron promptly. "I wouldn't want you to be the same as Alice. If you were, then I would feel disloyal. Ella, you don't have to explain a single damned thing about yourself to me. I know it all."

"Do you, do you really?"

"I know you better than any other person in the world."

Ella sighed. "Aaron, you're going to have to give me some time. I'll go back to London as arranged, see Fulham launched, and then have a good long talk with Greg to see what his plans are."

"You can't link your whole life to Greg," said Aaron. "I love the boy like my own son, you know that, but if William decided he was going to live in Hong Kong, or France, or Canada, or wherever, I wouldn't give up my practice here and move to be closer to him." The logic of what he was saying was irrefutable.

"I know," said Ella. "I know what you're saying is right, but I still need the time, Aaron. Can I have it?"

"Whatever I have is yours," he said, "and if it's a little time you need, you've got it. Just don't hang around too long. We've wasted so much time already—we're halfway through our lives, and what we have left is precious."

"I promise," said Ella.

They kissed, and instantly they both forgot the future, for nothing was relevant to either of them but that moment in each other's arms.

Chapter 37

London—*February 1985*

To the world, the opening of the West London Meyer Centre was a triumph. Beneath the surface, however, the people most concerned with the creation of the Meyer Centre were far from united in their triumph. Joseph Meyer was there, of course, looking terrible. Margot was there, too, as Stephanie had insisted, as were Greg and the Irvines.

Ella and Stephanie had devised a table plan that kept Joseph a good distance from Stephanie, Margot as far away as possible from Ella, Greg at the opposite end of the table from Margot, and Tim strategically placed some distance from them both. It seemed to Ella that the complexities of the various relationships would almost be a joke if they weren't so sad. Perhaps the saddest of all, in many respects, was the decline of her own relationship with Stephanie. The Meyer Centre was a considerable achievement. For two women who had built their own businesses from scratch, it was the crowning glory of all their activities to date, making Stephanie's country hotels and Ella's apartment buildings pale into insignificance by comparison. Yet the relationship between them was horribly strained, and the reason seemed to be Tim. Several times during the last frantic days before the opening Ella had tried to broach the subject of Tim with Stephanie, but each time she had been cut short until finally, in a fury, Stephanie had said, "Oh, for Christ's sake, Ella, you may be obsessed with my ex-husband, but I'm not. Just leave it, would you?" There seemed to be so much misunderstanding, of which the most significant was clearly the tragedy of Stephanie and Joseph—running the Meyer empire in tandem, both grieving for the same man, and yet worlds apart.

Margot had aged, Ella noticed with a degree of satisfaction of which she was not proud. Whereas in the past there had been a timeless quality about her, and although she was extremely attractive, she now looked as though she could well be forty. Greg had greeted her warmly on his arrival, and despite Ella's nerves about their reunion she could not help but admire the way her son handled the meeting. He seemed perfectly at ease, and having spent some minutes talking to Margot, he turned his attention to the Irvine girls.

Ella let Stephanie and Joseph take center stage during the press reception, and then at last the questions stopped and the champagne flowed once more. She sat alone and watched the proceedings with weary interest, receiving a number of impressions . . . of Stephanie and Joseph having a short but violent exchange in which Joseph seemed to be pleading; of Greg and Belinda kissing in a doorway; of Tim talking earnestly to Stephanie, who looked about to crack; and of Margot in avid conversation with an extremely good-looking man, clearly of Arab extraction. "Who is he?" Ella whispered to Stephanie.

"He's a colleague of Joseph's," said Stephanie. "His name's Prince Ahfaad Rochlieu."

"He's gorgeous," said Ella.

Stephanie gave her a sharp look. "A snake in the grass, I should imagine. He's an interesting combination—half Arab, half French. His position with Joseph is not unlike mine, inasmuch as he owns a number of hotels in the Middle East and he and Joseph have kind of become partners. The hotels are still separately owned, but they undertake a lot of activities together—marketing and so on."

"It's funny," said Ella. "He's the first man I've ever seen beside Margot who seems to look right with her. They sort of fit together, do you know what I mean?"

"I don't have your obsessive interest in relationships," said Stephanie. "I can't say I can get worked up about it one way or the other." She turned away dismissively.

Margot was enjoying herself more than she had in some time. Part of the reason was Greg. It was nice to see him again, but she could now recognize how totally unsuitable the relationship had been. Ella had been right, she realized, ironically. He had grown up, certainly, filled out, matured, and he had acquired some polish that had not been there before. The second source of pleasure was the Meyer Centre itself. It was a triumph, not only for Ella and Stephanie, but also for Joshkers Bank, which was known to have sponsored the deal to a great extent. Of course, Meyer had played a dominant role, but the Centre had a different feel from Meyer's other locations, an individual stamp. The third reason for Margot's pleasure that day was meeting Ahfaad Rochlieu. Joseph had introduced them early on in the day, and Margot could not remember having met anyone who fascinated her more. He was startlingly good-looking—tall and dark with large brown eyes and high cheekbones. She recognized immediately not only a superb intellect but, in all probability, a brain superior to her own, which was a challenge indeed. As the opening celebrations drew to an end and people began to drift away Margot found herself lingering, reluctant to leave Ahfaad's side. The thought of never seeing him again appalled her.

He seemed to sense her feelings, for he suddenly said, "We'd better have dinner together, hadn't we?" She nodded; it didn't occur to her to disagree. "Why don't you come back to my house? I have an excellent chef who can prepare almost anything you'd like." Margot hesitated. "Are you afraid my Eastern blood will get the better of me and I'll have you shipped off into white slavery?" Ahfaad raised a mocking eyebrow, but his intelligent eyes watched her intently.

She laughed. "No, and I'd be fascinated to see your home." It was an unusually candid remark for Margot.

Ahfaad's house was in Eaton Square. It had been two houses once, since he had bought properties adjoining each other.

"Do you live here all alone?" Margot asked, impressed by the size and grandeur before they had even entered the front door.

"Not always." He grinned at her.

"I am sorry." She was embarrassed. "I didn't mean to pry."

The spectacular exterior in no way prepared Margot for the opulence inside the house. She had an impression of curving staircases, priceless paintings, and a beautiful chandelier as she was steered down the hall and past the drawing room to a smaller room at the back of the house overlooking the garden. It was completely dark outside, but floodlights played on the garden, in the center of which was a magnificent fountain. Ahfaad's obsession seemed to be with silks—the curtains were silk, the sofa and chairs rough raw silk—all in muted shades of green and blue. There was an instantly recognizable Picasso in the hall, which, Margot had no doubt, was genuine. Books lined two of the other walls—beautifully bound in leather, volume upon volume—but somehow they were too perfect, and Margot suspected no one ever took them down and read them. A butler appeared and poured champagne, and Margot stood by the window, gazing out at the garden.

"You're a very beautiful woman, Margot," said Ahfaad quietly. "I'd like to drink to that." Margot inclined her head in acknowledgment. "Someone told me—Joseph, I suppose—that you are half English, half Korean. Is that right?" Margot nodded. "A mongrel, then, like me—we're always the best, certainly the strongest."

Margot laughed. "I'll agree with you there."

"Are you going to tell me your story?"

Much to her own surprise, for a full half hour Margot talked of the past, reliving the terrible days in Korea. After

Ella's blackmail she had taken steps to annul the marriage between herself and Terry. This meant that at last she was able to talk about it, and, unbidden, the story came pouring out.

"It must have been extraordinary for you," Ahfaad said. "One moment a child, the next a married woman, and then a child again. Why have you never married again?" he asked.

He was a strange man. His questions could have been construed as impertinent, yet somehow Margot did not resent them. "I had an affair with a married man for some years—sixteen, to be precise. That and my job were sufficiently absorbing that I never really thought about marriage nor missed it."

"And the affair is over now?"

"He died," said Margot.

"I'm sorry. And is there no one else at present?"

Margot grinned. "Is this some sort of interrogation?"

"Most certainly it is. I have it in my mind to woo you, Margot Haigh, but first I must know about the competition."

"I don't like the thought of making it too easy for you," said Margot, smiling, "but it is fair to say I am—how shall I put it?—between liaisons at the moment."

"Excellent." Ahfaad laughed triumphantly and refilled their glasses. "I, too," he said, "am between liaisons. I think this calls for another toast." They raised their glasses—they were both a little tipsy, but pleasantly so.

"Are you going to tell me about you and your life now?"

Ahfaad grinned briefly. "After my inquisition, I can see I'm going to have to, aren't I?"

"I rather think so," said Margot.

"My life pales into insignificance compared with yours in terms of achievement. My mother was an Arab princess from a minor principality, my father a wealthy and influential Frenchman—the Rochlieus owned chateaux and vineyards, even a castle or two. My parents met during the war. It was a passionate affair, by all accounts. I was born in

1943, here in London. My father was present at my birth, which was unusual in those days, but it was as well, really, because it was the only time we ever met."

"Oh, I'm sorry," said Margot. "He was killed, then, during the war?"

"Yes, a German ambush went wrong. My mother took me back home to her parents. I barely remember her. She was killed in a helicopter crash just after my fourth birthday. Sabotage was suspected but never proved—it was the usual sort of infighting that goes on in our part of the world." He smiled, but the smile did not reach his eyes.

"Poor little boy," said Margot, "an orphan at four."

"A very rich and privileged orphan. I inherited all my father's money and the estates in France, and my Arab grandfather showered on me all his wealth, since I was the eldest grandson. I was well cared for—indeed, lavishly cared for—and loved. My grandmother died when I was fifteen, my grandfather when I was eighteen, so I was a man by the time I had to fend for myself—besides which I've had the benefit of an English education here at Eton. Having coped with the early years of that, I was equipped to cope with anything." Margot laughed. "Yes," said Ahfaad, "from the desert to the most illustrious playing fields in the world—a life of strange contrast, not unlike your own."

"And now," said Margot, "how do you spend your time?"

"About six months of the year at my home outside Cairo, the rest of the time in Europe, partly for pleasure, partly for business. I do all the fashionable things—ski in the right places, spend the prescribed amount of time in the south of France, and do my Christmas shopping at Fortnum and Mason."

"Is it important for you to do the right thing?" Margot asked, intrigued.

Ahfaad shrugged. "It's like playing a game. It's what is expected of me. It requires me to bed the occasional famous actress and be seen from time to time with minor European royalty. It's fun, it's quite hard work, but since I'm stuck with the image, I might as well enjoy it."

"It's why you're familiar, I suppose," said Margot.

"Very probably," said Ahfaad. "By contrast, I know quite a lot about you. Did you know Joseph Meyer is a great admirer of yours?"

Margot shook her head. "No, I didn't. I barely know him. My only contact with the Mr. Meyer is through Stephanie Bonham, and the only project with which we have jointly been involved is the Meyer Centre."

"Nonetheless," said Ahfaad, "he's watched your progress over some years. The phenomenon of truly successful women fascinates him. That's why he tolerates Stephanie—he'd have booted her out years ago if she'd been a man."

"I don't see how the relationship can last a great deal longer in its current form," said Margot. "It worries me, because so much of Stephanie's success depends on her business relationship with Meyer. Since Alex's death it seems to have hit an all-time low."

"Yes . . . I agree," said Ahfaad. "Still, it's my belief that there's a big shake-up ahead."

"What do you mean?" Margot asked eagerly. Ahfaad looked wary. "My lips are sealed," Margot insisted.

"I'm only guessing," said Ahfaad, "truly. He's said nothing to me, but I would suspect that Joseph will sell his Meyer interests quite soon."

"Sell! Joseph? I can't imagine him parting with everything he's built up."

"Why not?" said Ahfaad. "If he can sell off Meyer while he's still young enough and well enough to do a good deal, he can at least safeguard the future for his employees."

Margot smiled. "I wonder . . ."

"Stop scheming," said Ahfaad. "Remember that what I have told you is in confidence and, in any case, is only an opinion."

Margot studied him in silence for a moment. "I'm surprised you told me at all. I imagine that Meyer selling up must be of interest to you."

"Not really," said Ahfaad. "It would just mean more responsibilities and more work. Of course, I could bring in someone to run it for me, but that would rather destroy the whole point of the exercise. No, it's not for me. Now, are we going to eat? What would you like—French, Italian, Arabic, Greek, Spanish?"

"Don't tell me you have a chef for every nation housed in your basement."

Ahfaad laughed. "No, just one man—but he is a genius."

"To tell you the truth," said Margot, "I'm not really hungry."

"Then I will order some crudités. No one can make crudités like Henri—his sauces!" Ahfaad rolled his eyes, got up, and crossed the room to ring the bell.

An extraordinary man, Margot thought, watching him. Despite all his money, he seemed oddly untouched. Margot had always been attracted to wealth and power—she knew that—but never before had she come across it so understated. He refilled their glasses. "I've had more than enough," Margot protested.

"Maybe." Ahfaad smiled and, coming over, sat beside her on the sofa, not touching her, but close. He looked deep into her eyes. "There's something about you, Margot, something I can't exactly explain, but it's as though I've been looking for you for a long time. You talked about recognizing me when we met. I recognized you, but not because I had seen your face splashed across the gossip columns. I think I recognize the person for whom I've been searching." He hesitated. "You think I'm crazy?" Margot shook her head, feeling suddenly close to tears. "We're very much the same," Ahfaad continued. "We're both mongrels, as I said, both orphaned early in life. In many respects we're rootless, we belong nowhere. Maybe, just maybe, with one another will we feel truly at home. You think I'm talking like an idiot? Perhaps, but I think we might have quite a future together."

Margot said nothing but stared back into his great brown eyes. She could not speak to confirm or deny—her heart was suddenly too full of emotion she could not express. All she knew was that Ahfaad's words mirrored exactly her own feelings.

Chapter 38

Gloucestershire—*March 1985*

Stephanie sat in the car for some time simply staring at the house. It was a beautiful, clear day; daffodils sprinkled the lawn, the orchard was in full blossom, the honey-colored Cotswold stone seemed to be shining with exuberance in the spring sunshine. She wound down the car window and took deep breaths of fresh air. She had spent the last two months in London and Paris, commuting frantically between the two, and smelling of exhaust had become a way of life. Just sitting in the car, she found herself already beginning to relax—it was extraordinary the effect Wickham always had upon her. How long had she been away? Six, seven years?

Her natural instinct on being asked to spend Sunday with Tim was to turn down his invitation. No, the children would not be there, he had told her—Millie was now living permanently in London, and Belinda, though still living at home with her father, was away for the weekend with Greg, staying with college friends of his. So what was the point of the invitation, Stephanie was almost tempted to ask, but she had been immediately attracted by the idea and accepted—a day away from London, away from the solitary misery of her life, was irresistible.

She must have been sitting outside the house for at least ten minutes before Tim came to join her. Middle age suited him, Stephanie thought as he walked toward her. He had become quietly self-assured. He had the same thick brown hair, only slightly flecked with gray, and his face, if anything, was better looking for a few lines. His figure was as trim as ever. He stopped by the open window of the car. "I left you alone with your thoughts for a few minutes, but I think it's time you came in now." She smiled, accepting his hand as he helped her out of the car. They exchanged kisses lightly, impersonally, on the cheek.

Inside, nothing much had changed; there were fires lit everywhere, and everything was polished and shining. The furniture was the same, the paintings hung in the same places, there was the odd new piece of upholstery, a bit of paint here and there, but no fundamental differences. Stephanie let out a sigh of pure joy.

"Nice to be back in the old place?" Tim asked.

They had naturally gravitated toward Tim's study, as always the coziest room in the house. She sank onto the sofa in front of the fire. "It's strange, you know—in dreams I always come here."

"How do you mean?" Tim asked.

"It doesn't matter what I'm dreaming about or who I'm with in my dreams. The setting is always Wickham. I wonder, perhaps, whether I haunt you sometimes."

Tim smiled. "Not noticeably."

They talked for some time about the children. "Lunch is ready whenever you are, incidentally," Tim said after a while.

"Is Mrs. Maggs here?" Stephanie looked up sharply.

"No, I gave her the day off."

"You should marry again, Tim," said Stephanie.

"So I'm always being told. The trouble is I don't have much time for a social life these days, what with the two farms to run and the kids home at weekends."

"Two farms?" said Stephanie.

"My father died a couple of months ago—I didn't let you know because I realized how busy you were. As you know, my mother's been dead for five years now, and in that time the stubborn old devil wouldn't let me help him—he absolutely insisted he could manage on his own. As a result, the place is in a frightful mess—the house is falling apart, the land is a disaster. I've been trying to sort it out, but it's not easy with the responsibilities of Wickham to consider as well."

"Why don't you put a manager in here for a few years?" Stephanie suggested.

Tim shook his head. "No, I'm coping—it just wears me out from time to time."

"You need to be careful," said Stephanie.

"Yes, though I haven't had a seizure now in nearly four years," said Tim. "I attribute my success to better drugs and a calm emotional life. I think emotional traumas are really my undoing."

"I'm sorry," said Stephanie. "I must have caused you a few of those over the years."

"Past history," said Tim. "Anyway, enough about me. At the risk of incurring your wrath, I'm going to tell you you look worn out, but I suppose it's not surprising. I assume that as well as having to cope with the loss of Alex in a personal sense, you're also having to cover his work."

Stephanie liked the way he spoke naturally and readily about Alex—everyone else avoided the subject. "I am finding it very difficult being on my own," she admitted. "Alex and I didn't get on too well during the last couple of years, but it doesn't make losing him any easier."

"Of course not," said Tim. "It must have been such a terrible shock, apart from anything else—such a waste of life."

"Yes." They were both silent for a moment, but it felt to Stephanie as though Tim was waiting for something. To cover the silence she found herself saying, "I don't know what the future holds for me, really. Joseph and I aren't speaking to each other, which doesn't make for a very happy working environment, and there are various other complications."

"Like being pregnant?" said Tim quietly.

Stephanie stared at him. "W-what do you mean? How do you know?"

Tim smiled. "I realized you were pregnant at the opening of the Meyer Centre in February. It was one of the reasons I asked you down today, to see if I could help."

"But how could you possibly know?" said Stephanie.

"I've seen you pregnant twice before, remember? There's a certain look about you."

"I didn't think I'd put on any weight," Stephanie protested.

"You haven't—well, a little, perhaps, but not so most people would notice. Let's face it, I am more experienced than most on the subject of Stephanie Bonham, mother-to-be."

"It's Alex's child, of course," she said.

"Of course," said Tim. There was a moment's silence, broken only by the shifting of a log in the grate. "Does Joseph know?" Tim asked, at last.

"Yes, and he's putting a lot of pressure on me. He wants the child, of course, but I'm damned if I'm going to let that happen."

"Why?" said Tim. "He's just lost his son, and I'd have thought you'd be grateful for his help in raising the child. After all, you're not exactly the most maternal of people, are you?"

"That was unnecessary," said Stephanie.

"I'm sorry," said Tim. "I just imagined you would welcome sharing the responsibility with Joseph."

"I don't want my child, boy or girl, to end up like Alex. Joseph is so suffocating, so demanding. I don't want my child to feel that he has to spend his life in the Meyer organization and that he's being groomed for stardom from birth. I want him to grow up with the benefit of a normal childhood. I want him to be free to make his own choices. Joseph ruined Alex, but he's not going to ruin my baby."

"All right, I accept that, but how will you manage with a baby and your career?" Tim said.

"A nanny, I suppose," said Stephanie defensively.

"With Joseph demanding to be involved, it's not going to

be easy. He'll expect you to bring up the child yourself, I should think."

"I know." Stephanie stood up and wandered to the window seat. She stared out across the drive. In her mind's eye she could see herself and George bicycling up the drive as children, faces pink with exertion, laughing, carefree.

"Why didn't you have an abortion?" Tim asked suddenly.

"This child was neither intended nor planned," Stephanie felt compelled to explain. "It was an accident, but the moment I knew I was pregnant I also knew I couldn't possibly get rid of the child."

Tim stood up and came to join her by the window. "This is possibly a contentious thing for me to say, but I'm going to say it anyway. Perhaps you wanted to have this child because it represented the way back to Wickham—an excuse, if you like."

Stephanie's head jerked up. She stared at him. "How do you mean?"

"You don't see the child being raised in a London flat with a series of nannies. You see it growing up here, having the childhood that you and George had, that Millie and Belinda enjoyed. I've been watching you. Just in the short period you've been back here it's obvious Wickham still holds the magic for you in a way I suspect nowhere else does, and nowhere else will ever be able to do."

"Yes, that's true," Stephanie murmured.

"Then I'll move out," said Tim decisively. "I can still run the estate so that you won't have to bother with that, but the house will be free for you to bring up your child. Once Mrs. Maggs knows you're pregnant she'll relent and help you in every way possible—you know how she adores babies."

From nowhere great tears began to roll down Stephanie's cheeks. "Oh, Tim, no, no," she said.

"Don't cry." He set down his glass and drew her gently to him until her head was resting on his shoulder. "Look, Stephanie," he began, still holding her close. "I've always known that this is your home and that one day you would want it back. Leaving it will be a wrench, of course, but perhaps a change of scene would do me good—in fact, I know damn well it would. I'm stuck in a rut."

"Stop it, stop it." Stephanie thumped ineffectually with small fists against his chest and then burst into a fresh bout of crying.

Tim held her firmly. "Now what?" His expression was warm, even amused.

Stephanie made a superhuman effort to control herself. "Of course I wouldn't let you leave, Tim, not for one moment. You are the most impossibly generous, kind person in the world to suggest it, but you're also an idiot. Wickham is you, you are Wickham now—it's I who am the visitor. I wouldn't consider your suggestion for even one moment." The tears returned, and she pressed her damp face against the rough tweed of his jacket. "Sorry, I'm making you all wet," she mumbled.

"Come and sit by the fire." He drew her back to the sofa and sat her down, his arm still tightly around her. "Then why not let the child be brought up here anyway?" he said after a pause.

Stephanie raised her eyes to his. "I left you to bring up our children, and that was bad enough. I can hardly expect you to raise another man's child."

Abruptly Tim removed his arm and stood up, his expression unreadable. "Of course that's not what I'm suggesting. Clearly this baby is your responsibility and nothing to do with me. However, this is a big house, and there's no reason why the baby and nanny shouldn't be installed in one part of it and I in another, if this is where you'd like the child to be brought up."

Stephanie eyed him cautiously. "But why should you share your home with anyone, Tim—particularly a small baby, with all the noise and clutter? And let's face it, this is not just any baby. This baby is the result of your wife's unfaithfulness, the son or daughter of the man who took me away from you. You could hardly be blamed for not feeling very well disposed toward the child."

"I love children," said Tim. "I expect I'd get fond of the little devil in time—and if not, it doesn't really matter, does it? Maybe it does seem a generous gesture, but frankly it's no great sacrifice. Indeed, if you could make the nanny impossibly glamorous, nubile, and under twenty-five, it would provide the ultimate incentive." He smiled, but it didn't reach his eyes.

Stephanie felt a stab of anger at his words that both surprised and confused her. "I expect that could be arranged," she said, sharply.

Tim stared at her, and a slow smile spread across his face. "You don't like the idea, do you?"

"Tim, don't let's play games," said Stephanie wearily. "It's a very kind offer, but I think it's unworkable."

"You're wrong," said Tim. "It *is* workable, and I'm sorry if I was flippant. Let me try and put it right by saying that I would actually welcome the opportunity to see a little more of you than I have in recent years—it would be nice to see you on weekends, which presumably you will spend here with the baby. I honestly think you should accept my offer. Look, put it another way if you like—I owe you one. Does that make you feel better?"

"You don't owe me anything," said Stephanie. "It's all the other way around. You know that."

Tim shook his head and came to sit on the sofa beside her once more. "I'm not denying you've caused me a great deal of pain over the years, but you also gave me the greatest gift of all. You gave me life, a proper life, a full, normal life like everyone else."

"If you mean I gave you Wickham," said Stephanie, "I think I should remind you that we created it together, and in any event, it's you who have sustained it."

"Of course I don't mean Wickham," said Tim dismissively. "What you gave me was far more valuable than this." He gestured around him. "You gave me a sense of self-worth. You made me realize that I could live like any other person. My accident robbed me of any concept of normal living, yet marvelously, miraculously you gave it back to me." Their eyes met and held, memories flashing between them. "There is no more valuable gift you could have given anyone," Tim said softly. "So is it such a big deal, under the circumstances, to share this house—which is, after all, yours—with your child?"

"You're a very special person, Tim," Stephanie said. On impulse she leaned forward and kissed him gently on his lips. It should have ended there, an acknowledgment of his kindness, his generosity, but the moment their lips met it lit a fuse between them, and their arms were around each other, their kisses frantic, their embraces at once familiar and yet new, intoxicating after their years apart. Stephanie could feel tears on her face, but whether they were her own or Tim's she had no way of knowing. All she knew was that it felt right to be in his arms, and when he stood up, took her hand, and led her up the staircase to their old bedroom it did not occur to her to argue. Once there, he undressed her and made love to her with a tenderness and compassion that Alex had never once shown her in all their years together.

By morning they were as much in love as they had ever been.

Chapter 39

New York—*June 1985*

The heat of the city hit Ella the moment she stepped from the plane at Newark Airport. All the way across the Atlantic she wished she had told Aaron she was coming so that he could have met her. Now, tired and anxious, she would have appreciated his support more than ever, though in her heart of hearts she knew this was the better way. First she had to find out, or rather confirm, what had gone wrong. She needed to give herself wholeheartedly to the business, and only when she had straightened things out could she tell Aaron she was back. Without doubt this was the worst crisis of her career, threatening to destroy everything she had achieved.

Since the opening of the West London Meyer Centre Ella had remained in England. She had been dabbling with property in the City of London, enjoying an English spring and frequent visits from Greg, often accompanied by Belinda. The relationship between herself and Stephanie was still tense, though a little easier. Ella had been genuinely pleased to hear that she and Tim were back together, and all she could hope was that as Stephanie's pregnancy advanced she would mellow a little toward her. It had been a pleasant spring and early summer except for missing Aaron. They had spoken regularly on the telephone, and Ella had promised to spend the summer in New York, for Greg was planning a trip abroad once he had finished college.

This tranquil period had lasted until just a week ago, when the bombshell struck in the form of a telephone call from Michael Gresham. He had begun without preamble, clearly very angry. "You have to be the most stubborn woman I've ever met. What's wrong with you? Can't you take advice from *anyone?*"

"Michael, I don't know what you're talking about," Ella had said. "Can you calm down and start again?"

"I warned you," he ranted, "I warned you back at Christmas to get out while the getting was good. When I didn't hear from you I wondered whether Jackie had forgotten to pass on the message, but she assured me she had told you, and since then you haven't even bothered to answer my letters. I know I'm only a humble lawyer, but I've seen the signs coming way ahead of most people, and if you'd just taken my advice at the time—"

"Michael, will you listen to me for a moment? I truly don't know what you're talking about."

He let out a sigh of irritation. "Last Christmas I came to

New York on business. I knew you were in England, but I had a long talk with Jackie and explained that I was worried about the oil market in Houston. The price was dropping slowly but steadily, and I had a feeling it was going to have a devastating effect on the city. I asked her to get hold of you urgently, and she promised to contact you as soon as possible in the new year. This she did, as you well know. What I've been trying to get across to you is the importance of shedding some of your property fast. Back in January the prices were still holding up and you could have gotten out with all your money intact, whereas now—"

"I never received that message," said Ella flatly.

"You're kidding," said Michael. "I spoke to Jackie from Toronto. I called her specially to make sure she'd passed my views on to you, and she said she had."

"I was in almost daily contact with her around that period," said Ella. "We had some lease renewals coming up in New York. Believe me, she never mentioned a thing."

"Shit." There was a silence on the other end of the phone for a moment. "Have you been receiving your mail from New York?"

"Yes, of course," said Ella. "Jackie faxes me daily everything that comes in."

"Then at least you have had my letters—why didn't you react to them?"

There was a stunned silence for a moment. "Michael, there has been no letter from you."

"God damn it, what's Jackie been up to? She could well have cost you your business, Ella—it's that serious. Don't you read the papers?"

"I know that oil prices have been a bit unstable recently," Ella admitted.

"Unstable! The market's plummeted, and as a result this is a sick, sick town, Ella. People are being fired, companies are going under, even one or two banks are going."

"Jack . . . ?" Ella began.

"No, no, he's all right at the moment, but he's not having an easy time."

"Then why hasn't he been in touch with me?"

"Because I told him that I'd already contacted you. I told him there was no need to worry you because I was keeping you up on what was going on. We both thought it was odd you hadn't reacted to any of my letters, but we assumed you were being your usual pigheaded self—choosing to ignore advice, particularly when it comes to the selling of your precious properties. It never occurred to me . . . Jesus, I see it all now."

"See what?" There was a long silence on the other end of the line. "See what, Michael?" Ella persisted.

"It's my fault," said Michael. "At the back end of last year I took Jackie out to dinner one night and somehow ended up in her bed."

"I don't understand, Michael. What are you saying?"

"Well, I spent Christmas Eve with her. Anyway, I wanted out, so I told her it was probably best if we ended our relationship because you would be coming back to New York shortly."

"What the hell did I have to do with any of it?" Ella said.

"Shit, Ella, I was looking for an excuse. I told Jackie that I thought it was pretty crass of us to carry on an affair in front of you. I told her that the trouble in Houston would undoubtedly bring you back from England, and for that reason it would be best if we split."

"Let me get this straight," said Ella. "You're saying that Jackie has deliberately avoided telling me about the trouble in Houston so as to keep me here in England?"

"Can you think of another explanation?" Michael asked.

"Have you seen her since Christmas," Ella asked, "in any capacity?" Her voice was hard as flint.

"No, I haven't. I was in Toronto on business until the end of February—a difficult case that dragged on. When I got back to Houston I found the shit had really hit the fan, and I've been here ever since, sorting out my clients' various messes. Oh, hell, Ella, I'm so sorry. I should have known."

"How bad is it?" Ella asked.

"Bad. At a guess I would say your property's worth no more than fifty percent of its 1984 value."

"Fifty percent. So at least it's still holding its own as collateral."

"Possibly, yes, though I don't know enough about your borrowing arrangements. It can't last, Ella. Things are getting worse. This is a city under siege. It's in deep, deep trouble."

"I'll straighten things out over here," said Ella, "and I'll be with you as soon as possible. I'll go via New York, talk to Jackie, and then I'll fly straight down. I'll let you know which day. Could you tell Jack what's happened?"

"Yes, I will," said Michael. "And Ella, I'm sorry, really sorry."

"Yes, I know you are," said Ella.

On the plane, and now in the cab on the way to Lexington Avenue, Ella tried to rehearse and re-rehearse how she was going to handle Jackie Partridge. She had not told anyone she was returning to New York; it seemed better to have surprise on her side. The shock of suddenly seeing her walk through the office door would leave Jackie vulnerable and give her no time to think of an excuse for what had happened.

"Ella! It's Ella! Isn't this just great?" Jessie waddled forward and wrapped Ella in her arms. "Boy, what a wonderful surprise! Haven't we missed you. Let me look at you." Jessie held her at arm's length. "You look well and happy—England must suit you, but we sure miss you, don't we, Jackie?"

Jackie stood a few paces behind. "Yes, of course," she said. "Hello, Ella . . . what a surprise. Why didn't you tell us you were coming?" Ella thought she could detect an edge to Jackie's voice, but on the face of it the girl seemed pleased enough to see her.

"I'll fix you some coffee," Jessie fussed. "When did you get in? I bet you're bushed."

"I've only been in about half an hour," said Ella. "I've just been up to the apartment to freshen up. Coffee would be wonderful, thanks." She took her time. She drank the coffee and worked her way through the pile of correspondence Jackie gave her, made a couple of phone calls, and accepted the light lunch Jessie brought to her desk. Only then did she ask to see Jackie. "Come in and shut the door," she said. Jackie came in and sat down, apparently unruffled, notepad and pen at the ready. "I've come back to the States quite specifically to see you and to sort out the mess in Houston. I assume I don't need to say any more than that."

"I don't know what you mean," Jackie began.

"Let's not waste each other's time, Jackie. I know what you did, and I also know why you did it. What you may not realize is that your actions may well have cost me my entire business."

At her words Jackie's face crumpled, and she burst into great gasping sobs. She began searching uselessly for a handkerchief, and Ella reached into the drawer of her desk and threw her over a box of tissues. "I'm so . . . sorry," Jackie said. "I knew what I was doing was wrong, but I couldn't help myself. I love him so much."

Ella let out a deep sigh. "Michael and I have worked out your motives. I'd just like to check them."

"Michael! Michael knows what I've done?"

"How else do you think I know?" said Ella. "He called me in London in desperation because of what's happening to the Houston real estate prices."

"Oh, God." Jackie burst into another fit of crying.

"When Michael first alerted you to the problem in Houston he thought I could get out with all my money intact. Now he calculates the price of real estate has dropped by fifty percent. If it drops any more, Jackie, I'll be ruined."

"Oh, no. Oh, Ella" was all Jackie could manage.

Ella was fast losing her temper. "I was born in Kentucky with nothing. You may think there's poverty in England, but you haven't seen anything compared with the poverty in Kentucky forty years ago. My home was a shack. How do you think it feels to have come this far only to have my business thrown away by a stupid lovelorn girl? It's unbelievable—you've been in a position of trust all these years. God knows I've paid you a decent enough salary and looked after you well. Was loyalty too much to ask?"

"I—I've nothing to say," said Jackie, "except that I'm terribly sorry, and that I'll go right away, of course. I—I think I must have been a little mad. It's just that there was nothing, no one in my life. I'm so lonely, and when Michael showed an interest in me I couldn't believe it. He's so handsome, so successful, and he was interested in me. When—when he told me there was no future for our relationship because of you, I could only see you as the enemy."

The anger left Ella as suddenly as it had come. The bleakness of Jackie's words struck a chord in her understanding. "Look, Jackie, I'm not trying to say this to be unkind, but it's vital you keep a grip on reality. Michael just used me as an excuse. He didn't care about hurting my feelings. Michael's a philanderer, a charming, unscrupulous philanderer. He doesn't care about you, or me, or any of the other girls he's bedded. There's no point in loving Michael Gresham, whoever you are."

"But I do," Jackie wailed. She began sobbing in earnest, close to hysteria.

With a sudden rush of irritation Ella leaned forward and slapped her hard across the face. Jackie screamed.

Jessie burst through the door. "What's going on here? What's happening?"

"Leave us, Jessie, please," said Ella.

There was no aspect of her life from which Ella had ever excluded Jessie before. A look of hurt and bewilderment crossed her face. She retreated, shutting the door carefully behind her, but, Ella was sure, staying close enough to hear what she could through the door.

The shock from the slap had stopped Jackie's crying, and Jessie's intrusion had calmed the atmosphere. "Tell me something about your life in New York," Ella said. "Do you have girlfriends?"

Jackie shook her head. "No, not really. There was an English girl I met on the plane coming over. We were quite friendly for a year or so, but then she married an American and moved to Philadelphia. She writes sometimes."

"So what do you do in the evening?"

"Take work home, usually, and have a TV dinner. Sometimes Jessie asks me to her house for dinner with her family."

The bleakness of Jackie's life was all too apparent. To be lonely anywhere was bad; to be lonely in a big city was terrible. Of all the experiences of Ella's life, loneliness to this extent was unknown to her. There had always been somebody to call on, and then, of course, there was Greg. It had been her intention to order Jackie out of the office, to threaten her with legal action. Now an odd feeling of compassion made her hesitate. Was she getting soft? She stood up and wandered over to the window. Jackie had done wrong, quite deliberately withholding vital information, but Jackie was not entirely to blame. Ella knew she had been neglecting her business in the States; if she had been on the ball, she would have known what was going on in Houston.

Her decision was so sudden it startled her. She turned from the window. "I don't want you to leave, Jackie."

Jackie stared at her. "W-what?" she managed.

Ella came back and sat down at her desk. "There are various reasons, the most philanthropic of which is that clearly this job is a major part of your life. If I dismiss you for what's happened, then I can't in good conscience give you a reference, and you'll find it difficult to get another job."

"Ella, I can't believe this," Jackie began.

"I'm not all heart," Ella said, her voice harsh. "If I manage to save my business, it will be because I've put a lot of effort and thought into the Houston operation. If I dismiss you now, I'm going to have to find someone to take over in New York. In the past you've run this office extremely efficiently, and that's what I'd like you to continue to do. Of course, against the advantages of having you here I have to weigh the fact that I don't know whether I can ever trust you again."

"You can," Jackie blurted out. "You really can, Ella. It was just Michael—"

"Enough," said Ella. "Let's say I'm prepared to take your assurances. There is, however, a third element to my decision."

"What's that?" Jackie asked nervously.

"I don't think it would do you any harm to see the consequences of your actions. Whatever happens, I'm going to lose a great deal of money. I may even lose everything, and I think you should be here to see the end of this particular saga played out. It's a lesson you won't forget in a hurry."

"Ella, I'll do anything, anything," Jackie burst out, tears in her eyes again.

"I want you to go home now for the rest of the day, and when you come in tomorrow morning I want it to be as though this thing never happened between us. I want no tears, no hysterics. It's over, finished—what we have to do is try to pick up the pieces and save this business."

"Will you . . . will you have to tell Jessie?"

"Yes," said Ella, "I've never had any secrets from Jessie, and I can't start now."

"Thank you," Jackie muttered, "thank you for everything. I'm so sorry, I'm . . ."

"Jackie," Ella said, her voice gentle. Jackie raised her head. "Because of what's happened I believe you won't ever let me down again. Am I right to have that faith in you?"

"Absolutely," said Jackie, her eyes shining.

"OK, take off and I'll see you tomorrow. I plan to be in the office tomorrow morning and then fly down to Houston in the afternoon."

It was after six by the time Ella felt she had done all she could for the day. She had spent long hours on the phone to Houston, which had confirmed that everything Michael had predicted was already coming true. Tessa had a string of lease defaults, and on most of them Michael had not recommended taking legal action because there was no money there to claim. As for re-renting any of the premises, it seemed out of the question; there was far more real estate available than people wanting it.

On the stroke of six Jessie came in with a bottle of wine and two glasses. "Cocktail hour," she said.

Ella grinned. "I guess I need that."

"I knew it," said Jessie, pouring the wine. "Now, will you tell me what's going on, honey, or will I have to beat the living daylights out of you to find out? You know your Jessie—she likes to know the score." Briefly Ella told Jessie the story.

"Men are shits," said Jessie. "So you're looking for a new member of the team?"

Ella shook her head. "I'm keeping her on." Jessie stared at her in silence. "Well, I felt—" Ella began in an effort to justify her decision.

"No need to explain, and I love you for it. Hell, I love you anyway, but I really love you for this. You've made the right decision—that Jackie, she'll sure as hell never let you down again."

"That's what I figure," said Ella.

The joy in Aaron's voice was all Ella needed to drive away her dark forebodings when half an hour later she called his apartment and told him she was in New York. "How come you didn't tell me?" he said when he had recovered from his surprise. "I have the place knee-deep in women, and I suppose I'll have to clear them out now that you're in town."

"You certainly will," said Ella. "My place or yours?"

"I'll come to you. I should think you're tired out after the journey."

It was not until several hours later, lying sated in his arms, that Ella was able to tell Aaron what had brought her back to the States. Aaron listened in silence. When Ella had finished he let out a sigh. "I know this is the wrong thing to be thinking, but I'm glad you're home, even given the circumstances that brought you back here. It's worth it just to have a sight of you and know that you'll be around until you've sorted out this mess. I like the way you handled Jackie, too—you know something, Ella Kovac? You're an old softie underneath."

"It's your fault," said Ella. "You're making me soft. You're making me see that there are things besides my business and my son. I've started to appreciate leisure in a way I never have before, and I spend far too much of my time thinking about you rather than the next real estate deal."

"That's as it should be," said Aaron. "So when are you going to marry me?"

"I can't decide anything at the moment, not while all this is going on. You do see that, Aaron, don't you?"

"Not really," he said. "Either we're right for each other or we're not."

"You know we are, but would you please give me a little space until this is over?" Ella asked.

"I guess so." Aaron's disappointment was evident in his voice.

They kissed and were interrupted by the telephone. Ella reached out and picked up the receiver. "Hello," she said.

"Mom? Mom, it's Greg."

"Greg! Are you OK?"

He laughed. "Why is it that whenever I call you unexpectedly you always assume there's something wrong with me?"

Ella turned over in the bed and shifted herself into a sitting position. "That's a mother for you."

"I guess," said Greg. "How's New York?"

"Same old city. Where are you?"

"I'm in London, at Holland Park."

"Alone?" Ella teased.

"Never you mind," said Greg with a laugh. "Actually, Mom, I was calling for a favor. My exams are over next week, and I thought I might bring Belinda to the States, just for a week or two, to show her around. Would that be OK?"

"Of course it would be OK," said Ella, "and is the next question 'please can I have some money, Mom?' "

"Something like that," said Greg with a laugh.

"OK, I'll transfer some funds into your account first thing tomorrow. When can I expect you two?"

"The middle to end of next week, I think," said Greg. "My last exam's on Tuesday morning."

"Call me when you have a flight."

"Yes, of course, Mom. Thanks."

"How is he?" Aaron asked when Ella replaced the phone.

"Fine," said Ella. "He's bringing his girlfriend over, I guess to see his roots. It must be serious."

"What's he going to do now that he's finishing college?"

"He wants to find a farm manager's job somewhere on a big estate in England."

"No thoughts of bringing his qualifications back home?" Aaron's voice was a little wistful.

"No," said Ella, "I think he's firmly entrenched in England. Part of it's this love affair with Belinda, but it's not as simple as that. He seems to fit in over there—the trouble is, for him the States mean city life."

"He could always go back to Kentucky. As soon as you've dispensed with your problems you could set him up with his own place there."

Ella shook her head. "No, he has friends in England now, and I think he'll make out very well. It'll be good, though, to have him over here even for a week or so."

"I'll call William in the morning," said Aaron. "He's coming back home next week, too, so we can have a real family reunion."

"Will we tell the boys about us?" Ella asked.

Aaron smiled before he kissed her. "I don't think we'll have to, do you?"

Chapter 40

Across the dining table Aaron and Ella raised their glasses to each other in a silent toast. Between them, in pools of candlelight, sat Greg, Belinda, and William. It was proving to be a wonderful evening. Greg and Belinda had flown into New York the same afternoon, and William had returned from college the previous day. It was the first time that the Connorses and Kovacs had been together in a very long time.

Greg suddenly rose to his feet. "I'd like to raise my glass to Mom," he said, "for such a great meal."

"I agree," said Aaron. "To the chef." They drank to Ella's health while she beamed at them.

Greg cleared his throat. "There's another thing." He glanced at Belinda. "Belinda and I had something of an ulterior motive in coming to New York. We've just gotten engaged."

The room exploded around him; there were kisses and congratulations. Ella found herself with her arms around her son, tears streaming down her face. "I kept wondering," she admitted, "but I guess I thought you guys were a little too young." She looked at Belinda and laughed. "Are you sure you want to take on this big baby?"

Belinda's face creased into a smile, so like her father's. "Quite sure," she said.

"We are young—I know that, Mom," said Greg, "but where the hell am I going to find another girl like Belinda? If

I don't marry her right now, some other guy will get her. She's one of a kind."

His words brought fresh tears to Ella's eyes. Aaron came to her side and slipped an arm around her. "Hey, this is supposed to be a happy occasion."

"I am happy," said Ella. "It's just—well, terrific. William, there's some champagne in the kitchen. It's not awfully cold, but let's open it anyway."

They drank to the health of Greg and Belinda, then Aaron made coffee and they all went into the living room. "So how are you proposing to support this future bride of yours?" Aaron asked with mock severity. "As godfather," he explained to Belinda, "I have to ask this kind of question."

"Well, that's the amazing thing," said Greg. "To be honest, we hadn't really made any plans, but when we told Tim he suggested that we take over his old family home—Monkswell Farm. He's been finding it difficult to manage both Wickham and Monkswell since his father died. It's a beautiful house, Mom. The farm has huge potential, and Tim's literally giving it to us. It's just unreal, like a dream come true—our own place right from the beginning, and a chance to build it ourselves the way we want it."

His eyes were shining, and Ella had never seen her son so happy. Despite his youth, she realized she had no doubts that he was doing the right thing. She knew that Aaron would be thinking, as she was, that Greg's settling in England would force upon her a choice as to where she made her home. However, even the uncertain future of her relationship with Aaron could not eclipse the happiness she felt.

"How does your mother feel about your engagement?" she asked Belinda.

"She's really pleased."

I wonder, thought Ella—she and Stephanie seemed to have drifted so far apart. Clearly Stephanie still saw Ella as someone who could prove a threat to her marriage. Somehow they would have to overcome that now that they were to be related by this marriage. If she had to sell her interest in Fulham to save her company, would it upset Stephanie? It seemed unlikely that she would be able to afford to put in a bid to buy her out, but Joseph Meyer or someone from outside the partnership might be interested. Either way, Ella thought with a sinking heart, it was not going to endear her to Stephanie.

"Actually, she's preoccupied with the baby at the moment," said Belinda. "It's due next month. Daddy's hoping it will be a boy. It would be nice for him—someone to inherit Wickham." Clearly, from the way Belinda was speaking, she had no idea that this child was not her father's, and Ella wondered how Tim and Stephanie were going to handle the situation.

Later that evening Ella and Aaron found themselves alone. William had called a girlfriend and arranged to take Greg and Belinda out on the town. "The stamina of the young," Aaron said. "Can you imagine flying in from England and feeling able to stay out all night?"

"Love will find a way," Ella suggested.

"I hope that's true." Aaron took her in his arms and kissed her. "Are you happy about Greg?"

"Very," said Ella. "It's not what I had planned for him, but he's made his own life the way he wants it, and that's all that matters."

"She's a wonderful girl," said Aaron. "I hope William is as lucky." He hesitated. "I nearly said something about us, and then I didn't know what to say or how to say it, and I wasn't sure you would be pleased anyway."

Ella reached out and touched his cheek. "I think it's a little premature to start making announcements about us, don't you? I have to get my business sorted out first—in fact, I was thinking of flying back to London later in the week."

"Why?" Aaron said. "The problem's in Houston."

"I know, I know, but I think I can raise some money in England." Ella explained her plan for selling the West London Meyer Centre.

"It sounds kind of drastic," said Aaron.

"The circumstances are drastic. I really don't have any alternative."

"Do you think Meyer will play ball?"

"Bound to. He'll know I'm over a barrel and won't be able to resist the chance for a good deal."

"And then you'll come home?" Aaron queried.

Ella hesitated. "I've been thinking about that, too. I have to make some money fast, and at the moment I think I'm more likely to do that in the UK than here in New York. I'm starting to get a feel for the London property scene, particularly the docklands and in the City. I think there's a killing to be made, and I'll need to act fast." She was carefully avoiding his eyes. "Then Greg and Belinda say they want to marry before Christmas, and their wedding will obviously be in England. There's not much I can do in Houston that Michael can't handle for me. I'm clearly not going to invest in any new real estate, nor can I sell off what I've got, so it's really just a question of watching the rents coming in, which is something Michael and his office can do far better than I." She grinned at Aaron, hoping to relieve the tension that was mounting between them. "New York runs like clockwork under Jackie, so it seems sensible to concentrate on the UK market."

"Sensible!" Aaron spat out the word. "Does our relationship matter at all to you, Ella?"

"Of course it does. It's just that I can't let my business go down the tubes, Aaron. I've put my whole life into it."

"It's only money." Aaron released her, walked over to the window, and gazed out into the night sky. "You've always told me that the whole reason for your obsessive involvement in business was to secure Greg's future. Greg's future is secure. You heard him this evening, Ella. He wants to do it for himself. He has your independence, and God bless him for it. What it means, however, is that whatever steps you take now, Ella, should be for yourself, not for your son."

"You're not being fair," said Ella. "How would you feel about it if I asked you to give up your work, give up your patients, and come to live in England with me? You wouldn't do it, would you?" She met his eye challengingly.

"That's a pointless argument," said Aaron. "New York is our home. I'm not asking you to leave your home, I'm asking you to come back to it."

"New York is *your* home," said Ella. "I'm not sure it's mine anymore. I like England, I like London, I like the way of life."

"Ella, isn't it time you let go of that boy now that he's made a life of his own?"

"It has nothing to do with Greg . . ." Ella stopped in midsentence, recognizing that what she was saying sounded ludicrous. "OK, it has *something* to do with Greg, but not everything. Look, Aaron, you're wedded to your work just as much as I am. Surely you can see that after years and years of building something I can't just throw it away."

"I'm not suggesting you throw it away," said Aaron. "It's just that you've made this decision without even consulting me."

"Why should I consult you?" said Ella angrily.

Aaron turned away. "Why indeed? I thought our happiness, our future, was bound together. Clearly I'm wrong. You go your own way, Ella. Make your own decisions and don't give me another thought." He strode toward the front door.

"Aaron, try to understand. Please don't leave me like this—not tonight, when everything was so happy with Greg coming home."

"I've given as much as I can give," said Aaron. "I don't want to stay here pretending we have a future together when clearly we have not. You're going your own way, Ella, making your own life. I have to do the same. I can't wait around for the next ten or fifteen years, hoping your business decisions will bring you to New York just long enough for us to marry and settle down. How could I ever feel secure in our relationship knowing that at any moment you might take off on some new scheme? I'm used to marriage where decisions are joint, where one partner considers the other's point of view and requirements. I'm not sure I can cope with anything else."

"I'm sorry, but I don't know what you mean," said Ella, helplessly intimidated by a building fury she had never seen in Aaron before.

"I mean that you're afraid to commit yourself to a proper adult relationship with all the responsibilities that involves. You're an emotional cripple. Over the years I've tried to help you all I can, but my life has taken its own beating of late, and I'm simply not prepared to lead some sort of half life waiting for you. You're right about my dictating the terms, and I'm doing so now. For us to have any future together we have to be married, we have to live in the same home, in the same city, at the same time. I'm quite happy to tolerate the odd trip to Houston on business or to the UK to see Greg and Belinda, just as I hope you would tolerate the odd medical conference or lecture tour I take part in from time to time. But that's it—we live together as man and wife or I'm through. So you go back to the UK, you sort out the sale of the Meyer Centre, and if you want us to be together, you come straight home. If you don't, then I'll know the answer." Without another word he turned and left the room.

Ella stood where he had left her. She had never felt more miserable in her life.

Chapter 41

London—*August 1985*

Ella and Joseph Meyer sat beside each other in the waiting room at Queen Charlotte's Hospital, pretending to read old issues of *Punch* and *Country Life.* They had arrived independently within hours of hearing that Stephanie had given birth to a son, and now both sat waiting for the opportunity to see her.

In the six weeks since Ella had returned to the UK she and Joseph had become firm friends. The negotiation for the sale of her shares of the West London Meyer Centre had been surprisingly speedy and straightforward. They had met regularly on the excuse of clarifying a particular point or signing a document, but mostly because they enjoyed each other's company. They were two of a kind, Joseph had pointed out on more than one occasion—tough on the outside, soft inside. Ella supposed he was right. Although her success was not in Joseph's league, they had both come from nowhere and in many respects had paid a similar price for their success. At the moment, however, the easy companionship they now shared was strained. They sat waiting for the summons to see Stephanie, both uncertain as to what sort of reception they could expect.

Stephanie had been extremely angry at Ella's decision to sell her shares. She saw it as a capitulation to Meyer and was bitterly opposed to finding herself in the position of being the minority shareholder, with Joseph holding the majority. Ella had tried to explain the desperate nature of her business in Houston, which had deteriorated terrifyingly in the preceding month, but Stephanie, already highly emotionally charged, simply would not listen.

The door opened, and Tim came into the waiting room. He looked tired, and Ella wondered whether the strain of helping Stephanie in recent months had adversely affected his condition—certainly he did not look well. "Look," he said awkwardly, "I'm terribly sorry, but I'm afraid Stephanie won't see either of you. It's really kind of you to have come, but she just doesn't feel up to it."

"Is she all right?" said Ella.

"She had a fairly difficult time." Tim hesitated. "I have to be honest, though. It's just that she's not terribly . . . well disposed toward either of you, and she feels she can't cope under the circumstances. I'm so sorry."

"The baby," Joseph said, "is he OK?"

"He's fine," said Tim. "We're going to call him Matthew—Matthew Alexander."

"That's good," said Joseph, "very good."

Tim smiled uncertainly at Joseph. "Actually . . . the baby's in the nursery at the moment. Would you like to come and see him?"

Joseph was out of his seat in seconds. "That would be kind, so kind."

Tim smiled. "Come on, then. One sneak preview coming up."

The baby lay fast asleep. Ella had only met Alex Meyer once, but even she could see the likeness. She heard Joseph's quick intake of breath beside her and turned to see that the old man had tears running down his face. She slipped her hand into his, and instantly he gripped it for comfort. "He . . . he's so like Alex," he said brokenly.

"Yes, I thought that," said Tim. "It's strange—Stephanie won't acknowledge the likeness. I don't know why."

Ella glanced up at him and saw in that instant how much the situation was hurting him. Not for the first time, she recognized that Tim Irvine was a very special person. She turned to Joseph. "Come on, I'm going to take you out to lunch."

"No." Joseph shook his head, tears still tumbling down his cheeks.

"Yes," said Ella firmly. She looked up at Tim. "Thank you for showing us the baby, and give Stephanie our love."

"I will," said Tim.

"Is your car here?" Ella asked once they were outside the hospital. Joseph nodded blindly; he was clearly in a state of shock. Ella found the car, told the chauffeur to take them to the Savoy Grill, and sat in silence, still holding Joseph's hand, as he sobbed quietly throughout the journey.

At the Savoy he seemed to pull himself together a little, and after a trip to the men's room he returned looking pale but dry-eyed. "I don't know what you must think of me," he said.

"The same as always," said Ella, "that you're just great. Come on, I've got a table. We'll go straight in."

"I couldn't eat anything," said Joseph.

"You'll do as you're told."

The ghost of a smile crossed his face. "Bossy woman."

In the end she tempted him to a Dover sole and a bottle of Chablis. He did little more than pick at his food, but it kept him occupied. "It must have been a terrible shock for you to see how like his father Matthew is," Ella ventured at last.

"I didn't know you already realized that Tim was not the father. I thought for a moment I'd betrayed young Irvine's kindness by being very tactless."

"Yes, I know," said Ella, "but I think you and I are probably the only two people who do know the truth. I'm not sure how they're going to handle Matthew's future, are you?"

Joseph shook his head. "I just know that I'm to be no part of it. My only grandchild, yet I can't even see him."

"I think you need to give them time," said Ella. "Try and see things from their point of view. They have so much pressure on them at the moment. They're trying to rebuild their marriage, and they've had to do it against the background of Stephanie carrying another man's child—and not just any man, but the man who took her away from her husband in the first place. They need to work on their own relationship before they can give consideration to you and your feelings. It's hard, but it's understandable."

"You're a very wise young woman," Joseph said, smiling at Ella.

"I'm damned good at sorting out other people's problems," Ella said with a wry smile. "Not so hot when it comes to my own."

"A woman like you shouldn't have problems," said Joseph. "Now, if I were thirty years younger . . ." There was a twinkle in his eye, and Ella laughed aloud.

"That's better, that's more your style." He sobered instantly, and she regretted her words. Leaning across the table, she took his hand once more in both of hers. "I know how you feel about Matthew. I have a son, remember? When I think of anything happening to Greg . . . well, it feels like there'd be no point in going on living. As for Greg's child, it will be as much a part of me as Greg is himself. I know patience is not an easy thing to expect of you. With all due respect, you're not a very patient man, but if you insist on playing the grandfather now you'll lose Matthew for good. I believe your biggest ally is Tim. The man has a heart of gold—you saw that for yourself today in the hospital. He couldn't bear to send you away without you seeing your grandchild. I'm sure he'll work on Stephanie over the next few months. Give him time. I believe he'll see to it that you play a part in Matthew's life."

"But how long?" Joseph asked desperately. "I'm not a young man, Ella. Who knows—I may not be here this time next year, and babies change so fast. I want to see Matthew grow up, I want to be a part of it."

"I know it's hard," said Ella, "but you have to bide your time. Look, I tell you what—why don't you let me have a word with Tim? I'll see him in the next day or so while Stephanie's still in the hospital. At the moment I don't think Stephanie is any more fond of me that she is of you, so I need to see Tim alone. I'll explain to him how you feel, tell him a little about your life, and make him realize just how important Matthew is to you."

"I'm not some pathetic old man who can't speak for himself."

"Oh, Joseph, for heaven's sake," said Ella, "no one could ever think of you as pathetic, nor old either, come to that—you're ageless. It's just that if you talk to Tim you'll lose your calm—you'll start screaming and yelling about your rights, and then you'll lose your temper and remind Tim that he isn't even a blood relation to the boy. Once you've done that you'll have blown it completely, because that will be something Tim won't forgive. Now, are you going to let me handle this one, or are you going to behave like a goddam idiot?"

"All my life I've been bullied by women. . . ."

Joe Allens was already crowded by the time Ella arrived. That was just how she wanted it—she had deliberately chosen to meet Tim in an atmosphere that lacked intimacy and could be guaranteed to be busy and noisy. Joe Allens, in Covent Garden, was perfect. She searched the sea of tables and caught sight of him in a corner, his hand raised, a smile of greeting on his face. She picked her way through the tables toward him. He stood up and kissed her warmly on the cheek. He had already ordered a bottle of wine and poured her a glass.

"Shall we toast Matthew?" Ella suggested.

"Why not?" said Tim with a smile. "To Matthew."

"You must be wondering why I asked to meet you," Ella said without preamble. "You must have thought it was a little odd."

"I'll tell you what I did think," said Tim. "I started wondering when was the last time I saw you entirely alone without the kids, and I realized we hadn't been completely on our own once since France—not in all those years."

Ella toyed with the stem of her wine glass. "Do you still hate me for how I behaved?"

"Of course I don't," said Tim. "I understand completely."

"How can you understand?" Ella burst out. "If you love someone, what difference should it make that they have"—she searched for words—"an illness you didn't know about? It should just be something you accept as a part of them."

"It's not just an illness, though, is it?" said Tim. "It's very distressing, particularly for the onlooker. The mistake was mine. I should have told you about it from the beginning, but somehow our relationship had become so intimate so quickly that each day it became more difficult to tell you."

"I can understand that," said Ella.

"It would have been terribly unkind if you had pretended you could cope with it when really you couldn't. Then we would have limped on in some sort of half relationship that could have destroyed us both."

"I feel the same," said Ella, "except for the guilt."

"Banish the guilt," said Tim. "After all, you and I are going to be related very soon, and so we have to get along, don't we?" He grinned. "Are you pleased about Belinda and Greg?"

"That's a silly question to ask," said Ella. "You must know I am. You're being very generous to them. I want to talk to you about that."

For some time they discussed details of their children's future life and the wedding arrangements, for it had been decided that Greg and Belinda would be married on November 10. They argued amicably enough about who would pay for what and eventually paused long enough to order a meal.

Released from the restraints of guilt that had haunted her for so long, Ella found she slipped naturally into a kind of intimate camaraderie with Tim. They laughed, shared jokes, and teased each other, and behind it all was the common link of their former intimacy and a future that would be shared through the marriage of their children.

It was only over coffee that Ella brought the conversation around to the main reason for their meeting. "I wanted to talk to you before Stephanie came out of the hospital," Ella began. "I know she doesn't want to talk to me at the moment."

"It's true," Tim admitted. "She's angry you sold out to Meyer. I don't know anything about it, but I gather you have some kind of financial problem."

"In Houston, yes," said Ella. "My properties have lost value because of the drop in the oil market. Many of them are now unoccupied. My income has dropped drastically, and I can't sell at the moment because I'd never get enough to cover the interest on my loans."

"That's rough," said Tim. "I'm sorry you're having these problems. I had no idea."

"I did explain it all to Stephanie," Ella said, a little harshly.

"Yes, I'm sure you did," said Tim, "but she's been preoccupied over the birth of this baby. She'll come around in time. It's just that the last thing she wants at the moment is to let Meyer get an even greater hold over her, and she felt that the sale of your shares gave him just that."

"I can see that," said Ella, "but I really had no choice." She hesitated. "Anyway, that's not why I wanted to see you. I wanted to talk to you about Matthew."

He set down his coffee cup with a look of surprise. "Matthew?"

"I'm really here as a kind of ambassador, but I haven't been sent—it was my idea to come."

"Go on," said Tim, looking apprehensive.

"How much do you know about Joseph Meyer?"

"Not a lot," said Tim. "I know he's very rich and powerful. Stephanie sees him as a threat, and I can understand why—he's a man used to having his own way. He ruled his son with an iron hand, he tried to rule Stephanie, and she's terrified that he'll get his hands on Matthew. I can't say I blame her."

"May I tell you his story?" Ella asked.

"Yes, of course," said Tim.

When Ella had finished, Tim was silent for some time. "The daughter . . . is she still alive?" he asked at last.

"Yes, she's in a home in New York. Joseph pays her a monthly visit, but he says she has no idea who he is."

"So Matthew is all he has left, is what you're saying," said Tim.

Ella nodded. "I—I'm not suggesting, of course, that you hand the child over to him, or that you make Joseph part of Matthew's everyday life. The very best thing that could happen to Matthew, in my view, is that his name should be Matthew Irvine, that he should be brought up as your son and given the same sort of childhood that you gave Millie and Belinda. All I'm asking is that you not cut the old man out of the boy's life completely. Stephanie worries that Joseph will have a suffocating hold on Matthew's life as he did on Alex's, but that's absolutely out of the question. Joseph brought Alex up alone because his wife had died. In Matthew's case, not only does he have you and Stephanie, but long before he's a man, Joseph will be dead. I don't know whether Stephanie's aware of this, but Joseph has had a heart condition for some years. He could die at any time, and I suspect that after the years of deprivation he suffered, he won't live to a great age. His mind is as clear and astute as that of a young man, but the flesh is weak."

"Does Stephanie know about his past?" Tim asked.

"I imagine so," said Ella. "In the early days they had a very good relationship."

"Well, I'll do what I can," said Tim. "I agree with you that it's not such a big deal to make an old man happy, but at the same time you have to recognize that Stephanie hates his guts. I don't quite understand the background of her feelings toward him, but they are strongly entrenched, and in addition, she feels very protective toward her new baby. It's strange actually—she is much more motherly toward Matthew than she ever was to Millie and Belinda."

"Do you mind that?" Ella asked.

"No," said Tim, "I'm pleased. Stephanie's lack of involvement in Millie's and Belinda's childhood worried me on every level. I minded for her sake, too—I felt that she was missing out on such a lot. Maybe with Matthew it will be different. I've told her that I will look on him as my own, that I will love him as much as our daughters, and it's true—the fact that he isn't mine makes no difference at all. Nonetheless, I think in her mind she feels a greater degree of responsibility toward him than she did toward the girls because he isn't mine, and that can only be a good thing."

Ella smiled. "So you're optimistic about your future together. That's wonderful."

"Yes, I am," said Tim. "We've both changed and mellowed, and we have so much shared past. I feel this time we might be all right."

"I'm glad," said Ella, "very glad."

Riding home in the taxi a few minutes later, Ella realized that her words were true. Although she had spent years missing Tim and wishing she could have another chance at their relationship, she found now that she viewed him as nothing more than a dear friend, for Aaron occupied all her thoughts. That she and Tim would be linked forever by the marriage of their children brought a great sense of pleasure and comfort, but nothing more.

Inevitably, her thoughts turned to Aaron. She had not returned to New York after selling her Fulham shares. Instead, she had written him a long letter and tried to explain why. Joseph Meyer had been instrumental in introducing her to a number of valuable contacts, and she was now heavily involved in the development of the docklands. It was a good, sound project that should bring her a great deal of money, and with Houston temporarily secured by the Fulham money she had been able to deposit with Jack Smith, she felt she had to stay in London. She knew Aaron would be angry, but in her heart she could not help but believe that he would understand her predicament and give her a few months longer. "I'll be back in New York for Christmas," she had promised him. "I'll just see Greg settled, and by December I should be able to leave the docklands project for a month or so. Please come over for Greg's wedding—we need you to be there." Aaron had not replied for some weeks. When he had done so it had been via a curt note saying that she had clearly not taken seriously his ultimatum, and that it should be understood that everything between them was now over. He added that he would attend Greg's wedding, since he was Greg's godfather, but only on the understanding that he was coming as a family friend, nothing more.

Ella had been devastated by the letter, yet she still could not believe it was true. She had not known how to respond, and so she had not replied at all. As the weeks ticked by she found herself growing more and more apprehensive about the future of her relationship with Aaron. She knew the only way to safeguard the future of her business was to continue in her course of action, and even the threat of losing Aaron could not divert her.

When the taxi stopped outside her house she paid off the driver and wandered inside. It was still her haven, and it still brought her comfort, but an increasing sense of loneliness seemed to be seeping into her soul. Greg was so preoccupied and happy, and he and Belinda spent most weekends at their new home now. She had acquired an increasing circle of friends in London, but they were mostly business contacts. Ella realized that but for the genuine warmth and intimacy of her friendship with Joseph Meyer her sense of isolation and loneliness would have been complete. It was a high price to pay for success.

Chapter 42

London—*November 1985*

It had not been Ella's intention to arrive early for her meeting with Margot—indeed, it had not been Ella's intention to arrive at all. At Greg's wedding she received word that Margot needed to see her urgently, and Ella's immediate reaction was to issue a rebuff. They had not met alone since the evening at Margot's home when Ella had threatened to expose her past. What had stopped Ella from refusing now had been the situation in Houston, which had worsened considerably since the summer. It was only the fact that Jack Smith refused to foreclose on her that had so far kept her business from crashing. Jack had been putting considerable pressure on her to pour more money into Houston, but Ella was resisting; she simply could not drain her London and New York operations of any more working capital without affecting them. They were healthy in themselves, and when she saw how quickly Houston had absorbed the Fulham money, it seemed crazy to throw good money after bad.

It was this set of circumstances that had her waiting in the foyer of the bank at Mansion House, for Ella was well aware of Joshkers' shareholding in Sunbelt Industrial Bank. At her most recent meeting with Jack he had hinted that he was under a considerable obligation to Joshkers, which had granted him a loan to keep his operation in business. If there was one thing that Ella had learned during her years in business, it was that nobody ever did anything for nothing, and she presumed that if Joshkers Bank had bailed out

Sunbelt Industrial, they would now wield a considerable amount of power down in Houston. Despite her personal feelings, this was certainly not the moment to cross Margot.

The two women eyed each other across Margot's desk. To Ella, Margot seemed like a dangerous, wild animal—sleek, powerful, and predatory. Margot noted the dark circles under Ella's eyes, the pale complexion, and the definite lack of normal Kovac bounce. Houston, or something, was certainly taking its toll on Ella. They exchanged perfunctory greetings and paused in conversation while coffee was delivered.

"So, Margot," Ella said as soon as the coffee had been served, "you wanted to see me urgently. I assume it's about Houston."

Margot shook her head and began her inevitable doodling on the pad in front of her. "No, not precisely," she said. "Actually, it's about Meyer Hotels." She paused dramatically for a moment to allow her words to sink in.

Ella frowned. "I don't follow you."

"There's a buzz going around the city—a reliable buzz—that Joseph's thinking of selling out."

"It doesn't surprise me," said Ella. "He's old, tired, and disappointed. Without Alex his work has ceased to have much point for him."

Margot looked up from her doodling. "I'd heard you two had become friendly. He's an impressive old guy, isn't he?"

"Very," said Ella shortly. It irritated her that Margot always seemed to know everything about everyone. With Fulham long sold, her relationship with Joseph was now entirely personal and no one's business but her own.

"I won't beat around the bush," said Margot. "What I want you to do is to put in a bid for the group before it goes on the open market. I think he would be very susceptible to your taking over the helm—he greatly admires your business achievements, and he's clearly fond of you personally. Money, I suspect, will be of secondary consideration to seeing that his baby goes to the right person."

"Hold it a minute," said Ella. "You're saying you want *me* to bid for Meyer Hotels—the *whole* of Meyer Hotels?"

"That's right," said Margot.

"You have to be joking!" Ella burst out. "It has to be worth several hundred million dollars. Even if I could raise that kind of money, real estate is my business."

"Let me put this another way," said Margot. "You're in a mess in Houston, right?"

"At present, certainly," Ella tempered.

"At present, and probably for some time into the future. I don't see Texas getting over this problem quickly. Even the banks are starting to drop like flies. It will be some time before we see any upward turn, and there's some falling yet to do."

Margot's cool appraisal of the situation sent a chill of fear through Ella, but she remained outwardly calm. "OK, Houston's not doing so great, but I have my other two operations."

"You do," said Margot, "but they're not big enough or busy enough to cope with the crisis you're facing in Houston. If you acquired Meyer Hotels, you could indulge in a little asset stripping. Looked at in the context of your total holding, Houston would then seem like small fry. By cashing in some of the Meyer assets you could give the Houston operation a much-needed shot in the arm, or simply cut your losses and bail out—whichever seemed most appropriate. Either way, you could cope."

"Just supposing I was to go along with such a preposterous suggestion, Margot—and I have to say now I will not—your advice seems to be in some conflict. On the one hand you're saying that Joseph Meyer might be prepared to sell to me out of sentiment, because he thinks I'll look after his group. In the next breath you're saying I should dismember the group in order to get myself out of the shit in Houston."

Margot let out a sigh of irritation. "Ella, we're not talking fairy tales here, we're talking about good business sense. What you do with the group once it's yours is up to you.

What I'm saying is that I think Joseph would be prepared to cut you a very special deal, particularly if part of that deal included a long-term commitment to take his grandson into the business, if the boy so wishes."

Ella's eyes narrowed as she looked at Margot appraisingly. "How the hell do you know about his grandson?"

"Does it matter?" said Margot. "The fact is I do. In normal circumstances, if Stephanie wasn't so pigheaded, I imagine Joseph would hand Meyer over to her lock, stock, and barrel if she promised to act as custodian for her son's future. However, since she's not prepared to make that kind of commitment, I suspect Joseph is looking for another way of selling Meyer while still making sure that Matthew has an entrée into the group, if he so wishes. You're the obvious candidate, in my view."

"Maybe I am," said Ella, "but there's no way I'll be a party to this. I can only repeat that I don't want to go into the hotel business, I don't want to find myself heading an operation the size of Meyer, and most important of all, I'm not prepared to double-cross Joseph. I'm sorry, Margot, the answer is no."

There was a silence for a moment or two. "Yes, I suppose I expected your reaction, and although I regret what I'm going to have to say next, it does not surprise me that it's necessary for me to do so." Ella suddenly felt very cold; there was menace in the air, a sense of foreboding. The image she'd had of Margot as she had entered the room now seemed stronger than ever—she felt like a defenseless victim waiting for Margot to pounce. She forced herself to concentrate as Margot began speaking. "If you're not prepared to put in a bid for Meyer, then I'm afraid I have no alternative but to advise Jack Smith to foreclose on you in Houston."

"He won't do that," said Ella, her heart beating so loudly she could barely hear her own words. "I was talking to him on the phone only this morning. He has made it perfectly clear that he will stick with me for the duration."

"He's not in a position to make such assurances to you anymore," said Margot. "He's deeply in debt to Joshkers, and he has agreed to our right of veto on all major decisions. Lexington Kovac is a major decision, as far as a branch of his size is concerned. If we tell him to pull out, he'll have to do just that."

"Blackmail," said Ella.

"If you like to call it that," said Margot coolly, "but then you and I are no strangers to the term, are we?"

At that moment the telephone rang on Margot's desk, making both women jump. Margot picked up the phone. "Yes, OK, switch it through to Janet's office and I'll take it there. Sorry." She stood up. "I'd better take it. I'll ask my secretary to send in some more coffee. A few minutes alone will give you a chance to think things out. At the risk of sounding threatening, I can only repeat that I'm very serious in what I say. Bid for Meyer, or we pull out of Houston. The choice is yours, of course." She strode from the office, a tall, elegant figure.

Left alone again, Ella took her cup and walked over to the window. What puzzled her about the ultimatum Margot had issued was her motive. Why should Margot be so eager for her to take on Meyer Hotels? It would mean big banking business, but the motives had to go deeper than that, surely. And why threaten to pull out of Houston? It made no sense. It wouldn't just be Lexington Kovac she would be hurting, it would be Joshkers as well. Indeed, the collapse of Lexington Kovac could mean the collapse of Sunbelt Industrial. Maybe that was it; maybe in the world of banking politics this was what Margot wanted to achieve. It seemed to Ella at that moment that her world was collapsing around her, yet—though she knew her mind should be probing the proposition just put to her—she found her concentration ebbing away.

It had been a strange year. However happy she might be about it, the fact was that she had lost Greg. He was a married man now, and she knew she would have an increasingly small part to play in his future life. Margot was threatening her with the loss of her business, and most important of all, it appeared she had lost Aaron Connors. Aaron had come to Greg and Belinda's wedding, as he had promised to do, but he had refused an invitation to stay with her. He had simply flown in the day before the wedding and flown out again the day after.

The sound of the door opening jerked her thoughts back to the present. "Sorry about that," said Margot. "Now, where were we?"

The supercilious smile, the glint of triumph in her eyes, the total confidence that she was already the victor, made any alternative decision in Ella's mind impossible. Suddenly she did not care about the implications and the ruin it would bring to her. "I won't do it," she said. "You'll just have to make that call to Jack and tell him to go ahead and foreclose. I'm not bidding for Meyer under any circumstances."

"You know," said Margot after a pause, "when I was anticipating this meeting it did actually occur to me that you might be stupid enough to react this way, so it's just as well that I can force your hand."

"What the hell do you mean by that?" demanded Ella.

"I can force you to do as I wish over this Meyer bid, Ella, because I own twenty-five percent of your business."

Chapter
43

New York—*December 1985*

Laurence Merman had aged beyond recognition. Ella, angry and preoccupied as she was, was nonetheless startled by his appearance. When she had last seen him he had been a suave, well-groomed, middle-aged man. Now he was definitely elderly, and his appearance, although not untidy, gave the impression that he was a person who no longer cared what he looked like. Nonetheless, as she entered his office, the smile of pleasure at seeing her was genuine, and just for a moment she forgot the reason for the visit and responded to his embrace. "The rest of us get older, you stay the same. How long is it since you were last here, ten years?"

"Must be, I suppose," said Ella. She looked around the little office.

"Coffee, or something stronger?" Laurence asked.

"What have you got?" said Ella.

"Scotch, or some wine in the fridge."

"Scotch would be nice."

Laurence raised his eyebrows. "This is a new side to my girl. Scotch at lunchtime?"

"I don't normally drink at all at lunchtime," said Ella, irritated, "but I think the circumstances warrant it."

Laurence frowned at her as he poured two hefty measures of whiskey and handed one to her. "What circumstances?" he asked.

"Why did you do it, Laurence? Was it out of spite? It can't have been because you needed the money."

"Do what?" Laurence asked.

"Sell your stock to Margot Haigh, of course."

At her words he blanched slightly and tossed back his whiskey. "It certainly wasn't spite," he said, "and you're wrong about the second motive, too—it was money."

"But how could it have been?" said Ella. "The Café Colettes are still booming, aren't they?"

"They're on the mend," said Laurence, "but I guess you haven't been around New York too much recently. I had to sell some to keep afloat, and the business as a whole has been running at a loss for the last three or four years."

The fact that he had not tried to bullshit her in any way, coupled with the despairing note in his voice, drained much of Ella's anger. "I don't understand, Laurence. What went wrong?"

"Colette," he said after a pause. "She died." He reached for the whiskey bottle and topped off his glass and Ella's.

"Laurence, I'm so sorry, I had no idea. When?"

"Just over a year ago."

"I should have known," said Ella. "You should have contacted me."

Laurence shook his head. "No reason to do that—you and I went our separate ways. No doubt you've had your ups and downs over the last few years, and I haven't been there for you, have I?"

"No," said Ella, remembering her feeling of resentment at the way he had dropped her after their affair was over. "If you needed money, why didn't you come to me?"

"I don't know. Maybe I would have, but it was Margot who suggested I sell to the bank, and it seemed like a sensible thing to do. I couldn't see it would do any harm to you."

Ella set down her whiskey glass. "Laurence, you didn't sell out to the bank, you sold out to Margot Haigh."

"Same thing," he said.

"No," Ella thundered, "it's not the same thing. Margot holds that stock personally."

"Personally! But why?"

Ella shrugged her shoulders. "To have some sort of personal hold over me, I suppose."

"I thought you two were good friends."

"Were. What I still don't understand, Laurence, is why you didn't tell me what you intended to do."

For a moment Laurence avoided her eyes and played nervously with the tumbler in front of him. "Because Margot asked me not to. She asked that the stock remain in my name and that I not tell you or anyone about the sale. I'm afraid I complied."

"But you must have thought her requests a little odd," Ella insisted. "Didn't you wonder why the bank didn't want to put the stock in its name in the ordinary way?"

"I guess I did," Laurence mumbled, "but at the time I could think of nothing but Colette, the fact that she was dying and that I was running out of cash. Selling my stake in your business on the open market would not have been easy. Real estate's so volatile, and although you have a track record, I wouldn't have known where to begin."

"You could have tried offering it to me," Ella said.

"Yeah, I should have done that, but somehow I felt awkward getting in touch with you and asking you to help me fund Colette's death. I can't explain it. It just felt wrong, though I guess it's what I would have done if Margot hadn't made the suggestion." Laurence raised his eyes. "Ella, I'm real sorry. I behaved like a shit, and I know it. If I could just try and get across to you the feeling of panic and hopelessness. I guess when we're desperate we all become pretty damned selfish. At that moment, Ella Kovac's business was the last thing on my mind. I'm not proud of it, but that's how I felt."

"Don't," said Ella. "There's no need to go on, Laurence. I understand, I do. I just wish to God you'd told me about it." There was a deep, melancholy silence between them. They were both a little drunk. "Supposing we go out and eat something," said Ella, "before we both fall over, and I'll tell you about the trouble I'm in and see if you can come up with any bright ideas."

The lunch with Laurence was pleasant enough. They found themselves talking about old times, about Greg as a little boy. Slowly, painfully, like someone removing a bandage from a raw wound, Laurence told Ella about Colette's final months and his slow but steady attempts to get his life back together since her death.

Ella explained to Laurence the corner into which Margot had pushed her. Margot's revelation about her stock holding in Lexington Kovac had explained her motive for wanting Ella to buy Meyer Hotels—pure greed. The stock would be worth a great deal of money if such a deal could be pulled off. Margot's motive was simple—personal ambition.

Laurence listened politely and asked a few questions, but it was clear to Ella that he was going to be of no use in helping her decide what to do. He had completely withdrawn.

If she could have been angry with him, it might have helped ease the sense of pressure and stress she was feeling, but there was no joy in kicking a man when he was down. They were old friends, they had shared a lot of good times; recriminations were useless.

Back in the office she dealt with a few queries Jackie had accumulated and signed the mail. Jackie's gratitude at not being fired was pathetic in its intensity. She couldn't do enough for Ella, and this, at least, was a comfort.

As soon as Jackie left the office Jessie waddled purposefully into Ella's room and sat down. "Tired?" she asked.

"A little," said Ella. "I'm packing up, actually. You go home, too."

"Not until I've said what I have to." Ella put down her pen and pushed back her chair wearily. When Jessie had something on her mind there was no way you could avoid hearing all about it—her persistence was terrifying. "It's about this trouble you're in," said Jessie. As soon as Ella had flown in from London she had told Jackie and Jessie the full story, and clearly Jessie had been brooding on it.

"Yes," said Ella wearily.

"You need someone to talk to, someone not involved in this business, someone who knows you well, who can come to a decision as to what you should do. I wish I was clever enough to help you, but I'm not. The kind of mess you're in at the moment, Ella, you need a friend, a good friend."

"You're right," Ella admitted, "but there's no one right now."

"There's Dr. Connors," Jessie said.

Ella shook her head vehemently. "We're not friends anymore, Jessie."

"That's bullshit. You two will always be friends. You go back to when you were kids. OK, you might not be so friendly right now, but friendship like that you can't break altogether. You go and see him, tell him your troubles. He'll help you sort it out."

Ella smiled, close to tears. "It's a nice idea, Jessie, but it isn't practical. He'd slam the door in my face."

"He would not," said Jessie. "He cares about you a very great deal, that man."

"Did care," said Ella.

"Does care," said Jessie. "I'm not supposed to tell you this, but he phones me every week to see how you're doing."

Ella stared at Jessie in astonishment. "Aaron calls you?"

Jessie nodded, triumphantly. "Ever since you first started spending so much time in London. It's a kind of habit now—he calls me, and I tell him how you're doing. Not business stuff, he's not interested in that—just how you're sounding, how Greg is . . . that kind of thing."

Her words momentarily silenced Ella. Then, almost to herself, she said, "Then why won't he have anything to do with me?"

"Oh, Ella, how come you still don't know the first thing about men?" Jessie let out one of her gales of laughter. "Pride, men have pride, it's their biggest downfall. Your Dr. Connors, he's a nice man, a good man, but underneath he's just the same as all the rest. He loves you very much, but he's not prepared to play number two to your business, and since he can't see he'll ever be number one, he's kind of opted out—yet he can't quite, because he loves you so much."

Ella stared at Jessie. "If you're right, his position is impossible, and it would be better if I didn't get in touch with him—it would be unkind."

"No position is impossible," said Jessie. "He loves you, you love him, you have all those years and years of past friendship. You're in trouble right now, and you need him. Go to him and tell him just that. I lay my life savings—every dollar I've ever earned—on the fact that there'll be no door slamming. Now are you going to do as I say?"

Ella took a deep breath. "I'll call him, as you suggest. If he slams the door in my face, I expect a check from you on my desk by ten o'clock tomorrow morning."

"You've got it," said Jessie with a grin.

By the time Ella reached Aaron's apartment she was incredibly nervous. She gave her name to the concierge and waited with mounting trepidation while he called up to Aaron's apartment and told him she was there.

"He said to go up," the concierge said. "You know the way?"

Ella nodded. She was over the first hurdle; at least he would see her. She stood nervously in the elevator, which seemed to take an age to reach the twelfth floor. When the doors opened Aaron was standing there, a formidable sight, still in his dark suit from work, his face inscrutable. "Hello, Ella," he said coolly.

She stepped out of the elevator. "Aaron, I'm sorry to arrive unannounced like this, but . . . I need help, and you're the only person who . . ." From nowhere came a storm of tears. All the tensions and stress of the last few days burst out. The mask slipped from Aaron's face; he smiled, a beautiful smile, full of love, and the sight of it made Ella cry all the harder. He opened his arms, and she fell into them.

When Ella had finished telling Aaron the whole sorry story she sat back, feeling oddly relaxed and cleansed. It was a very long time since she had taken anybody so completely into her confidence. For years she had been operating alone, making her own decisions.

She knew, or thought she knew, exactly how Aaron was going to react. There was no way he would want her to become involved with Meyer. It would mean she would lose everything. But somehow, sitting in Aaron's familiar apartment with his arm around her as dusk settled over the city, it did not seem so terrible.

He was silent for a very long time. When at last he spoke his words astounded her. "Well, there's not really a choice, is there? You have to go ahead. It's the only possible option."

"You mean . . . you think I should buy Meyer?" Ella said stupidly.

"Of course."

"But I thought it would be the last thing you would want me to do. It's an enormous group, Aaron—running it would be a twenty-four-hour job, and the headquarters isn't even in America, it's in Geneva. I suppose I could move it back to the States, but it's unlikely to be easy, particularly in the early days." She stared at him incredulously. "I never thought it would be what you'd recommend."

"You wanted me to tell you to let Margot pull the rug out so that you could blame me instead of yourself?"

"No," said Ella, and then she paused. "At least I don't think so," she added truthfully.

"I've thought about that conversation we had in your apartment so much in recent months," said Aaron.

"Me, too," said Ella.

"And a lot of what you said was right," said Aaron. "It's not making the situation any easier between us—if anything, my beginning to understand your point of view makes it more difficult. One thing you said, though, did strike home. You asked me if I would be prepared to give up my career for you. At the time, if you remember, I sidestepped the issue by saying it wasn't relevant, because in truth it wasn't. However, I've asked myself that question, Ella, many, many times since. My work is so much a part of me—and that's not just since I've been widowed. I guess I do spend a little more time at the hospital than I did when Alice was alive, but not that much. The truth is that if I gave up my work, I somehow wouldn't be me any longer. What would I think about all day, do all day? I guess I'd find it very difficult to have any confidence in myself if I had no real reason to get up in the morning." He shrugged his shoulders and smiled sadly at Ella. "So I guess what I'm saying is that you built this business from scratch, you've put all your life into it, you've seen it flourish and grow, and now it's under threat. You can't desert it now, Ella, you have to fight. If you fight and lose, you've done your best. If you fight and win, wonderful, but not to fight at all . . ."

His unconditional support, Ella knew, should have brought about a surge of confidence and a renewal of hope for the future. Instead she felt oddly let down. "So what you're saying is that you're reconciled to the fact that you and I have no future together?"

Aaron removed his arm and turned to face her, taking both her hands in his. "Yes, I suppose that's what I'm saying," he said. "I recognize the sort of person you are, Ella, and now I can respect and admire you for it, rather than resent you. Of course you must go for this chance. You'll probably make a fine hotelier—you've made a pretty damned fine everything else—and it would be crass of me to stand in your way. Maybe one day . . . who knows? Either way, any way you look at it, I'll always be here for you. I want you to know that. Whatever our circumstances, the friendship goes on, right?"

Ella nodded dumbly, close to tears again. She knew his words should have brought comfort, but instead she felt a deep sense of desolation. What he was saying was crystal clear. Their relationship was back to where it had been when Alice was alive, and Ella realized with an awful clarity that this was not how she wanted things to be. She wanted Aaron to wrap her in his arms, to tell her that he would look after her forever, that she should forget her business, Margot, and Joseph Meyer—that they could all go to hell. But she had left it until too late. He no longer needed her as he had once. He was free of her emotionally in every way except friendship. He was throwing her back out into the jungle to continue to struggle to survive. How could she tell him it was no longer what she wanted—no longer what she wanted at all?

Chapter 44

London—*March 1986*

Although it was still early March there was a definite promise of the summer to come. Margot and Ahfaad lounged on the terrace in their dressing gowns, breakfasting on mimosas and croissants. As had become their habit, Margot was spending the weekend with Ahfaad. For once, they had nothing planned—the whole two days stretched ahead uncluttered by business commitments or social occasions. Margot stretched out in the sun like a sleek cat. Ahfaad eyed her appreciatively—her auburn hair and creamy skin were perfectly set off by the apricot negligee he had bought her in Paris several weeks ago. It was good to see her out of her inevitable black—the pale, soft color made her look younger, less austere, almost vulnerable. He smiled to himself that such an adjective could ever be used to describe Margot Haigh.

"What are you smiling at?" she asked.

"Nothing. I was just admiring you—you're a very beautiful woman."

Margot smiled back. "Well, I'm wearing a very beautiful negligee."

They sat in contented silence, the newspapers still unopened on the table. "What shall we do this weekend?" asked Margot.

"I thought we might get married," said Ahfaad.

Margot stared at him. His expression was quite unreadable; it was impossible to tell whether he was serious or not. "You're joking!" she said, testing the water.

"I'm not. I've never been more serious in all my life."

Margot looked positively flustered, and her discomfort made Ahfaad smile. "You see," she said triumphantly. "I knew you were joking. What shall we do, seriously?"

"I wasn't joking, Margot," said Ahfaad. "I'd like to marry you, and there's no better time than the present."

"I might not want to marry *you,"* Margot suggested.

"Whyever not?" said Ahfaad. "We're completely right for each other—you know that."

"If this is a proposal," said Margot, "it's not very romantic."

"We're not romantic people," said Ahfaad. "Besides, marriage is a contract and should be regarded in the most businesslike manner possible. We have the same interests, we like the same sort of people, we enjoy talking about business, we have a truly wonderful time in bed, we enjoy the same restaurants, we like to travel . . . it sounds like the ideal recipe for marriage to me."

"And love?" Margot asked.

Ahfaad threw back his head and laughed. "Love! You of all people, Margot. All right, I love you. Is that good enough?"

Margot looked at him doubtfully. "What about children? I'm forty-four, Ahfaad. I'm too old for children now."

"I know how old you are," said Ahfaad, "and it's of no significance to me."

"You mean you don't mind not having any children?"

"I have to say I don't somehow see you in the role of earth mother"—he smiled—"and no, I don't mind not having children. The kind of domestic routine they demand would bore me. I loathe other people's children. I suppose it's possible that I might become attached to one of my own, but it's not a subject about which I feel strongly. If you were twenty-four and made the statement that you did not wish to have children, I would not try to press you. Does that answer the question?"

"Yes." Margot seemed genuinely ill at ease.

"You don't seem very pleased at my suggestion, Margot. Is it possible that I have misinterpreted our relationship?"

"No, it's not that," said Margot, "it's just that I never imagined you would ask me to marry you. I thought we suited each other now, but ultimately you would look to a younger woman to provide you with a family. In other words, I did not see us as having a long-term future."

"You underestimate yourself, my darling," said Ahfaad. "You have made me your slave." His tone was bantering, but the expression in his eyes was warm. He leaned forward and took Margot's hand. "Come on, open your mind to the prospect. If we were to marry, what conditions would you wish to impose on the relationship?"

"Conditions! None that I can think of," said Margot. "I'm very happy with the way we live now. I suppose I would have to give up my house and move in here with you." She sounded a little doubtful.

"Certainly it is customary for a husband and wife to live under the same roof," said Ahfaad. Margot tried to ignore the pangs of dread she instantly felt at the thought of leaving her home after so many years. "No other conditions?" Ahfaad pressed. Margot shook her head. "I have just one condition for you. I would like you to stop working for Joshkers Bank and come to work for me instead."

"Complete takeover bid, then," said Margot. "Body, soul, and business brain?"

"Something like that," said Ahfaad. "I don't like the idea of your working for someone other than myself. In other words, I don't want anyone else having a call on your time. I don't think that's unreasonable."

"I think it's wholly unreasonable," Margot said. The dazed expression had left her face, and she sat bolt upright in her chair. "I think it would be positively unhealthy for me to work for you—we'd be in each other's pockets all day and night, and I'd have no sense of independence."

"Precisely," said Ahfaad. "That's the way it should be."

"You have to be mad!" said Margot. "There's no way I'm going to sacrifice my independence to you or any other man. I love my job. If I wasn't so devoted to Joshkers, I wouldn't have stayed with them all these years—there have been plenty of opportunities to leave along the way. I think there's a good chance that before I'm much older I'll get the chairmanship, and I don't mind admitting that's what I'm after. I'll be the first woman to obtain such a position in the male-dominated banking world, and I like the idea."

"I don't understand why it's so important to you," said Ahfaad. "You've nothing to prove. You can compete with any man in a man's world."

"Well, it is important to me," said Margot with a touch of a smile. "I'm a well-known personality in the banking world, particularly here, but also in the States. I'm simply Margot Haigh, and whether I'm male or female is of no relevance anymore. I have a reputation for being tough, aggressive, and ruthless. It is a reputation I protect, because any concessions I make are viewed as weakness or emotional female reactions. I'm not about to give it up—not when the end is in sight."

"I hear what you say," said Ahfaad after a pause, "and I admire you very much. Nothing you've told me is unknown to me, but Joshkers is a small bank, and I think you could do a lot better. Together you and I could expand and develop my business interests. You have some wonderful contacts, you have a natural commercial flair, you are a prodigious worker—the world is our oyster."

"So that's why you want to marry me," said Margot with a strained smile, "for my business acumen."

"No, goddammit, it isn't." It was Ahfaad's turn to feel uncomfortable. "Look, I'm not used to this any more than you are. Women have always been an expendable commodity so far as I am concerned—decorative, nice to have around, a satisfying diversion at the end of a busy day, but not to be taken seriously, not part of real life. This attitude has worked very well for me—until now. Now, in you, I know I've met my match—you are not an expendable woman, you are equal to me in every way, and for that reason I want you—but I want you completely. As you say, a complete takeover bid. I don't think that's asking too much."

Margot found his small speech oddly affecting, and she recognized that in all probability his words were true. It was a daunting thought that she was the first woman to have really had an impact on Ahfaad. She considered the thought of marriage to him. It would provide her with the security she had always craved and more personal riches than most women could imagine, and yet to be totally beholden to him for everything was out of the question. If he cared for her, as he said he did, he must recognize this. "I would like to marry you very much," she said, "but not at the expense of giving up my job at Joshkers."

"Then I'm sorry," said Ahfaad firmly, "but I'm afraid I shall have to withdraw my offer."

The sense of sorrow and loss Margot felt at his words was profound, and it shocked her—she just hoped her feelings did not show. "As you wish," she said brusquely. "So where do we go from here?"

"We go on as we are now." He stood up. "What about a ride in Hyde Park? It's a beautiful day. A good idea?"

"Yes," said Margot.

"Splendid. I'll go and change."

She watched his long, lean figure as he strode across the patio and back into the house. The subject was closed. She wondered when and if it would ever be raised again.

Chapter 45

Geneva—*March 1986*

It was the first time the three of them had met around a conference table together in a very long time. They sat in Joseph Meyer's elegant office while his secretary poured coffee. Stephanie found herself gazing out across the lake. It was a beautifully sunny day, reminiscent of that first time she had met the Meyers. She had been so naïve then. It was amazing, looking back on it. . . . Thank God for Tim. He had picked her up, dusted her off, and set her back on the right track. It was strange—in all the years that she had known him, she had never before appreciated his strength of character. She had always mistaken his easygoing nature for weakness. Now she knew different.

Stephanie turned her attention to the table. Margot and Ella were sitting glumly next to each other, not speaking at all. Stephanie was vaguely irritated. With Greg married it seemed ridiculous that their old feud should continue. Joseph, by contrast, sat at the head of the table, relaxed and apparently in good humor. He met Stephanie's eyes briefly. The look was neither hostile nor friendly, just interested. Stephanie was the first to drop her gaze.

Joseph waited until his secretary had withdrawn. When at last he spoke his tone was measured and friendly, and as usual, he commanded absolute attention. "You all know why you're here," he said. "I've decided, after careful deliberation, that it would be sensible to dispose of the Meyer Group while I still have my faculties. I intend to make public my intention to sell on August fifth of this year.

However, in the meantime I am prepared to entertain a bid either from you, Stephanie, or from you, Ella, with the obvious advantage that should I accept either of your offers, it will be before the group becomes available on the open market. Details of exactly what is involved in the Meyer Hotel Group are contained in these files." Three identical bulging files were waiting for them on a side table. "Also contained in the files are accounts for the last ten years. My accountants and my attorney have been instructed to accept calls from you at any time with any questions you may have."

He turned his attention to Margot. "Margot is here because she has indicated to me that Joshkers would be prepared to back either one of you in the purchase of the Meyer Group. I have not quoted an asking price because I feel it is better that you make your own assessment of its worth. There are, however, two conditions of purchase. I do not want the group broken up and sold off or my staff's future put in jeopardy. For this reason, included with your bid should be a detailed ten-year plan as to how you see the group progressing and how you intend to run it." He hesitated and drank some coffee. "The other condition is in respect to my grandson, Matthew. Here again I am not laying down any ground rules. I am simply saying that I would like him to have the option of some involvement in the future of the group should he decide, upon reaching maturity, that the hotel business is for him. Of course"—he looked directly but briefly at Stephanie—"by 'some involvement' I am not suggesting that he should be given the post of bellboy in one of the hotels. I am expecting a directorship, a shareholding, and a substantial say in the overall running of the group. He is, after all, a Meyer by blood, if not by name." His voice hardened perceptibly. Stephanie felt herself bristling with anger but said nothing. Joseph's gaze swept around the three women. "Any questions?"

"How and when would you like to receive the bids?" Margot asked.

"I would suggest," said Joseph, "that we set a date of August first for our next meeting, in New York. In order to give me and my advisers time to digest the contents of your proposals, I would ask that you submit bids to me here one week prior to the first of August. We can then meet and discuss them"—he smiled—"shall we say at high noon at the Meyer headquarters in New York?"

"You're not giving us very much time," said Stephanie.

"It's as much time as you're going to get," said Joseph abrasively. "Most of the business world would give their eyeteeth for the opportunity I'm giving you. I'm not interested in complaints."

Stephanie remained undaunted. "What about bidding for part of the group," she said, "assuming that only a part interests us?"

Joseph looked at her disdainfully. "I've already indicated I want a package for the group as a whole, which protects my staff. I presume you're thinking in particular about the European operation. I'm not prepared to sell that separately from the operations in the States or the Middle East. Each has its own contribution to make. The group, as you should know, has been painstakingly built up to provide just this kind of balance. I'm not prepared to entertain a bid for any one part of the group—it's all or nothing." He stood up. "Are there any more questions?" No one spoke. "Well, if you'll excuse me, I'm a busy man. I'll see you all on the first of August."

In the elevator on the way to the ground floor the women stood silently, each holding her copy of the Meyer file. "What about lunch?" Margot said as they came out into the foyer.

"No, thanks," said Stephanie, "I have to get home. Tim's expecting me. If I hurry I can catch the midday flight." She smiled a little warily at the other two. "See you around." Ella, who had not spoken once since entering Meyer's office, managed a brief smile in return.

"How about you?" Margot said.

Ella looked at her coolly. "No, thanks."

"I think we should talk," said Margot.

"What about?" Ella asked.

"Don't be obtuse, Ella, and don't sulk. You're being given the opportunity of a lifetime, as Joseph Meyer said—you should be pleased."

"If I was still my own master, I might be," said Ella.

Margot chose to ignore her. "I assume you're staying at the Meyer Hotel?" Ella nodded. "Let's at least go back there, dump these horrendous-looking files, and have a drink."

In the bar half an hour later Ella and Margot sat over two glasses of peach champagne. "We need to talk strategy," said Margot.

Ella shook her head. "No way."

"Why?" Margot asked.

"If Stephanie puts together the sucessful bid, you will be backing her, right?" Margot nodded. "Then in your capacity as her banker it's hardly appropriate for you to be privy to the details of the proposal I'm putting together."

"I won't let Stephanie outbid you," said Margot. "I've a twenty-five percent stake riding on this, remember."

"Precisely," said Ella, "so from Stephanie's point of view it would not be ethical for you to be involved in the details of my bid. You could use the information to mess up her chances of success."

"It won't work, Ella," Margot said.

"What won't work?"

"Putting in a stupid bid that won't be accepted. If you do that, I'll still pull the plug in Houston. The deal we have is not only that you should bid for the Meyer Group, but that you should bid with the intention of winning."

"I'll do that," said Ella, "but I'll do it my way."

"Without access to the figures you're preparing I have no way of knowing whether what you say is true."

"Then you'll just have to trust me, won't you?" said Ella. She leaned back in her chair. "You're forcing me to bid for the Meyer Group against my will. In order to save my business I'm doing so, but I would remind you that it is my business—and it is I who will decide the details of the bid. The only figure I will be passing on to you for consideration is the amount of borrowing I consider necessary in order to fund such a purchase. Your fact file from Joseph will enable you to decide whether the degree of funding is justified by the amount of the collateral. You've put me in the position of having to go up against Stephanie. If there's going to be a fight, it will be a fair one—your alternative is no fight at all."

Chapter 46

New York—*July 31, 1986*

Matthew Irvine enjoyed his first Concorde flight very much indeed. At eleven months old he showed no desire to walk but was a prodigious talker in a language entirely his own. Stephanie found herself wondering whether it had really been necessary to bring the nanny with them.

Their suite at the Meyer Hotel was the epitome of comfort—a room for Nanny and Matthew with their own bathroom, and a large reception room, beyond which lay Tim and Stephanie's bedroom and bathroom. "I wonder if this is significant. It has to be one of the best suites in the hotel," Stephanie said after they had inspected it.

"Ah," said Tim with a smile, "but what you have to work out is the nature of the significance. Is Joseph giving us these marvelous rooms as a consolation prize or because he sees you as the future chairman of Meyer Hotels?"

Stephanie looked at him and gave a despairing shrug. "Who knows?"

"Are you nervous?" Tim asked.

"Very." She bit her bottom lip, pushing the hair back

from her face—a gesture from her girlhood. "It's as though everything I've done to date, so far as my work is concerned, has been leading me toward this point."

Tim crossed the room and took her in his arms. "But if Meyer sells to Ella instead, you'll still have the franchise, and Ella won't screw you."

"She will, she's bound to," said Stephanie. "I've shown you the figures. The franchise is up for renewal in eighteen months, and whoever is the owner of the Meyer Group by then will want to rethink the terms." She dropped her eyes. "It was the early days of Alex and me, and when I look back on it now, to some extent he must have let his heart rule his head."

"Who could blame him?" said Tim.

Stephanie looked at her husband and, reaching up to him, kissed him, a long, lingering kiss that left them both trembling. "It's amazing to think," said Tim, "that here we are, due to be grandparents in just a few months, and you can still set my pulse racing with a single kiss. Not bad for an old married couple, not bad at all."

Stephanie fingered his lapel. "Do you think you're right about Ella?"

"I know I'm right about Ella."

"Even so, she'll want more money for the franchise—she'll *have* to increase the fee."

"Maybe she will, but she'll recognize that you need time to adjust. In my view, the problem lies not with Ella achieving the successful bid but in neither of you doing so. If Joseph is unhappy with what both of you have to offer, then I suppose you could be in for a rocky ride." He hugged her tight. "Still, there's no point in crossing that bridge—one step at a time." He bent forward and began nuzzling her neck, slipping his hands inside her shirt. "What you need, Mrs. Irvine, is an early night."

"I ought to go over the figures," Stephanie protested, "in case he puts me through a third degree."

"There's a bottle of champagne on the bedside table," said Tim. "You go into the bedroom and open it. I'll tell

Nanny we're having supper in bed and don't want to be disturbed until the morning."

There were tears in Stephanie's eyes. "I do love you, Tim. So many wasted years," she said, stroking his cheek. "I behaved like an idiot."

"Not wasted years," said Tim. "There's no good looking at it like that. Would we appreciate what we have today if we hadn't lost each other along the way? I doubt it. We've been given a second chance, and we're not going to blow this one."

"There's something I've been meaning to say to you," said Stephanie. She looked at him, feeling embarrassed, awkward—suddenly so different from her normal self.

"What is it?" said Tim, at once amused and alarmed.

"When this Meyer thing is over I wondered whether . . . well, I wondered whether we might have a go at having another child."

A look of joy flared into Tim's face but disappeared as quickly as it had come."You don't have to do this," he said.

"What do you mean?" Stephanie asked.

"You don't owe me a baby just because Matthew isn't technically mine."

"I know that," said Stephanie, "I just think it would be good for us all—good for you, good for me, and good for Matthew to have a brother or sister."

"You're really serious, aren't you?" Stephanie nodded. "Do you think you'll be able to cope with the baby and Meyer?"

"If I get it," she reminded him, "yes. As you say, we'll make time." They kissed again.

Across town the atmosphere was not by any means as harmonious. In Aaron's apartment overlooking Central Park Ella, whiskey in hand, stood by the window, her expression troubled, the atmosphere tense and agitated. "Look," said Aaron, clearly exasperated, "the die is cast, right? You've put in your bid, and it's either acceptable to Meyer or it isn't. At this point in time there is absolutely nothing you can do about it. If he chooses Stephanie Irvine's bid, so be it."

"How can I make you understand?" said Ella angrily. "It's no good saying 'So be it.' My whole business life depends on this deal. How can I get across to you the importance of my succeeding and the implications of my failing?"

"I have successes and failures in my work, too," said Aaron.

"Yes, but it's not the same thing at all," Ella said dismissively.

"No, I think you're right there," said Aaron. "I think mine are a great deal more important." Ella swung around and stared at him. Aaron met her gaze, unrepentant. "Let me tell you a story," he said. He stood up and began replenishing his whiskey glass. "In the early hours of this morning I delivered twin girls. The woman in question has been married for sixteen years to a man she loves. They were never able to have children because of my patient's gynecological problems, but last year she miraculously became pregnant. Everything went well until she went into premature labor. Unfortunately she was out of the city and made the fatal decision to return here to New York, to me, rather than seek medical advice in Seattle, where she was. By the time she reached me, proceeding with labor was inevitable—there was nothing I could do to delay the contractions. I made the decision to let her have the babies normally, rather than by cesarean, because she already had such a well-established labor. The birth was relatively easy and quick because of the small size of the babies, but they both died within a few hours of birth. What I haven't told my patient yet is that due to a variety of medical complications, I am sure she will be unable to bear another child. She and her husband are now too old to adopt, and the combination of their loss and the fact that I can give them no hope for the future will probably break up their marriage."

"We never talk about your work," Ella said in a small voice, after a lengthy silence.

"No, we don't," said Aaron, "and normally that's the way I like it. I'm only citing this example because—"

"I know why you told me about your patient, Aaron," Ella said. "I may be a fool in many respects, but I'm not that insensitive. What I'm talking about is the loss of a few million bucks. When compared with the loss of two longed-for children, my aspirations seem pretty insignificant."

"Not insignificant," said Aaron. "I'm just saying that there is life going on outside your business world. Sometimes I think you expect Lexington Kovac to protect you from what's happening to the rest of the human race. OK, so losing this deal might be bad for you, but it really isn't the tragedy you believe it to be."

"But you wanted me to go after Meyer," Ella said, exasperated, "and that's half my problem. You wanted me to do it, Margot's forcing me to do it. The position I'm in is not even of my own making."

Aaron laughed. "You can't have it both ways. If you're saying you wouldn't even have put in a bid if it wasn't for Margot and me, then you have no reason to worry about the outcome. If you lose, you'll have won, so to speak."

"Stop trying to be clever, Aaron." Ella drained her glass and sat down in the chair opposite him.

Aaron sighed heavily. "We're going around in circles," he said. "I guess the best thing to do is to stop talking about it. What would you like to do? Should we go out to eat, call out for something and stay home . . . or go to bed?"

Ella stood up. "Tomorrow's a big day and I'm tired. I guess I'll go home, Aaron." She saw the expression on his face and softened. "Look, thanks anyway. It's just that I'm not very good company tonight."

"I should be able to help you more," Aaron said.

"Why should you? It's my problem. We all have them, as you have so competently illustrated." She picked up her jacket from the back of the chair and walked to the door.

He put his hands on her shoulders to restrain her from leaving. She stood poised for flight, anxious to go, it seemed to Aaron. He let out a sigh, released her, and turned away.

"Look, Ella, forget everything that's happened, everything we've said to each other. The truth is that I love you, and, God help me, I want to spend the rest of my life with you. I don't know whether it's relevant to you right now, but that's how I feel."

"I love you, too. I always have—ever since I was a kid. Given that fact, don't think I'm not tempted to abandon everything and simply let you take over." Her expression was defiant, but Aaron could see she was close to tears.

"Then why don't you?" Aaron asked.

Ella seemed to consider the question for some time. "Because I have to play this final scene alone and give it all I've got. I can't simply give up without a fight."

"And whether you win or lose, do we have a future together?" Aaron's expression was grim.

Ella met his eye. "I don't know, Aaron. It depends."

"Depends on what?"

"On whether you'll still have me." There were no tears now, just an awesome sadness that completely silenced Aaron. There seemed nothing more to be said.

Without another word Ella turned and hurried out the door. She was already at the elevator when Aaron reached her. She looked at once forlorn, vulnerable, and absurdly young, and all his instincts were to grab her, drag her back into his apartment, and hold her tight all night, to ward off the demons that seemed to be invading her head. Somehow, though, it was not possible. Pride and hurt held them apart, so they simply gazed at each other helplessly as the elevator carried her away.

Chapter 47

New York—*August 1, 1986*

Joseph Meyer was clearly enjoying himself. All three women were aware of it and in different ways resented it. Ella was so jumpy that Joseph's almost frivolous attitude toward the morning's meeting had her at screaming pitch. Margot, ever the professional, wanted him to cut the small talk and get down to business, and Stephanie, always uncomfortable in his presence, simply wanted to be back in her apartment with Tim and Matthew.

After coffee and the exchange of pleasantries that seemed to last forever Joseph opened his briefcase and drew out what Stephanie and Ella immediately recognized as their proposals. He laid them side by side in front of him. "As you can imagine," he said, "I have studied these proposals very carefully." The silence and concentration in the room was awesome. "Stephanie's bid is a little higher than yours," he said to Ella. Ella's heart hit the floor. "But she is not proposing to buy the Meyer Group outright—she is suggesting the slow withdrawal of my interest over a five-year period. Her reasons for making the proposal are very sound from her own point of view, though I'm not at all sure they are from mine. I'm an old man. I may not be here in five years."

He turned to Stephanie, who was already planning how she was going to break it to Tim that she had failed. "Ella is prepared to pay me almost immediately for the acquisition of the group, subject only to verification of the projected figures for the current year. However, her offer is less than yours." Hope flared in Stephanie. "Over the question of the staff and their future, you have both been extremely vague. I have no doubt that this is because you are not prepared to commit yourself to maintaining my staffing levels, and this worries me, because this is one of the main requirements of the sale. If you are committed to my staff, then you will be committed to running Meyer as the hotel group it is today. Without that commitment, for all I know you could turn the hotels into ball-bearing factories, destroying everything I've built.

"Then there is the question of Matthew. Predictably, Ella has been far more generous in what she's prepared to do for the boy than his own mother." He shot Stephanie a none-too-friendly look. "Against this, of course, I have the fact that while Stephanie's attitude toward her son may seem ungenerous compared with Ella's, this may not reflect an accurate picture of the future. In Ella's case, she is entering into a contractual agreement. Knowing her as I do, I am confident she will honor that agreement to the letter when Matthew comes of age, if involvement with Meyer is what he wants. However, I have to balance this against the fact that while Stephanie may not be offering him so much at this stage, it is because she wishes to protect him from me and what I stand for. Because the boy is her son, if he shows a very real interest in the business once he has reached maturity, there will be a tendency for Stephanie to be more generous than the terms of her proposed contract would suggest. Indeed, he would be the natural successor to her position as head of Meyer, whereas Ella would not be unreasonable to consider her own son as a more appropriate heir."

There was a lengthy pause during which Stephanie and Ella exchanged a look—it was neither hostile nor competitive, but sympathetic. God, thought Stephanie, I don't know whether we're more terrified of succeeding or failing. The silence persisted for so long that Margot intervened. "So, Mr. Meyer, put us out of our misery. What have you decided to do?"

"Nothing, at the moment," said Joseph.

"You mean you're going to offer it on the open market after all?" The three women stared at him with ill-disguised hostility.

"No, let me explain," he said. "You two are not the only ones to have done your homework in the last few months. I have been looking very thoroughly at both your businesses. Stephanie's is well run and highly profitable and has a great deal to commend it. It is, however, small. Yours, Ella, is far more impressive in terms of size, but while the New York operation runs like clockwork, the UK business is still in its infancy, and Houston is clearly a disaster." It had been ridiculous, Ella thought, to imagine for one moment that a man of Joseph Meyer's stature would not have investigated the extent of her problems in Houston. He was continuing to speak, but her mind was reeling away—the thought of bankruptcy and the collapse of her business suffocated her sensibilities. "And so," Joseph was saying, "bearing in mind that my primary concern is for the future of the Meyer Group, I think it would be sensible to ask you to consider a joint purchase."

Stephanie and Ella stared at each other in shocked silence, each trying desperately to judge how the other would react. Not removing her gaze from Stephanie's face, Ella said, "That's ridiculous. It's out of the question."

"Why?" said Joseph. "I don't see that at all. Your partnership in Fulham proved highly successful. Now, as well as having established a very satisfactory business relationship, you are linked by the marriage of your children. Indeed, I'm told there is a grandchild on the way. I'm sure it will have been pointed out to you by Margot—and indeed it must be obvious to you yourselves—that you each have qualities the other lacks. It seems to me to be a perfect arrangement."

Ella turned to face him. "You seem to have conveniently forgotten the Centre des Arts. The only reason Meyer became involved was that I pulled out. Our relationship may be stable, but it's hardly close." She glanced, embarrassed, at Stephanie but pressed on determinedly. "Maybe, just maybe, it would be worth considering our handling another project together, but when I suggested the idea to Stephanie last year she was dead set against it. Even so, an individual project would be far more appropriate than our permanently joining forces in a business sense, which is what I assume you're suggesting."

"Obviously it would be the neatest and cleanest way to put together a bid," said Joseph. "Since the Meyer Group is so much bigger than either of you, it would seem sensible to pool your resources and operate as one business." He glanced at Stephanie. "What do you think?"

"I agree with everything Ella says. We've worked hard to establish our own businesses and our own corporate identity. If either of us had wanted a partner, she would have taken one years ago."

I think you're both being very shortsighted," Margot said harshly. "I have always wanted you two to work together. Putting in a joint bid for Meyer has to make sense—in fact, it's the obvious answer."

"For you, maybe," said Ella.

"What's that supposed to mean?" Margot said warningly.

An awkward silence followed, broken at last by Joseph. "I have to admit I had not expected this kind of reaction to my proposal," he said. "In fact, I'm disappointed. It seems to me that I'm bending over backwards to help you two, and you're not even prepared to meet me halfway. If you don't want the opportunity of a joint bid, fair enough. We'll go public on the sale next week. But I have to say I find your attitude extraordinary."

Stephanie and Ella glanced at each other. "Am I right in saying," said Stephanie, "that you will not consider either of our individual bids, even if we rework them?"

"That's right," said Joseph. "Before this meeting—before I had even received your proposals—I had already decided that neither of you was substantial enough to cope with the Meyer Group."

"Then why didn't you tell us?" Ella asked.

"Because I wanted to see the nature of your proposals, to

see how serious you were. Clearly you have both put a great deal of work and thought into the proposed acquisition, which is why I'm prepared to entertain the idea of a joint venture."

"Well," said Ella. She glanced at Stephanie and was rewarded by a slight nod. "I guess we'd better take a look at it. How long are you giving us?"

"Until ten o'clock tomorrow morning," said Joseph.

"That's ridiculous," Stephanie burst out.

"We can't do it by then," said Ella.

"You have to," said Joseph. "I'm not prepared to delay any longer. Besides, you've done all the preliminary work. You know exactly what's involved. It's simply a question of reworking the figures to reflect your slightly different approach as partners. Margot will help you, I'm sure."

"Yes, of course I will," said Margot, "and I must say I think it's an inspired idea." Stephanie mumbled something incomprehensible under her breath.

"Good," said Joseph, standing up. "That's settled, then. This room is at your disposal, of course, plus any office facilities you may require. We'll meet here at ten o'clock tomorrow morning." He smiled, clearly pleased with himself and the chaos he had created. Ella and Stephanie watched him depart with undisguised anger.

"I'll order some more coffee," said Margot. Stephanie and Ella ignored her.

"It's ludicrous," Ella exclaimed. "The whole idea is crazy. Why do you want the Meyer Group, Stephanie?"

"To protect my franchise."

"Precisely. You don't want to head up the whole group for its own sake any more than I do, do you?"

"Not particularly," Stephanie admitted. "Five years ago, possibly, but today . . . well, I don't know. My priorities have changed somewhat."

"And I'm in exactly the same position," said Ella. She saw Margot watching her carefully. Part of the agreement between them had been Ella's undertaking never to disclose to anyone Margot's stockholding in her corporation. "As you heard from Joseph himself," she said carefully, "I've got trouble, big trouble, in Houston. The only reason I want the Meyer Group is that some careful asset stripping will solve my Houston problem. Jesus, Stephanie, I'm not the kind of partner you want—my business is in a mess right now, my heart isn't in the project as a whole, and we have the fiasco of Centre des Arts still lurking in the shadows to haunt us."

"Don't worry about that," said Stephanie. "Fulham more than canceled out the Centre des Arts."

"All right, if not Centre des Arts, then what about Tim? How do you feel about working with me, given all the circumstances of the past?"

"Do we have to discuss this in front of Margot?" Stephanie asked uncomfortably.

Ella shot Margot a look of undisguised loathing. "Well, she's clinging here like a leech until we've decided what we're doing, so I suppose we have to."

"I'm not at all worried about Tim affecting our relationship," said Stephanie. Her expression was unreadable and her words final. Ella realized she'd gone a little too far—it was clearly not a subject Stephanie was prepared to discuss.

The coffee arrived, and the three women sat in an explosive silence as it was poured. After the waiter had gone Margot took charge. "Joseph is absolutely right when he says you're being given the opportunity of a lifetime. What you have both achieved to date is commendable, but it's in a different league from the Meyer Group. Your potential for growth and prosperity by heading up such an organization is phenomenal. Joseph obviously wants you both to have his group. For various reasons he admires you both, and he sees you as the candidates most likely to honor a commitment to Matthew, which clearly has to be of major concern to him. Given your individual circumstances, I don't really see how you have any grounds for not taking him up on his offer."

"That's the trouble," Ella said. "That's what I've been trying to say all along. We're not doing this because we want to, we're doing it because we don't have any choice."

"I simply don't believe you have no interest in running Meyer," said Margot. "You've both always been ambitious."

"People change," Stephanie said.

"Maybe, but not to this extent. Still, I suppose I can't force you."

Stephanie stood up and wandered over to the window. "I think we're going to have to go ahead with it, Ella," she said at last.

"I agree. It just makes me so mad."

The three women spent the rest of the day poring over the figures, and as each new schedule was agreed to it was retyped by a girl they had brought into the conference room for the day. At four o'clock Margot suddenly said she had an important appointment and excused herself. Left alone, Stephanie and Ella ordered fresh coffee and continued working, though now it was simply a question of tidying up the loose ends. Shortly before six Stephanie said, "Why don't we take a break? There're only these few figures left to type now. We could take a shower and maybe have some dinner together. What do you say?"

Ella, bone-weary and dispirited, was about to refuse when suddenly she realized the suggestion had appeal. "I'd like that," she said.

"You can shower in our suite, if you wish."

"No, thanks," said Ella, thinking of Tim. "I'll go back to my apartment for a change of clothes. Shall we meet in the bar at about seven-thirty?"

Several times during the day Tessa from Houston had tried to contact Ella, but she had refused all calls as they worked on the figures. On arriving home at her apartment she found several messages from Tessa on the answering machine asking her to call, and a message on her hall table from Jackie saying that Tessa needed to contact her urgently. She went to lift up the phone and then hesitated—whatever it was, it could wait, for undoubtedly it would be bad news. The ever-increasing cash flow problems of Houston were starting to wear her down, and she knew that if she was to make any sense in front of Joseph Meyer tomorrow, she needed to keep her confidence intact. Whatever Tessa's news, it was likely to have the reverse effect.

Ella showered and then collapsed on her bed in a bath towel, still wet. She had promised to telephone Aaron with news as to how the meeting had gone. She dialed his number only to be rewarded by his answering machine telling her that he would be working late at the hospital that night. For a moment she toyed with the idea of calling the hospital and then dismissed it—her news could wait. She remembered his story of the previous evening and felt humbled by it. Instead she lay back on the pillows, her eyes closed.

Stephanie and Ella enjoyed a pleasant dinner. Over coffee, it was Stephanie who raised the question of Tim. "I'm sorry I cut you short this morning when you mentioned Tim," she said to Ella, "only I was damned if I was going to discuss it in front of Margot—it's none of her business."

"I'm sorry, too," said Ella. "It was tactless of me. I guess I just wanted to say how pleased I am that you two are back together again, and that I'd never do anything to jeopardize your marriage—even assuming I could, which I doubt."

"I appreciate your saying that," said Stephanie, "and I know it's true."

"If we are going to work together," said Ella, "inevitably the combination of business and the children will throw us all together a great deal. It might be reassuring for you to know that there is someone I care about very deeply. I may marry him one day, if he'll still have me."

"Really? That's terrific!" said Stephanie with genuine warmth. "Is he English or American?"

"American," said Ella. "I've known him all my life. He's a doctor—a gynecologist. He lives right here in New York. His name's Aaron Connors."

"So what's stopping you from marrying him?" Stephanie asked.

"Oh, the pressure of work and my commitments away from New York."

"If you love him, don't let that stand in your way," Stephanie said. "I learned that lesson the hard way."

"I know you're right," said Ella, "but it's easier said than done."

Stephanie smiled, full of understanding. "Don't I know it. I spent all those years running away from personal commitments, and I can't tell you how deeply I regret it now."

"I'll remember what you said," said Ella.

"And I'll remember what *you* said," said Stephanie. "I don't think our working together will be so bad, do you?" Ella shook her head and smiled. "Look," said Stephanie, "you're exhausted—me, too. Why don't we meet in the conference room at eight-thirty tomorrow and finish off the figures then?"

"I give in," said Ella. "It sounds like a wonderful idea."

Back in her apartment Ella found that Tessa had phoned again, but it was too late now to return the call. Too tired even to undress and take off her makeup, she collapsed on her bed and in seconds was asleep.

Chapter 48

New York—*August 2, 1986*

It had been a long wait. Stephanie and Ella had met at eight-thirty sharp, and by five to nine the remaining figures had been typed and checked. Now there was nothing to do but sit around. Both were becoming increasingly nervous and apprehensive—the more they had looked at the project, the more they were aware of the enormity of the task that lay ahead of them.

Joseph arrived at exactly ten o'clock. He still had the air of someone well pleased with himself, but he stopped short at the sight of Stephanie and Ella seated at the conference table. "You both look exhausted," he said, clearly dismayed.

"We are," said Ella.

The minutes ticked by, but there was still no sign of Margot. "It's not like her to be late," said Stephanie. "In fact, I don't think I've ever known her not to be on time in all the years I've dealt with Joshkers."

"Nor I," said Ella.

"We'll give her until half past," said Joseph. "If she's not here by then, we'll start without her."

They were all reluctant to begin the meeting without Margot Haigh, for in a way she had been its catalyst. However, as the time neared the half hour, Joseph, with a sigh of irritation, came and sat down at the table. "We'll begin," he said. "May I see your proposal?"

Stephanie handed it to him, and the two women sat in silence, watching him as he turned the pages—a nod here, a grunt there, a frown and a pencil note elsewhere. It occurred to Ella how strange the circumstances were—here was Joseph contemplating the disposal of his life's work without the aid of any adviser—even a lawyer. Yet it was typical of the man, and perhaps reasonable enough—after all, what adviser would be able to tell Joseph Meyer anything he didn't know himself?

The door suddenly burst open, and Margot swept in. She was dressed in black as usual, but there was a difference about her—her cheeks, normally pale, were flushed, and her eyes sparkled. Compared with the weariness of the other two women, she seemed full of vitality. "I'm so sorry I'm late," she said, "but I'm afraid it was absolutely unavoidable."

"I'm just looking over the proposal," said Joseph. "We waited as long as we could, but without even a call from you we had no idea whether you were going to turn up or not."

"I've been sitting in traffic for the last quarter of an hour," said Margot, "but I left the bank late, and there was a reason for that. Before you go any further with this meeting, I have something to tell you—a number of things, in fact." So arresting was her sudden appearance that nobody dreamed of arguing with her. She sat down at the far end of the table so she could see them all as she spoke. "I have just come from Joshkers, where I handed in my resignation. That's why I'm late." She looked directly at Joseph. "My reason for doing so is that I would like to put in a counterbid to Stephanie and Ella's. My backer is Ahfaad Rochlieu, whom you know well, Mr. Meyer."

"I'm sorry, I'm probably reacting a little slowly," said Joseph. "You're saying that you and Ahfaad wish to buy the Meyer Group?"

"That's right," said Margot. "We're prepared to offer you fifteen million dollars more than the price Stephanie and Ella are suggesting, and we are willing to pay the offer price in full immediately, with no retention. We are also prepared to give ten-year contracts to key personnel in all areas of the Meyer operation. In addition, so far as Matthew Irvine is concerned, we will gift him an immediate ten percent stock holding in the group, which will give him a major stake. Thereafter, on January first, 2015, we will give him first option to purchase the remaining stock at a substantial discount."

Stephanie and Ella were so flabbergasted that they were entirely speechless. Joseph, however, rallied immediately. "I think you may have been a little hasty in terminating your relationship with Joshkers," he said coldly. "Aren't you forgetting the original terms of my proposal? At our meeting in Geneva I made it plain that I would entertain a bid from either Stephanie or Ella, but that if neither of them could come up with a satisfactory bid then I would be offering the group on the open market. A bid from yourself and Ahfaad, however attractive, does not fall within the conditions I laid down at that original meeting."

"Of course not," said Margot, "but to proceed with their

offer is no longer possible." She indicated Stephanie and Ella's proposal. "As for offering the group on the open market, it will require at least another year's lead time to enable potential purchasers to do the work that Stephanie and Ella have undertaken in recent months. Besides, even if you did offer the group to the market, I very much doubt you'd get a better price than the one we're offering."

"Wait a moment," said Stephanie. "What do you mean that our offer's 'no longer possible'? It's a legitimate offer, carefully worked out, and one with which you entirely agreed up until four o'clock yesterday afternoon."

Margot swung her chair to face Ella—there was no visible sign of emotion on her face. "But that was before I knew Jack Smith's bank, Sunbelt Industrial, had gone down."

"Gone down!" said Ella. "What are you saying?"

"Sunbelt Industrial Bank went out of business at eleven o'clock yesterday morning. It simply ran out of money and closed the doors. I'm afraid Jack Smith shot himself."

Ella stared at her, and for a moment the picture of amiable, happy-go-lucky Jack came into her mind. It was impossible to imagine him taking his own life. "Are you sure?" she said in a faint voice.

"Quite sure," said Margot. "What this means, of course, is that you've lost everything so far as Houston is concerned, and I'm afraid that one of my last tasks for Joshkers Bank was to advise the board to foreclose on all your business activities, both here and in the UK. I'm sorry, Ella. It's unfortunate, but the days of Lexington Kovac are over."

"Unfortunate!" Ella burst out. "What the hell are you talking about, Margot? You're telling me my life is in ruins, and it's unfortunate! Why didn't I know about Jack Smith?"

"I don't know," said Margot. "When I arrived here this morning I quite expected to find that you had withdrawn your offer. When it was clear you had not, it was equally clear that you had no idea what had happened in Houston. I thought your office would have advised you."

Ella let out a sigh. The endless calls from Tessa yesterday, which she had ignored, were clearly to tell her what was going on. Still, what did it matter? "Nonetheless, Joshkers must have had some prior knowledge of what was going to happen."

"Not precisely," said Margot. "As you know, we've been extremely concerned about the Houston position for some time, but we had no idea that Jack was in such trouble. The first we heard about the problem was his clerk ringing to tell us that Jack was lying across his desk in a pool of blood."

The brutality of the words made Ella flinch. No one spoke, and Ella, to her surprise, felt nothing at all. "Under the circumstances," Margot continued after a stunned silence, "the offer from Stephanie and Ella is invalid. Stephanie, as you rightly assessed yesterday, Mr. Meyer, has not a large enough operation to tackle the acquisition of the Meyer Group alone. In any event, I sense in both Ella and Stephanie a lack of commitment. They were making a bid because they felt they had no alternative. However, in my view, their offer does not stem from a burning ambition to take Meyer Hotels to dizzy heights."

"When you go for the jugular you really make a first-class job of it, don't you?" said Stephanie bitterly.

Margot ignored her. "You don't know me very well," she continued, addressing Joseph exclusively, "but you do know Ahfaad. You've dealt with him over many years, and you know him to be an excellent hotelier, loved by his staff and slavishly admired by his guests. He has the kind of experience in big hotels both Stephanie and Ella lack. I should also tell you that Ahfaad and I were married last week in Cannes. We would like to run Meyer Hotels for the next twenty-five years, but at that stage we'll be more than happy to hand it over to your grandson, since we have no children of our own. In fact, both of us would find it extremely appropriate to do so—it seems only right. The discount we are proposing will be generous, and we will be guided by you on this. If Matthew is going to be the kind of man capable of running the Meyer Group, it is important that it is not handed to him on a plate. For this reason, Ahfaad and I think he should have to raise the money himself—the discount should make finding a backer none too difficult. The combination of Matthew's parentage and upbringing should ensure that he is the kind of young man you would wish to see heading your business empire. However, if he does turn out very different from what we all imagine, he will have neither the desire nor the ability to find the necessary funding."

Joseph let out a sigh and turned to Ella. "Have you any reason to suppose what Margot has just told us about Houston is untrue?" he asked.

"Of course I haven't been misleading you—" Margot began.

Joseph raised a hand to silence her. "Have you, Ella?" he repeated. Ella shook her head miserably. "And if this fellow Jack Smith has run out of cash, can you see any way you can save even some part of your business?"

Ella raised her eyes and met his. The formidable tycoon had vanished—she was looking into the eyes of a caring, anxious elderly man who was willing to help her in any way. But there was no way anyone could help her now. It was too late. "It was the one thing that hadn't occurred to me," said Ella. "I was fighting a hard battle down in Houston, but I was just about keeping my head above water, and I naturally assumed Jack was doing the same. I've been pouring the income from New York and the UK into the Houston operation to keep it afloat. This means, of course, that the corporate profits for the last couple of years are pretty much wiped out, and all of the Fulham money has been lost, too—but at least I've been coping with the situation. However, the bank going . . . I just hadn't expected that. Poor Jack."

"Yes," said Joseph, "what a stupid thing to do. Losing the people you love may be worth dying for, but simply losing money . . ." He smiled suddenly. "Remember that, Ella Kovac. What we're doing here is just playing a game of Monopoly on a grand scale. Today hasn't been a good day for you, but in the scheme of things, in the context of your life and happiness, it's nothing."

Hot tears gathered at the corners of Ella's eyes. "I—I

think I'll leave now, if you'll excuse me." She stood up hesitantly.

"Yes, of course," said Joseph.

"Would you like me to come with you?" said Stephanie.

Ella shook her head. "I'll call you later."

Stephanie waited until the door was closed, and then she turned to Joseph. "Are you going to accept Margot's offer?"

For the first time in many years Joseph looked at her without any trace of hostility. "What would you do in my position, Stephanie?" he asked.

When at last she replied, her voice was entirely without rancor. "I'd go with Margot, of course. She's giving you everything you want with a minimum of hassle—in fact, it's an offer you simply cannot refuse."

"I'm afraid you're right," said Joseph.

Chapter 49

At the sound of Ella's voice Tessa burst into tears. "Oh, Ella, have you heard?"

"Yes, I've heard, and I wish I'd been able to get back to you yesterday. You must have had one hell of a day."

"I didn't know what to do. What's going to happen now?"

"I'm sorry, but I guess you'd better start looking for another job. The bank may employ you for a week or two, but no more."

There was a stunned silence. "Lexington Kovac's really finished, then," Tessa said.

"I'm afraid so—the sooner you find another job, the better."

"But what about you, Ella?"

"I'll get by. Tessa, I'm surprised I haven't heard from Michael Gresham. I need to get hold of him—is he in the office?"

"No," said Tessa. "That was the other problem I had yesterday. He's been out of town for several days on some court case down in Mexico. He hates Mexico—everything always takes so long." She spoke fondly, and Ella found herself wondering whether Tessa was another notch on Michael's belt. It wouldn't surprise her. "I finally contacted him late last night. When he heard the news he said he'd catch the next plane out. He should be in Houston by now, and he said to tell you he'd call you as soon as he got here."

"Fine," said Ella. "I expect to be down with you tomorrow. Can you hold on to things until I come? Don't worry about your salary. I'll find that from somewhere."

"Oh, I'm not worried about that," said Tessa, "just about you."

"You can stop worrying about me, I'm fine." Ella replaced the receiver and then, taking a deep breath, buzzed down to the office below. For some reason she couldn't face sitting at her familiar desk—not now that it was no longer hers. With Joshkers foreclosing, all the properties would be on the market in a matter of days—her apartment, too. It seemed so unreal. Jessie answered the phone. "Could you and Jackie come upstairs? I need to talk to you," Ella said. When they arrived it was obvious that Jessie had been crying, and Jackie was close to tears. "So you know?" said Ella gently.

"We had a call from the bank this morning. They're sending someone over this afternoon to collect the books," said Jackie.

"They don't waste much time, do they?" said Ella. "Look, I'm really sorry, but as I told Tessa just now, you two had better start looking for jobs."

Jessie shook her head. "No way, not yet. We've already talked about it. We'll stay on with you until the place is sold over our heads. There'll be a stack of work to do, I guess."

"You can't do that," said Ella. "I'm not sure I'll be able to pay you."

"We've talked about that, too," said Jessie. "We won't accept a dime from you, Ella Kovac. You've looked after us all this time, and from now on we're going to look after you. Right, Jackie?"

"Yes," said Jackie. "You can't change our minds, Ella, it's what's going to happen. You're going to need some moral support during the next few weeks."

For the first time since leaving the conference room Ella felt close to tears, but she was not going to let them see her break down. "It's very kind of you," she said. "I accept, but you must take off all the time you need to look around for other work."

"OK," they agreed.

"Will you have anything left?" Jackie asked tentatively.

Ella thought for a moment. The house in London was in the corporation's name, as was all the UK property. Suddenly she remembered the little farmhouse in Provence, which had been transferred to Greg and Belinda, with the understanding that the whole family could use it. She smiled. "I have an interest in an old farmhouse in the south of France," she said, "and I have the clothes I'm wearing. That means I'm not much worse off than when I first arrived in New York." As she spoke the words she felt a strange sort of exhilaration. She dismissed the feeling—feelings could not be trusted at the moment.

Jessie started to cry quietly.

"Stop it," said Ella gently. "We did our best, Jess. We can't do more than that."

"You're so calm," said Jackie.

"It hasn't hit me yet." Ella looked around helplessly. "There must be an awful lot to do, but I don't know what. I've experienced most of what the commercial world can throw at me, but not bankruptcy—that's a new one."

"We'll be here," said Jessie. "We'll do everything. Now you should have a rest—you look exhausted. I guess the bank officials will want to see you this afternoon."

"I guess they will."

Both women stood up and left the office.

She sat for a long time, her mind a complete blank, before the idea of calling Aaron came to her. She knew she should be trying to contact Michael Gresham, but a strange lethargy seemed to have overcome her. When she dialed Aaron's number she was not surprised that his machine answered and informed her that he was at the hospital. She hesitated and then dialed the hospital number. A voice sounding not quite like her own informed a series of receptionists and nurses that it was urgently necessary that she speak to Dr. Connors. She probably sounded like a woman in labor, she thought, faintly amused. When at last she was actually asked whether she was a patient, she said she was—it seemed easier. Moments later she was put through. His voice sounded clipped and efficient. "Dr. Connors. How may I help you?"

"Aaron, it's Ella."

"Ella! I've been thinking so much about you. How did it go yesterday?"

"It's gone," said Ella.

"What's gone? You mean you lost the deal?"

"Lost the whole business," said Ella. "The Houston bank collapsed, and the director, Jack Smith, shot himself. It's the end of my business, Aaron."

"Jesus! Look, hold it a minute—I can't leave the hospital right now, but I'll transfer your call to another room where I can talk in peace." Minutes later, after a series of clicks, she heard his voice again—it was warmer, more intimate now. "I'm so very sorry, darling," he said. "How are you feeling? Where are you?"

"I'm at home. I'm all right, I guess."

"What happened? Tell me all about it." Sparing no details, Ella related the events of the last twenty-four hours. "The bitch!" Aaron burst out when she had finished.

"Not really," said Ella wearily. "All's fair in love, war, and real estate."

"Hell, no, Ella. She and Ahfaad must have been planning this thing for some time."

"I doubt it," said Ella. "I get the feeling it was a snap decision. Up until yesterday I genuinely believed she was going to back Stephanie and me. OK, she had a vested interest—the shares in my business—but I think she was figuring on going through with it. It was only the collapse of Sunbelt that made her look around for an alternative—that, coupled with Stephanie's and my genuine apprehension and lack of enthusiasm about a joint purchase."

"Nonetheless, I can't believe she couldn't see what was going to happen in Houston. There she was, forcing you to bid for a deal that you didn't even want, her only motive being personal greed, and all that while you could have been using your energies to look for ways of solving the problems in Houston. You've wasted so much time preparing for this bid."

"I honestly don't think any amount of time I'd have spent on Houston could have saved it. If I'd chosen to liquidate my properties, the amount of money I'd have lost would have forced the bank to foreclose on me anyway. Hanging around living hand to mouth and waiting for things to improve would have still ended with my being brought down by Jack and his problems."

"Poor guy," said Aaron. "Look, I appreciate that people behave in a strange way in business—I just feel that Margot shouldn't get away with it. As you say, she had a vested interest in your business, Ella—one you didn't even know about. She used that to manipulate you into a position to bid for Meyer when you didn't want to. Then she outbids you by playing her trump card just when the shit hits the fan. I don't reckon Joshkers Bank would like the way she's gone on too much." There was a long silence. "Ella? Are you still there?"

"Yes," said Ella. "Aaron, I think you may have hit on something. I don't know, maybe I'm clutching at straws."

"What sort of something?" said Aaron.

"Well," said Ella slowly, "Joshkers is going to lose millions of dollars with the collapse of Lexington Kovac. I can't begin to estimate how much—it depends what they realize from the sale of the various properties. Undoubtedly it will be the biggest disaster in their year, and there are going to be a lot of questions asked as to the validity of making such large loans available to me. It's going to look kind of odd, too, that up until just a few hours before the Houston bank crashed Margot was in serious negotiation with me and Meyer, which would have necessitated her authorizing even more enormous borrowing on my behalf, and there's her timely resignation . . ."

"Yes, yes," said Aaron impatiently, "we know all that, but I don't see where it's leading you."

"It means this," said Ella. "She was prepared to allow borrowing on a business she knew was already seriously flawed."

"Right," said Aaron.

"And why did she do that?"

There was silence on the other end of the phone for a moment. "Because . . . because she had a vested interest in your business," said Aaron.

"Exactly," said Ella triumphantly. "She had a conflict of interests—her loyalty to the bank opposite her personal greed in wishing to see Lexington Kovac succeed. I'm not sure, but I have a feeling that what she did may be a criminal offense."

"Jesus!" said Aaron. "You might be able to save the business yet."

"Look, I'll call you back," said Ella. "I need to speak to Michael Gresham right away. He's the best person to advise me on this—they don't come much more slippery than Michael."

Aaron gave a slightly hollow laugh. "So you've led me to believe over the years."

"Aaron, thanks."

"Don't mention it. Look, I should be through here by late afternoon. Shall I come over?"

"Oh, yes, please," said Ella without hesitation.

She sat for some moments gazing out of the window. From her vantage point on the sofa all she could see was the deep blue of the sky and the corner of the apartment tower next door. Suddenly the sun edged around the concrete balustrade at the top of the building, sending a shaft of sunlight piercing through Ella's window, cutting her living room in half. The band of golden light seemed like a signal. She lifted the telephone and dialed Michael Gresham's number.

Chapter 50

Joseph followed Stephanie hesitantly into the apartment. Her invitation, so unexpected, made him suspicious and jumpy. At the same time it was irresistible. Without preamble or explanation she had telephoned him ten minutes before and asked him if he would like to come and see his grandson.

Tim Irvine rose from a chair by the window and came across to shake his hand. He looked from one to the other—they were a charming couple. In different circumstances he knew he would enjoy their company, but clearly there was some sort of trade afoot, and he knew he had to be wary. His strongest emotions were involved; they must know that. Somehow he had to hold on to the fact that this was a business deal. He could not remember feeling more on edge and nervous.

Tim spoke. "Look, Mr. Meyer, I know what you're thinking. You imagine we have asked you here to try and change your mind about your decision to sell to Margot Haigh. Even worse, you think we're going to use your grandson to try and twist your arm. I just want to say here and now, before you even see him, that nothing could be further from the truth." The words were music to Joseph's ears, but still he could not believe them. He blinked nervously, unable to speak.

Stephanie reached out and laid a hand on his arm. "What Tim says is true, Joseph. Now that you're selling the company, it's changed everything. I didn't want you to force Matthew into a mold, but you've done the deal, and Matthew's a very lucky little boy. He has the opportunity, if he so wishes, to head up the Meyer Group one day, but the decision will be his. So long as you can assure us that you will never apply any pressure on him to take up the Meyer crown, we'd like you to be as much a part of his life as you wish."

Joseph stared from one to the other; there was no doubting their sincerity. "Thank you," he murmured.

"Would you like to see him now? He's playing with his toys in the bedroom." Joseph tried again to speak, but nothing happened. Stephanie took his arm and led him to the adjoining room. The child was sitting on the floor. "I'll leave you two alone," said Stephanie. Giving Joseph a gentle push, she retreated and shut the door.

For a moment he felt a sense of panic. It was a long time since he'd had anything to do with small children, and this one was little more than a baby. Curiosity got the better of him. "Hello," he said, and, walking over to the child, he sat down beside him on the floor. The sight of Matthew made him gasp aloud—at first glance he was entirely Alex's son. The same wild, dark curls, the big brown eyes, the high cheekbones, and the startling bone structure, already apparent beneath the baby chubbiness. There, however, the similarity ended. The eyes that regarded him with interest were kind and joyful—they twinkled and shone. Joseph smiled and was rewarded by a smile back, a dimple appearing on one cheek. For the first time in his life Joseph admitted to himself what he had always known: that he had never liked his son. Loved him, yes, loved him to distraction, but even as a tiny child Alex had been discontented and difficult, a reserved, awkward character who seemed unable to give love due to his own self-absorption. It was obvious, however, that Matthew was very different from his father—very different indeed.

When Stephanie came to join them twenty minutes later they were playing with building blocks—Joseph was stacking them, and Matthew was knocking them down, squealing with delight. They were laughing and obviously having a wonderful time. The only difference between them was that Joseph's face was wet with tears.

When Nanny bore away an excited Matthew for his supper Joseph joined Tim and Stephanie in the sitting room. "Would you like some tea, coffee, or something stronger?" Tim asked.

"Something stronger," said Joseph.

They opened a bottle of wine, and Tim poured three glasses. "Shall we drink to the future of the Meyer Group?"

"No," said Joseph, "I think we should drink to Matthew Irvine." He stressed the surname, a point not lost on Stephanie or Tim.

"To Matthew Irvine," they chorused.

"I could insist on some sort of protection for your franchise as part of the deal," Joseph said after a pause.

"No," said Stephanie, "Margot has made her offer, and it's a fair one—it's the best possible solution for you, for Meyer, and for Matthew. I'll just have to take my chances as they come. After all, I've known her a long time, and I can't see that she's going to gain a lot by putting me out of business—not if she wants to protect her reputation in the banking world."

"That's true," said Joseph doubtfully.

"Forget it, honestly," said Stephanie. "The subject's closed—we didn't ask you here to talk about business."

"You'll be returning to the UK soon?" Joseph asked.

"Tomorrow, we thought. I have so much catching up to

do, since I've spent so much time on this proposal in the last few months. I want to have everything looking good before Margot's henchmen start poking around." She smiled reassuringly at Joseph. "I hope you will come and see us whenever you feel like it. Where are you planning to be based?"

"In Geneva, I thought. I like it. New York . . . it's no place for an old man. I'll buy myself somewhere on the lake, so I guess we'll be neighbors, almost."

Tim and Stephanie smiled. His remark was not intended as any kind of joke. In the world in which Joseph Meyer moved, an hour and a half's flight by private jet qualified as neighborliness. "Well, as Stephanie says, you're welcome at Wickham any time," said Tim, "any time at all. We'll do the very best we can with Matthew, you know that. As far as I'm concerned, he is my son, and I will bring him up as such. However, Stephanie and I are both adamant that we should not deny him the knowledge of his true parentage, particularly in view of his inheritance. As soon as he is able to grasp a few simple facts we will explain to him about you and Alex, so that the knowledge becomes part of his growing up, not a sudden shock in later life."

"You have a very special man there, Stephanie," Joseph said. What he thought but did not say was that he had difficulty understanding why she had chosen his son over Tim Irvine.

"I know," said Stephanie.

"You know, the first time I met you, Stephanie," said Joseph, "I admired you very much, both for your business acumen and as a woman. I still do, and I do so regret the intervening years of difficulty between us."

"We both did and said things we shouldn't have," said Stephanie, "but we can put it all behind us now. We have a future. Let's look to that future and enjoy it."

"And you really want me to be part of it?" Joseph was close to tears again.

"On one condition," said Tim with a grin. "That when

you teach Matthew to play Monopoly, you'll tell him it's as good to invest in houses as it is in hotels."

Joseph threw back his head and roared with laughter. "I'll do that," he said, "I'll certainly do that."

Matthew had gone to bed, and Stephanie and Tim sat comfortably on the couch, arms around each other, kissing in earnest. Tim began unbuttoning the front of Stephanie's blouse. The phone rang. "Damn," he murmured, "let's leave it."

"I can't," said Stephanie. "I can never leave phones. I always think it might be something vital."

"Leave it just this once."

"No." She kissed him again and disentangled herself. "Hello," she said.

"Stephanie, it's Ella."

"Ella!" Stephanie caught her breath. "Ella, how are you? You must feel ghastly."

"No, I feel fine. Actually, I'm calling because we need to meet. It's important—something's come up."

"What sort of thing?"

"I'll tell you when we meet. Can you make it to my apartment in, say, half an hour?"

The thought of crossing town at the end of such an exhausting and emotional day held no appeal for Stephanie, but there was no question of her refusing. "Of course I'll be there," said Stephanie.

"Good," said Ella. "Perhaps I should warn you that Margot will be here as well."

"Margot! Jesus, why?"

"All will be revealed in half an hour," said Ella. "See you." The phone went dead.

Chapter 51

The door of Ella's apartment was opened by the handsomest man Stephanie had ever encountered. His tall, florid good looks were quite breathtaking, as was his infectious grin and twinkling blue eyes. "Lady Bonham, I presume," he said. "Come in."

"Are you Aaron?" Stephanie asked, full of curiosity.

He laughed. "No. My name's Michael Gresham. I'm Ella's lawyer."

Ella stood up as they came into the room. "Thanks for coming, Stephanie. Come and sit down. You've met Michael."

"I certainly have," said Stephanie. "You *are* a dark horse."

"He's just my lawyer," said Ella primly, but a smile played on her lips.

"More's the pity," said Michael sagely.

"This is all very mysterious," said Stephanie. "What's going on?"

"We only have about twelve minutes before Margot comes, assuming she's not going to make a habit of being late," said Ella. "I want you to listen very carefully to what I have to say, because I want to make sure I'm doing what you want before we proceed with this thing."

"What thing?" said Stephanie.

The air was electric with excitement when Margot arrived, promptly on time. Michael ushered her in, and Ella made the introductions. Margot, Stephanie noticed, was not at all at ease. The fact of having a lawyer present presumably unnerved her, but she put on a good performance of remaining cool. "I'm sorry if I sound callous," she said, "but I really am very busy today. Joseph's only agreed to go ahead with the deal on the condition that I have the whole thing tied up by the end of the month."

"This won't take long," said Ella. "I began doing a little thinking after our meeting, and it occurred to me that Joshkers Bank would not be too pleased with you if they knew the background of this particular scenario."

"I don't know what you mean," said Margot.

"I think you do," said Ella. "You have behaved unethically as far as the relationship between Lexington Kovac and Joshkers is concerned. You allowed Joshkers to continue supporting me despite the declining situation in Houston, and you were even prepared to recommend that the bank make available to me the enormous sums of money involved in the acquisition of my part of the Meyer deal."

"That is correct," said Margot. "I happen to have had a lot of faith in you, Ella. I still do. It was extremely bad luck that Jack Smith's bank went under. But for that I think you would have—"

"Cut the crap," said Ella. "Looking at it from Joshkers' point of view, I don't think there's any doubt that the way you behaved represents a serious conflict of interest. If Joshkers had known, or indeed were informed now, that you are a twenty-five-percent stockholder in Lexington Kovac, I think they would be very angry about the amount of money that you let them lose as a result of the collapse of my business."

"It's all part of the daily banking routine," said Margot. "You win some, you lose some."

"I'm sorry to disagree with you," said Michael Gresham, "but without doubt you have committed a criminal offense. You know as well as I do that if you had admitted to your stock holdings in Lexington Kovac at the time you acquired the stock, the bank would have either asked you to resign or, at the very least, given the account to a different officer of the bank. In addition, the idea that Ella should bid for Meyer was clearly ridiculous under the circumstances. It was obvious, and indeed it has been obvious for some time, that Sunbelt Industrial Bank was vulnerable. If I knew that, you must have been even more aware of it, since Joshkers owns stock in the bank and, I understand, made them a substantial loan. From Joshkers' point of view, the whole thing stinks, especially in light of your hasty resignation. This is not an idle threat, Miss Haigh. I have spent some hours studying the position—Joshkers could throw the book at you for what's happened, and if they ever learn that it is not Laurence Merman but Margot Haigh who holds that stock in Lexington Kovac, I have no doubt that they will."

Margot took a deep breath. "So what do you want?" She looked directly at Ella.

"I will make sure that your stock ownership in Lexington Kovac will never become public knowledge provided that you renew Stephanie's franchise on exactly the same terms as currently, except in fairness to you, from now on, the fee she pays will be index-linked. The fresh contract will run for a ten-year period from today and thereafter be subject to renewal. Let me make myself quite clear on what I mean by that—you will have no right to cancel the franchise now or at any time in the future. The franchise goes on for as long as Stephanie wishes. After ten years it will be assessed at market value by an independent third party, and Stephanie can either continue under the new terms or ask to be bought out."

There was silence in the room. "Is that it?" said Margot.

"That's it."

"I don't understand. Assuming your lawyer friend here is right—and I'm certainly not admitting that he is—why aren't you trying to help your own business? Why help Stephanie?"

"Because Stephanie's business is worth saving," said Ella. "Mine isn't. Because Stephanie's commitment to her business is still intact, and mine isn't. The heart went out of my ambition the day I found out that you were a stockholder in Lexington Kovac. If we did some sort of deal now to save my business, I know you'd insist on being a part of my future. There's no way you would release the stock to me. The business would never really be mine again, and I'd resent every last dollar I made for you. I've worked damned hard. I'm tired. I began with nothing, and I've got nothing again. I can cope with that. Besides, Margot, the real problem is that I can't cope with ever having to deal with you again."

"You sound very bitter, and I can understand that," said Margot, "but it wasn't my fault, you know. I didn't create the oil crisis any more than I was responsible for Jack Smith's bank going under."

"I know that," said Ella. "I'm not looking to you as a scapegoat, but you asked me the question, and I'm giving you the answer. Stephanie's business is a business worth saving. I doubt you'll be prepared to admit it, but neither Stephanie nor I held out much hope of your renewing her franchise unless you have some, shall we say, incentive to do so."

"I'll need guarantees."

"So will we," said Michael, "which is why I've drawn up two agreements. One is for you to sign, Miss Haigh, guaranteeing the terms and renewal of the European franchise of Meyer Hotels. The other is for you to sign, Ella, guaranteeing silence on the question of the stock holding."

"Laurence might talk," said Margot.

"Rubbish," said Ella. "Laurence's word is his bond. You know that, or you wouldn't have entered into the agreement with him in the first place."

Margot turned to Stephanie. "And what do you think of all this? Do you have the same aversion to working for me as Ella does?"

"I won't be working for you," said Stephanie, "or even with you. Franchisees work for themselves. I'll be accounting to you with my annual fee and commission on sales, and I can assure you that you will be well pleased with the results

I achieve. As to the gesture Ella has made, I think it's magnificent and very generous, not only to me but also to you."

"How do you mean?" said Margot.

"You and your banking subsidiary have ruined Ella. You can deny it and say you weren't responsible for the oil crisis, but as Michael has indicated, it seems likely that you have known of the imminent collapse of Sunbelt Industrial for some time. Revenge is sweet, and if I were Ella, I would be very tempted to turn you over to Joshkers Bank and take great pleasure in watching you being hauled through the courts. Not only is it what *I'd* be tempted to do—I suspect you would, too, if the roles were reversed."

For once Margot said nothing.

The documents were signed, and Michael rose, placed them carefully in his briefcase, and disappeared into the kitchen, returning moments later with a bottle of champagne and four glasses. "Some may say that this is hardly the moment for a celebration. We're sitting among the ruins of Ella's business, and none of you should lose sight of that. On the other hand, all three of you are facing a new beginning in your different ways, and being an Irishman, I believe the only way to seal any agreement is with a drink." He popped the cork, poured the champagne, and handed around the glasses. "Well, ladies," he said, "I would like you to raise your glasses to the deal you've just struck. May it bring you all happiness and fulfillment."

Just for a moment, despite everything that had happened, the three women smiled at one another, a sense of camaraderie briefly returning. "To the deal," they chorused.

Epilogue

New York—*August 2, 1986*

She stood in the center of the room in a short, striped nightshirt, her hair still damp from the shower, a riot of curls around her face, which was devoid of makeup. She looked sixteen, if that. Aaron closed the apartment door quietly and leaned back against it. He studied her in silence, and she returned his stare steadily. "It must be thirty years since I hauled you out of that pile of screaming kids."

"It is," said Ella, "almost to the day."

"I could do it again—rescue you from a battle zone, set you on your feet, and brush you off. This time, though, I'd want guarantees."

"What kind of guarantees?"

"That if you came under my protection, that's where you'd stay. That we'd plan our future together, not independently, and that you'd become my wife. What do you say?"

Ella looked at him doubtfully. "I'd still have to work. I'd go insane at home all day. You see, I've been offered this deal . . ."

Aaron threw back his head and laughed aloud. "You're

incorrigible—nothing changes. Tell me, will this deal take you out of town?"

"Sometimes," Ella answered.

"Out of North America?"

"No."

"Certain?" said Aaron. Ella nodded her head. "I think you'd better let me marry you, don't you?"

"Yes . . . yes, please," said Ella breathlessly as she ran across the room into his arms.